Tales of Hardooth 5

ENEMIES FROM BEYOND

Dara J. Carr

Tales of Hardooth 5

ENEMIES FROM BEYON

Dara J. Carr

Harrison House Publishing

Harrison House Publishing
www.theharrisonhousepublishing.com
info@theharrisonhousepublising.com
ISBN: 978099614709
Library of Congress Control Number: 2017959984
Harrison House Publishing and the "HH" logo are trademarks belonging to Harrison House Publishing.

PRINTED IN THE UNITED STATES OF AMERICA

This story is fictional. No actual person or event is depicted. Any similarity with any person, living or dead, or any event, is entirely coincidental and unintentional.

TXu 1-937-740

OTHER BOOKS BY

DARA J. CARR

The Semi-Dragon Tale

Revenge Cometh Forth

Here Are My Shorts (a collection of short stories)

Volunteer…Spy?

The Original Owlam

What New Things We Can Learn?

The Lies We Tell to Survive

Countless Enemies and Discoveries

ENEMIES FROM BEYOND

1

Wilfadge hung his head. "I'm sure glad we have the gorge to fall back on. If we didn't...we wouldn't have any home to go to." He looked up and leaned back in his chair. "The Teams that are spying on Algothon...stay there. The Teams that are spying on the Teltermak at Satroco Isle...no need to be there at all. Recall all Teams from other missions. We're going to harvest what we have here, take it to the gorge and disappear. We'll leave a sign at the *Tuzine* trading area. The sign will read: Trading of *Tuzine* is suspended indefinitely due to the fact that we're going to have to fight another war against the Teltermak. No *Tuzine* can be manufactured or traded while we're fighting a war."

Hadathoo frowned. "Are we going to continue manufacturing our drug in the gorge?"

"Of course we are! We can always make new rooms to store it there." He shook his head. "For the moment...we're leaving our beloved city. We'll hop all buildings into Spy and take all of our crops with us. We leave nothing...but the wall...in Home dimension. We even hop the trams into Spy."

Teelila cleared her throat. "What about the Rakab-Rosh? The Teltermak have mind-screwed them and unless we can... unscrew them...we may have to kill them."

Hoynama raised her hand slightly. "What about the tunnels...and the munitions factory...and some of the training that's going on? What do we do with them?"

Wilfadge looked up sadly. "If a munitions manufacturing plant has an accident, it usually turns out as very spectacular destruction. I suggest the one in Zee-Altha has a very bad accident...eventually...when it suits our best interest. As to the tunnels, steal a bunch of explosives from their munitions plant... before we blow it up...and collapse the tunnels. Collapse every taja of the tunnels...preferably with the diggers still in there."

Till looked around. "What about the drugs and the kite training?"

Wilfadge nodded. "If we can use ammunition that we steal from them...we use it for that purpose. One thing at a time. We disarm them and blow a whole bunch of them up in tunnels and on the kites and drug manufacturers."

Dwalooa drummed her fingers on the table. "What about the Rakab-Rosh? They're still headed this way. What about when they get here? What do we do?"

Wilfadge sighed. "They'll find a wall that is just a big circle with nothing inside the wall...except dirt."

Antrong frowned. "Are we going to fight back against the Rakab-Rosh...at all?"

"They're drugged. Once they get here, maybe the Teltermak will realize that they're not needed, because there are no Owlamites to capture...here...and they'll let the Rakab-Rosh get off of the drug...and then...the non-drugged antagonists should go home."

Shyshee looked at Wilfadge angrily. "What if they don't go home?"

"Then we look at that situation...if it happens...and act accordingly."

"So that's it," said Ahandi. "We run and let them take over our city."

"We number less than 30,000. The Rakab-Rosh number about 400,000...plus they have the Teltermak backing them. I don't like the odds because the Teltermak are everywhere and trying to make everyone else do their dirty work. We have to look at the full scope of where the Teltermak are and maybe start getting rid of a lot of them...before we attack and kill their puppets."

Team 7016 got the message about the mass migration. It did not affect them very much because they had moved the majority of their belongings to the gorge a long time ago. There was still some affection for the original building, however, it was getting rather old and the gorge was a safer place to live. The main thing they had to do was start moving crops from Owlam to the gorge. That was going to take a lot of hopping and Jumping. Seeing as how the Rakab-Rosh were nearly at Owlam, the hopping had to be done now, Jumping later...once everything was located in Spy dimension.

The next day, when all of the *Tuzine* customers showed up at the trading area (including a contingency of Teltermak customers) there was a lot of shock, anger and dismay after reading the big sign.

There was also a lot of hostile staring at the Teltermaks as well. No one bothered to try to find out if it were true. The anger at not getting the powerful antibiotic for an undetermined amount of time made everyone very hostile towards one race. There were fifty-six Teltermaks in their trading contingency. By the time the day was over, all fifty-six were dead. They were either shot, slashed to pieces, bludgeoned to death or hung from the signs over the trading stations. None survived and as a result, Home Base did not know, immediately, about the massacre. They also got the fact that there would be no more *Tuzine* from the Owlams…for an undetermined amount of time.

Each contingency left a note, of their own, at the trading stations before they departed. Each note basically had the same message: "We took care of the Teltermak hypocrites at the trading station. Please let us know, somehow, when the trading will start up again. We hope that it is a short war and we pray for your survival."

Hopping all of the crops was a lot of work. By the time all of the plants were in Spy, there were a lot of very tired Owlamites. Now that all of the plants were in Spy, when someone would go back to Home dimension and look out over the inner area, all they saw was a brown desert of…nothing.

Team 7016 Jumped back to the gorge, each one took a bath and they all went to their beds to get some strength back. They were rudely awakened during their slumber, with a mental communication that informed them that the Rakab-Rosh had arrived at the city of Owlam and were very surprised to find nothing inside the walls.

The Teltermak were also very infuriated about finding fifty-six of their own dead at the trading stations. After reading all of the signs and messages, they reported back to Home Base that someone had betrayed them to the Owlams and another plan was completely ruined…again.

To take out their frustrations about the information being leaked to the Owlams and the plan to take over everything here, they considered that the only ones who could have possibly given any information to the Owlams - the Rakab-Rosh. The immediate execution of all Rakab-Rosh was ordered, to make sure they got the traitor, and another slaughter took place outside the walls of the city of Owlam. Now, a fifteenth race, created by the firestorm weapons, was extinct.

Hadathoo looked at the report he was about to give to the Command Staff. "We should stay away from our home city…for about ten years. One: So the stench subsides. Two: That many dead bodies in one area…there's sure to be an epidemic…of some kind of nasty disease. I don't care to watch all of the decay of those bodies take place."

Wilfadge nodded. "So we stay inside the walls. Grab all of the plants and any belongings that are still there...we bring all of that here to the gorge."

Shyshee laughed. "What are we worried about the plants for? We can't trade the drug at home. What're we going to do... give our location...here...away to do some trading? Plus all of the plants are in Spy...why do we need to move them here?"

Wilfadge gave her a scowl. "No! We will...make surprise visits...to other places. We will never give away our location...here at the gorge. We will trade with other cities, towns and villages... all except the Teltermak villages and cities...and Algothon. Also...if someone decided to move in to our city walls...they'll build homes and such over the existing fields. What then? The plants will not get any sunlight at all...and they'll die...and we lose them all."

"So we're letting the rest of the world know that we're still here...just underground until we solve the Teltermak problem," said Hadathoo. "How long do you think we can get away with that?"

Wilfadge smiled and let out an evil laugh. "As long as we're capable of Jumping to anywhere on the planet...and not letting anyone follow us."

"We're going to have to figure out a way to keep other peoples out of the gorge and off of this high plateau...here on South Chilamte," said Till. "How do we go about that?"

"Excellent question," said Wilfadge. "I suggest that we all go home and start contemplating that very tactic…and then come back…after we've moved all of the plants out of Owlam to here."

Shyshee looked at the ceiling and smiled. "Aren't we forgetting about something? What about the Teltermak munitions plants…and all of their other endeavors…in that area? Are we going to forget about that…or…are we going to attack and punish them…for these transgressions?"

"First things first," said Antrong. "If they're manufacturing weapons in one place…they have to ship them out to other places. If they store them all in one place, all that would do is hinder their plans to attack and conquer another area. We need to get in that plant and look at all of the crates they're planning on sending out. Get some addresses off of those containers and then we'll get a good idea as to where all of their little dens and hideouts are located."

Dwalooa put her hands over her face and groaned. She dropped her hands. "Along that same line…where are they sending those mind controlling drugs? Maybe we should get a reconnaissance Team in there and start finding out where all of that stuff is going."

"We're forgetting about the kite school," said Hadathoo. "That'd be a place where they create new units and send them out…to a new area and create a new hideout. I think that we should somehow slow that school down…immediately…so they can't create or reinforce existing hideouts."

Teelila nodded. "A fire in the warehouse…where they

store the materials for making those kites should slow that down a little. Also a few nasty, if not fatal, accidents by several of the instructors should hurt that enterprise."

Antrong smiled. "A fire where they have all of the finished kites could be even more detrimental. Maybe we should hit that school hard…rather quickly."

Wilfadge nodded. "I want the shipment of drugs and the kite school stopped first. While they're putting out fires, in the school and drug plant, that should give us an opportunity to check all of their files and see what we can find out about locations. One location, of course, is their hideouts. The other locations – where are they planning on shipping the drugs too…and whom are they planning on doping next?"

"Don't forget the tunnels," said Ahandi. "We need to collapse those infernal things as soon as possible."

Wilfadge sighed. "Yes of course. Tell Eeleeg to get to work on it…NOW! He doesn't have to wait for any order. Just get in there, set some explosives and bring all four of them down… completely. That way…those monsters will have to start from scratch."

Eeleeg headed to the munitions plant in Zee-Altha. He called four other Teams to assist in finding all of the necessary explosives they needed to collapse all four tunnels. After reading several destinations on several containers, he advised Dwalooa and Hoynama of his findings – on destinations. He then continued searching for all of the equipment that he would need.

Ahandi and Antrong went back to the kite school in Axswain. They found a few areas where they could wreak havoc with the supplies used to make the kites. They also found a good area for destroying the kites that were already assembled. There was also the area where the instructors were housed. All they needed now was sufficient volatile materials to get their plan of destruction into full operation.

Teelila and Till headed to the drug plant. Since the mind controlling drug was still one of the high priorities for the Teltermak, the hundreds of barrels of the stuff had to be going somewhere. They sabotaged all of the trucks that were supposed to be moving the drug out, while they went through files looking for destinations.

Hadathoo and Shyshee went to Teltermak with fifty other Teams, looking for any information they could find. It did not matter how trivial it seemed, they wanted all information the Teltermak had. Find it, categorize it and get it to the Staff.

All of this was very taxing to all of the Owlamites, seeing as how they had to transfer all of the plants from Owlam to the gorge and get them planted. They had to plant them in Spy and then start hopping sufficient water to the plants to keep them alive. They did not have to worry about sunlight, because the same sun that shined in Home dimension also gave the necessary light in Spy dimension.

Moving entire crops was exhausting and time consuming. When you have an entire field of grain, all of the stalks had to be moved in small shocks. The undertaking left a lot of the Owlamites getting some sleep (whether they wanted to or not) in the field, next to the last plant they had hopped.

Wilfadge was not ready to be a bystander. He and his Team were taking part in moving plants as well. After personally seeing how long it took to move an entire field of grain, he did not criticize anyone for falling asleep...right in the middle of a transplant. He was beginning to think that burning everything in Owlam would have been a better remedy, if it had not been for the fact that they were hoping to move back some day and to have to rebuild from your own fires...that was a very irritating thought. Keep moving plants and make sure you leave nothing behind for the enemy...in Home dimension.

A meeting was called. Wilfadge wanted to know what was happening in the reconnaissance. What have we found out or destroyed?

Ahandi looked rather smug, however she still did not look happy. "We devised a way to take out the instructors and the manufacturing plant for the kites at the same time. We made our own underground storage area, one that the Teltermak had not found yet. We stored a bunch of volatile materials in there... and after over one hundred years...the stuff rotted to the point where...it blew up and...collapsed a lot of the ground around there...because it was only eight taja beneath the surface...unlike most of the other underground areas that are usually twenty to forty taja deep."

Wilfadge frowned. "So one blast took care of all of it?"

"One blast did," said Antrong. "We decided to have a very nasty chain reaction instead. We took out all but two instructors, we took out all of the building material and we got almost one thousand students in the blasts."

Wilfadge nodded. "That means that there is no more school for a while in flying."

"Not really," said Ahandi. "After they got the fires out... and started inventorying the remains. One of the higher ranking ones...on scene, conferred with someone at Home Base. It was decided that they should move the students...to the other schools... at Bising and Rakab-Rosh."

Wilfadge closed his eyes. "Brilliant! Get the inhabitants to move out...and take over a city that is already built." He opened his eyes. "We are now going to have to go check...all of the cities that those *chokwad* Teltermak got the original inhabitants to abandon."

Shyshee groaned. "That would be...Gabeesh-Or, Twakon, Parash-Zanab and Noga-Or."

Hadathoo sighed. "Not to mention the possibilities of Yagalom-Ayin, Maka-Or...and dare I think it...Perfor and Cacktash."

Wilfadge hung his head. "They have units on islands... why not all over the continents as well? We're going to have to do a lot of reconnaissance...again." He looked up and shook his head. "Any report on the drugs?"

Teelila nodded. "Yes, Sir. The primary targets, for the

drugs: Kalash, Rahanan-Sar, T'Mor, Cowpa and Argaman-Or."

Wilfadge stood up and glared back at Teelila. "That would mean, their next target…is the Turgon Wall. They want control of the Wall."

Teelila nodded. "Yes, Sir. That seems to be the meaning of that one."

"Send a message to the Turgon Wall…immediately… NO…send a courier…with a written message. We don't want the Teltermaks to know…that we're going to scuttle that plan as well. Get the message to all of our allies at the Wall and…give them a sample of the drug as well…so they know what to look for…as well as switching to drinking bottled water that they import in for themselves."

Till looked up at the ceiling. "What about water for the prisoners?"

Wilfadge scoffed. "If this drug gives you control over someone…it would mean the prisoners will become much more cooperative. Let them guzzle it all they want."

Hadathoo chuckled. "Don't we still have a Team that keeps an eye on the Turgon Wall for us? Isn't that Team 6909?"

Wilfadge stopped short looking a little confused. "If they give themselves away, then they won't be much good for spying now will they?"

Hadathoo leaned back snickering. "One of our computer geniuses came up with a way they can send a written message… it'll be accepted at the Wall Headquarters and appear that it came from the city of Owlam. All we have to do is contact any one of the four people there and they can send the message. The Teltermak will never know that it happened…until it's too late."

"Well then…send the message to Team 6909… telepathically," said Wilfadge.

Shyshee leaned back and closed her eyes. Moments later she opened them. "Officer Grade 4, Siynooma…of Team 6797… has been informed. She'll get the message to all of our allies at the wall immediately." She looked at Hadathoo and smiled. "There are three Teams at the Wall. Siynooma is the ranking one there."

Hadathoo nodded.

Wilfadge looked at the reports. "Can anyone tell me why it is taking so long to collapse the tunnels?"

"It's the placement of the explosives," said Ahandi.

Wilfadge smiled. "How is this a problem?"

"They decided to go with wires rather than a remote switch. Eeleeg said that once the explosions start, it could mess up a remote. Using a direct wire will keep the circuit intact and we can be more assured that the blasts will occur as planned."

Wilfadge nodded in agreement. "What kind of explosives are we using?"

"They've got some small explosives attached to cylinders for welding torches. They blow up the explosive, it in turn blows up the contents of the cylinder…which creates a great deal of shrapnel…not to mention that it collapses a good part of the tunnel…that has already been weakened."

"So they blow up the entrance and then cascade deeper into the tunnel."

"No, Sir, it goes the other way. If they blew up the one at the beginning of the tunnel first…it could cut the wires to the others. By blowing up the furthest one first, you keep your wires intact until they're needed. You cascade towards the entrance."

Wilfadge frowned. "How many explosions and how long does it take?"

"According to Eeleeg, there'll be twenty-five blasts in each tunnel. If you count slowly, from one to ten, you won't reach five before the last blast happens."

"Again, tell them not to wait. As soon as all explosives are in place…BOOM! They don't need to wait for any special order. I want to know afterwards that all four tunnels are…filled in." Wilfadge took a breath. "Now, is there anything new to report on the units they have…scattered everywhere?"

"Yes, Sir," said Dwalooa. "When Officer, Eeleeg was looking for what he needed…he noticed that the crates were marked as to which unit they were supposed to go to. The Teltermak don't have any organization other than to assign a new number – in numerical sequence – when they start a new unit. According to Eeleeg…the largest number that he saw was…33064." She cleared her throat. "We now know that the Teltermak have at least 33,064 units…that are active…somewhere in the world…today."

Hoynama leaned forward. "We also have no idea how

many are in each unit. You could have one unit of fifty personnel…
and the next one – sequentially – has over ten thousand. Until we
can identify them…other than things like…Team Drib…we still
have a lot of questions."

Shyshee had been sitting there with her eyes closed. She
opened her eyes. "I have a report from Officer, Siynooma at
the Turgon Wall. As soon as our allies got the message about
the Teltermak and the mind controlling drug…they arrested all
Teltermaks that were there as guards. They found twenty-eight
barrels of the drug that have not been used. They found no empty
barrels. They're currently…executing…all Teltermak who are at
the Wall…no matter what their position. According to Siynooma…
that's ninety-one…so far."

Wilfadge looked a little concerned. "Were they able to call
Home Base about their predicament?"

Shyshee giggled. "The first thing that our people did was
vandalize their radios. The Teltermaks tried to send a message…
but no radio was transmitting."

Wilfadge gave her an admonishing look for giggling.
"Getting back to some of that scouting…who should we send to
check out those other cities…to see if the Teltermak have taken
them over as well?"

Hadathoo scoffed. "I suggest that we send Team 7016.
Most of the time, their dumb luck has taken over and they get
more good information than what we were originally hoping for."

Wilfadge fought to keep from laughing. "You're right.
They do have some uncanny knack of finding out…all kinds of

things. Go ahead and send them out."

Shyshee cleared her throat. "What about the plants they're supposed to be hopping and Jumping?"

"Someone else will take care of the gardening and landscaping for them," said Wilfadge flatly. "The reconnaissance is more important."

Team 7016 did not like the assignment, however, they complied.

Two days later, Eeleeg set off the explosives. He reported back that there were a lot of very angry Teltermak. There were a lot of dead ones buried in the tunnels as well.

Hadathoo reported that the people in Headquarters were calling for the executions of all traitors who had taken part in this morbid act of sabotage…if they could figure out who the traitors were. He also reported that the bodies of the Rakab-Rosh were being cleaned up…for the ghastly Teltermak cuisine.

Since Eeleeg was the best expert on explosives and how to set off some devastating cascade explosions, he was given the task of bombing the drug plants in Galsino. The first thing he did was take a barrel of the mind controlling drug to Spy dimension and blow it up. He found out, much to his pleasure, that the drug was highly flammable. He set off four small explosions in the warehouse. The first explosion was rather small. The residual explosions rocked the entire city. The smoke cloud that went around the city appeared to have some permanent brain damaging effects on anyone who got a whiff of the smoke.

Team 7016 was back in seventeen days with a report. At first the Staff was a little upset at how they had been able to accomplish all of this in such a short time. Soolchakan reminded them that it was just a situation to find out what was happening at those places and not a detailed description. There were nine rather embarrassed faces after that comment, however, they would survive.

Soolchakan started his briefing: "Axswain, Galsino, Teltermak and Zee-Altha, you already know. Beetsik and Towlayaw-Or, have been turned into survival schools. The students have to learn to live off of the land…and seeing as how both of those races did not have sophisticated technology…like plumbing, the life there is rather tough. Bising and Rakab-Rosh are kite schools. Cacktash, Maka-Or and Parash-Zanab are all being used to manufacture munitions…as well as Zee-Altha. Gabeesh-Or, Ikogo, Noga-Or, Perfor and Yagalom-Ayin are all basic and advanced military schools."

Hadathoo interrupted. "Wait! You said…Ikogo? But… Ikogo wasn't on the list."

Soolchakan looked up hesitantly. "Yes, Sir, it wasn't. However, because it is an abandoned city, we checked, because the Teltermak seem to be taking over any and all abandoned cities… for their purposes."

Hadathoo turned to Wilfadge and gave him an "*I told you so*" look.

Wilfadge just wrinkled his nose at Hadathoo and then turned back to Soolchakan. "Anything else?"

Soolchakan looked back down at his report. "Yes, Sir. Along with Galsino manufacturing drugs, the other drug places are: Neksheth-Or, P'Lalfan and Twakon. The only other city… that they have all to themselves, of course, is Teltermak."

Wilfadge leaned back in his chair. "FOUR…drug manufacturing plants? It sounds to me as if they're planning on doping the entire world in order to take us all over passively…as drug addicts."

Dwalooa scoffed. "Five military schools and three kite schools. It sounds as if they're prepared for hostile takeover on a grand scale. Let's not forget four ammunition plants…each one utilizing an entire city to make all kinds of weaponry."

Soolchakan cleared his throat. "Yes, Sirs, weaponry… including the fact that Parash-Zanab…is also manufacturing pulse weapons…to include…*heelmashk* weapons."

Teelila looked at Soolchakan in shock. "Oh, not that nonsense again!"

Soolchakan nodded. "I'm afraid so."

Wilfadge spoke through his teeth. "Have they successfully made any of the *heelmashk* weapons yet?"

Soolchakan shrugged. "It appears they have five of them, Sir. They haven't figured out a way to get them out of the city… yet. It seems that they made them too large to go through any of the exits…through the gates of the walled city. I don't think they had that in mind when they first started making the things. They're all mobile...on flat-bed trucks, but they're still going to have to make a larger orifice in the wall to get the things out."

Wilfadge huffed. "Before they do...get with Eeleeg. Get him there...and sabotage all five...*each* one in the exact same way. That way they'll think that it's some kind of a design flaw... or manufacturing...or component flaw. Maybe they'll think again before building another one."

Three days later a Staff meeting was called. Wilfadge wanted a report from Eeleeg in regards to the destruction of the *heelmashk* weapons.

Eeleeg stood there with a strange look on his face. "Yes, Sirs...the *heelmashk* have been destroyed. Uh...they are... nothing but debris...but...I can't take credit for the destruction."

Wilfadge raised his eyebrows questioningly. "Oh? Why not?"

Eeleeg smiled sheepishly. "I...called those computer experts...and asked for a little help."

Wilfadge frowned. "Why?"

"Sir, you wanted it to look like a design flaw. If I just blew them up, that'd be a known sabotage and...that would start an investigation that could lead to...who knows?"

Wilfadge shrugged. "And?"

"Well, yes, Sir...the computer experts...told me to talk to

Officer, Kiyalee and…"

Wilfadge pounded his fist on the table. "ENOUGH OF THE SILLY PRELIMINARIES! WHO DID WHAT AND HOW?"

Eeleeg cleared his throat nervously. "I think…that… Officer, Kiyalee…should be the one to give you that briefing."

Wilfadge smiled. "So…where is she?"

Eeleeg closed his eyes and turned his head slightly to the right as he made a mental communication with Kiyalee.

A few moments later, Akantini was ushering Kiyalee into the conference room. Kiyalee had her cheeks puffed out a little and was chewing on a mouthful of…something. She looked around the room with a little trepidation as she continued trying to chew and swallow as quickly as possible. She finally got most of the mass down her throat and was smacking her lips a little and sucking a few things through her teeth as she put her left hand over her mouth trying to muffle some of the noise.

Wilfadge finally spoke up as he saw that she was finished chewing. "Officer, Kiyalee, according to Officer, Eeleeg, you were the one who was instrumental in befouling the *heelmashk* weapons. Could you please tell us what you did…so that it'd look like a design flaw?"

Kiyalee smiled. "Oh…that's what you want…yes, Sir." She started giving a full detailed description of what she had done in the circuitry.

Dwalooa sat there trying to uncross her eyes.

Teelila started flapping her hands in the air. "WAIT! WHOA! WHAT…are you talking about? What's a capacitor?"

Hoynama looked equally confused. "What's a cathode?"

Antrong was puzzled as well. "Relay…what are you relaying?"

Wilfadge smiled and chuckled. He cleared his throat. "Officer, Kiyalee…it appears that…you're going to have to simplify…your explanation."

Kiyalee was the one who looked confused now. "Huh?"

"Dumb it down," said Hadathoo as he looked around the table. "None of us are experts…or even novices in electronics. You need to give us an explanation…that any idiot could understand."

Kiyalee looked a little desperate. "Uh…simplify… uh." She chuckled nervously. She turned towards the door. "BONARAIN…I need your help!"

Bonarain came to the door looking apprehensive. "With… what?"

"They…want me to explain…what I did…and…HELP!"

Bonarain walked up to Kiyalee smiling. "Don't be so technical. Tell them…in terms that…everyone can understand… what you did."

"I don't know how," whimpered Kiyalee.

Soolchakan walked in shaking his head. He took Kiyalee by the shoulders and turned her to where she was facing the Staff.

He pushed Bonarain up behind Kiyalee to where Bonarain was resting her chin on Kiyalee's left shoulder. He placed his left hand on top of Bonarain's head and his right hand on top of Kiyalee's head. He closed his eyes and bowed his head. Both women looked a little startled as he was communicating with them mentally.

Bonarain smiled and closed her eyes.

Kiyalee's expression went from fear and surprise to one that looked as if she had just received a revelation. Her expression went blank and she cocked her head to the right. "I...messed with...some of the components...in the on/off switch."

"I can understand that," said Wilfadge with a pleasant smile. "Please continue."

"I...changed some of them around...so that...I could turn it on...but the Teltermaks couldn't...turn it off."

"I'm still with you," said Wilfadge.

"So...now...the thing is on and they can't do anything. I then...rearranged some of the components...in the firing mechanism."

"Very good," said Wilfadge with a nod.

"I also messed with the...workings...inside the cone... so that...it couldn't fire. That...built up a...sort of...pressure...a LOT of pressure...and...it blew back...inside the whole thing... and it blew the thing up."

"A backwash of pressure...where it blew back in, on itself," said Wilfadge. "Is that what you meant?"

Kiyalee smiled. "Yes, Sir."

"BACKWASH?" Eeleeg looked stunned. "I'd call it more than some simple backwash."

Wilfadge raised his eyebrows. "Oh? Then what would you call it?"

Eeleeg scoffed. "A massive surge! When that first one blew...it left a crater that was at least fifteen taja deep and over a kilotaja in diameter. There was *h'oolyach* flying everywhere."

Hadathoo snickered. "So it didn't just mess the thing up, it blew the *piddleeyanks* out of everything in the immediate vicinity as well."

"Immediate and for quite a distance," said Eeleeg. He then chuckled. "When the fourth one went up...it was next to the outer wall. They now have an orifice in the wall...that they could get a *heelmashk* out...once they clear away all of the rubble."

Wilfadge snarled. "So they could still build another one... and get it out?"

"No, Sir," said Kiyalee. "When the first one went up... or...just before it went kaboom...they saw there was some kind of major problem going on. They called the primary technicians out there...to see what they could do. All fourteen of THE primary technicians were there...with the one and only copy of the technical manual for putting that thing together."

"I hope you're saying what I think you're saying," said Wilfadge. "I still want you to elaborate...just to make sure."

Kiyalee looked puzzled again. Then she looked as if she had been slapped. She turned and looked back at Soolchakan. She turned back to the Staff and swallowed. "The fourteen...*primary technicians*...were the only ones who knew how...or had ever put that thing together. The primary technical manual...*absolutely*... was the only copy of how to put that giant puzzle together."

Wilfadge scoffed. "Why can't the other people figure it out...as how to put the thing together?"

Kiyalee turned to Bonarain. "Help," she said desperately.

Bonarain smiled.

Kiyalee turned back to the Staff and her face went blank. She had that dull look for several moments and then took a breath as she raised her eyebrows. She pointed around the table at the Staff. "Let's say that each one of you is one of the minor technicians that've been assigned to assemble one of the components. Okay, you put your piece together...but you have no idea where it goes... in the giant puzzle. The *holy* fourteen, of the primary technicians, they were the only ones who were even allowed to look at the main technical manual. They were the only ones who had ever put the things together." She took several breaths as she was getting instruction on how to simplify from a smiling Bonarain. "Each component may look different...but if you don't know where it goes...all of them are worthless. Each one of you makes your nine components, but...how do you put them together? Is it...1, 2, 3, 4, 5, 6, 7, 8, 9...or is it 9, 8, 7, 6, 5, 4, 3, 2. 1? Or is it 1, 3, 5, 7, 9, 2, 4, 6, 8? Or maybe there are a few other components, made by other personnel, who fit in between your pieces. Without that main technical manual...no one knows where each piece goes."

Hadathoo grunted. "Isn't there a possibility that some genius could fit them together...eventually?"

Kiyalee smiled. "There are over four thousand different components. All of the pieces have the exact same kind of a plug in, to put them in line, or connect them together. Since you can hook...component 1 up to...54 or 879 or 2,222 or any other... without even knowing which one is component number 1...you don't know where to begin. Since you have over four thousand... and the same plugs fit all of them...there are billions, possibly trillions of different combinations. I don't think they'll get that lucky on the first try."

Wilfadge growled. "Surely they have another manual... somewhere else...don't they?"

Kiyalee shook her head. "No, Sir...that was the *one* and *only*."

Eeleeg laughed. "And that '*one and only*' was turned to ashes...along with the fourteen primary technicians...in the first blast."

Kiyalee shrugged. "*All* of the technology...on building a *heelmashk*...is lost. It is now nothing but ashes...and part of lost history."

Hadathoo chuckled. "So, there is the strong probability... that for the rest of our lives...we'll never have to worry about another *heelmashk* weapon."

Both Bonarain and Soolchakan backed away from Kiyalee.

Wilfadge snickered. "Amazing! It took all three of you to simplify the explanation for us. Thank you. Now, what about their other pulse weapons...could we destroy all of them in the same way?"

Kiyalee scoffed. "Their pulse weapons are no match for our 459. We can shoot a satellite out of orbit with a 459. Their pulse weapons...if you were standing on the far east side of Owlam...and aimed at the west wall...the beam would fade and die, long before it got past the center of the city."

Wilfadge nodded. "So we can definitely outdistance them."

Dwalooa sighed. "It still appears that the only thing that we can do to the Teltermak, at this time, is harassment."

"First things first," said Wilfadge. "Officer, Eeleeg, do you need any special technical assistance in destroying a munitions plant...or drug manufacturing plant?"

"No, Sir, that's very simple. There's always a way to make explosives go off."

Wilfadge nodded. "Good! Your next assignment... confiscate all munitions that you think that we can use...then turn ALL of the Teltermak drug plants and munitions plants into rubble. Please get this accomplished at the earliest possible time. The less ammunition and drugs the Teltermak have...the more we can...maybe slow them...and figure out what their next move is."

Eeleeg smiled. "Yes, Sir." He vanished.

Dwalooa frowned. "How are we supposed to figure out

their next move?"

Wilfadge sniffed. "Don't forget – we now know where their Home Base Headquarters is located. We can drop in anytime… and listen to them. We've been doing the same to the Algothon for quite some time. Now, we watch the Teltermak bosses…very closely."

2

Once again, Officer Leader, Boneech was placed in charge of spying on the Teltermak. Now that the Headquarters area had been found and established as *the* only primary headquarters for all of the Teltermak, it was easy get all of the information they wanted.

The Teltermak were absolutely flabbergasted at how their classified information was getting out so quickly. Before they could encrypt the information and inform some of their forward teams of any new plans, in code, the forward teams were hearing it from the areas where they were spying…un-coded. It was bad enough that all of their plans to capture and enslave the Owlamites had been completely scuttled…again, but to have their classified information given out, by some intruder, faster than they could send it was humiliating, infuriating and bewildering.

Now to get a report that all four of the Teltermak drug manufacturing plants had gone up in flames, all in the same manner, followed rather rapidly by the complete devastation of all four munitions manufacturing plants, the High Command was ready to kill anyone, just to try to get whoever it was that was giving out ALL of the information so quickly.

Ultimate Leader, Ootgreeg was sitting there fuming as a doctor was putting a cast on his broken right hand. It was broken because he had put his fist through a hard wooden wall. He tried to ignore the pain as he was talking to his Second in Command: Army Assistant to the Ultimate Leader, Yoykongkong. "How do we find this...spy ring that is...causing us such relentless grief?"

Yoykongkong was just as frustrated, however, he was not into punching out some helpless wall. "I wonder if it is those Ghost Assassins that have been giving us grief...ever since that rotten Algothon attack. No matter what we've done to find them...they still elude us. The only clue that we have so far is that...no matter what happens...they always seem to be protecting the Owlams. Is it possible that the Ghost Assassins *are* the Owlams?"

Boneech was not sure whether she wanted to laugh in his face or give him a one way ticket to Jahong's Death. She was getting nothing from them right now because all they were doing, while the doctor was in the room, was venting.

One of Boneech's Team members, Officer Grade 7, Jojog was sitting there looking as if he had a bad taste in his mouth. "Can I get rid of one or both of those *bimyocks*?"

Boneech snarled back at him. "No, you can't touch them... yet. As long as we know that these two are the main biggies, we know where to go to find information. If we kill them we have to start searching...all over again to find out who is in charge. Forget about eradicating them...for now."

Jojog sighed. "Yes, Sir." He picked up his pad, sighed and continued taking notes.

Yoykongkong watched the doctor for a few moments. "Maybe we should call a full meeting of the highest personnel."

"Get serious," said Ootgreeg. "Do you know how long it'd take for all of the Army Leaders to get from where they are to here? By the time they got here, all of the information would be obsolete and we'd be fighting a different battle." He winced as the doctor repositioned the injured hand. "Besides, it seems that the Ghost Assassins are helping out more than just the Owlams now. All of our plans to take the Turgon Wall have gone *spiknok*. We can't get any of our personnel within a day's walking distance, without them getting captured...and EXECUTED! Our Great Wings are being shot out of the air everywhere...by everyone. All that we've done to further our cause...and everything is just going completely...*mombik*!"

"We can't just sit here and do nothing," said Yoykongkong. "If we do, then the Ghost Assassins and whoever else is causing us grief will get the upper hand."

Ootgreeg glared at him. "They already have the upper hand, you dumb *protch*! Right now, all of our personnel are running...in fear...for their lives. Since those Owlams made the announcement that WE are the ones responsible for the stoppage of *Tuzine* - manufacturing and sale – WE are the ones on the run... everywhere. Haven't you read the latest reports...or any reports?"

"Yes, Sir, I have and...I just don't understand who could do this or how. The Owlams were the only ones who haven't been affected by all of this and it seems that the Ghost Assassins are now protecting everybody. That bunch that was using others to fight their battles...that was genius. Then the Ghost Assassins... somehow snuck in and released all of hostages and..." He trailed off and shook his head. "They did it in a way...and at a time, during a nasty storm, where even we don't even know what happened... but it had to be them. Who else could've pulled it off?"

A Teltermak man walked in looking rather upset. He placed a document on Ootgreeg's desk and walked out. Ootgreeg snarled and picked it up and with a sour look started reading. He shook his head and dropped it back on the desk.

"Army Leader, Voyvashik. She's executed four hundred sixty-eight personnel for cowardice. It still hasn't stopped our people from running." He looked up. "What's the next step?"

"How many do we have to execute before someone finally grows some courage?"

Ootgreeg grunted. "Give the order that all of the executions stop. Since that message about the *Tuzine,* all Teltermaks, everywhere, are marked for death. Until we can stop the Owlam lie...that we're responsible...we all have to run. We may have to recall everyone...back here...to home. We need, as many as possible, still alive!"

Yoykongkong nearly collapsed in his chair. "That's almost eleven million people. We don't have the room...here!"

Ootgreeg looked up sadly. "Yes, we do. Between Teltermak and the other three cities, in the immediate vicinity, we have enough room for all. We can probably defend a smaller area a lot easier. Make the call and bring everyone home...until we can get this catastrophic mess under control."

Boneech was immediately in telepathic contact with the Owlam Command Staff. She informed them of the recall. They in turn relayed the information to everyone in the world where they knew the Teltermak were causing grief.

Yoykongkong left the room to go inform the radio operators of the Command decision to recall all personnel until they could get everything back under their control.

The radio operators all gave him a sad or sour look and started encrypting the messages. After sending them, the majority of them got the same response back. They gave the information to Yoykongkong. He walked back to Ootgreeg's office, muttering to himself with his head hung low. He walked into the office and looked up.

Ootgreeg saw his face. "Now what?"

Yoykongkong shrugged. "The usual…lately. On Ficara… Army Leader, Jinjisik had to abandon Twakon…after the fire destroyed the drug plant. He recalled everyone to Gabeesh-Or and…they're having a terrible time getting everyone in that city… alive." He looked at the paper in his hand. "The same thing on Aerisau. Army Leader, Aboontkom abandoned the drug plant in P'Lalfan and recalled everyone to Parash-Zanab. Many of the units were massacred attempting to get to that city." He sighed and checked the paper again. "Army Leader, Voyvashik on South Chilamte…same thing. Abandon the destroyed drug plant in Neksheth-Or and recall everyone to Perfor. So far, less than one fifth have been able to get to Perfor. Army Leader, Zidz, on Neopaure, most of his personnel are deaf…after being in the city of Cacktash…when the ammunition plant blew up. The ones who can still hear…still have some hearing loss and seem to have a permanent ringing in their ears. They're recalling all other units on Neopaure…but…as bad as their hearing is, they don't know if the outer units are responding." He heaved a sigh again. "On Lusaratia, Army Leader, Fannkozzok reports that the units are attempting to get to Noga-Or and join forces. On Cifpasica, Army Leader, Thoobwot is attempting to get everyone to Bising. On Satroco Isle, Section Leader, Dooldorok has given up the potion factory. There's no reason to defend a bunch of empty refrigerators…since it seems that the prime ingredients for all of the potions are currently out of our reach."

Ootgreeg raised his left fist to slam it down on his desk. He stopped and looked at the cast on his right hand. He grimaced in pain and held his breath in order to keep from screaming out loud. He held his right hand against his chest and rubbed the cast with his left hand. "Any good news?"

Yoykongkong shook his head. "Section Leader, Kishkoosh reports hostile forces massing around Axswain. Section Leader, Gooloo reports hostile forces massing around Galsino. Section Leader, Gockzoyon reports hostile forces massing around Zee-Altha. Section Leader, Blobsot reports hostile forces massing around Beetsik. Section Leader, Quock reports hostile forces massing around Ikogo. Section Leader, Roshosho reports hostile forces massing around Rakab-Rosh. Section Leader, Argoosik reports hostile forces massing around Towlayaw-Or." He looked up from the reports. "I've checked with our city guard. We have hostile forces massing…here…around Teltermak. Either the Owlams…or the Ghost Assassins…have turned everyone against us. Not even this kind of hatred was put against the city of

Algothon."

Ootgreeg closed his eyes. "So, no matter where we are…we're having to fight our way out of a mess…just to get to somewhere else…where the mess is just as bad. We have to find out…who those Ghost Assassins are. We can forget about those rancid Owlams…for the moment…and try…TRY…to find out who our main enemy is. They've been hiding…far too long."

Boneech and her Team were all sitting there laughing, holding their sides because of the pain from the laughter.

Yoykongkong looked back down at the report. "Should we tell the Axswains? They're in a rather vulnerable position… on that island."

Ootgreeg looked up angrily. "They are not our concern. They had to run from the Ghost Assassins as well. They left far more behind than what we did. They don't even know what happened to their people and none of them seem to care. NO! Leave them to their own defenses. If the Ghost Assassins care about them, they'll go after them. Maybe that'll give us some time to get our people back from some of those islands because the Assassins are going after them…even though they number less than three hundred."

"What…you think that the Ghost Assassins will finish the Axswain off?"

"If they do…I don't care. All I care about is my people and how this entire thing is suddenly…so beyond our control."

"Just try to get as many of our people back…alive…as is

possible."

"Yes."

Yoykongkong walked out of the office. He left Ootgreeg to his melancholy attitude. The empire was failing fast because everyone seemed to be against them. They still had no way of knowing who their main adversary was or how to find and/or stop them. The elusive monsters just killed without remorse and were somehow able to maintain their secret, even after all of these years since the change.

Everywhere on the planet the Teltermak were running. All tribes of Heyyah and all races of the Elf people were attacking the Teltermak with one thing in mind: Stop the Teltermak and the *Tuzine* trade returns.

For the next eighty years the Teltermak were on the run and their numbers dwindled drastically. They were still able to use their Great Wings to escape a lot of the trouble. As the reports of killing Teltermak came back, by one method or another, to the Owlamites, they did everything that they could to keep track of how low the numbers of the Teltermak were becoming. At the eighty year mark, they triple checked all of the figures. So far, there had been over fifteen million Teltermak killed. Either the numbers were being embellished greatly or the Teltermaks, even during war, were still procreating, making every effort to keep their race alive.

The *Tuzine* trade had been continued, with Owlamites making visits to cities, towns and villages all over the world. The

Owlamites continued to tell races everywhere that as long as the Teltermak were kept at bay, the *Tuzine* trade could continue… unabated.

The news of the drug going back on the market got back to the Teltermak ears. The main frustration there was that they could do nothing about what the Owlamites were doing or saying. The reports of the Teltermak being the ones responsible for the non-availability of the drug made everyone mad…including the Algothons (who had to go through other people to buy their doses…at a rather grand markup in price).

They traded with almost everybody. They even traded with the P'Lalfan and Ikogo people. The only thing that either could offer was fish, however, there were several fish, which cooked and spiced to perfection, were very tasty…and even went well with kwatha.

Senior Officer, Till continued to look to the heavens at every opportunity. He was suffering some frustration of his own in the fact that many of the flying cameras were starting to blink out and quit after just over two centuries of orbiting the planet… with no preventive maintenance being performed on them. He was down to three – and he could not really rely on them. He had to switch from one to another in order to keep an eye on any one place in the heavens…if he happened to see something interesting.

He was able to see most of the planets in the solar system, however, he could not really learn anything new about them… except that they orbited Holgotho, the central star, at different distances. He checked the Algothon archives and was able to find all of the rumors and legends about the planets. He now knew that all of it was nothing but rumor and superstition. These were not entities, they were planets and gas giants, most with their own satellites.

Till was able to get all of his newly acquired knowledge of the planets to all of the Owlamites. At first, numerous Owlamites were shocked at the revelations about the planets, however, once he was able to get all of the information out, with evidence, they accepted the new information with different emotions and reactions.

Hadathoo and a few other top members of the Staff were thinking of new ways to use this information against races and areas that considered the planets as some form of deity. Even with the technology that was available, there were still people that were of the opinion that those planets were more than just a giant rock floating around a star. A few wiser heads decided that if they did too much of destroying entire theological ideologies…in a short time, then it would be the Owlamites and not the Teltermak that other races would be attacking.

The Teams that were spying on the Algothons were also reporting back that the people of that city were once again attempting to flex their muscles and trying to take over the world again. Once again, the Owlamites had to "remove" a few of the more intelligent ones in order to make sure they did not manufacture any more of the firestorm weapons. There were many among the

Owlamites who were concerned as to just how crowded Jahong's Death was becoming with all of the debris they kept sending there.

Word came to the Command Staff that the Teltermak were tunneling again. This time, however, they were tunneling in a different direction. They were tunneling east of the city of Teltermak away from the city of Owlam. The ones in Axswain were tunneling north away from Owlam. The ones in Galsino were tunneling west away from Owlam.

The ones in Zee-Altha had long abandoned that city. There was nothing left after the ammunition manufacturing plant had exploded. All that had been left behind, other than ruins, was a giant crater, or two, in the middle of the city walls.

Once again, Eeleeg was tasked to investigate the tunnels. He checked all ten of the tunnels going away from Teltermak. All of them were going directly east for over fifteen kilotaja, with no sign of any turns. The ones from Axswain went very deep in order to go under the large canyon that was directly north of the city. They also kept on a northerly path for over fifteen kilotaja. The ones going out of Galsino were the same. They all went directly west, with no turns, for over fifteen kilotaja. Eeleeg reported that until he found out about any turns, there was no point in investigating them any further.

Many on the Command Staff were still very apprehensive about giving the Teltermaks any leeway. They had proven themselves to be totally treacherous in the past and there was no reason to believe that these tunnels led to anything different.

There had to be some deceitful plan going on somewhere. The Teltermak could not be trusted, even with their own possessions.

Six years later, all of the Teltermak tunnels were detonated…by the Teltermak…at the end in the cities themselves. Boneech had observed all of the Teltermak citizens going into the tunnels. She had seen it before. They had drills – many drills. They would all head for the tunnels to see how long it would take to use them as an escape path. Then one day, they all disappeared in the tunnels and…BOOM! No more tunnels and not a clue as to where the Teltermak had escaped to.

Once again, the Owlamites had to guess where the Teltermak were and keep a watch for the crafty monsters. Start anew in the vigilance of keeping track of them…once they found them. The only clue was the destroyed tunnels and the Teltermak had made sure that the trail was completely clogged with too much debris. Even if someone was able to dig the tunnels out, it would be several years before they got to the end and the trail could be very cold by then. Even Eeleeg was not sure where they had ended.

The only option was to wait and see where the Teltermak popped up again. It was estimated there were around 500,000 at the time the tunnels were destroyed. They would have to appear somewhere…eventually.

The Owlamites were constantly informing other races that they should keep the vigil going as well. The Teltermak had proven they were capable of just about any kind of evil plot, for the purposes of taking over anything and everything. There was no reason anyone should think they were hiding just for self-preservation. They were hiding to increase their numbers and start another plot of domination.

Many of the personnel who were mechanics kept on going to Kiyalee with wonder in their eyes. That old 161 was still in good working condition. She had rebuilt the engine at least a dozen times. She had rewired it at least six times. She had rebuilt the transmission at least eight times. She had to machine certain parts, because there was nothing else available. Somehow she still managed to keep that antique thing working…and looking good.

Kiyalee did not look at it as something marvelous. She was rather disgusted with the laziness of others, in that they had not kept their trucks in operational condition. They would rather trade for a new one than renew the old one.

Till kept looking to the skies. One time one of the adjustment on one of the cameras went awry. He found himself looking at something out there that had a strange shape and some blinking lights. After magnifying it and checking on it in the Algothon archives, he found that he was looking at another one of the Algothon satellites. The cameras in it had long ago conked out, however, the adjustment rockets that were used to keep it in a synchronized orbit were still functioning. Once they conked out, the orbit would decay and the entire thing would be burned up on reentry.

He now had to get some new information from the archives. Reentry? Orbit decay? Burn up on reentry? Synchronized orbit? Adjustment rockets? He found himself learning an entirely new, rather complicated, vocabulary.

He assigned some of the tasks of researching these new terms to his Team. Officer Grade 3, Ababi, Officer Grade 6, Hoodeefa and Officer Grade 7, Choychata did not share his enthusiasm, however, they were on his Team and he was the Team Leader, so the three women had to learn the new jargon, whether they liked it or not. They found that none of this came up much in conversation with others at any party or celebration. Someone might show an initial interest, however, once they got into the explanations, the conversation would change to something else… that everyone could get involved with. Now they knew what the computer specialists, the shipwrights and other experts felt like when learning a specific area.

Some of the other Command Staff complained to Wilfadge about the obsession of the most junior member of the Staff. Wilfadge did not concern himself with any of the extracurricular activities of any of the Staff, as long as they did not interfere with the main workings of the Staff and the protection of the Owlamite race.

Three years later, the Teltermak were found. They had reestablished themselves on Satroco Isle. They once again had their big potion processing plants and their big refrigerators. Boneech was again assigned to keep track of them. Find out if they are planning any more world domination, find out if they are processing potions again so we can find out what that main ingredient is. Find out if they have harmed anyone else...again. Find out, find out, find out. Just keep an eye on them and see what they are plotting again.

On the Neopaure continent, there were several different Heyyah tribes and races of Elf who decided to get together and form a sort of a cooperation area type government. They looked at the occurrences of the past and decided that there was strength in numbers and cooperation. Since it had been Algothon that had caused the strange manifestations of the Elf races, it was decided they should be the ones who were chastised the hardest...if anything untoward happened on the continent.

These co-ops formed countries: Agrosha, Ajeemank, Koryapor, and (the one that Algothon was stuck in the middle of) Mataberee. The Algothon people found that if there was any attack, by them, on anyone else, the Algothons would be dealing with enemies that now had military that numbered close to something that was greater than the population of Algothon. If they did not watch what they were doing, they could end up under siege...from several sources. They could end up cut off from any and everybody (not that there were any allies of theirs anywhere in the world).

The city of Algothon attempted to put up a friendly façade, while they secretly (or so they thought) tried to rebuild their nuclear arsenal. They were constantly stopped as they continued the attempts as the most brilliant physicists kept on having silly and fatal accidents in their homes and on the job.

Another thing that stopped Algothon from rebuilding their arsenal was an extreme lack of any more fissionable material. Their primary source had been found as they were originally digging their underground storage bunkers. Now that source was tapped out. They would have to come up with some subtle reason for others to trade with them for that particular material. It seemed that there was no subtle way. The city leaders and the scientists (that were still left over) had several meetings about what terms they could use, however, they still could not come up with anything that would not alarm a prospective seller, as to the intentional use of the materials. The majority of the skepticism and pessimism was mentally induced on them by Owlamites.

There were many others on different continents who saw this cooperation between cities, towns, and villages. They started communicating with other communities on their continents to see if they could achieve the same goal. There were all kinds of diplomatic meetings all over every continent.

Some of these communications came to the city of Owlam. Wilfadge and the rest of the Command Staff were very worried about this new phenomenon because it might end up in a situation where they would have to give up all of their secrets to their allies. This would also mean they would have to tell the truth about some of their fabrications - such as a mulitfastidigeous thonlock communicator, which would mean they would have to admit to their mind reading capabilities…and other nasty secrets that they did not want anyone to know about. They could end up just as isolated as the Algothons.

The Owlamites looked at the way the things had been set up at the Turgon Wall. They did not have problems with anything except for the fact that the administrators from the Argaman-Or and the Towtoo were such sticklers for the letter of the law. Nothing would be kept secret from any ally – who worked at the Wall. This was a primary rule in order to be in any position of administration at the Wall. These same two races were pushing for a united group, just like on Neopaure, and the rules of "no secrecy from allies" was being pushed hard by the same two races.

The Owlamites would have to give up their secrets about *Tuzine* as well. They would have to share their capabilities of dimension hopping, the 459 pulse cannons, all of the goodies they had stolen from the different races and who knows how many other stunts, major and minor, they had pulled against enemies. They would have to figure out some way to put it across to their allies that they were totally xenophobic, otherwise they would have to share all…or disappear altogether. This was a debate they did not look forward to, however, the way the Towtoo kept pushing for a united continent, the pressure was getting increasingly difficult to argue against.

Disappearing into the gorge in that mammoth high plateau in the northern part of South Chilamte was looking more inviting with each new communique from the allies at the Turgon Wall. They still wanted to keep the city that they had owned for thousands of years. They also wanted their independence from outside interference. They wanted to keep their secrets…if for nothing else - survival. The debate raged on for years.

Word came in from Aerisau that four countries on the largest continent had formed there: Ekogib, Festrema, Monokland and Tuvalow.

Each new treaty that formed a new country on any continent put even more pressure on any city or group that wanted to remain independent or neutral.

Twenty years later, the pressure was becoming almost beyond control for everyone to become part of one of these new countries that were sprouting up everywhere.

On Cifpasica, there were now three of these countries: Dreeland, Lanopa and Pebonottoms. On Lusaratia, there were four countries: Chinivak, Lower Oosam, Nookamin and Vonver. The crazy thing with Lower Oosam was that they had formed a united country with a portion of Ficara, which was called Upper Oosam. Different continents, however, one united country, governed by the same government, with the capitol city – Saditelo - located in Lower Oosam.

Once this agreement between Upper and Lower Oosam had been accepted by all parties concerned, the continent of Ficara, very quickly, started their own batch of new countries: Buzitari, Chogine, Grenboling, Jebeltau, Parth, Slateel and of course – Upper Oosam.

South Chilamte soon fell in line with this new ideology. Falamin, Joktel and Peegruch soon became countries on that continent, with the big high plateau becoming known as High Country.

North Chilamte seemed to be the continent that held out

the longest, because of several disagreements between certain factions. Eventually they came into line with: Cheseet, Eang, Hasindol, Ithagum, Paselter, Tabrow, and Varnast. The Owlamites found themselves right in the middle of one of the largest countries to be formed on any of the continents - Paselter. Everything had been formed around the city of Owlam, with them still trying to hold out.

On South Chilamte, the Owlamites had the gorge. It almost cut that entire giant, high plateau in half. Nobody wanted the gorge because whenever it rained, which was quite often in that tropical zone, the entire bottom of the gorge was turned into a raging river that flowed north and emptied out, through a series of underground rivers that had been cut through the northern area of the plateau, through thousands of years of erosion, into the Central Talanka Ocean. Of course that was the water that did not get claimed into the reservoirs of the Owlam hideaway area in the gorge.

For years the different Elf races and the tribes of the Heyyah in the new country of Paselter kept hounding the Owlamites to join in on the unified country. They were told that if they did not join, it would weaken the entire group, because someone was in the center who refused to join. That could justify others who did not wish to join. The harder the outside interests pushed the Owlamites, the harder they pushed back.

The Towtoo and the Cowpa sent emissaries to Owlam who were very intelligent and were very good debaters. Each one attempted to use their power of persuasion in order to bring the stubborn Owlamites around.

The problem the emissaries had was that the Owlam Command Staff would invite them in and give them a nice banquet – before any debates were to begin. While they were sitting there eating, the Owlamites would perform some intense mind-reading and by the time the debate began, they had an answer for each argument before it was even voiced by the visiting parties. They also had several minds cooperating with each other in order to have a valid argument against each new idea the others brought up.

Each one of the diplomatic missions went back to the united group to start over, because the Owlamites had, somehow, shown themselves to be more obstinate and even greater debaters than the team that was sent there. They had to come up with new arguments that should be used for enticement and not any form of coercion.

There were many who were getting suspicious as to how the Owlamites were able to victoriously accomplish such lofty verbal battles. Every time they had a meeting to try to come up with positive arguments, they had every desk, chair, pad, pencil, person, wall, floor and ceiling checked for listening devices. There was even talk that all of the personnel who entered the room, should do so naked in order to prove they had no form of recording device on their person. That one was scrapped because they decided that that was just too paranoid.

Someone finally mentioned the idea of telepathic communication and mind reading. At first it was mocked as impossible. Then they started thinking back to the Cacktash and Perfor and the unusual capabilities that they had manifested.

Now, mental telepathy was being looked at more seriously. Are the Owlams capable of that sort of communication? If they are, then in reality, they could be a serious threat to anyone attempting to call them friend. Some claimed that mind-reading could be an excellent form of spying on an enemy. Maybe that was how the Owlams had been so successful in destroying the Sodle.

The new question: If the Owlams were mind-readers: How do you stay on their good side? If they can read minds, then they would be fully aware of any form of mendacity or manipulation that was used against them. You could not spin anything.

There were some who got a little radical and were suggesting that some kind of force be used against the Owlams in order to bring them into line. Those peoples were quickly admonished and reminded of what happened with the Teltermak. That group of conquerors had tried to go against the Owlams and the Owlams had won by cutting off *Tuzine* to everybody, thus enraging everybody and having the entire world attack and almost obliterate the entire Teltermak race. No one wanted to follow suit and be the next race that was hated by all.

On Satroco Isle, the Teltermak were doing everything that they could to come up with the formula for manufacturing the precious *Tuzine*. There were now over 7,000,000 different recipes that had been attempted and none of them worked. Of course the Owlamites had a great deal to do with all of the failures.

The spies who were fouling the mixtures were getting bored with the same routine. The complaint was sent back to the Command Staff that they should just order the complete annihilation of the Teltermaks and that would solve a lot of problems.

The argument against the genocide was that the Teltermak were still the only ones who knew what that mysterious "prime ingredient" in their potions was. No matter what source the Owlamites had dug into to find this ingredient, there was nothing written down. This was an even better kept secret than the *Tuzine* recipe. Kill all of the Teltermak and you destroy the knowledge of the potions. Maybe the potions were worth something, however, until you know how to make it, you still need the primary chef in order to keep the possibilities alive.

The answer always came back: Keep on fouling their mixtures until we can find out more information about the potions. Once we have the secret of the potions, then we can start thinking about the final deadly solution of the Teltermaks…who were once again making noises about world domination.

These debates went on for another twenty-five years of parity. Twenty-five years that marked the 260th anniversary of the dropping of the firestorm weapons all over the planet of Hardooth. 260 years of finding out about themselves and others on the planet. 260 years of keeping secrets and stealing secrets from others.

3

Wilfadge was bored. He decided to take a vacation with his Team. They were going to get away from the city of Owlam and the gorge and go explore a few places they had never been to before.

Master Officer, Ahandi had decided on a vacation with her Team as well. She departed for places that were personally unexplored as well.

Shortly after that Master Officer, Teelila took her Team… somewhere.

Master Officer, Dwalooa stood there smiling at Hadathoo. "According to Supreme Officer, Wilfadge, there has to be at least one Master Officer here on duty at all times. Since you are the junior ranking Master Officer…" Her grin got bigger. "…you just got nominated for the position…until one of the other Master Officers gets back from their vacation. It has been a while since I had a vacation as well…so…I and my Team are going on one."

Hadathoo gave her a sullen smile. "Have fun," he grumbled. "I'll just sit here with four Senior Officers…and their Teams…and my Team…and be bored."

She grinned. "I knew you'd understand."

"Does anyone know where you...or any of the others are going?"

She snickered. "You know that any one of us is only one little telepathic message away from returning...if it is really important enough."

He turned away. "Yeah, yeah, yeah," he said sullenly. "So go! The sooner you go, the sooner you get back...the sooner I can go on a vacation."

Dwalooa and her Team vanished.

Antrong looked around at the other Senior Officers. "How many of us really need to stay here?"

Hadathoo just gave him a blank stare.

Till and Hoynama both snickered. Shyshee just huffed and sat down.

Antrong shook his head. "So if you gotta be miserable - everyone has to be miserable. Is that it?"

Hadathoo let out a low growl. "Of all five...the Master Officers and the Supreme Officer, it has been longer since I was on a vacation than any of them. They all decided to do this now... just to have fun at my expense. So why do you really think that I'm miserable? When was your last vacation?"

Shyshee huffed. "I'd like to have a vacation...sometime before Wilfadge's two hundredth anniversary as the *Voice of Power*."

Till frowned. "When is that anniversary?"

"Next year," said Hoynama. "He's had the title for 199 years."

Till just nodded and sighed. "Has it really been that long since all that *h'oolyach* happened?"

Antrong laughed. "Don't give me any garbage about how it seems like it was just yesterday! When you think of how many times we've had to chase the Teltermak off, we've fought off the Galsino, the Zee-Althans, the Axswains…and a few others…who are now extinct…believe me…it was NOT just yesterday."

Hoynama cleared her throat. "So who gets to stay here and keep you company, Master Officer, Hadathoo? We really don't all need to be here. Some of us could go home and…water the plants...you know, the plants that we use for Tuzine."

Hadathoo sighed. "Cast lots between the four of you. Only one has to stay. The other three can go…pee on a *Shoonshook* weed."

Shyshee lost the bet.

Till went back to his computer to watch the heavens. Most of the time it was always the same thing, however, he still could not get enough of it.

Ababi and Hoodeefa were not as interested in gazing at the stars as Till, however, they did go to their computer screens and turn them on. They both stared at the screens trying to look as if they were interested.

Choychata went to the kitchen to make some dinner.

Till adjusted the camera so that it was aimed at Zhagool. He decided he wanted to take a closer look at some of the craters that dotted the surface of the larger moon. At the moment he had nothing better to do. He aimed the camera at a central point on the moon and started to use the telephoto lens to get the closer look. He had it magnified to about one fourth of the capability of the camera.

Suddenly something flew past the large crater he was focusing on.

Ababi jumped back from her screen and nearly fell out of her chair. "What was that…that…whatever it was?"

"I don't know," said Hoodeefa. "It looked like…it had some lights on it."

"That's ridiculous," said Choychata. "You probably saw an asteroid…or meteor of some kind…and it has some shiny parts on the exterior. We've seen those things before."

"Not like that," said Till. "This thing…is…not an asteroid…or any other…natural object. I think…we've got some visitors…from…who knows where."

Hoodeefa scoffed. "Now, you're getting really ridiculous… Sir."

Till pulled back on the magnification. Now the entire moon was in the screen. All four of them were looking at their screens trying to see if they could find what the strange thing was…or where it was…or if it was.

Choychata was getting bored with the search. She leaned back to stretch…and saw the thing again. Some large object, with blinking lights, that came around the moon. It was some kind of satellite that was orbiting the moon. She pointed at it, however, before she got it out that she had seen it, the other three saw the thing as well.

"I think that thing is some kind of…spacecraft," said Till excitedly. "I think we're being visited…by someone from…only the Great Maker knows where." He had a chilling sensation of joy over this new discovery.

Hoodeefa swallowed. "So…what do we do…about this?"

Till smiled. "Are we taping it?"

"Of course," said Ababi. "We always do. Are you saying that we should send this tape…to everyone?"

Till scoffed. "You think anyone will ever believe us without a tape?"

Choychata snarled. "I can see the *chokwad* thing and I still don't believe it myself."

They all watched as the thing continued on the orbit and disappeared around the backside of the moon again.

Till smiled. "Stop the tape and send it and we'll get ready for the next appearance on the other side. I'd like to get more than one tape of that thing."

Hoodeefa rubbed her eyes. "This isn't happening…is it?"

Ababi sneered. "Yes it is. All this time we've been looking

out there and finally we see something." She looked at Till. "How long do we keep an eye on that thing?"

Till looked around triumphantly. "We keep watching it… as long as we can see the silly thing. The more we can see of it… and learn anything about it that we can…the better for all of us."

Hoodeefa frowned. "How is that better, in the long run, for all of us?"

"Suppose that thing is hostile," said Ababi. "If it is…we might just be able to do something about it…with a 459…or two."

Till laughed. "Are you telling me that you want to start a shooting match with someone who is capable of space flight?"

Ababi snarled back at him. "How sure are you, that they're NOT hostile?"

He sighed then huffed. "We're just going to…have to allow them to shoot first. That's the only way that we'll know whether or not they are hostile…or not."

"Yeah? How many people are going to have to die before we finally shoot back?"

Till shook his head sadly. "Hopefully…no more than one."

Akantini showed the tape to Wilfadge. He laughed it off at first. After watching the film showing three orbits, he stopped laughing.

"So…Senior Officer, Till finally found something out there…in the cosmos," said Wilfadge. "I wonder what the Algothons would do with this information."

Akantini scoffed. "Probably send a firestorm weapon after it. They were looking out there as well."

Officer Grade 5, Nashisi showed the tape to Ahandi. "Sir, what do you think of that?"

Ahandi yawned. "If Supreme Officer, Wilfadge isn't worried…why should I worry? Till finally has some proof that there are other beings out there…if he didn't fabricate this tape."

"Okay…uh…what do we do in the meantime?"

"We came out here to relax. SO RELAX!"

Nashisi shrugged and sat down. "Yes, Sir."

Officer Grade 4, Sorn informed Teelila about the tape. He was rather skeptical of the tape himself. He did not try to hide his pessimism about it as he told her about it.

Teelila frowned as she watched it. "I don't know if I believe it either. I just don't see that this is sufficient proof. He might have made this up…just so he can keep on watching, the stars…as if they do anything but twinkle."

Sorn nodded. "Do you have any answer for him, Sir?"

She stood up. "Right now, my main concern is a bath. My

neck feels filthy."

Officer Grade 5, Zhorbik brought the tape to Dwalooa. He cleared his throat to try to not look as if he were laughing. "Sir, this is from Senior Officer, Till. According to him, it *is* proof that there are other beings out there. He says that the tape is definitive."

Dwalooa plugged in and watched the tape. "That's no proof. I could probably do something similar...with some of the programs that I found in the Algothon archives. I don't believe it either."

Hoodeefa sadly shook her head. "None of them believe it. They think that we made it up. They're all...laughing at us."

Till stood there gritting his teeth. "I'm going to call Antrong and Hoynama. Maybe if they see this here and can see that we're not fooling around with anything, then maybe someone will believe us.

Choychata turned to Till. "They've changed their course, Sir. They're...headed towards...Hardooth. They look as if they're coming...at a tremendously fast speed."

All four of Team 31 were now looking at the monitors.

"As fast as they're moving, I don't think...uh...not gonna take very long to get here," said Ababi. "I just hope...they're friendly."

Till leaned closer to the monitor. "Magnify the thing.

Zoom in on it. See if you can find...a window...preferably on the Bridge of that thing...and maybe we can get a good look at them."

Hoodeefa started turning the knobs. It was a little difficult keeping them zeroed in on a moving target, however, she was able to make all of the necessary adjustments. She turned the lens towards what appeared to be a window of some kind. There appeared to be two of the passengers on the craft looking out the window back at them. She quickly magnified the window. "Ugly lookin' things, aren't they?"

Till sighed. "After what we've seen of some of the Elf races, it's a little difficult to call someone from another world ugly."

Hoodeefa shook her head. "I agree...they're ugly. Looks like they have the body of a Heyyah and the head of a bug."

"No telling what their legs look like," said Choychata. "We can only see them from the waist up."

Till snickered. "We could probably see a lot more of them...if we wanted to."

Ababi looked at him suspiciously. "What do you mean by that?"

He shrugged. "We can see right into that ship. We can see the hallway behind them. It's possible that we could...Jump... right in behind them...in Spy of course and take a look around."

Ababi sneered at him. "And who is the brave soul that is gonna be that stupid?"

He sneered back. "I figured it'd be you."

Ababi looked back and forth from Till to the screen. "Sir… are you…serious?"

He shrugged. "We want to know something about them. The best place to start…is on their ship."

She swallowed hard. She looked closely at the area directly behind the two aliens. She sat there with her lower lip quivering. She closed her eyes and Jumped. She opened her eyes and looked around. She was on the alien ship, standing behind two…whatever they are. She heard them babbling in a foreign tongue that she had no clue as to how to even start trying to understand it.

"**You made it**," sent Till. "**I knew that you could do it**."

"**Congratulations**," sent Hoodeefa.

"**Shut up**," snarled Ababi mentally. She did a little looking around. "**You're not going to believe this, but…I'm on the Bridge. It seems there's a wall behind these two and… there's several more of the…uh…whatever they are…in this same area…looking at all kinds of monitors**."

Till snickered. "**What's on their monitors**?"

Again Ababi snarled. "**How should I know**?"

"**Well go take a look**!" Till mentally scoffed at her. "**You won't know until you look**."

Ababi shook her head and walked up to see the monitors of the two aliens that could be seen in the window. She rolled her eyes as she looked at a bunch of characters that she could not identify at all. She headed up five stairs to the other part of the Bridge. She looked at the first monitor that she came to. "**Uh... Sir...this first monitor...is showing an aerial map of Aerisau. A very...good map too. The thing seems to be pointing out all of the villages, towns and cities**."

Till sat there thinking. "**Okay, what's on the next one**?"

She slowly walked to the next one. "**A map of Cifpasica**."

Till nodded. "**It sounds as if they are exploring the planet**."

"**Yes**," sent Hoodeefa. "**But exploring and mapping... for what**?"

"**I think that they're setting us up for conquest**," sent Choychata.

"**Let's not jump to conclusions...yet**," sent Till angrily. He contemplated for a few moments. "**Can you try to read their minds**?"

Ababi squawked. "**Read what?! I can't read anything that's on their keyboards! How am I supposed to tell what's in their minds**?"

"**Try! See if you can get a feeling...or an attitude... or something that might help us**."

Ababi rolled her eyes. "**Maybe you should get that... teacher from Team 7016. Maybe she can do it**."

"**Good idea**," sent Till with a smile. "**I'll call her up right now**."

'I was joking,' thought Ababi to herself. She shook her head and went ahead with the suggestion of attempting to read their minds. She was shocked at what she received. It did not seem possible. She went back to concentrating on reading their thoughts and it was there again. Maybe she should wait until that teacher was here and explain what she found then.

Bonarain looked up angrily. She had just popped a very large, tasty lump of kwatha in her mouth and now some *bimyock* was calling her out for a job. She listened to what was being sent and was sure that someone was playing a prank. She concentrated on the apartment number she had been given. Jump to the front door of apartment 1-31 and then knock. She made the Jump – with her kwatha. She stood there looking at the door. Instead of knocking, she spooned out another lump of kwatha and while she was chewing on that she kicked the door, instead of knocking.

Someone called out for her to enter.

She hopped to Ghost dimension and walked through the door. On the other side she hopped back to Home. She stood there, loudly sucking a few pieces of kwatha through her teeth. "What's so *chokwad* important?"

Choychata pointed to a monitor. "That thing...on the screen...some kind of alien ship...form another world."

Bonarain gave it a quick glance. "Right! Sure it is!" She looked back down in her mug as she spooned around for more lumps. "Okay, what's the joke?"

Till cleared his throat. "Put the mug down."

Bonarain continued spooning. "Why?"

"Put it down…now," he said emphatically through his teeth.

She glared back at him as she placed the mug on a table.

He looked back at his monitor. **"Ababi, it seems that Officer, Bonarain doesn't believe us. Why don't you come back here and Jump her onto the ship…so she will believe us**?"

A moment later Ababi was standing next to Bonarain. Ababi smiled apprehensively. "Hop to Spy."

Bonarain rolled her eyes and scoffed. She hopped to Spy.

Ababi took Bonarain's hand and Jumped both of them back to the spaceship. Now Bonarain was no longer looking skeptical - she was totally in shock as she looked around the Bridge of the alien craft.

Ababi smiled. "Now…do you believe us?"

Bonarain tried to say something, however, nothing but a croak came out. She cleared her throat several times. "All right… if this is a hoax…you've gone to some great trouble to…" She frowned. "What do you need me for?"

"I tried to read their minds…and…I got this strange imagery."

Bonarain smiled sheepishly. "Imagery?"

"Yes...should I send it to you...or do you want to try reading their minds?"

Bonarain did not change her expression. "Why don't you...send it to me...and then I'll...give it a try myself."

Ababi closed her eyes, cleared her mind and sent the imagery. She opened her eyes when she finished and saw Bonarain staring back at her in horror.

Bonarain again had to clear her throat. "That...is what you...got?"

Ababi nodded.

Bonarain walked over to one of the aliens. She lowered her head, clenched her eyes shut and started reading the alien's mind. She stepped back, opening her eyes in fear, as if she had been slapped. She had learned several things – some were baffling and others needed no explanation. She knew they were in deep trouble.

By now, the alien ship was down inside the atmosphere of the planet. It was flying along at a speed of Mach 14 (whatever that meant). Suddenly, beams of destruction were coming out of several places in the ship and creating explosive havoc on the surface of the planet.

Bonarain closed her eyes and sent out a panicky warning: **"We're under attack! Everyone go to Spy...or Observation...or Ghost! We're under attack from a... hostile...force...from another planet!"**

Every Owlamite received the warning, however, did not

heed it because they thought it was another part of the joke being played on them by Team 31. After seeing a few of the blasts hitting the surface and seeing the destruction that resulted, they all hopped to other dimensions…the ones that were still alive. For others it was too late.

Till sent out a desperate message to Bonarain: **"Who's doing the shooting? If you can…stop them**!"

Bonarain looked around the Bridge. She pointed at four of the aliens that were pressing all kinds of buttons on their consoles. "Those four…they're the Gunners!"

Ababi did not wait. She was there before Bonarain was and before the aliens could even comprehend what happened, all four Gunners were relocated in either Jahong's Death or Stink. The shooting immediately stopped.

Ababi looked at Bonarain. "How did you know…they were the Gunners?"

Bonarain had a look of fear on her face. "The imagery… that you sent me…and my own mind reading efforts…I can understand these *doovofts*!"

Now Ababi was the one with the shocked look on her face.

Bonarain looked at a man standing in the center of the room. "He's telling others to get there to the weapons consoles and start shooting again.

Ababi and Bonarain had to get rid of nine more of the aliens before all of them stopped in their tracks, trying to figure out where and how their comrades had disappeared…and were disappearing. The Captain was no longer screaming orders for anyone to man the consoles as he was equally mystified by this strange occurrence.

Bonarain looked around. "Officer, Ababi…I need the rest of my Team…here aboard this ship! I need their help!"

Ababi mentally sent the request to Till.

Till came back angrily. **"Go get them! Those bimyocks are obviously hostile and she's the only one who can understand them. If that is what she needs, get her Team on that ship…NOW!"**

Ababi Jumped to the Team 7016 apartment door. She went through the door. She saw Soolchakan sitting at a table eating something. She did not ask. She grabbed his shoulder. She was going to hop him to Spy, however he had heard the warning and was already there, even though he seemed rather lackadaisical about it. She Jumped him to the ship.

Soolchakan had been in a seated position while eating. Here, there was no chair and he unceremoniously ended up falling to the floor. He got up, still with a mouthful of food and a fork in his right hand.

Ababi gave him a helpless smile. "I can't explain… Bonarain can." She Jumped back to 7016's apartment to look for another member of Team 7016.

A few moments later Kiyalee was involuntarily Jumped aboard, covered with engine grease stains and had a wrench in her hand. She looked around in shock as well. "What's going on…

and WHERE AM I?"

Soolchakan shrugged helplessly. "I don't know!"

Bonarain waved at them from the Gunner's station. "I'm over here! I need help!"

Soolchakan looked around. "Right! You're there! You need help! With what?"

"Keeping all of the *h'oolyach* on this ship, away from these consoles!"

Soolchakan and Kiyalee did a quick move to where she was standing.

Soolchakan quickly looked over the console. "What's so special about this one...and why do we have to keep them away?"

Bonarain let out an exasperated grunt. She grabbed hold of his ears, pulled him close, placed her forehead against his and started sending the strange new imagery to him, in a force-feed manner. He winced when she grabbed his ears, however, he did not fight her. He accepted the information. She let go of him, once she had finished the imagery. He staggered backwards in a drunken manner. He shook his head and blinked several times trying to clear his thoughts. He looked down at the console and then up at the aliens in shock.

For the first time, he noticed the aliens. They were mostly around seven taja in height. Their bodies, from the neck down, looked basically like any normal Heyyah. The head was very different. The eyes were silvery and multi-faceted. They had what appeared to be at least six brown antennae growing out of the top of their heads in rows of three on each side, which hung limp down the sides of their heads. There did not seem to be any form of a noticeable nose or ears. The mouth was a wide slit and showed no lips. Other than the antennae, there seemed to be very little hair on the top or sides of their heads. When they spoke it was a droning, alto monotone that seemed to overuse the "D" and the "P" in their words.

Several of them were slowly, cautiously approaching the weapons console, waving their hands as if they were looking for some kind of invisible force field.

The ship's Leader (or what they called: Tomontain [O-7]) was screaming at them to get to the console and resume firing. This was when Soolchakan realized that the imagery he had been force fed, taught him how to read, write and comprehend the Jowfoonda language. Jowfoonda – the aliens that were currently attacking Hardooth.

Kiyalee had walked up to where Soolchakan and Bonarain were standing. She looked around in fear and shock. Bonarain grabbed Kiyalee by the ears and force fed her the same information that Soolchakan had received.

Ababi reappeared on the Bridge with Chyning. Chyning was *not* happy. She was dripping wet, including her hair, and wearing nothing but a robe. Before Ababi was pulled Chyning out of the bathtub, she had obtained some pulse pistols and brought them aboard the ship as well. Chyning was now the one looking around the Bridge with a great deal of apprehension on her face. She slowly made her way up to stand with the rest of her Team, trailing water the entire way. As soon as she reached the rest of the Team, Bonarain now force fed the information into Chyning's head as well.

After finishing with Chyning, Bonarain sank to her knees. She looked around the room and then collapsed onto the floor.

Soolchakan looked over at Ababi. "Get Bonarain out of here. She's no good to us right now. She's completely mentally exhausted from...what she taught us!"

Ababi was a little upset over the order, because Soolchakan was a Grade 5 and she was a Grade 3. Unfortunately, Bonarain had not given her the information, so now it was a rescue for a fallen Owlamite and leave the Owlamites who had necessary information for combatting these – whatever they are – to do the fighting. She grabbed hold of Bonarain and Jumped back to the Team 7016 apartment.

She grunted in disgust as she looked around the dining room. All of the apartments had the exact same floor plan, however, the decorations were all different. Ababi was thinking of Jumping Bonarain to the second floor, where the bedrooms were, however, she did not want to Jump right into the middle of a table or chair... or some other decoration. Then she realized that they were still in Spy dimension. Everything upstairs was in Home. She once again Jumped with Bonarain. They went to the second floor and she saw their names were on the doors. She dragged Bonarain to her room, right through the door. She hopped the bed into Spy and got Bonarain up on it. She loosened all of Bonarain's clothing. She saw an overstuffed chair. She walked over, hopped the chair into Spy, sat down realizing that she was somewhat tired as well. All of that Jumping had worn her down considerably. She made a mental call to Till, letting him know that she was temporarily out of action, leaned her head back and rested. She was tired, however, not enough to go to sleep, yet.

Back on the spaceship, Chyning picked up the pulse pistols. "Who wants one?"

Kiyalee was ready to accept one until Soolchakan grabbed it. "Don't you dare give her one of those things!"

Kiyalee snarled and showed her teeth to Soolchakan.

He snarled back at her. "Go find the engine room!"

Kiyalee scoffed. "What am I supposed to do there?"

"You're the mechanic…figure it out. See what you can do to foul their engines…or allow us to take over this big bucket."

Chyning looked around a little frantic. "What are we supposed to do?"

"Keep these…Jowfoonda…away from their weapons console."

"How?"

He reached out and touched the shoulder of the nearest alien. He hopped the creature into Shogoot's Search. He turned to Chyning. "I picked Shogoot's Search because…that's the one that dissolves them in some kind of liquid acid. I don't know what the other dimensions will do to them, but acid should…well I hope it'll…" He shrugged.

Chyning scoffed. "I'll do it my way." She walked up to the one that was closest to her and kicked him in the…well it should be the groin…as hard as she could. The creature grabbed its groin and started spinning around. The antennae all stood straight up. There was a strange high pitched buzz coming out of its mouth. Then it fell to the floor and started convulsing as a green liquid started coming out of its mouth. After a few moments it stopped moving completely.

Kiyalee looked away holding her hand over her mouth. "Okay, that's disgusting. Now, how do I find the engine room?"

Soolchakan pointed to a sign, near a set of double doors, on the wall. "Follow the signs," he said.

Kiyalee walked over to the sign, looking back at him angrily. "How am I supposed to find it when I can't read…?" She looked up at the sign and froze. "Uh…I can read it." She stood there with her mouth hanging open for a moment. "I…uh…I'll go to the engine room," she said helplessly. She walked through the door.

Chyning came up to Soolchakan. "And all we have to do is keep all of these Jowfoondas away from this…weapons console… right?"

"Right!"

"I don't think I can do much kicking. I hurt my foot… when I…kicked…him…it or…whatever that thing is."

He scoffed. "You hurt your *foot*? Look what you did to… him…it…that!" He turned his pulse pistol on. He aimed at the closest Jowfoonda and shot the beam right between those huge bulging eyes. The head exploded and green ichor splattered everywhere.

The Tomontain was now screaming even louder for someone to get to the console and resume firing on the planet. Chyning grunted in anger, took her pulse pistol and aimed at the Tomontain's chest. The man's entire torso exploded making an even bigger mess on the Bridge. Chyning put her hand over her mouth as if she were going to be sick.

Soolchakan shook his head. "They're extremely fragile. I don't remember any pulse pistol…doing that kind of damage to any…creature on Hardooth. It usually just leaves a hole."

Chyning regained a little of her composure. "So we kill all of them. That's what we're supposed to do. What difference does it make if…we hop them to Shogoot's Search or…detonate them?"

He sighed. "Since we're the only ones…right now…who understand their language…and writing, we're the ones who'd have to…drive this ship…for the moment."

"Why, do we want to keep it?"

"The Command Staff might want to keep it. We could learn all kinds of new things about this…mechanism."

A man (?), wearing the rank of Chinchik (O-5), started barking orders. He/she/it was commanding someone to get to the weapons console and resume firing. An alien, wearing the rank of Vilvak Second (O-2), challenged the Chinchik to try.

The Chinchik was not amused and ordered the Vilvak Second to move faster or be executed. The Vilvak Second crept closer and Soolchakan hopped him/her/it to Shogoot's Search.

"**I found the engine room**," send Kiyalee. "**We've got a big fat problem though. I'm not a physicist. You need a physicist in order to understand all of the *h'oolyach* about these…engines**."

Soolchakan grunted in anger. "**They're engines! Learn them! Do something! Find out what you can understand…and we'll go from there**."

"**HOW? All of their technical manuals are… written at a level that…I've never seen before**."

"**Then start reading the minds of some of the personnel in that engine room and see what you can get from that**."

Kiyalee scoffed at the thought. Then she looked at the ones who were working the engine consoles, preventative maintenance consoles and trouble-shooting consoles. She shrugged and started digging through their minds. After a few moments, her mind was reeling at all of the information that she was getting from these highly educated Jowfoonda. It seemed a little staggering to the mind that what she was considering above her, was normal stuff to them.

Chyning growled at Soolchakan. "Are we going to have to read some minds here…in order to understand all of this… *h'oolyach*…in this room?"

"We don't have much choice. We have to learn…
something…anything…we can about this…ship."

"But we can't read minds and kill at the same time!"

He hopped another Jowfoonda into Shogoot's Search. "Do
you want to kill or read?"

"I'll kill," she huffed!

"Okay, I'll start reading. Keep the *doovofts* off of me."

She shrugged and started grabbing Jowfoondas and
sending them off on a one-way trip to Shogoot's Search.

Soolchakan shouted in pain. He held his head and growled.

She looked at him confused. "What's the matter?"

"That…last one that you…hopped. I was reading *his*
mind…at the time."

"Well…POINT at the one you're reading," she shouted
angrily! "I can't tell…which one…if you're not pointing. SO
POINT!"

He shook his head. He looked around trying to clear his
head. "No! Hold off on killing. Each one seems to have some
information that we need. Start gleaning information. Kill…only
if you really have to."

"Can I kill em' after I read em'?"

"Yes, why?"

"Cause the first one I'm gonna erase is that loudmouthed

Chinchik! He's gettin' on my nerves."

"Go ahead. I found a communications officer that has some very interesting information. Just make sure that you have all of the information that we can get from him before you…give him a shove."

"By the way…how come we can understand these *bimyocks*? I've never taken any kind of…foreign language course. But I understand these…outworlders…and their weird language."

"When Bonarain wakes up, we'll ask her. She force fed us some imagery and it…is the only thing I can think of…as to why…or how."

"But…how…?"

"ASK BONARAIN WHEN SHE WAKES UP! For now… read minds and glean information."

She gave him a pouty look. She faced off against the loudmouth Chinchik and started delving into his mind.

Back in the engine room, Kiyalee was getting a crash course in quantum physics and normal physics. She was learning things that she never knew existed and was not really sure how to explain them. She was learning all kinds of things about light-speed engines that used forces she had never heard of before.

Most of the maintenance personnel were using their computer consoles to get the information they wanted. There were hard copies of all of the manuals on shelves in the room. She shrugged as she looked at the books. Since the Jowfoonda were using their computers, they did not need the books, at this time. She quickly Jumped all of the manuals back to her bedroom, for later perusal. Then she Jumped back and went back to reading minds.

Chyning got tired of reading the mind of the Chinchik. He/her/it was the ranking security officer on the ship and he/she/it was not a very nice person. It had executed fourteen of underlings for (what seemed to her) trivial acts of insubordination. There was a woman in the science section that he had the hots for (okay, this *bimyock* is male). Everything else was security regulations. She was finally able to dump the bellowing buffoon into Shogoot's Search.

Soolchakan found out all he needed from the communications officer. He sent that unfortunate soul into Shogoot's Search and looked for another victim. He growled in frustration because as soon as he got rid of the communications officer, someone else immediately sat down in the chair and kept the communications going. He decided to leave that one alone for a while.

A Honroodo (O-4) came onto the Bridge with several enlisted personnel. They were attempting to discover how personnel were disappearing without a trace. They had their weapons drawn, however, none of them could figure out what they were supposed to shoot at…or why…or where…yet.

Chyning scoffed. "You get the idea that maybe Bonarain should have mind-clogged a few others with this stuff before she knocked herself out?"

"That would've been nice…but…the three of us…took

everything out of her. We'll have to wait until she wakes up…and then find out how it's done…and then maybe we can force-feed a few more…and get some help."

"Do you think we'll really need it?"

"I've picked up some very interesting…and terrifying information from that communications officer."

Ababi reappeared on the Bridge with three others in tow. "Hello," she said cheerily. "I'd like to introduce you to: Officer Grade 5, Oolsena, Officer Grade 6, Zayza and Officer Grade 7, Yeenfa. They're the Team members for Senior Officer, Antrong of Team 30. They're here to assist you…in your discovery." She looked around a little confused. "Where…is your other Team member?"

Soolchakan snarled about the interruption. "Officer, Kiyalee is in the engine room learning what she can in there."

Oolsena scoffed. "Are you saying that you can read all of this…*h'oolyach*?"

"Yes," he said flatly. "Bonarain force-fed all of it…from some kind of imagery. Now, will you shut up, so I can glean some more information from these people?"

Oolsena now looked angry. "Why don't you feed some of it to us, so we can help?"

"Because I don't know how she did it! Now…SHUT UP!"

Oolsena made a mental communication with Antrong.

Antrong showed up a few heartbeats later looking rather

upset. "Why aren't you getting my Team indoctrinated in this stuff? You can read it, why don't you get them educated?"

Soolchakan was ready to send Antrong into Shogoot's Search. "Bonarain did it! How she did it...I don't know! She didn't tell me! You'll have to ask her! She collapsed after she force-fed all of the information to me, Kiyalee and Chyning. Ababi took her out of here. Ask Ababi where Bonarain is!"

Ababi's shoulders sagged. "Officer, Bonarain is out cold. When she force-fed the information to the rest of her Team, she... mentally collapsed and I had to take her back to her bedroom... and put her in bed. She's out...for...who knows how long."

Antrong closed his eyes and clenched his teeth. He opened his eyes and glared at Soolchakan. "So you can't give us the information, what're we supposed to do...watch you while you get it all?"

Soolchakan glared back. "I'm not getting *h'oolyach* as long as you keep interrupting me. If you want to be useful... SHUT UP AND LET ME GET THE INFORMATION!"

Antrong was ready to strangle Soolchakan. He turned to Chyning. "Can you give me any information?"

Chyning huffed back at him. "Same thing! I'm trying to get information and all you're doing is being an unnecessary interruption!"

He walked over to Chyning. "I'm going to have to interrupt you anyway. I need to know if this ship can be landed... voluntarily or otherwise...on the surface."

Chyning was flabbergasted. "I don't know! You'll have to ask Kiyalee! She's the one with the engine expertise."

"Where is Kiyalee?"

"In the engine room."

Antrong growled. He closed his eyes. "**Officer, Kiyalee, this is Senior Officer, Antrong, can you hear me**?"

Kiyalee growled at the interruption. "**Yes, Sir, I hear you**."

"**Good! Now, can this ship be landed on the surface**?"

"**Not at this speed**."

"**What…how fast are we going**?"

"**Right now? We're going Mach 14**."

His jaw sagged and he stood there looking rather dull normal. "**What is…Mach? What does the 14 mean**?"

"**Mach means the speed of sound. The 14 means that we're going 14 times faster than sound moves**."

He shook his head rapidly. "**What kind of *h'oolyach* is that? Sound doesn't move**."

"**Apparently it does and we're going 14 times faster**."

"**That's ridiculous! It doesn't feel like we're moving at all**."

"Really? Look out a window."

He scoffed. He walked over to the spot where the navigators were looking out the window that Ababi had first seen through for the Jumping. When he looked out and saw the terrain whizzing by at a speed that he could not comprehend, he got a little dizzy. He looked away and tried to focus on something else. **"All right…we're moving fast…incredibly fast. Is there any way that you can slow them down…and force them to land**?"

"Only if I damage an engine…or maybe a nacelle or two."

Again he looked confused. **"What…is a…nacelle**?"

"Don't have time to explain. Do you want me to do whatever it takes to make them land?"

He sighed. **"Yes! Make them land."**

Kiyalee shrugged. She used what she had gleaned so far and checked a few of their switches, knobs and other things on the different panels. She hit three different switches and nearly got thrown off of her feet. There was a near panic in the engine room as all of the personnel started jabbering at the same time. One of them walked over to the panel and corrected her sabotage without hesitation. She grunted in disgust and threw the switches again. He corrected again. She growled in frustration. She hopped the panel into Spy and hit the switches again. The Jowfoonda technician jumped back a little when the panel disappeared. He went back to his console and started making the corrections through his computer terminal.

Kiyalee looked around frustrated and angry. 'Looks like I'm going to have to act like Chyning,' she thought. Four roundhouse kicks to the heads of four Jowfoonda technicians and now there were not enough conscious Jowfoondas who could keep up with her sabotage.

Back on the Bridge, Soolchakan was a little surprised. "They're beginning…some emergency landing…thing. They're going to land the ship…in a desolate area and…try to figure out what's going on with the engines."

"About time," muttered Antrong.

Soolchakan frowned. "What's that supposed to mean?"

"I told her to make them land this thing. She argued with me about some silly notion about…moving sound."

Soolchakan groaned. "It's not a silly notion. There's a lot of stuff in their technology that we don't understand. I've just started to scratch the surface. Before we start laughing it off, we need to try to understand it. I found the same thing in the minds that I've been reading. Sound DOES move. It moves very rapidly and this ship is capable of moving a lot faster than that and that's one of the ways that they measure their speed. Just because you've never heard of certain types of technology, doesn't mean that it doesn't exist. Think about those potions that the Teltermak made. We don't know what's in them and we're not even sure how they work, but the Teltermak made them and built an entire complex around them."

Antrong was ready to start admonishing him for insubordination, however, he realized that just the existence of this ship proved that someone had technology that was above and beyond what Owlam had. He backed down because he knew that Bonarain had put something in Soolchakan's head that made him understand…something…beyond what any Owlamite knew. Better to keep your mouth shut and listen, for the time being. He could do nothing other than stand there frustrated.

Soolchakan had gone back to listening to some of the jabber that was going on among the people on the Bridge. Chyning was still doing some mind reading as well. Both were picking up all kinds of information on the Jowfoonda, their hierarchy, their running of the ship and a few other idiosyncrasies of this alien race.

Chyning walked over to the communications console. "Who is this guy talking with?"

"I don't know," said Soolchakan shaking his head. "Whoever it is, they certainly have a lot of questions."

She nodded. "Whoever it is…is NOT on this ship."

He sighed. "Let's see what happens…if we…disappear another one." He grabbed hold of the one on the radio and the Jowfoonda was immediately hopped to Shogoot's Search.

Another Bridge officer quickly ran to the radio and picked up where the one that had vanished left off.

Chyning folded her arms. "They certainly have a lot more courage about that radio. They're still afraid of the weapons consoles…but no one hesitates to get to the radio."

Soolchakan nodded. "Mm-hm. They feel some strong

need to keep in touch with the others…on the other end of that radio."

Antrong had been listening. "If they think it's so important to keep in communication with someone else…I think that we should break their communication line."

Soolchakan shook his head. "Not until we know if there are any consequences."

Antrong scoffed. He sent a quick mental note to his Team. The four of them all started concentrating. They waited until the Jowfoonda had successfully landed the ship on the surface. They did not know what country or continent they were on, they only knew that they were no longer flying.

Antrong took a deep breath. "NOW!"

Soolchakan, Kiyalee and Chyning knew something had happened. They were not sure exactly what, however, the ship had an immediate reaction. All of the lights turned off and banks of red lights turned on in every room of the ship. Every single Jowfoonda dropped what they were doing and ran for small exits that seemed to be opening up everywhere.

Kiyalee Jumped from the engine room to the Bridge. "WHAT DID YOU DO?"

Soolchakan held his hands up. "I didn't do anything." He pointed at Antrong. "I think he did something."

"We hopped this ship and everything in and on it to Desert dimension," said Antrong with an air of arrogance. "Now…what is all of this jabber that the ship is griping about?"

Kiyalee snarled. "You turned on the ship's self-destruct system when you hopped it, you *melafathan bimyock*! Now... we're gonna lose everything!"

Antrong scoffed. "Shut it off!"

Kiyalee snickered. "Oh...just shut it off?" She glared at him. "How?"

"I don't know," Antrong said angrily.

"I DON'T EITHER," shouted Kiyalee! "According to the countdown that I'm hearing, we have about twenty more heartbeats left before this ship blows up...with an explosion that'll make the firestorm weapons look like minor fireworks. I don't know about you, but I'm getting out of here...back to Home." With that she vanished.

Soolchakan grunted and gave Antrong a dirty look and vanished.

Chyning stuck out her tongue at Antrong and vanished.

Antrong's entire Team 30 all vanished. Antrong himself stood there looking around rather disgusted. He finally Jumped.

Fourteen heartbeats later the ship blew up...in Desert dimension...leaving a crater that was fifty taja deep and four kilotaja in diameter. The sand was turned to glass for at least twelve kilotaja in every direction.

4

Kiyalee sat in the dining room counting slowly. When she reached fifteen she looked at Soolchakan and quietly said: "Boom. That ship is gone. There's nothing there in Desert dimension...but a mess." She shook her head and sighed. "I think that the mother ship is on the way here...to find the lost child." She looked off to the side. "We could be in grave danger."

Soolchakan hung his head and grunted. "I wish we had something more than memories of that thing."

"We do," said Kiyalee with a grin. "I swiped some technical manuals off the ship before it blew."

He looked up with a surprised grin. "Really? So we can read up on that thing?"

Kiyalee shrugged. "Trouble is...I don't know how long... or soon...the mother ship is gonna be in getting...here...and start blasting away at the surface...just like the other one did."

Both Soolchakan and Chyning groaned.

Kiyalee looked at her fingernails. "We need to get that information to the Command Staff quickly...before Antrong gets over there and starts telling lies about us. He's the one who made that stupid mistake...not us."

Soolchakan shook his head. "You're right. We need to be there to tell our side of the story." He rubbed his eyes. "Let's get over there."

Chyning waved her hand at Soolchakan. "Shouldn't we check on Bonarain first?"

He looked at her and sighed. "You go ahead and check on Bonarain. Kiyalee and I will head to the conference room. You can join us there…afterward."

Hadathoo was in the Supreme Officer's main workroom attempting to contact Wilfadge. He was doing everything he could to make the mental connection, however, he was finding nothing. After several useless tries, he switched to Ahandi. Maybe she would respond – nothing. He next tried Teelila – nothing. Now Dwalooa – again nothing. Now he was really getting worried. He next went to contacting the Vice Commanders. Antrong, Till, Hoynama and Shyshee all responded. All four confirmed they could not get any of the other Master Officers or Wilfadge.

Hadathoo clenched his fists on the desk. **"We need to have an emergency meeting…with whomever we have left.**"

The four Vice Commanders agreed and all of them headed for the conference room.

Hadathoo merely had to walk to the conference room from where he was currently located. He walked out into the hallway and found several Owlamites sitting in the hallway looking rather stunned.

The four Vice Commanders all Jumped into the hallway and were equally confused at the sight of all of the other personnel that were present.

Officer Grade 3, Nayna was the first one to come out of her trance and stand up. "Sirs…I was with…Supreme Officer, Wilfadge…in a rather sunny area…relaxing. There were…some other…races of people there and…I didn't want to be bothered… by them. I hopped to Spy dimension…and I was there when…a huge beam of light came down…and destroyed everything there… including…Supreme Officer, Wilfadge."

Officer Grade 4, Akantini walked up beside Nayna. "I was there too. One heartbeat, everyone is relaxing…having fun…the next moment…there's nothing but dust."

Hadathoo closed his eyes and clenched his fists. "So… Wilfadge is dead. Who is next…on the list…as the…*Voice of Power*?"

Nayna sniffed and wiped a tear. "The next one on the list was…Ahandi…but she was at the same place…and…she and her entire Team…gone."

Officer Grade 4, Sorn stood up. "I was on…Team 21… with Master Officer, Teelila. She was next in line after Ahandi. I was in Spy dimension as well…because of some stupid prostitute who kept on pestering me and…well that doesn't matter. Master Officer, Teelila, Officer Grade 6, Amafee and Officer Grade 6, Noyafa…my Team 21 are all…gone."

Officer Grade 5, Zhorbik stood up. He walked up next to Sorn. "The next one in line...after Teelila was Master Officer, Dwalooa. She went to the same resort...as the others." He gave a deep mournful sigh. "Team 23 has lost Master Officer, Dwalooa and Officer Grade 5, Ah-Aba. Officer Grade 6, Uvanimi and I... are the only ones left of Team 23." He looked at Hadathoo sadly. "Sir...you're next in line for the *Voice of Power*. You, Sir...are the new Supreme Officer...and the *Voice of Power*."

Hadathoo closed his eyes and let the information sink in. "All right," he said shakily. "Now...we need to find out... how many we lost...and where. We also need to find out about... whatever it was that attacked us and when...to expect the next attack. I suggest that all of us stay in Spy dimension...until we find out something...that says we're safe to go back."

"That ship is gone," said Antrong. "I was on it...when it went to...an automatic self-destruct system."

Hadathoo looked at Antrong confused. "When...did it blow up...and where?"

"It blew up...in the Desert dimension, Sir," said Antrong with a shrug. "Why it blew up...I don't know."

Team 7016 (minus Bonarain) had Jumped into the hallway by now. They had been listening to the current casualty list given by surviving Team members.

Kiyalee walked up to Antrong. "You know why it blew up! I told you why! Don't say you didn't!"

Antrong glared at Kiyalee. "*You* are being insubordinate!"

"She's also being truthful...Sir," said Soolchakan adamantly!

Hadathoo held his hands up. "HOLD ON! One at a time. I'm going to get all of the information...but...not jumbled." He lowered his hands and looked around at a group of very silent Owlamites. He then realized that as the *Voice of Power*, he had given a command and any command by the *Voice of Power* WILL be obeyed. He huffed. "All right...let's try to get this done chronologically. Who first noticed this...spaceship?"

Till raised his hand. "I...saw it...when it was orbiting Zhagool."

Hadathoo raised his eyebrows. "Let's go in the conference room and...start sorting things out."

Everyone followed Hadathoo into the conference room. Hadathoo walked up to his normal seat. He placed his hands on the back of the chair and looked down. He sighed and walked over to the end of the table. He took the position of the Supreme Officer and slowly sat down. He looked up at Till. "You were saying?"

The four Senior Officers sat down.

Till sniffed. "Yes, Sir, I saw the ship orbiting Zhagool. I wasn't sure what it was at first, then it changed direction and started heading towards Hardooth...at an incredibly fast speed. We were able to focus on it...with the Algothon flying cameras. The computer kept it in focus as it got closer. Officer, Ababi was able to Jump aboard the thing...and establish a landmark...a better one than what we'd seen through the camera. She couldn't understand any of the…aliens, so…I figured that the teacher…on Team 7016 might be able to help. I contacted her and…she…did something. I had Ababi Jump the rest of Team 7016 aboard and… well…my information is a little sketchy…after that, because I don't really know…what Officer, Bonarain did."

Ababi, Soolchakan, Kiyalee and Chyning all gave their renditions of what happened. After they were finished, Antrong was sitting there red-faced and looking a little uncomfortable.

Hadathoo gave Antrong a nasty look and cleared his throat. "So there is this very strong probability that another… outer space…ship, bigger and meaner, is headed this way…to find that scout ship…is that correct?"

Kiyalee nodded. "No, Sir. It's not a probability…it's a fact."

Hadathoo hung his head. "Before it gets here…" He looked up. "Officer, Nayna. You're the most experienced at… those wretched role calls. Start another one so we can find out if we lost anyone else…in this latest attack. While you're doing that…we all need to find a way to…watch the skies…and see if we can find this…mother ship." He looked at Kiyalee. "Especially since there is no clue as to where it is or how long it'll take to get here." He glared at Antrong. "And we have none of their technology to help us track the silly thing."

Till cleared his throat. "Sir, Officer, Choychata is currently watching the skies with the one really good Algothon camera that we have left."

Shyshee gave Hadathoo a weak smile. "What should we

do if we do see the silly thing?"

Hadathoo looked at the three members of Team 7016. "Try to take over the entire ship...without setting off any... destruct systems. We're going to use the people that we know can understand these..." He frowned. "What did you call them?"

"Jowfoonda," said Soolchakan slowly and concisely.

Hadathoo nodded. "Yeah...them."

Hoynama leaned forward. "So...what do we do?"

Hadathoo grunted at her. "We assess the situation when we find the *chokwad* thing. Meanwhile, everyone who is alive, answers the roll call. You're a LEADER! LEAD and make a few decisions on your own." He glared at Antrong. "*Wise* decisions."

When Bonarain woke up, she was horrified at the information she received about more Owlamites on the list of the dead. She was instructed by Hadathoo to teach more people the Jowfoonda language. She informed him that if she gave the information slowly, she could give it to more Owlamites, with less exhaustion on her part.

Teams 254, 255, 256, 257 and 258, the computer operators, were given priority on learning the language along with the computer repair Teams, 1000, 1001, 1002 and 1003. Hadathoo decided that the Command Staff should be next...as soon as he replaced the deceased ones with live ones that had a full Team.

Nayna continued the roll call. Teams 13, 20, 123, 180,

341, 658, 1028, 1727, 2162, 2391, 2773, 3247, 3625, 4566, 5017, 5413, 5708, 6573, 6819 and 6929 were all wiped out completely. Teams 21, 23, 55, 1076, 1419, 2536, 3736, 5263 and 6056 all lost at least one member. Hadathoo was now going to have to do some reassigning of his own, in order to maintain the integrity of the Teams. Twenty-two men and seventy-five women had died in the Jowfoonda attack.

The Command Team was going to need four new members, plus the current ones needed to be reassigned. Hadathoo became the new Supreme Officer. Senior Officer, Antrong was promoted to Master Officer and became the Sector 1 Commander. Senior Officer, Till was promoted to Master Officer and became the Sector 2 Commander. Senior Officer, Hoynama was promoted to Master Officer and became the Sector 3 Commander. Senior Officer, Shyshee was promoted to Master Officer and became the Sector 4 Commander.

Officer Leader, Yamananee was promoted to Senior Officer and became the Sector 1 Vice Commander. Officer Leader, Beemella was promoted to Senior Officer and became the Sector 2 Vice Commander. Officer Leader, Deelka was promoted to Senior Officer and became the Sector 3 Vice Commander. Officer Leader, Wymini was promoted to Senior Officer and became the Sector 4 Vice Commander.

Now came the job of reassigning the surviving personnel of partial to complete some incomplete Teams. Once again, they had to upset a few Teams in order to make an attempt to get back to normalcy for all. Nine Teams that were now partial, along with several others from before were put together in order to try get all in the routine of survival for the entire Owlamite race.

Officer Leader, Ota called in from Algothon and reported that the city of Algothon had been hit hard by the Jowfoonda. There were three strikes that hit the city and had caused massive damage. One strike in each part of the city. None of the Owlamites were injured because they were all in Spy dimension when the attack hit. The Algothons had no clue whatsoever where the attack had come from.

Officer Leader, Boneech informed the Command Staff that Teltermak had been hit. The new kite school was nothing but dust. The Teltermak were blaming the attack on the Ghost Assassins and were horrified at how even more powerful this new weapon was.

Officer Grade 5, Yaza of Team 6909 reported that the Turgon Wall had suffered no attack at all. They had seen a beam hit, somewhere on the west side of the wall in (what was now being called) the Land of the Turgons. She had no idea what the Jowfoonda could have possibly been aiming at, considering the fact that the Turgons had no technology at all and they were the only ones on the west side of the Wall.

Hadathoo called a new meeting to order. The new Command Staff along with their Aides were all there, with Team 7016 (minus Bonarain) there to give any information that they could on this mother ship that was headed to Hardooth.

Kiyalee was brought up first. "Sirs, I don't know what I can tell you. Those engines on that ship…are something the likes of which I never dreamed possible. Their terminology is something very new as well. The engines need a quantum physicist in order to keep them running...or built. They measure their speed... according to the speed of sound and..." She swallowed hard. "... also...the speed of light."

"Hadathoo leaned forward. "I heard Antrong saying something about that earlier. You say that they measure their speed...according to...something that..." He looked off to the side clenching his eyes shut, attempting to understand the concept. He looked back at Kiyalee. "Sound...moves? Light...moves? How...fast?"

Kiyalee chuckled nervously. She set up a large rollway board in the room. "My Team and I...did some figuring. We did some converting of the Jowfoonda mathematics." She wrote a *very* long number on the board. "This, according to Jowfoonda math, is how fast light moves, in one heartbeat." She wrote another *very* long number. "This...is that same number converted into kilotaja."

Hadathoo raised his eyebrows. "That? That is how far it...light...*moves*...in ONE LOUSY HEARTBEAT!"

"Yes, Sir." She looked around at the faces of the other personnel on the Staff. "I know that it sounds...incredible, but... that is how they measure the speed of those special...quantum engines." She sighed. "You know that constellation of five stars... in the southern sky? The ones we call the Grand Alignment?"

"Of course," said Hadathoo. "What of it?"

"The one in the middle, Sir. According to what I can get

from the Algothon archives, and converting it with Jowfoonda mathematics, the one in the middle is exactly thirty-nine light years from our planet. What that means, Sir, is moving at this speed…" She pointed at the kilotaja figure. "…and that speed is every heartbeat – moving at that speed, it takes thirty-nine years for the light of that star to get here…where we see it. The light we see from that star was emitted thirty-nine years ago. We're just now seeing it." She was looking at numerous sets of shocked, wide eyes.

Hadathoo stammered. "So…if that star…were to… suddenly blink out…we wouldn't know…of the death of that star…for…thirty-nine years…after the fact."

She smiled. "Yes, Sir, you've got it."

Hadathoo's shoulders sagged and his eyebrows went up. "I did?"

Kiyalee chuckled. "Yes, Sir." She cleared her throat. "Sound though…moves much slower." She erased the numbers on the board and wrote another number. "This is the speed of sound…in the Jowfoonda math." She wrote another number. "This is that same number converted to our mathematics." She turned back to the Staff. "This is how fast sound moves. It moves that fast…in one heartbeat. They call that: Mach."

Hadathoo looked at Antrong. "It'd be nice if we still had that ship…in order to test out these theories."

Antrong cleared his throat and hung his head.

Kiyalee shook her head. "It's not theory, Sir. They can do

it. I just, like you said, don't have one of the ships here to prove it."

Hadathoo smiled. "Okay, thank you. I think that you've twisted our brains enough with that information." He turned to Soolchakan. "What can you tell us...of the chatter from the Bridge of that ship...?" He scowled at Antrong. "...before it blew itself up?"

Soolchakan stepped forward. "Everything that I got, from those people, was that it was just a scout ship. They were coming here to observe and test our capabilities. The first part...when they were orbiting Zhagool, they did some long range observations. After they finished that, they came closer to Hardooth and started orbiting this planet and started taking pot-shots at some of the inhabited areas that have technology. They were going to show off their power and see if we could do anything about it. Test our planetary defenses to the maximum."

Hadathoo nodded. "All right, they've seen that we can stop them."

"Not really, Sir," said Soolchakan slowly. "They were not sure...what was causing their personnel to...disappear into thin air. They knew they were disappearing from the weapons console and the communications console, but...they had no idea that it was us. They were under the impression that it is some crazy phenomenon that is a part of this immediate area."

Hoynama scoffed. "They have no idea that it was someone from this planet that did that to them?"

"I heard that too, Sirs," said Chyning. "They called

it confusing and…some other word that…apparently didn't translate." She shrugged. "I think it was a cuss word."

Hadathoo rolled his eyes at the last comment. "All right, so they think it is some oddity…where…on or above the planet?"

Soolchakan shook his head. "They never got the time to explain. People were disappearing on them above the planet. When Kiyalee forced the thing to land, the whole ship disappeared so…they may think that the closer they get to the planet…the worse it gets…for them."

Hadathoo growled. "Any idea when that…mother ship… is going to get here?"

Soolchakan shook his head and shrugged.

"And meantime, we have no Jowfoonda that we can talk to…in order to find out what's going on," said Shyshee.

"Sir, that's not necessarily true," said Kiyalee thoughtfully.

All eyes went to her.

Kiyalee smiled at them. "When that countdown to self-destruction started…all of the Jowfoondas headed for escape pods. When they had two people in each one, they launched the things out of the scout vessel. If they were able to get far enough away, from that scout vessel, before it blew up…they could still be alive. I looked at the specs on the pods, in those manuals, and there is enough air and food…for two…Jowfoondas…for thirty-three days."

Till looked confused. "Are those…pods…capable of those

speeds that you showed us a little while ago?"

Kiyalee shook her head. "No, Sir. They're only capable of a short burst…that's supposed to get them away from the ship before the blast. In outer space, they'd just keep on going. In the atmosphere…they have a very limited range."

Hadathoo smiled. "So that means that there could be a bunch of them…walking around in Desert dimension…wondering where the mother ship is and if it'll come rescue them."

Deelka looked around the table. "Maybe we should get some of those Teltermak kites out of storage…and do a little exploring of Desert dimension…see if we can find any of them."

Hadathoo nodded. "Good idea, Officer, Deelka. Take care of it."

Deelka's jaw dropped. She started to say something, stopped herself and then looked off to the side. "Yes, Sir."

Till started chuckling.

Hadathoo looked down his nose at Till. "Is there something that you'd like to share with us?"

Till smiled. "Love to. When that mother ship gets here… we need to do everything we can to capture it. Officer, Kiyalee already has some knowledge of it. Those computer operators and repair personnel, they'll know some things about it as well. Once it's here, we capture it…and use if for our purposes." He looked around the table with a triumphant smile. "We've lost almost all of the Algothon flying cameras. If we can capture that Jowfoonda ship, we can use it to scan the skies, for other possible aliens. We can use it to look at the Algothons…and look for the Teltermak…on the surface of Hardooth. We can utilize it for all kinds of things."

Hadathoo nodded. "Yes…IF…we can capture it."

Till grinned. "Sir, we should certainly try."

Hadathoo looked at Soolchakan and smiled. "You may be the ones leading the way on this…capture mission. If Officer, Bonarain can get enough people trained…before it gets here…we'll see…who is leading the capture attack then." He pondered for a moment. "Officer, Till, can you use what few remaining cameras you've got…to look for this mother ship?"

Till sighed and shrugged. "At this time…there's only one that I can totally depend on. The main problem with that – I don't know what direction the mother ship is coming from."

Hadathoo frowned. "Where did that scout ship come from?"

"It was orbiting Zhagool when we accidentally spotted it." Till shook his head. "It could have been doing that for some time. As I said – we accidentally spotted it."

Hadathoo nodded. "Get somebody on that camera…and see if you can have another…accident."

Till smiled. "Officers Ababi and Hoodeefa are currently doing just that. They're doing some scanning with it to see if they can find anything…different."

"How far out can you see?"

Till snickered. "Sir, we've found a fourteenth planet in our system. I checked on it in the Algothon archives. They originally discovered it about twenty years before they launched the firestorm attack. They named it Denhahbon."

Shyshee scoffed. "What kind of a name is that?"

Till shrugged. "It's the name of some ancient god in Algothon mythology."

Hadathoo frowned. "Why didn't we know about it from before?"

"Because it is way, *way* out there."

Hoynama waved her hands at Hadathoo and Till. "People! We're getting off of the subject. We don't need to be counting planets, we need to look for that mother ship."

Till sighed. "Ababi and Hoodeefa are looking for the ship. The only reason I mentioned that new planet was so that you know that they know that it won't be the planet. If they happen to see Denhahbon in the sky, they won't mistake it for the ship."

Hoynama leaned back nodding. "Good."

Choychata walked up to the conference table. "Sirs... Ababi reports that they found something."

Hadathoo looked up. "Something? I was hoping for a better word than that. What kind of...something...did she find?"

Choychata closed her eyes and concentrated. "She says... it's...another scout ship. This one is orbiting Niygool."

"They're being cautious," said Wymini. "One scout ship has disappeared without a trace. They're not risking the mother ship...yet."

Beemella grunted. "How far do we let them go with this one?"

"Not too far," said Hadathoo. "We can't allow them to decimate the entire planet on a scouting mission."

Antrong looked at Till. "Can we get someone on board this one without causing any problems yet? I mean if we can get someone on it and have them look around for a while...maybe they can dissuade the Jowfoonda from coming near us again...at all."

Hadathoo stood up. "Officer, Soolchakan, do you think that you can make the Jump to this new scout ship?"

Soolchakan shook his head. "The Jump to the ship is not the main problem, Sir. Once I'm aboard...all I can do is observe. We need at least one computer operator and one computer repair up there to do some deep digging in their computer system."

Hadathoo used the *Voice of Power* to call Bonarain and her class to the conference area. Bonarain showed up with nine Teams, all looking rather confused. "Officer, Bonarain, are these people ready to go aboard one of those ships and...take over?"

Bonarain shook her head. "No, Sir. That'd be at least eight days from now...at the speed we're going."

"How were you able to do it with your Team members?"

"Sir, I was able to slam it into them…because, after all this time, I know them. I don't know these other people that well."

"You've been in their heads for almost four days now. You should know something about them."

Bonarain smiled sheepishly. "A little…yes, Sir…but…not as well as I know my own Team members."

Hadathoo grunted. "Pick one from the operator crew and one from the repair crew. Slam it into them and then worry about the others later."

She looked around at all of her students. "I…don't know which ones are operator and which ones are repair."

Hadathoo pointed to his right. "All of the operators…over there." He pointed to his left. "All of the repair…over there." He glared at Bonarain. "Once they're all separated, pick one from each side! Pick the one that, to you, seems to have been the most apt student so far…and do that slamming into the mind."

Bonarain looked at the repair personnel. She sighed and walked over to Officer Grade 3, Atsuska. She grabbed Atsuska by her ears and once again had her forehead up against someone and was force feeding imagery. Atsuska made several grunts and gasps as she was getting information at an incredible rate. When Bonarain let go, Atsuska fell backwards and was caught by her Team members and steadied.

Bonarain staggered over to the operators as if she were drunk. She made (as direct a line as she could) to Officer Grade 5, Ini. Again the foreheads were together and Ini was fluttering her hands out to her sides and making a few strange noises in her throat as she was being force fed.

Soolchakan walked up behind Bonarain. As soon as she let go of Ini, she collapsed and was caught by Soolchakan. He smiled at Hadathoo. "Excuse me for a few heartbeats, Sir." He vanished with the unconscious Bonarain. He reappeared a few moments later alone. "Officer Bonarain is resting in her bed, Sir."

Hadathoo smiled. "That's nice." His demeanor changed to something sterner. "Are you ready to take them to that… Jowfoonda ship?"

Soolchakan smiled. "It's not if I am ready." He looked at Atsuska. "Are they ready?"

Atsuska looked a little confused.

Soolchakan sighed. "Are you ready?"

She shrugged. "I don't know."

Soolchakan rolled his eyes. {Are you ready?}, he asked in Jowfoonda.

She glared back at him. "I told you – I DON'T KNOW!"

Shyshee looked confused. "What'd he say…that second time?"

Chyning smiled at Shyshee. "He asked her, in Jowfoonda, if she was ready."

Atsuska looked shocked. "You…did?"

He grinned at her. {Yes, I did}, again in Jowfoonda.

She sighed. {I guess I am}. She shook her head. {WEIRD}!

Soolchakan turned to Ini. Before he could say anything to her, she held up her hand to stop him.

{I understood all of that...what you said to her...and... vice versa. I guess that I'm ready as well}

Shyshee threw her hands up in disgust and flopped back in her chair. "I hope that someone knows – and understands - what's going on."

"Yes, Sir," said Soolchakan. "They're ready."

Antrong chuckled. "How nice."

Hadathoo had a curious smile on his face. "Please...tell me, Officer, Soolchakan: Why was Officer, Bonarain able to do this...slamming into your minds...three of you? Today...she was only able to do two...and once again she is...spent. Why?"

Soolchakan smiled back. "We know her and she knows us. We didn't fight her when she force fed us the information. Atsuska and Ini did fight her."

Atsuska looked affronted. "I did not...fight her!"

Chyning cleared her throat. "Yes, you did."

Kiyalee scoffed. "All those...grunts, groans and squeaks... and all of the arm flapping...yes, you did fight her."

Now Atsuska looked like a guilty child. "I...didn't mean to."

"Neither did I," said Ini.

"Don't worry," said Soolchakan. "She'll be able to teach some more…tomorrow."

Hadathoo sat back down. "Fine! Now, the five of you, do what you can to get on that ship and…try to take control of it. Control it so that we can utilize it without it blowing itself up."

Soolchakan sighed. "That's the plan, Sir. Now…if someone could take us to where Officer, Ababi is…so we can get a good look at the ship…that'd help immensely."

Till pointed at Choychata and then pointed at Soolchakan. Choychata smiled and walked over to Soolchakan. Before he could say anything, she Jumped him to apartment 1-31 and Master Officer, Till's private observatory.

Choychata smiled. "I'll be back with the others. Kindly move off of our Jump platform so we don't join with anybody."

Soolchakan let out a little chuckle as he backed off of the plank. He stood there waiting as Choychata Jumped Kiyalee, Chyning, Atsuska and Ini into the apartment.

Now that all of them were in the apartment, Choychata led them to where Ababi and Hoodeefa were watching the mother ship as it orbited Niygool.

"I thought it was supposed to be a scout ship," said Chyning.

"Originally it was," said Ababi. "The mother ship came in just a little while ago."

Atsuska looked at the ship on the screen. "Why is this one…orbiting Niygool? From what I understood…the first scout ship was orbiting Zhagool…why the difference?"

Ababi answered without taking her eyes off of the screen. "Niygool is further away. They probably think that they're safe… as long as they stay a little further away."

"That makes sense," said Soolchakan. "We didn't get aboard and…cause that much trouble…until they started moving closer to Hardooth."

Ini cleared her throat nervously. "So…how…do we get aboard…that thing?"

"We Jump," said Chyning merrily.

Ini sniffed. "What…if we miss?"

Soolchakan looked at her and smiled. "Don't…*miss* that is."

Kiyalee stared at the screen. "So what part of that thing is our target?"

They all studied the ship as it came into view. It was a very long cylindrical ship with several armatures on each side. On each armature there was one of the ball shaped scout ships attached – except for one empty armature. It appeared that these were parking or riding locations for the scout ships. On the rear of the mother ship there were two smaller cylindrical objects attached at the top of the ship. According to Kiyalee, those would be the nacelles that contained the light speed engines of the ship.

"That ugly thing is the mother ship," said Kiyalee.

"I think you're right," said Chyning. "All of those ball shaped things on the sides...are all scout ships...that're docked with the mother ship."

Soolchakan bit his lip. "If...all of the scout ships...are the same...then we could use the same kind of landmark...that we used for the one that we were on before. We've got thirteen to choose from."

Kiyalee sounded concerned. "But it won't be...the same landmark. It'll be the control panel...on a different ship. It's not like that time with the Algothon Navy. Those ships had...different numbers on them. I can't see any difference...in those crazy little parked scout ships."

Soolchakan frowned. "All right, we...think of one of the control panels...and it's dark...in the room...and the panel...is off. That'd be...one of the scout ships in the rear of that mother ship. They look dark. There might be...no one on board them and...we could study them...or that one...a little better...without interference."

Kiyalee swallowed hard. "You...first," she said nervously.

Soolchakan hung his head. Someone had to be first. Someone had to take that leap into finding out...something. He looked up and prepared himself for who knows what? He pictured the control panel the way he had seen it in the occupied scout ship. He now put a blank panel, with no one around, into his imagery" held his breath...and Jumped. He stood there with his heart pounding. He had made it. He let out a sigh of relief.

He calmed himself and listened for any unusual noises. He heard nothing - at first. He heard two voices that were somewhere on this Bridge. He walked up the stairs to see the rest of the Bridge. There were two Jowfoondas kneeling near a console and they each had a toolbox close by.

'Perfect,' he thought. 'This one is under maintenance. The maintenance is being done on the Bridge. That means…this one is down for a while and a wonderful spot for us to have some fun.' "**Soolchakan calling Atsuska. Can you hear me**?"

"**YES**," came back a frantic reply. "**You blocked us and we couldn't find you!**"

He nervously chuckled. "**Sorry about that. I made it. I'm on one of the scout ships.**"

"**Which one**?"

He thought for a moment. He did not have a clue which one he was on. He walked back down to the observation window that the navigators would be looking through. "**It appears… that I'm on one of the rear scout ships on the starboard side**."

The reply came back sounding rather confused. "**What's a…starboard**?"

Chyning broke in. "**That's the right side of the ship.**"

There was a long pause. "**Uh…the right side…if you are looking from the rear…or looking at it…from the front**?"

Chyning now sounded a little insulting (on purpose). **"They call it the starboard side so that no one'll ask that question."**

Another pause. Atsuska sounded a little irritable. **"Landmark the *chokwad* thing and Jump us in."**

He looked around at the Bridge. He shrugged. The Ship Leader's chair seemed to be a pretty good landmark. He stood in front of it and looked for something unique about this chair. He felt very sure that each chair would be identical on all of the scout ships, so he pulled out his knife, hopped the point into Home, popped a few stitches in the seat cushion and put his knife away. He nodded as he stared at the damage he had done. He Jumped back to apartment 1-31. He grabbed Atsuska and Ini and Jumped back to the ship.

"The two of you, stand off to the side. I'm going to Jump the others to this same spot."

The two women backed away from the chair without any hesitation.

He Jumped back to 1-31, grabbed Kiyalee and Chyning and Jumped back to the ship.

He noticed that Chyning was rubbing her cheek and looking very angry. "What happened to you?"

Atsuska chimed in. "When she got smart with me I backhanded her."

He nodded. "Yeah, she needs a good smack-down every now and then."

Chyning opened her mouth and a very strange sound came out of the orifice. She had her fists clenched down at her side.

Soolchakan looked at her sternly. "WHAT?"

Chyning gave him an angry look, turned to the side and folded her arms across her chest with her lower lip sticking out slightly.

He shook his head. She was now nearly three hundred years old and still acting like a child. "The two of you, move away."

Chyning stormed away. Kiyalee backed away looking a little confused.

He Jumped back to 1-31, grabbed Hoodeefa and Choychata and Jumped back to the ship.

Both women hollered at the same time. "WHAT DID YOU BRING ME HERE FOR?"

He smiled. "While Atsuska, Ini and Kiyalee are doing… whatever they need to do with the computers, you two, Chyning and I will be exploring the mother ship…and a scout ship, looking for some landmarks in there. We'll also be mapping out the different ship's facilities, like the dining area, the medical area, the Bridge, weaponry, sleeping quarters, maintenance and any other thing that we happen to come across."

Atsuska walked up to Soolchakan, still looking a little aggravated. "That sounds like a reasonable plan. NOW…what is starboard?"

Soolchakan had to explain certain nautical terms such as: Fore, aft, bow, stern, port, starboard and anything else that he could think of.

Atsuska listened intently. After the explanations were done she looked at Chyning. "See! If you'd just explained it, in a civil manner…you wouldn't have gotten *hit*."

Chyning glared back at her and then turned away, still pouting.

Kiyalee held a hand up. "Uh…why am I supposed to stay here…with the computer experts? I don't know that much about those things."

Soolchakan sighed. "You've had a chance to watch some of them working with the things…in maintenance. Those guys are doing some repair…so you might know more than you think you know. Stay here with Atsuska and see if you can lend a hand… even though your knowledge is…limited."

Hoodeefa and Choychata departed the area to start the exploration.

Atsuska shook her head. "What…primarily…are we looking for?"

Soolchakan felt like slapping Atsuska. He cleared his throat and turned to her with a smile. "You are looking for the self-destruct system and trying to find a way to deactivate it… at least on one of the scout ships…if not the mother ship as well. That way, we can take-over the entire operation of all of these ships."

"What if we accidentally set of the self-destruct? How do we know if..."

Kiyalee interrupted. "Oh don't worry! If you set it off... there is a *tremendous* warning that it *has* been activated."

Atsuska sighed. "Okay. I'll take your word for it." She looked at the two maintenance men. "Can you wait until we... have some kind of control...over these two?"

Soolchakan looked at them and sighed. "What do you need from me to help you with the computers?"

Atsuska shook her head. "I don't know yet."

He shrugged. "Start by reading their minds."

"Let's start with the one on the left," said Ini.

All of them started concentrating on him...and all of them felt disgusted.

Chyning growled. "Reminds me of a certain pervert that I had to babysit on that Bising ship. All he could think about was what he was going to do to his girlfriend...when he got home."

Atsuska frowned. "We can't read Teltermak minds. How did you know what he was thinking?"

"He liked the sound of his own voice," said Chyning with disgust and contempt on her face. "He also couldn't keep his hands...off his...crotch."

Ini waved her hands. "Forget about that! What's the other guy thinking?"

They all concentrated on him. He was checking the readings on his electronic device.

"Let's see if we can find if he has some kind of password to get into the computer," said Soolchakan. "We'll be able to do what we want…if we have the password of a technician."

There were several more tense moments of mind reading.

Ini leaned back and shook her head. "He has a *very* focused mind."

"So does the other one," said Chyning. "While you guys were trying to get a password from that one…I tried the other one. He's still being…perverted."

Kiyalee huffed. "The only way that we're going to get them to use their password…is to force it." She got closer to the console they were working on. They were on the underside, while she looked at the readout on the screen. She smiled. She grabbed hold of the power cord, hopped it into Spy, unplugged it momentarily, plugged it back in and then hopped it back to Home.

Both men noticed the console shutdown.

The pervert was a little surprised. {What did you do Shkrook}?

{I didn't do anything. I was checking the readings…and it died}.

{Well you had to have done something}!

{Hey, Changchog, they said they were having all kinds of problems with this console…maybe that was one of the problems…

as well}.

Changchog grunted. {All right…maybe. Let's turn the thing back on and watch what happens}.

Shkrook got up and walked around to where Kiyalee was waiting. He hit the switch to turn the computer back on.

Kiyalee signaled Chyning. "Help me watch him. We might get it done more accurately if both of us are watching."

Chyning nodded and headed over to the console and got her nose up close.

"Get ready," said Kiyalee.

The computer finished the start-up and the prompt for the password appeared on the screen. Shkrook started feeding his password in the blank. As he fed it in, both Kiyalee and Chyning hit a random key.

Shkrook's head jerked back. {Incorrect password! What}?

He grunted and fed it in again. Again, Kiyalee and Chyning each hit a random key. When it came up with the "incorrect" again, he slowly hit each key carefully with his index finger. Both women were writing each character on their pads as he fed it in. When it accepted the password, this time, the two women compared notes.

Kiyalee shuddered. "This is weird. Ten days ago…I never heard any of these monsters talk. Now…I can speak, read, write and understand…everything they say."

Atsuska cleared her throat. "Did you get the password?"

Kiyalee gave Atsuska a big grin. "Yup!"

"Good! Let's go to another console and get into their system."

Easier said than done. They got away from the two technicians and found they could not log on to another terminal as long as Shkrook was logged on already.

Atsuska sighed in frustration. "We need to get him off of that busted one before we can log onto this one."

Soolchakan turned to Chyning. "Are you still a little upset over being smacked?"

She snarled at him.

"Go take your anger out on those two Jowfoondas."

She walked over to them with a scowl on her face. "I need them to be standing up."

Soolchakan took out his knife, hopped the blade into Home and scraped the edge of the console he was near. Both Jowfoondas noticed it. They did not get up they just stared in that direction. He scraped the console again. This time both men stood up. Two spinning kicks later and both Jowfoondas were laid out flat...minus a few teeth (if they had any to begin with).

Soolchakan momentarily surveyed the damage. "Now, shut that computer off."

Chyning pulled the cord, the way she had seen Kiyalee do it. The computer immediately died.

Atsuska used the password to sign on at the other terminal. She watched the screen and grinned. "We're in."

"Good," said Soolchakan. "Chyning and I will be exploring this scout ship…and then later the mother ship. Let us know if you need any help." He looked at the two KO'd Jowfoonda. "Let us know if you need help…with anything."

Atsuska snickered. "I'll be sure to call."

He turned to Chyning. "Let's map this *chogo* out."

Chyning pulled out her pad and started taking notes as they walked along.

5

Hoodeefa and Choychata were walking around in the mother ship.

Hoodeefa shook her head. "This thing is...*huge*! It's about two and a half kilotaja in length. How did they ever get it off of the ground?"

"Especially without wings," said Choychata.

"Maybe they used rockets...like the Algothons have."

"Maybe."

So far they had been on three decks. There was a main hallway in the center that went from bow to stern. There were several side halls that branched off at set intervals.

"Drawing this thing out...won't be a challenge," said Hoodeefa. "*Everything* is at 90 degree angles and measured very regularly."

They stopped and looked around bored.

"We've been on three decks now – 12, 13 and 14, according to that map they have on the wall," said Choychata. "All of this stuff...so far...has been crew quarters, a few medical stations and some dining facilities."

"I wonder where they store all the food," said Hoodeefa.

Choychata just shrugged.   "Funny thing is…in those dining facilities…I don't see any kitchens…yet they're all eating something."

"Let's find another deck…and see if there's anything different there."

"Up or down?"

"We're on 14. We've seen 12 and 13. Let's try 15."

They descended through one of the many spiral stairways on the ship. Deck 15 seemed very different. On this deck, the personnel were dressed differently. Instead of the dark green pants and light green shirts, these people were all wearing some kind of jumpsuit. Some were dressed in brown, some in yellow and some in blue. They had the regular crew quarters, dining facilities and medical stations, however on this deck there were slides that went down a deck further.

Hoodeefa looked at the slide with consternation. "Should we try it?"

While pondering the issue, one of the blue suits sat down on the slide and disappeared down the chute.

The two women shrugged at each other and then jumped on the slide. They were now on deck 16. This was a totally different environment. There were hundreds of small single-seat ships parked in neat rows from bow to stern on this deck. From what the women observed of the personnel on this deck, the brown suits were pilots, the blue suits were mechanics and the yellow suits were some kind of coordinators.

The small ships were mostly cylindrical. There was a pointed nose with several small objects that were pointing forward on the nose cone. The women guessed they were the business end of some kind of pulse weapons. Why they needed six of them was a mystery, however, they would leave that up to someone else to figure out. There was a seat for the pilot just behind the middle mark of the ship. There were six, what appeared to be wings, however they seemed too short to keep anything airborne. Each of the wings had another pulse weapon barrel on them. This made twelve pulse weapons. Again a mystery as to why they needed that many. The only thing that they could guess was that if one got damaged, they still had plenty of firepower to keep on going. In the rear there was some kind of…thing. It did not look like the exhaust cone of a rocket like the Algothons had. The women could not even guess at the power plant inside this small ship. They remembered that Kiyalee had said something about quantum physics and since they had no idea what that was, it must be the science that had designed these engines and was beyond their personal scientific capabilities.

Hoodeefa looked out an observation port. "I…uh…think that we're…in the bottom of the ship."

"Why?"

"Look out the window. The window is almost in the floor and…the floor is kind of rounded here…as if it…is the bottom."

Choychata took a quick glance and turned away holding her stomach. "Oh! There's nothing down there but…" She looked out the window again. "There's not even air out there. It's a void. There's nothing beneath us." She took a few quick breaths. "I was looking at that…big set of doors…in the front of the ship. I guess if they want to launch these little…ships…they open those doors first."

"But that would let all of the air out."

"Look at the sides here. You see a bunch of lockers with… some kind of suit…with a helmet…hanging all over the place. They're all yellow and blue. Maybe…when they open those doors…the mechanics and…coordinators…get in those things."

Hoodeefa shuddered. "Well I don't wanna be here when they do open that…door. Let's get upstairs."

"Which deck?"

Hoodeefa shrugged. "When we came out of that scout ship, we were on 12. Let's go up to 11. We haven't seen any of that part…yet."

"What if it's just like 12?"

"Then we go to 10!" Hoodeefa grunted in disgust.

Chyning followed Soolchakan making all kinds of annotations on her pad about the layout of the scout ship. They found where the command personnel stayed on the ship (when they were on a mission). They found all of the crew quarters for maintenance, gunners, communications, medical, science and security. They found no cooks or food storage.

They were baffled because they had not found any personnel who were in charge of cooking the food. They found dining facilities, but no kitchen. They found tables, flatware, some plates, glasses and fancy serving platters. They found no ovens or anything else to cook on or with.

She looked at him. "Do these people…eat?"

He scratched his head. "They have…flatware…that's similar to ours. They have glasses and plates. They have mugs and serving platters. They have to eat…something! They have to eat…it…somewhere but…I'm stumped."

"IT! They eat…IT! But what? Where?"

"They eat at a table."

"No, I mean…where's the food?"

"I…don't know."

He was suddenly called mentally.

"This is Officer, Ini calling Officer, Soolchakan. Can you hear me?"

"Yes, I can hear you. What did you need?"

"One of the Jowfoondas is waking up."

Soolchakan stood there pondering. **"And…**?"

"What do I do?"

"Which one?"

"Which one…what?"

"Which one is waking up?"

"I'm not sure if it's...WHAT DIFFERENCE DOES THAT MAKE?"

"Try knocking him out again."

"I'm not that good at kicking...maybe Chyning could...."

He stood there with his eyes and fists clenched shut as he bit his lower lip. "GET A TOOL OUT OF ONE OF THE TOOLBOXES AND SLUG HIM WITH IT!" He waited for several moments. "Did you slug him?"

"Uh...yes."

"Is he out cold...again?"

"Yes."

"Okay, now put the tool in the hand of the other mechanic."

"Uh...why?"

He groaned. "Those two *bimyocks* have bruises on them. If someone comes in there and finds them out cold...and there's no sign of them fighting each other...there's an investigation. If there is evidence that they cold-cocked each other...that's as far as the investigation will go. It'll be determined that they fought each other. No one will worry about us."

"Should I...get another tool...and belt the other

one?"

'No,' he thought without sending. 'Just kiss and fondle him a little.' **"That sounds like a plan."**

"Okay, I've smacked the other one with a tool. I'm putting the tool in the hands of the other one. Now... like you said...it looks like they fought each other."

"Good job." He hung his head and moaned.

Chyning shook her head. "Did that really just happen?"

He looked up dull-eyed. "I'm afraid so." He closed his eyes and groaned. "Let's get back to mapping this big tin bucket."

Hoodeefa and Choychata had found nothing worth looking at on decks 11, 10, 9, 8, 7, 6 or 5. They found that there were a lot of personnel on this ship and they had to have quarters in which to live in their off duty time. On deck 4, they found some game rooms. There were several games (that made no sense to them, seeing as how they could not read the rules...yet). They watched several of the Jowfoondas playing some of these games but still did not understand the goal or rules. The gymnasiums were very different. Here they recognized practice dummies, punching bags, running tracks, exercising machines and barbells. They spent very little time in the gymnasiums because there was no question about what was going on there.

They went up to deck 3 and found many of (what appeared to be) the different Commanding Officers of the different areas of the ship. The living quarters on this deck were much larger and lavish. All of the personnel on this deck seemed to be wearing uniforms that had all kinds of flashy decorations on them.

They also found the Legal department…which was currently performing a court martial of some type.

Hoodeefa turned on a small recorder to catch all of what was being said so she could get this turn of events translated.

The person who appeared to be the judge did not have any form of a gavel. He had a stick that he used to smack a small gong that was on the desk. He said something and hit the gong. A man who was dressed only in a loincloth (and a lot of chains around his arms and legs) started screaming back at the judge. The judge got up and walked away. Four men in gray uniforms took hold of the man and pushed him into a large hollow glass ball and closed it, trapping him inside. They rolled the ball over to the wall and hooked a line to it. The ball was then rolled into a small alcove that was only large enough to hold the ball. A sliding door was closed and now they could no longer see the ball.

Hoodeefa and Choychata both looked at each other puzzled. They walked up to where several observers were looking out the window of the spacecraft. They both gasped in shock as the glass ball, with the man inside, was launched out into space. It appeared as if it were intentionally fired at Niygool.

After the ball was launched, all of the personnel moved to a large screen that showed the ball going down to the moon below. Apparently they had some camera that remained focused on the ball as it descended. The man inside was floating around helplessly inside the ball screaming. No one was listening because there was no microphone inside the ball. His slit of a mouth was moving, however, the two women could not tell whether or not he was terrified because they could not read anything in those insect type eyes.

Hoodeefa pointed at the screen. "Look...that line they hooked...to the ball. It's trailing after the thing."

Choychata scoffed in confusion. "What's going on?"

"Either it's a very nasty experiment...with an involuntary lab rodent...or it's an execution."

Choychata stuck out her tongue. "Yuck! That...is a *horrible* way to go."

The line hooked to the ball suddenly went taut. The ball split in half and the man was expelled toward the surface of Niygool. The two women now clapped their hands over their mouths. The man would have been expelled toward the surface, however, as soon as the ball opened, his body blew up in a huge bloody mess. The green blood splatter was frozen solid almost instantaneously. Now all that the two women saw was a blood splatter and some bones that were continuing the slow fall toward Niygool.

The ball was closed and the line was used to retract the ball. All of the personnel who had witnessed the execution now walked away to do...whatever.

Choychata swallowed hard. "You...recorded...all of... that?"

Hoodeefa simply nodded.

"That's a sight that…I wish I could…un-see."

"You and me both!"

Atsuska was looking over all of the data that she had brought up on the screen. She shook her head. "I just don't see how we're going to bypass all of that *h'oolyach*. We may have to…give up on this…capture scheme."

Ini shrugged. "There's just three of us here. Maybe… when some of the others are here…they may be able to come up with something different."

Atsuska scoffed. "You mean like…how to bypass the safety guards?"

"Who knows? Someone just might." Ini looked at Kiyalee.

"Don't ask me," said Kiyalee. "I'm a mechanic. I don't know nuthin' bout computers. I may be able to work on some of the electronics…but this stuff…is way above my learning."

They heard one of the Jowfoonda men moan. Kiyalee closed her eyes and shook her head. She walked back over to the one that was stirring and hit him again. She held the tool up over her head and watched to see if he was still stirring. When he did not move she dropped the tool and went back to the screen.

Atsuska frowned. "They sure don't stay asleep very long do they?"

Kiyalee looked to see if there was any blood on her hands. "If they don't stop that…I'm afraid that I may do some permanent damage to them…if I haven't done that already."

Soolchakan and Chyning came back from mapping the scout ship.

He looked at the two victims. "Find anything that you can use?"

Atsuska shook her head. "These…Jowfoondas…they don't trust anybody."

"Okay," said Soolchakan. "That's a good idea, but…there should be some way to bypass their safety protocols."

Atsuska scoffed. She looked at Kiyalee. "Show him!"

Kiyalee picked up a flat piece of equipment.

Chyning looked at it puzzled. "What is that thing?"

"It's a small and very portable computer," said Kiyalee. "It's a little larger than ours, but it's a lot more complicated in what it can do." She laid the computer upside down. She used a precision tool to take a panel off of the computer. "There," she said as she pointed. "That disc is the hard drive. There's that silvery coil around it…and that's the self-destruct mechanism for this portable."

He frowned. "Does everything…have a self-destruct… thingy…in it?"

Atsuska nodded. "All of the technological pieces have one…yes."

Chyning shook her head. "So if we run off with that

thing…it'll blow the *h'oolyach* out of the hard drive."

"No," said Ini. "In the case of the portable, that coil will heat up to an incredible temperature and…*melt* the hard drive." She pointed to a small object attached to the inside of the computer. "That's the tattletale switch. If we take the portable out of here… on any mission that hasn't been authorized by…some high and mighty muckity-muck, that little component sends a message back to the mother ship. If there's no authorization code fed in…within a certain amount of time…instant immolation."

Soolchakan nodded. "So there's no way to take it out of there and keep the hard drive…or the portable."

Atsuska sighed. "We can't do anything with it unless we put it in maintenance mode."

Soolchakan frowned. "If you put it…in maintenance mode…what happens then?"

Ini smiled. "We can take the whole thing apart."

He rolled his eyes. "So…?"

Atsuska looked confused. "So…what?"

He grunted. "Put the thing in maintenance mode, take it apart and put it back together…*without* the tattletale or the destroyer coil."

Atsuska stood up and held her finger up as if to admonish him. She opened her mouth and froze. Her expression changed from anger to confusion to pondering. Her wrist went limp, her shoulders dropped and then her arm flopped down at her side. She stood there staring off into space. "That just might work."

Chyning walked away laughing hysterically.

Ini looked confused. "What's with her?"

Kiyalee gave a patronizing grin. "You two are the computer experts and it was him who came up with the suggestion on how to handle it. That's what's so funny."

Atsuska blushed in anger. She hit several keys on the Jowfoonda console. "Take it apart." She folded her arms and glared at the still giggling Chyning.

Chyning could not stop laughing. She was holding her sides and moaning in pain, however, she would continue giggling while holding her sides.

Atsuska got up, walked over to the two Jowfoonda techs and kicked each one of them in frustration.

Kiyalee had the coil and the tattletale switch sitting off to the side. She put the rest of the computer back together. After the last screw was in place she shrugged. "Okay! It's time to…test the theory."

Atsuska looked at the portable. "Give it to the giggling *bimyock* and have her Jump…somewhere on Hardooth. Then come back."

Chyning came over and picked up the portable. She turned it over and looked it over. She sniffed and then disappeared. Everyone on the ship looked at the tattletale switch and the coil. Nothing happened. Chyning reappeared with the portable.

Atsuska nodded. "No alarms...no damage...no... nothing."

Soolchakan smiled. "Is it still in...maintenance mode?"

Atsuska looked at the active console and back at Soolchakan. She nodded with a worried look on her face.

He smiled. "We're not gonna know...unless we take the chance."

Atsuska sighed. She hit some keys on the console. She looked at Chyning. "Jump again...and we'll see."

Chyning licked her lips and looked, almost fearfully, at the portable. She disappeared. Once again, the four Owlamites looked around and listened. Nothing. Chyning reappeared looking apprehensive.

Atsuska went limp in her seat. "I don't believe this. I was thinking of some overly complicated way...to bypass all of their safety protocols and...the answer was so simple. Just...fool it into thinking it's being worked on...and...don't reinstall the tattletale *or* the destroyer coil."

Ini snickered. "Okay, so what do we do with that tattletale switch...in the meantime?"

Soolchakan shrugged. "Hide it."

Hoodeefa and Choychata were on deck 1 - the Bridge. They were looking around at all of the consoles and all of the people working them.

Hoodeefa shook her head. "Do you understand any of this…stuff?"

"Nope! I think…before we do anything else…we get someone up here who can understand these…monsters and…let them worry about what's being said."

"Should we record some of it?"

"Why not?"

Hoodeefa pointed. "Hey, that guy that's talking to the one in the fancy golden vest…isn't that the one who was the judge… downstairs?"

"I think it is…maybe."

"Let's record what he's saying. Maybe…it'll shed some light on what happened to that guy…and why."

"Do we really want to know?"

"If I don't find out, I'll wonder about it…forever."

"I guess you're right. Might as well."

They got up close in order to record the conversation. The two Jowfoondas were talking in a curiously jovial manner. Both of them laughed (or appeared to laugh) about something. While Hoodeefa was recording the words, Choychata took a few pictures. The uniform of the one in the chair was just *too* fancy with that golden vest and all of the adornments. He had to be of a very high rank in order to get away with all of that stuff.

The judge finally walked away and the gold vested one

turned his attention to other matters of the ship.

They got bored with just walking around the Bridge. They decided they had enough information for now and headed back to the scout ship where the sabotage was taking place.

Atsuska looked at the growing pile of equipment that was currently in maintenance mode, where the tattletale and destruct mechanisms had been removed. "Now...if we could just do the same...to the scout ship."

Soolchakan gave her a questioning look. "What's the problem there?"

She sighed. "According to this...the ship's commander must be notified...of something of that magnitude. I don't think that we'd get away with it...or bypass that particular command."

Ini picked up a stack of the portable computers. "I could Jump all of these back to Hardooth and...we'd have something for everyone to look at...once they all understand Jowfoonda."

Atsuska nodded. "Right. Along with all of the other things that we've changed and misappropriated." She looked at the two bloodied and battered Jowfoonda. "What should we do with them?"

"Leave em where they are," said Chyning. "Let them explain...how they fought each other over...nothing."

Atsuska smiled. "That's a good idea. Leave someone here to watch what happens when the others find them." She stared at

Chyning and her smile got even bigger. "It'd have to be someone who isn't helping with the computers or the computer systems."

Chyning now had a sick look on her face. "What about Hoodeefa or Choychata? Why couldn't they stay?"

"They don't understand the Jowfoonda language," said Atsuska patronizingly.

Chyning sat down and glared at Atsuska.

Atsuska closed her eyes. **"This is Officer, Atsuska calling Officer, Hoodeefa, can you hear me**?"

"This is Officer, Hoodeefa, what did you need, Sir?"

"How near done are you with your mapping?"

"We've been from bottom to top. We found most of the facilities and…are guessing at a few others. Why?"

"We were thinking of heading back and looking at all of the data. If you have sufficient information on all decks, I think that someone will be interested in it… especially someone who speaks the language of these monsters."

"Yes, Sir. I'm interested in getting a certain conversation translated all right. They executed someone on the ship. I'm wondering what carries the death penalty on a spaceship."

Atsuska opened her eyes in shock. **"I agree. Come**

back here to the scout ship and we'll all go together."

"**Uh...Sir, we're kinda...lost!   We're not sure... where to Jump to in all of this**."

Atsuska hung her head. "Officer, Soolchakan, have you been listening to this?"

"Yes, I have."

"What's your suggestion?"

He smiled. "**Go ahead and Jump back to your apartment on Hardooth.   We'll all go to the Command Staff conference room from there and give a report**."

Atsuska shrugged. "Sounds good to me. Okay...everyone who's going back to Hardooth now...grab some of this equipment and...let's go."

Chyning looked away and snarled. She watched as each of the others picked up a load of equipment and vanished. Now that she was alone, she looked around the room at all of the notebooks and written manuals that were all over the place. She figured they were there in case something went wrong with the computer, there was a hard copy of any of their instructions readily available. She picked a thin one to pull down and read. One – because it was thin. Two – just like her position in the Team, the binder was green. As a matter of fact it was almost the same shade of green as her shirt.

She walked over and took one more look at the two

victims. She returned to the desk, flipped the binder open and started reading. It was a quick reference guide for conquest of a planet. She was a little startled at that thought for a moment. She decided that this would tell a lot about who these people were and what they had intended to do.

According to the book, the first step was observation. Determine what the capabilities of the sentient life form was capable of as far as technology was concerned. Under normal circumstances it would be a Chinchik (O-5) who was in charge of the observation. Once the observation stage was over, a Tomontain (O-7) was dispatched to further decide where the main targets should be, based on technological advances of the area. Once the attack was started, it was to maintain as much chaos, panic, disaster and confusion as possible, while destroying major targets. She sat back and pondered, wondering how hard Algothon had been hit. Their city was probably one of the most advanced as far as technology was concerned.

Once most of the technology was destroyed they were to find a primary landing zone and establish their presence on the planet. If it was determined that there was a danger to the landing party, there would be the requirement for more reinforcements before anything was allowed to get out of the control of the current landing party. The best opportunity to take over a planet would be to appear as if they were some kind of deity and control the citizenry through their superstitions.

She snickered. "I think that we stepped on your initial landing party. Got rid of them as well."

If there was any form of resistance to the initial landing party, all members of a sect, group or nation were to be exterminated for the transgression of fighting back.

She sat back with her eyes wide open. "It ain't bad enough we get a bunch of *h'oolyach* from the Teltermak...now you *doovofts* wanna do the same."

If the group, to be exterminated is extensive, call in as much reinforcement as is necessary in order to establish total dominance of the planet as rapidly as possible.

She giggled. "Your problem is that you don't know who did it to you. You can't even find your missing child."

One of the two Jowfoonda victims started moaning. She ran over to him and gave him another kick in the head. "On no you don't...not now." She slowly walked back to the book while looking back at him. "This stuff is just getting interesting."

She sat down to read some more and heard another noise. She groaned in disbelief. There were three more Jowfoonda personnel coming onto the Bridge of this scout ship. She might not get to finish this thing...now.

The three Jowfoondas were officers. The ranking one, a Honroodo (O-4) called out: {Zizh Tosko (E-6), Shkrook! What's going on with the repairs}? He stood there waiting for a response. He turned to one of the others with him. {Vilvak Second (O-2), Winthok, where's that damaged console}?

The indicated officer pointed. {It's the backup navigational console, Honroodo, Bikbish}.

Bikbish grunted. {So what are they doing…where and why}?

The three officers walked over to the console. As they approached, the third officer noticed the two bloodied men, unconscious on the floor. He pointed and stood there with his mouth wide open.

Bikbish looked at the man. {What's your problem, Vilvak First (O-1), Foogoo}?

Foogoo finally found his voice. {There, Honroodc, Bikbish…the two technicians…they've been fighting each other… and…look}!

Bikbish looked over the console and growled. {Call Security in here}!

Foogoo pulled a small communicator off of his belt and held it up to his mouth. {Security is needed on the Bridge of Scout 9…quickly}.

A quick acknowledgement came over the radio.

Chyning huffed. "Now I know I won't be able to finish this *chogo* thing now."

Another call came in on the radio. {This is Yambagin Cho (O-9), Shalashak! Why do you need Security on the sleeping scout ship}?

All three men snapped to attention. Bikbish responded. {Yambagin Cho, Shalashak, this is Honroodo, Bikbish. Nothing to disturb you with at this time, Sir, we've discovered that two men have been in a fight}.

Another call was heard over the radio: {Yambagin Cho, Shalashak to Kooz Office! Report to the Bridge of Scout 9 immediately}.

A quick acknowledgement came over the radio.

Chyning brightened up. "Kooz? You *bimyocks* are going to call the Legal Office down here…now? You're going to hold a court-martial…right here…right now? *This* is getting better every heartbeat." She sat there grinning, eagerly awaiting to find out what was going to happen next.

Nine Security personnel came running into the room. {Where's the fight}? Said the one in charge.

Bikbish pointed at the two men. {They've knocked each other out, Honroodo, Toyan}.

Toyan walked over to see. He scowled at Bikbish while panting heavily. {You might've informed us that the fight was over before we *rushed* all the way here Honroodo, Bikbish}.

Bikbish nodded. {Noted for further reference, Honroodo. My apologies}.

Toyan turned to his men. {Holster your weapons}. He shook his head and pulled a radio off of his belt. {We need Medical personnel in Scout 9. Two men injured}.

A quick acknowledgement came over the radio.

Toyan looked back at his Security detail. {Take positions}.

Four of them stood around Shkrook and four stood around Changchog.

The six Medical personnel were the first to arrive. They walked around the two injured Jowfoondas doing a quick assessment of the situation. They broke into two sets of three and began a further examination of the two victims.

{This wasn't an argument…this was a battle to the death}, said one of the doctors. {These men have sustained…some horrible physical damage}.

Four Legal personnel arrived. They had simple gray uniforms. One had a black circle on his chest, one had a brown circle, one had a yellow circle and the last had a red circle.

The black circle spoke first. {How badly are they hurt? Is it worth my time now to put them on trial}?

The doctor looked up. {We'll be able to get them talking. As to why they did this, I'm glad that I don't have to figure it out}. He went back to taking care of his patient.

Chyning was taking in all of the crowd that was gathering, wondering if she could pull some mischief on them. She watched the red circle Legal man walk over to where she was sitting. He picked up the binder she had been reading, closed it and replaced it on the shelf.

"I was reading that, you *doovoft*! Now you've lost my place."

As he walked away, she tripped him. He went sprawling on the floor. He sat up and turned, looking for any object that he might have stumbled over. His shoulders sagged as he saw nothing. He got up to go back to his place and she tripped him again. He propped himself up on his elbows and grunted in frustration.

Bikbish raised his eyebrows. {Are we having trouble with walking, Koozloomon}?

Chyning looked at the man startled. Koozloomon? According to what she had learned from Bonarain in the force feeding of the language, Koozloomon was the term for "executioner". She snickered as she realized who she was messing with.

He got up and looked down at his feet as he walked very carefully to where he was supposed to stand during any legal event.

The man with the black circle on his uniform put a small gong on a working station. He sniffed as he looked around at the entire situation. {Are we ready to begin the preliminary hearing}?

{Yes, Koozgofon}, said the man with the brown circle.

{Yes, Koozgofon}, said the man with the yellow circle.

Chyning sat there with her mouth agape. Koozgofon was the term for a trial judge. They were getting ready to have a trial right here and now. She was now wondering which circle was the prosecutor and which one was the defender. She knew that she would not have to wait very long to find out.

The judge held up what looked like a stick. He pressed something on it and another stick in the hand of the man with the brown circle lit up.

{Proceed, Kooztoyso (Prosecutor)}.

{Thank you, Koozgofon. What we see here is plain and simple. Two men got into an argument over…probably something very trivial. They beat each other to a bloody mess. Their injuries appear to be extensive. We don't really need a doctor to prove that fact. Since we cannot allow that kind of behavior on this ship, it is recommended that we go to trial and I also recommend the death penalty for both parties involved. It doesn't matter what their difference of opinion was…we don't allow this kind of… activity…between members of the crew}. He took a step back.

The Koozgofon nodded. He hit another button on his wand. The light went out on the stick in the prosecutor's hand. {Koozyast (Defender), do you have any rebuttal on this subject}?

The light turned on in the stick held by the Defender. {I most certainly do, Koozgofon. My learned opponent has forgotten the edict of the Commander of this expedition. Yambagin Cho, Shalashak stated that we had received some insane ravings, over the communicator, from the Scout Ship Number 8…just before the mysterious disappearance of said ship. Since it seems that everyone aboard Number 8 went insane prior to that baffling disappearance, we were instructed to look for anything that appeared…out of the ordinary. The acts of these two men, whose previous records are both unblemished, acting like brawling criminals…would certainly fall under that guideline. My suggestion, before any more trial negotiations occur, is to take them to the hospital and have them thoroughly examined, physically, psychologically and if necessary…spiritually. Only then can we truly discuss any form of guilt or innocence on their part}. He took a step back.

The Koozgofon nodded. He changed the lit stick to the Kooztoyso. {Any comment}?

The Kooztoyso stepped forward. {I thank my learned opponent for reminding all of us about the Commander's edict. I agree completely with the examination of these two men. If it is something that happened *to* them and not because of their tempers…we need to find this out…before the entire ship goes crazy. My one stipulation of change to what the Koozyast said is that I recommend they be given truth serum…to determine if they actually were fighting about some…trivial matter…or if this was indeed an involuntary act of insanity}. He took a step back.

Again the lit stick changed.

The Koozyast stepped forward. {No contest against truth serum. Get the men to the hospital as quickly as possible and get the investigation completed}. He stepped back.

The Koozgofon nodded. His stick lit up. {I agree as well. We need to find out exactly what happened in here. The men will be examined thoroughly and we will proceed after we get the findings from the medical personnel}. He looked down at the doctors who were working on the men's injuries. {Please get them to the hospital now, in order to perform all of the necessary examinations}.

One doctor stood up. {Now stop right there! You have now turned these two over to me! Since I now have the control over them, *I* will be the one who will decide when and how they're moved. I'm not telling you how to do your job, don't *you* tell me how to do mine}!

The Koozgofon nodded. {I surrender to your expertise}

Toyan smiled. {So I and my personnel are not needed here anymore}?

The antennae on the Koozgofon's head started wriggling and he sounded angry. {On the contrary...you might be needed if these men awaken and decide to renew their argument. If this is some insanity...because of our proximity to that planet...you will be needed...if for no other reason than to aid the doctors in getting the two patients to the hospital...without further injury... to themselves or anyone else}.

Toyan nodded. {We will render any and all assistance necessary}.

Chyning shook her head. This language had a strange habit of overuse of the D and the P, unless it was proper names and titles. 'Strange language,' she thought. She ran over to the exit to get there before the Kooz personnel departed. On the way out, she tripped the executioner again. She watched the six antennae on his head go crazy with movements as he lay there grumbling. She snickered as she headed back to find that green binder again. That binder was something that the Command Staff would want to see before making any final decisions on the Jowfoonda.

Atsuska and Ini were able to turn on all of the stolen computers as well as all of the other pieces of purloined equipment. The only aggravation was that they only had one password. They were going to have to go back to the Jowfoonda ship and obtain a lot more passwords unless they could find one that would open everything…like a password from the ship's Commander. Until they had another password or one that could open up several items they were limited in learning about these components.

They had to wait for almost a full day before Bonarain woke up and was able to continue teaching the Jowfoonda language to the other computer personnel.

While the class was going on, Soolchakan went to the ship to relieve Chyning. He was able to watch two more of the Jowfoonda go into the scout ship and work on repairing the faulty console.

Chyning returned and informed the Command Staff of everything she had observed after the others had departed the ship. She also informed them about what she had read in the green binder. (She did not tell them about messing with the executioner).

Hoodeefa and Choychata played their recordings for Atsuska, Ini and Kiyalee who translated all of the conversations that were on it. It seems that the individual who was executed was an incorrigible. He had committed his tenth transgression and despite his expertise in his job, he was considered something that was not worth keeping.

Hadathoo contemplated all that he had heard from the ship. "All right, we now know that they're conquerors and they wish to conquer our planet. We have the report from Officer Leader, Ota that the Jowfoonda attacked all three sections of Algothon, so…they're definitely out to destroy the technology of the planet before doing the takeover. How do we stop them?"

Beemella shrugged. "Either we destroy the entire ship, by making them think that they're all insane or we take it. The problem with taking it though...we have to make sure that there are a lot more personnel who learn that language...and how to work those...uh what did she call them...nacelles?"

Antrong cleared his throat. "The nacelle is the cowling around the engine. It is the *engine* that we need to learn a lot more about and what Officer, Kiyalee called...quantum physics." He shook his head. "We were all brought up as watchers...because we didn't show any aptitude for...chemistry or...physics...or a lot of other things. We're all going to have to step up...and learn... whether we like it or not."

Hoynama frowned. "Are we all going to have to take the aptitude tests again?"

Hadathoo rolled his eyes. "Those tests were burned up by the firestorm weapon. We don't have any more copies of them."

Shyshee chuckled nervously. "Is it possible that...someone else...like the Algothon have some of these tests...or something similar?"

Hadathoo grunted and closed his eyes. "Ota is going to think me mad...if I tell her to try to obtain some kind of aptitude tests from the city of Algothon."

Till grunted back at him. "Do we have another choice? Should we ask the Kalash or maybe the Cowpa if they have something like that?"

Hadathoo sighed and stared at Till for several moments.

He closed his eyes again. He opened his eyes again and looked at the door looking as if he were waiting for something to happen.

One of Hadathoo's Aides, Officer Grade 5, Yoytay ushered a rather confused looking Officer Leader, Ota into the room.

Ota smiled. "Did you summon me, Sir?"

Hadathoo smiled back. "Yes! We have a very unusual request and...I thought that it'd be better if we asked you in person...in case you have any questions."

Ota smiled again and clasped her hands together. "Yes, Sir?"

6

They had to find time for everyone to take the aptitude tests that Ota had obtained. They had to figure out who was going to administer the tests…in a fair and impartial manner. They also had to figure out what the answers were and how the results pointed to the capabilities of each member of the Owlamite race.

After two months, they finally had all of the results and it was rather unpleasant. All of the Owlamites showed that they were in the job that they should be in. They were watchers, observers, some medical personnel and farmers. The only ones who showed any new aptitudes were the ones that had been given special assignments such as the computer operator Teams of 254, 255, 256, 257 and 258. There were the Teams that were computer repair: 1000, 1001, 1002 and 1003. Then there were the Teams that had been assigned as shipwrights: 2000, 2001 and 2002.

The medical Teams – 221, 222, 223, 224, 225, 226, 227 and 228 did not help much as far as the quantum physics. They were where they were supposed to be.

Hoynama looked over the information with just as much mental defeat as the rest of the Command Staff. She looked at Hadathoo and smiled. "Sir…if I remember correctly, when that Algothon navy was headed our way…there weren't any shipwrights."

Hadathoo looked up sadly. "How is this supposed to help us?"

"Well…Sir…as I recall…the…*Voice of Power*…ordered those three Teams to study and learn all about ships." Hoynama smiled as she looked around at all of the other personnel. "They were ordered to become shipwrights and they did. If someone of the Owlamite race…is ordered to become something…by the *Voice of Power*…it happens."

"She's right," said Shyshee. "I've been looking over some of the notes from all of the other meetings of the Command Staff… and the *Voice of Power* at that time…gave an order…and the personnel followed that order. That's why we have the computer personnel and the shipwrights."

Deelka scoffed. She shook her head as she glared at Shyshee. "NO, you have to be intelligent enough to understand this stuff before you can learn it and utilize it. We're all watchers and observers because that's all we have the smarts for."

"No," said Yamananee. "Intelligence is irrelevant. I was a teacher for a while and I found out, from observing my students, that if a person does not want to learn something, it is almost impossible to teach it to them. If a person *does* want to learn something, or has a great interest in that subject…it is impossible to stop them from learning as much as they can about that particular subject. I saw some of my dumbest students excel in one certain subject, because they liked it and were greatly interested in it. I saw other students that I thought were extremely intelligent… look like an absolute *bimyock* in certain areas because they were totally uninterested." She smiled at Hadathoo. "You have to use the *Voice of Power*...to get someone interested in this...quantum physics. Once you give them the proper...motivation...stand back and watch them learn."

Hadathoo pondered the thought for a few moments. "How were the Teams chosen that are currently our computer experts and shipwrights?"

Shyshee smiled and shrugged. "The Supreme Officer just...chose them at random."

Hadathoo grunted in exasperation. "So I...randomly choose...who is and who is not going to be a genius?"

Shyshee nodded. "I'm afraid so, Sir."

Hadathoo sighed. "Where's the latest roll call...of intact Teams?"

One of Hadathoo's Aides, Officer Grade 7, Wees, brought him the list with a confused look on her face.

Hadathoo looked through the list. "Does anyone have any suggestions?" He looked around the table and received no help." He looked at one specific area on the list. "Officer Leader, Hrombisk...he's the lowest ranking Officer Leader. I'll take his Team first...in order to have someone in charge of...that group." He went through the list taking a few notes as he went through it. Once he finished his list, he prepared himself to use the *Power*. "Team 85, Team 207, Team 435, Team 1599, Team 2495, Team 3143, Team 3703, Team 4111, Team 5445 and Team 5999... report to the Command Staff conference room...NOW!"

Beemella looked surprised. "Ten Teams?"

Hadathoo shrugged. "It's a complicated subject. The more that we can get learning this stuff, the better. Maybe they'll even help each other learn this...*chogo* stuff."

Yoytay was ushering all of the Teams into the conference room. It was getting rather crowded as each new Team was brought in.

Once they were all in, Hadathoo took a deep breath. "From this day forth, all forty of you will have a great desire to learn all that you can about this new science that we've discovered. These sciences are called physics and quantum physics. Most of what we learn will be aboard that Jowfoonda spaceship that is currently orbiting Niygool. You're going to get with Officer, Bonarain, and learn the Jowfoonda language. You're going to get with the computer experts and learn their computer system. The more that you learn, the more eager you will become to learn even more about those sciences. However, your primary interest will be in physics." He leaned back in his chair. "You are all...now dismissed." He looked at Shyshee. "Is that what you had in mind?"

Shyshee smiled. "Pretty much, yes...Sir."

Antrong cleared his throat. "So far, we've been messing around with this situation for a while. They have, of course, gained no new knowledge of where their scout ship disappeared to, without leaving any form of a debris field. We've been attempting to gain access, unlimited access, to their computer system, in trying to figure out a way to bypass that...infernal self-destruct system. All that we've obtained is a few passwords that...don't get us any further than we already are now. They found out about our *obtaining* several small components...as well as finding the parts that we removed from them, and are still mystified as to where those components are."

Hoynama scoffed. "So far, all you've done is rehash information that we all know. What's your point?"

Antrong nodded. "Again, it has been almost three months. They're patient, in conducting their search and haven't called in reinforcements. We're patient as well and haven't done anything major...to give away any of our capabilities. I suggest...that we lose some of our patience and do something...rather aggressive."

Hadathoo shifted in his chair. "I'm listening."

Antrong leaned forward. "Let's get our Teams of computer experts and the physicists aboard that ship. Let's also get numerous spy Teams aboard. Then...we hop the entire ship, I mean *everything*, into Desert. If that self-destruct system turns on...there's a good possibility that since they're all there and the ship is intact...they'll deactivate the self-destruct...if for no other reason than to investigate the strange phenomenon that just happened to them...and then we'll learn how to deactivate it...and then we can take the ship completely...without any fear of losing it. Officer, Bonarain has been able to train many of our people in the Jowfoonda language...we have a good sized group that could go on board...and observe just about everything they do while understanding everything they say."

Wymini looked a little skeptical. "Are you sure that we

want, or can, utilize all of that ship?"

"We've lost almost all of the flying cameras that the Algothon put up there," said Till. "If we don't get some kind of new…technological eyes up there…we could end up with another group coming in here…that we don't see coming…and this new group could be more powerful and destroy or enslave the entire planet."

Hadathoo chuckled. "It could also spare us from the activity of…wasting any more time on the Algothons. Those *bimyocks* are continually trying to build new firestorm weapons. If we can't convince them to stop, I'm sure that the Jowfoonda vessel has the capability of forcing them to stop." He sighed. "Let's not rush into it. Let's give it a few more months…thus giving our new physicists a chance to learn something about that ship."

Yamananee shook her head. "Are you sure that they're going to remain patient?"

Beemella snickered. "The communications that they've been…sending out into deep space…they're warning their own to stay away…for the moment. We've been messing around with a few of their systems, watching how they repair them. They keep on sending out messages that state: Things are going wrong that should not. Stay away until we've solved this problem." She wiggled her eyebrows at Yamananee. "They're mystified and frustrated…but they seem to be infinitely patient in trying to solve a problem. If they can solve that problem then they can take over this planet…and according to what is in that green binder… subjugate everyone on this planet as their slaves. Apparently, the thought of several million slaves…of different species…is something they find worth waiting for."

Yamananee looked disgusted. "What a bunch of *doovofts*? They remind me of the Teltermak."

"I don't know which one is more irritating," said Hadathoo. "Both seem to want us as slaves…and the crazy thing there…I'm understanding more of why the Jowfoonda want us as slaves rather than why the Teltermak want us. The Teltermak keep destroying other races…but they want to own us." He shook his head. "Irritating!"

For the next four months, Bonarain was kept very busy training more Owlamites in the Jowfoonda language and writing. Since quantum physics was way over her head, the physicists had to learn on their own by reading the information located in several different tutorial programs (stolen from Algothon as well as the Jowfoonda). The Jowfoonda were baffled and a little upset over the fact that their tutorials kept running themselves…and no one was reading them (at least no one that they could see).

Some of the Jowfoonda technicians attempted to shut the program off before it ran through the entire course and ended up in some of those strange fights. There were two fatalities and numerous critical injuries. The ship's Commander decided to give the order that the programs should run their course and see if there were any injuries as a result of that. Since no one got hurt when they left it alone, they now decided to see what was going on in the internal workings of the computers that made random programs activate. All of their troubleshooting activities came up with nothing unusual. Their questions remained the same: Is this some unusual space energy that is prevalent in this area? If there is such an energy – what do we do about it?

The day was drawing close. The day that the Owlamites were going to hop the entire Jowfoonda ship (named Ispododokodor – whatever that means) was going to be hopped into the Desert dimension. All of the Medical Teams were on board. All of the computer Teams were on board. All of the shipwright Teams were on board. There were 500 other Owlamite Teams on board... including Team 7016. All of them were doing any and all final preparations in order to record virtually everything the crew did in the kind of crisis that might result from the hop.

Team 7016 was going to be on the Bridge with several recording devices, watching and observing certain key officers as they performed their duties when the crisis struck. At the moment – they were bored.

Chyning had a disgusted look on her face. "Did you read that report from Doctor Toysay?"

Bonarain was shocked. "YOU...you READ...a report... on your own?"

"I was bored," Chyning whined. "We got all of our stuff in place...on the first day of preparing all of this *h'oolyach*. Some of those Teams...they...waited until the last heartbeat to...get in here and get set up."

Bonarain chuckled. "So you were actually bored enough to read something...that you were supposed to read?"

Chyning wrinkled her nose. "It wasn't mandatory reading...and that's what made it interesting."

Kiyalee hung her head. "We should have known. If it's mandatory, she doesn't read it. If it's not mandatory...she does." She scoffed.

Soolchakan sighed. "So what was so interesting about this...non-mandatory document?"

Chyning smiled. "According to a study, done by Doctor Toysay and Doctor Thongola, they finally figured out what the Jowfoonda are eating...and where they're getting their food from."

Now Bonarain's interest was piqued. "I was kinda wondering about that myself. No one has found any kitchens or stoves...so far."

Chyning smiled. "Those places where all of the Jowfoonda eat, correct, there's no kitchen or stoves...nothing. BUT...all along the walls, there's all kinds of box like recesses in the walls. Each one of them have twenty of these funny looking little nozzles in them and a keypad above them." She leaned closer to her Team members. "When someone punches in a code on that keypad, it tells the computer what they want to eat. They put a plate in the recess and those nozzles start spraying all kinds of weird energy onto the plate...and food appears out of...seemingly nowhere."

"I've seen that," said Kiyalee. "They get their food...from out of thin air."

Chyning giggled. "They can't create something...from nothing."

Bonarain huffed. "So where's it coming from?"

Chyning giggled again a little harder. "They're recycling their own dung. They have a big vat on the ship that collects all of the sewage. It treats the sewage, removing all of the toxins and burning them…and then it takes the raw chemicals and minerals and turns them into something nutritious."

Kiyalee looked nauseous. "Recycled…MANURE? They're eating…!"

Soolchakan sighed. "Don't be surprised. We do the same thing."

Kiyalee now looked horrified. "NO…we DON'T!"

Soolchakan leaned closer to Kiyalee. "You planted that *iskinadon* tree in our gardening area…right?"

Kiyalee nodded with her hand over her mouth.

"What do you use to fertilize the tree?"

Kiyalee scoffed. "I use…animal manure…but…it's not the same thing."

"Yes it is. The tree filters the manure and turns it into *iskinadon* fruit. These people have figured out a way to do the filtering…with technology rather than a tree."

"That's totally disgusting," said Kiyalee horrified.

"No, that's necessity," said Soolchakan. "Either they do it with technology…or they'd have to have a garden on the ship…that's probably five times the size of this ship." He nodded.

"Even though it sounds disgusting…it's still efficient in the use of recycling anything that they have on board."

"Let's change the subject," said Bonarain as she placed her hands on her queasy stomach. "Let's check our area again."

"We've checked it six times," said Soolchakan.

"Let's check it again," said Kiyalee emphatically.

Chyning sat there giggling.

Hadathoo sighed. "The day has come. It's time to let all of our people know that we're going to execute this…scheme." He Jumped aboard on the ship's Bridge. He looked around at the eight Teams that were going to record all of the Jowfoonda on the Bridge. He closed his eyes. **"The time has come. I will go over it again, in order to make sure that no one has any questions. There are two Teams that are going to hop this ship to the Desert dimension. Team 88 under, Officer Grade 1, Cheensaya and Team 89 under, Officer Grade 1, Shivima. The amount of energy that it will take to hop a ship this size…those eight people will probably be exhausted by that one act. Team 86, under Officer Grade 1, Plykatha and Team 87, under Officer Grade 1, Nasaneenee will assist in hopping all eight of the exhausted Team members back to their homes. The rest of you will stay on board and record everything that your target Jowfoonda does and says. If the self-destruct program kicks in, you have about thirty heartbeats until it goes off. If they do NOT deactivate it…or cannot…get**

**back to your homes in the gorge. If they deactivate it...
PLEASE...find out how to turn the *chokwad* thing off.
Get any and all passwords and codes that you can. We
only have one chance at this...maybe. If we can get all
of that information, then we can OWN this ship. For over
260 years, we've allowed the Algothons to live, so that
we could learn from them. If we can get this ship...we no
longer need the Algothons. We'll have something much
better to learn from. Are there any questions**?" He waited
several moments and received nothing. "**Officer, Cheensaya,
it is now in your hands. You will notify all personnel just
before you execute the hop. Remember...we don't want
to lose anyone. If your life is in danger...get out of here.
I'm going back to the Command Staff conference room
to listen in on any sendings that I can receive. Good
luck**." He Jumped back to the Staff conference room in the gorge.

Soolchakan turned his recorder on. He was not sure what
he was going to get from one of the navigators, however, it had to
be recorded.

Bonarain was standing next to a security officer. For the
most part, they had not seen any of these people move, unless they
were being relieved for a meal or for the day. They usually stood
there waiting for something to happen...which was a long wait.

Kiyalee was next to one of the gunners. She snickered
wondering what he was going to shoot at...once the hop was
executed. The only thing he could really do was turn his console
on...and wait until he had a target.

Chyning had the real fun job. She was next to a supply officer. She had no idea what that guy could possibly do in a crisis…maybe go count some of the supplies? What could he possibly do that was in any way important in a crisis?

Cheensaya did a quick roll call of the eight personnel that were going to do the simultaneous assisting in the hop. She called out a short countdown to all personnel on the ship…and then the hop happened. All eight of the personnel who participated in the hop were dizzy but conscious. They were Jumped back to their homes anyway.

All lights went off and the banks of red lights on every deck came on. The self-destruct program kicked in and started the countdown.

Yambagin Cho, Shalashak grabbed the armrests of his chair. {What's going on? What happened? Report…somebody}!

{We've gone through some kind of portal}, said one of the science officers. {We've moved into a completely different… dimension}.

Shalashak looked around. {How? We didn't do anything? Give me a reason to stop the self-destruct}!

One of the communications officers stood up. {I found some of the crew of scout ship 8! Apparently they came through the same…portal and have been stuck here ever since}.

{That's a good reason}, said Shalashak. {Computer! Recognize my voice! Yambagin Cho, Shalashak, Commander of the Ispododokodor! Ignore danger and desist with the self-destruct!

Command…reboot…reset and turn off the self-destruct}!

There was a series of buzzes, beeps and whirring sounds. The bank of red lights went off and dim lights came on. A computer voice spoke: {Does the Executive Officer agree}?

Another Jowfoonda stood up. {This is the Executive Officer, Yalkaska (O-8) Skikshoy! I concur with the Commander! Reboot…reset and turn off the self-destruct}!

There was another series of noises from the computer. All of the lighting went back to normal. There was a huge amount of sighs of relief from both Jowfoonda and Owlamite.

The Commander and the Executive Officer both went to an array of command consoles. Both of them keyed in a code and then keyed in another one to reset the self-destruct program. There were two Owlamites who were closely watching (and filming) every move they made as they fed in the clearance and reset codes.

Shalashak went back to his seat. {All right! All sections report! Are there any casualties? Is there any damage}?

All subsections reported in to their section chiefs who reported to the Bridge. No injuries and no damage. Just a lot of frazzled nerves at hearing the self-destruct system turn on plus a lot of confusion.

{Now, how many escape pods have you found}?

The science officer shook his head. {All I've found…so far are sixteen that are still sending out their beacon. We'd have to make a full sweep of the planet in order to find all of the ones that've broken down}.

Everyone on board, Jowfoonda and Owlamite all had the same question in their head – if not spoken: Planet? What planet? Shalashak did voice the question.

The science officer hit a few keys on his console. The view screen now showed the planet that they were orbiting, complete with longitude and latitude lines. {The planet that we are orbiting…at this time, Yambagin Cho}.

{Have you located any of our people}?

{Sir, there are only forty-one of the personal locaters that are showing life. All others are just sending out the locater signal…showing a corpse}.

{Is the signal of the Tomontain that was in charge of that vessel one of the live ones}?

{Negative, Sir. The highest ranking one that is registering life…is a Vilvak Second…Dconchoonod}.

Shalashak grunted in disgust. {All right, what have we got on this planet}?

Officer Leader, Hrombisk was the one in charge of the observation and takeover. He looked at the view screen and reported back to the Command Staff. **"Sirs, we're currently orbiting a planet…that I do NOT recognize. If I remember correctly, when we sent that scout ship into Desert dimension, we had forced the thing to land…on Hardooth. This mother ship was still flying…and orbiting. We're orbiting a planet…that takes up the same space…as Hardooth… but in a different dimension."**

All of the members of the Command Staff were all looking at each other wide-eyed with elation and a little trepidation. Till could not hide his enthusiasm. He sat there bouncing and giggling.

Hadathoo let out a slight laugh. **"Officer, Hrombisk, please keep reporting everything that you see and hear about this planet."**

Hrombisk was feeling quite a bit of elation himself. **"Yes, Sir! This planet appears to be...inhabitable... er...inhabited. The planet is rather different than ours. It seems to have...one massive continent...and one massive ocean. According to figures that the Jowfoonda are finding, the ocean takes up 71% of the planet surface. The continent takes up 28%, with the other 1% being taken up by a smattering of small islands that surround the continent.**

The continent...stretches all the way from a point at the north pole to a point at the south pole. It is a good 22,000 kilotaja from north to south. From east to west...it is just over 11,000 kilotaja at the widest point and 8,500 kilotaja at the narrowest. It also appears that...in the northern area, where the continent is the widest, there is a very large area that is inhabited by a sentient race. The same in the southern part of the continent. What's really unusual is the central part. The only inhabitable area, in the center, is along the east and west coastlines. The entire central part of the continent is nothing but one gigantic desert. From the equator, it appears that the desert stretches about 3,500

kilotaja north and about 4,000 kilotaja to the south. The inhabitable coastlines, east and west, only go in about 50 to 100 kilotaja.

From what the sensors on this ship are reading, there is minor technology and industry in the inhabited area. I'd say that the people of this planet...just recently discovered electricity. There doesn't seem to be any internal combustion engines. There are numerous, very large, very heavy external combustion machines that travel only on rails. That appears to be the only thing connecting all of the towns and cities on the planet.

Currently the Jowfoonda are attempting to pinpoint the exact location of their personnel. I don't know what this tracking system is, but they can zoom in on the EXACT location of each one with...incredible accuracy."

Shalashak pounded the armrest of his chair. {Why are there so few that are still alive}?

The science officer hit a few more keys on his console. The picture on the view screen spun a little bit and showed a dark circle in the desert. {Sir, this appears to be where the scout ship was...when it blew up. All of the escape pods, that deployed, went out in a circular pattern. As you can see...when I pull the magnification back...the blast site is 1,366 *kistoo* from the western, coastal inhabitable area of the planet. The only ones who survived are the ones who were in pods that ejected towards the inhabitable area. All of the others, that ejected...further into the desert...the personnel in those…only had enough emergency nourishment for thirty-three days. If they didn't have enough intestinal fortitude to make the walk…to the closest area that is tolerant to life…they didn't stand a chance}.

Shalashak growled. {What a fate! You escape in a pod to get away from the blast and die slowly from heat and starvation}. He shook his head. {See if we can get to our people without arousing much attention from the indigenous inhabitants}.

{I doubt that seriously, Sir. It appears that our people…are actually living in some of the local villages}.

{Why would they make friends with…peoples that we're going to enslave}?

The science officer shook his head. {You'll have to ask *them* that question…once we rescue them, Sir}.

{Can you zoom in…on one of our people and see what kind of interaction they're having with the locals}?

{Standby, Sir}. The science officer started fiddling with a few dials and keys on his console. {I've located one…and…I can…zoom in on him…and…according to the readout from his in-planted monitor, that is Quibid Tosko (E-4) Babad}.

Everyone was looking at the view screen. All of the Jowfoonda gasped in shock.

Shalashak stood up with a scream of rage. {He…he's in chains! He's being treated as a slave…by THEM. This is an OUTRAGE}! He turned to his right. {Vidimgombo (O-6), Oonjoosh! Get your attack force ready NOW! Get down there, locate all of our personnel, rescue them and get them back up here. I want to find out what's going on. NO ONE...absolutely no one...enslaves a Jowfoonda}.

Oonjoosh stood up. {Sir, we haven't located all of our personnel yet. How are we...}?

{WE'LL HAVE THEM LOCATED BY THE TIME YOUR FORCES LAUNCH}, roared Shalashak! {We'll have good locations for all of them}.

Oonjoosh turned to his console and started barking orders into a microphone.

Hadathoo looked at the Command Staff with some hesitancy. "Should we get involved in this?" He looked at all of their expressions of horror. He nodded. "I didn't think so."

Hrombisk had to think fast. **"Get some Teams down there with the fighters. The fifteen Teams that are closest to that bottom deck, get down there now and get in the seat with the fighter pilots. Watch and learn how they launch, maneuver, attack and then come back and land on the mother ship. We don't want to waste this opportunity."**

"Officer, Hrombisk, this is Officer Grade 6, Konnok, Team 4494. These *doovofts* are getting ready to launch a lot more than sixty fighters."

Hrombisk growled to himself. **"Irrelevant! We're just trying to learn about those craft. We're going to observe them doing an actual attack and watch how to fly them.**

We're not trying to stop them."

Konnok sent back: "**Understood. Sorry about the confusion.**"

"**Officer, Hrombisk, this is Officer Grade 4, Totaka, Team 5600. I'm in the launch area and they're getting ready to send out...one ship that's much larger...than any of the fighters. Should someone be aboard that one**?"

Hrombisk scoffed to himself. 'You have to ask?' "**Absolutely! Why don't you do that**?"

Totaka shrugged. She looked at the larger ship. "**Understood.**"

The giant doors at the bow end of the ship opened up. All of the fighters launched out into space and started the immediate descent to the planet. The larger vessel with Totaka aboard was the last one to launch.

While the fighters were all aimed at the planet and flying down forcefully, Totaka noticed that the ship she was on seemed to be slowly and almost lackadaisically just losing altitude. She carefully watched the pilots as they made easy maneuvers and observed their monitors for information from the mother ship. She wandered into the rear section of the ship and found a room where there was nothing but seats. Ten seats to a row, fifteen rows and an aisle way down the center.

Totaka snickered to herself. "**Officer, Hrombisk, this is Totaka. This larger vessel is a personnel transport ship.**

Once they've found and rescued all of their personnel... they're going to take them back to the mother ship on this thing."

Hrombisk nodded in approval of the tactic. **"Sounds good. Go ahead and stay aboard and watch how they fly that ship."**

"Yes, Sir."

The attack was totally one-sided. The local population had no clue as to how to defend themselves from airborne invaders. The weaponry they had was useless against the metal shells (and electromagnetic shields) of the fighters.

When the Jowfoonda slaves saw the fighters come down and demolish everything around them with surgical precision, some laughed, some rejoiced and others let out a sigh of relief. As soon as all of the locals around a Jowfoonda were slaughtered, the Jowfoonda personnel gathered in a group to watch the slaughter and wait for the transport vessel to come and pick them up.

There were three villages that were attacked and virtually annihilated by conventional weapons from the Jowfoonda fighters. Once the transport vessel had collected all of the Jowfoonda citizens, Shalashak gave an order and there were much larger conventional bombs that came out of large weapons on the mother ship that turned the three villages and everything in them to rubble. No houses, no carts, no livestock, no dead bodies, no gardens, no metal, no wood, nothing was spared. Everything was incinerated. The three villages were now nothing but large piles of charred debris on the landscape that was being charred even worse by fires that no one was left to put out. There was no sign of life there at all or that there had ever been a village there before, except for the empty roads that led up to the charred rubble.

Now the fighters and the transport vessel all returned to the mother ship. On deploying, the transport ship was the last to launch. It was now the first to return to the large parking bay on the mother ship. After all of the fighters were returned to their places in the bay, the large doors were closed that the bay was again pressurized so the activities could go back to normal.

As the rescued Jowfoonda disembarked from the transport, the Owlamites expected to hear cheers or welcome home or something. Nothing. They expected the rescued ones to be happy that they had been rescued. Nothing. Everyone seemed rather melancholy over the entire situation. The Owlamites were confused and disturbed by this...nothing.

The ones who had been slaves all looked a little haggard. They had very little clothing on. There were whip marks and other scars all over their bodies. Their antennae did not wiggle around like the other Jowfoonda antennae did. Some were missing antennae, some were missing one of the insect-like eyes. Two were missing an arm. There were ten females who had a strange red hue on their arms.

"Supreme Officer, Hadathoo, this is Officer Grade 4, Viniski of Team 4596. We're watching the ones who were rescued come back...and no one is celebrating. I've seen people that were more jovial at a funeral. Very

strange, Sir."

The Command Staff sat there contemplating.

"Maybe it's just their way," said Shyshee.

"As Viniski said," said Yamananee, "…very strange."

"Let's not judge," said Hadathoo. "Let's just…wait and see how this turns out. Let them do what's right in their culture. I don't understand it either, but…let's see."

The forty-one personnel were herded into a large room on the deck, just above the flight deck. They all walked in and sat down in chairs that had been arranged in rows, facing a large desk.

There were several armed security personnel standing along each of the walls. Viniski counted sixty security personnel. She could not understand why the freed slaves would need to be guarded. She could hardly wait until something happened that gave them an idea of what was going on.

The four gray-clad members of the Legal Office walked in. The judge with the black circle on his chest led the way. He walked up to the desk and placed his little gong on the desk. The prosecutor, with his brown circle, sat to the judge's right. The defender, with his yellow circle, sat to the left. The executioner, with his red circle, stood behind the judge.

The Koozgofon looked around. He stood up and struck the gong. He held his stick up and it lit up. {This court is now in session. We are asking the question: Why did all of you Jowfoonda citizens allow yourselves to be taken as slaves? Why did you not take over on this planet and enslave the local indigenous trash?

To be the primary one to answer these questions and all charges against you, we choose the ranking one who survived the crash of scout ship 8 – Vilvak Second, Doonchoonod. You will step forward}.

One of the men came forward. He was missing a large portion of his left eye group and all three of the antennae on the left side. {Yes, Sir, I am prepared to answer for all}.

The Koozgofon nodded. {How do you say? Are you guilty or not guilty of allowing yourselves to be taken prisoner and used as slaves}?

Doonchoonod scoffed. {We did not *allow* it. We had no choice. We had *nothing* to back us up}.

The Kooztoyso stood up. The Koozgofon looked at him and put his stick down. The prosecutor's stick lit up. {You say that you had no backing? You had and have always had the backing of the Jowfoonda Empire. How dare you to say that you had no backing}?

{Sir, the backing that we had on that planet was nothing. The scout ship was gone, blown up. Where was the Ispododokodor? All we had was a bunch of used up and spent escape pods and empty bellies. There was no one that we could contact, other than ourselves, and that was sadly insufficient to subjugating anyone or anything on the planet. We would have needed backing from something a little more powerful than our own hunger…such *as* the *power* of this ship. Where were you during this crisis? Why did you wait so long before coming to our aid? Why did YOU not bother contacting us at any time before this rescue? As such…

how am I or any of the survivors guilty of any negligence}?

The Kooztoyso was a little startled at the statements. He stuttered and made a few unintelligible sounds. He turned away from the defendant and looked as if he were trying to figure out a new question. His antennae were wiggling, randomly, all over the place.

The Koozgofon stood up. His stick lit up as the Kooztoyso's stick went out. {It seems that we have a difference of opinion here. Justifiably so. The answer to the question from the defendant about our not contacting you…we have now found out that…you on the scout ship 8 went through some kind of dimension shifting portal. When we came to find the scout ship, we found no debris and no communication transmissions. Now…after all of this time, the Ispododokodor ended up being sucked through the same kind of dimensional portal. How…we do not know. We have not been able to find any form of an energy emission that explains it. Here we are now…and…it seems that since you received no backup from the Jowfoonda Empire…we cannot properly judge you for your actions. Instead…what we will do…now…is obtain a report from you on exactly what did happen. We would appreciate it if you start from the beginning. The beginning, in this case, is the time you suddenly found yourself in a different dimension. That is unless you have something that happened before the dimension shift that…is relevant}. He hit the gong with his stick and the light in it went out. He sat down.

Doonchoonod looked relieved about what he had just heard. His shoulders sagged a little his breath came out fast and loud as if in relief. He straightened up and started his oration. {The strange things started prior to the dimension shift. We had all of the technological targets lined up and Tomontain Dodigish ordered the attacks to commence. Almost immediately, things started getting odd. On the Bridge, all of the Gunners...just vanished. No sign of them, no trace and no technological trail. They just... vanished. The Tomontain ordered other personnel to get to the Gunner stations immediately. Everyone that went to those stations vanished. Then the communications officer vanished. Several times, someone else took the seat...and vanished. No matter who went to the Gunner station or the Communication station...they vanished...without a trace}. He hung his head and cleared his throat. {The Tomontain...suddenly...his chest just...exploded. There was blood everywhere from the explosion. Chinchik Gogos was the ranking one on the Bridge at the time and he took over immediately. Suddenly he disappeared as well. Personnel were vanishing all over the Bridge and we could not replace anyone fast enough. Then something went wrong with the engines. Vidimgombo (O-6) Chooj showed up on the Bridge and ordered an immediate emergency landing. No sooner had we landed... the self-destruct alarm went off. None of the Command personnel attempted to shut it down. We all headed for the escape pods and...got out of there. I felt a jolt when the pod blasted out of the mooring. I felt another jolt when scout ship 8 blew up. I and Han Tosko (E-5), Tiggit were in the same escape pod. We took the food...and headed for an area we had seen while the pod was still in the air. We got there in about eleven days...and...within two days...we were...} He hung his head. {enslaved}.

The Koozgofon stood up and his stick lit up. {Did Vidimgombo Chooj make any attempt at deactivating the self-destruct system}?

{No, Sir. As a matter of fact, he stood there frozen…and did nothing until the countdown was around 20 or 21. He then headed for an escape pod himself}.

{He got into an escape pod…without saying anything}?

{He said nothing, Sir. He jumped in the pod…and launched it}.

{He…was…ALONE}?

{As far as I know…yes, Sir}.

The Koozgofon turned to his right. {Have we found…the life monitor for Vidimgombo Chooj}?

{Yes}, said the Kooztoyso. {It appears…from the report… that he died of starvation…next to the pod…after eating all of the food. He never left the pod}.

The Koozgofon shook his head. {Recover the pod and let the body rot where it is. There's no point in retrieving the body of a fool who can't make any command decisions under pressure without panicking}.

The Kooztoyso looked at a computer screen. He stood up. He held up his stick. The Koozgofon touched his stick and its light went out. The stick in the hand of the Kooztoyso lit up. He looked back at his computer screen. {Bibrit Tosko (E-7), Viskint, step forward}.

One of the women came forward. {I am Bibrit Tosko, Viskint}.

{I chose you because you are the ranking female in the group. The red on your arms shows you to be pregnant. You and all of the women are pregnant. Why}?

She placed her fists on her hips and huffed. {As you recall, Sir, we were enslaved. We had no say in the matter. They forced us to copulate with the men and allowed us no form of birth control. They were forcing us to make another generation of slaves for them. We had *no say* in the matter}.

{How could they have even known what to do…in order to force you to procreate}?

She huffed again and shook her head. Her antennae were wriggling all over the place. {Their genitals are located in the same place as ours. Their…act of copulation is almost the same as ours. AGAIN…we had NO choice in the matter}.

The Koozyast stood up. The Kooztoyso lowered his stick and the stick for the Koozyast lit up. {Once again, we have to remember that…our personnel on this planet, did not have any power of the Empire behind them. They were forced to acquiesce. We find ourselves in a difficult position. We cannot prosecute them for what they were powerless to or not to perform}. He sat down.

The Koozgofon stood up. His stick lit up. {We do find ourselves in a rather unique situation. All of the representatives of the Empire…in this dimension…wherever it is, are on this ship. The personnel who were on the planet…for an involuntary and extended period of time, cannot be punished…because they actually did no wrong. They survived to give report…once rescued}. He looked around. {Is there anyone else who has anything to add to these proceedings before I close them}?

A man stepped forward from the side. {Koozgofon, I do}.

The Koozgofon turned to him. {State your name and your business}. The light went off in his stick.

{I am Vilvak Third (E-3), Oshkiy. I have retrieved the personal log of Vidimgombo, Chooj. We found the escape pod he ejected in and pulled the personal log from it}.

The Koozgofon nodded. His antennae all stood straight up. {He was the one in command…at the time of the destruction… so…I guess we need to hear anything that might have to be ruled upon. Continue}.

Oshkiy bowed slightly. He held up a small pad. {According to the log…I think that he shamed the rank of Vidimgombo completely. The log contains nothing but a bunch of rambling and whining. There is also another complaint…by him. He complains…after 26 days…that there is insufficient food on board an escape pod. On day 31, he complains that he has run out of food}.

The Koozgofon held up his stick and it lit up. {Each pod is supposed to have enough nourishment for two people for 33 days. Was that pod…short of victuals}? He turned his stick off.

Oshkiy sighed. {The…litter that surrounds the pod…and was left in the pod, shows that it was fully stocked. He was by himself and therefore had 66 days of food. He devoured it all…in 31 days…and then starved to death}.

All of the Kooz personnel hung their heads.

The Koozgofon stood and lit his stick. {The…man Chooj… who was formerly a Vidimgombo…is now and forevermore… reduced to First Tosko (E-1). If there are any offspring or widow that make a claim to his estate, they are to be informed of his negligence and irresponsibility…in a crisis…when we finally obtain the capability of getting back to our dimension and informing them. Any decisions that he made aboard this ship, while he wore the higher rank, are to be investigated and ruled upon. Again I say, retrieve the pod he escaped in…and leave the body to rot where it lays}.

Viniski stood there shaking her head. "Such nice people. I wonder what they'd do with a traitor."

7

Hadathoo kept on tasking the Command Staff, trying to come up with a way to take the Jowfoonda ship intact. How do we get the ship, get rid of the Jowfoonda and keep the ship without that self-destruct program going off? The Command Staff, in turn, kept on tasking the computer experts to dig deeper into the Jowfoonda for the answer to the question

Officer Grade 3, Sankiki of Team 254 kept on coming back with the same sad story. The self-destruct program had no shutoff switch. It was armed and ready to go off if it detected anything that fell into the pre-programmed line-up of reasons for destruct. She and the other personnel who were computer operators and repair could not find any way to bypass the program.

They were forced to allow the crew to survive because they were the only ones who had the authority to turn it off after it had been started.

Kiyalee had found the location of the bombs that were planted in the ship. There were six of them in the mother ship and one in each scout ship. After finding them she had given the report to the Command Staff.

Hadathoo now looked at Kiyalee's drawing, showing the exact location of each bomb. "You'd think they wanna keep this thing," he snarled. "They made sure that no one else can have it."

Shyshee shook her head. "I understand the logic, Sir. If they can't have it…no one can. It's my toy and I'm the only one who can play with it."

Till looked at the report from the physicists. "They've shown us…how to run the ship…if we can take it. We could take it…now…if it weren't for those…firestorm weapons. We can take it and run it…but we don't have a way to turn off the program."

Wymini grunted in disgust. "If they're so determined that no one else can have it, I suggest that we go ahead and make them blow it up. Then they'll be deprived of enslaving the Desert dimension planet."

Deelka cleared her throat. "Couldn't we just…hop the firestorm weapons…into another dimension…and see what happens?"

"No," said Antrong. "Our physicists have already found a program that would shut the entire ship off…all except for a suicide program that would send the ship hurtling, at an incredible speed, straight into the nearest large mass. That would be the planet. The silly thing would auger in…somewhere on the planet and…destroy their atmosphere, a little like the firestorm weapons did to our planet." He shook his head. "We have to shut both of them off…completely…before we can get rid of that Jowfoonda crew and own the ship."

Hadathoo called a meeting of every Team that was working on the puzzle. He got all of them in the main auditorium to inform them of what had been found so far and see if anyone had any constructive way of bypassing the Jowfoondas. The room was silent for a very long time.

Kiyalee finally stood up. "Why don't we try putting the whole ship into maintenance mode? We can take all of those little components, use their internal program to make them think that they're being repaired…and then put them back together without their little destruct mechanisms…why can't we do it on a larger scale?"

All of the computer repair Teams started buzzing on how that could be done and how it could work. They were all discussing it among themselves and came up, very quickly, with a way to do just that. The main stumbling block there, though was they needed the Jowfoonda to be distracted, in order to execute the sabotage before the change was noticed.

Soolchakan stood up. "We don't need to attempt any distraction. The Jowfoonda are currently trying to enslave the planet of the Desert dimension. All we have to do is…oh say we…start fooling around with their attempts…in one place…get most of, if not all of, their attention on that one place…and while they're trying to figure out why they're having such a difficult time in that place…we strike."

Hadathoo saw the faces of the computer repair personnel. The smiles on their faces told him that the phony maintenance plan could work. He turned to Soolchakan with a grin. "Do you have such a place in mind?"

Soolchakan shrugged. "Sir, if you look at the continent…I mean a certain area in the northwestern part of the continent…

there is a place there, where there are four very large communities. All four are clustered in a rather small area and it would take a large number of their army, in order to control all of that area. If we could give the native citizens a bit of help…that could be the distraction that's needed."

Bonarain stood up. "The main thing that we'd need to do, in order to pull that off, is to keep their single-seat fighters from being able to clobber the natives from the air. How are we going to pull that off?"

Soolchakan smiled and shrugged. "Just hop the business end of all of their guns into Ghost dimension. That way...they see the things going off…but not damaging or affecting their targets in any way at all. That should cause some consternation among the Jowfoondas…enough to distract them."

Hadathoo chuckled. "Does anyone have anything else to add to that plan?" He looked around. No one said anything. "All right! Let's get some personnel into that area and…start… *improving* their defenses…or befouling the Jowfoonda offensive weapons and slow the conquerors in their process."

The Jowfoonda had taken over 80% of the populated area of the planet. They had waited until last to get the four big cities in the northwest. They wanted to show the natives that since they had taken all the other places the only way for the native race to keep their cities intact was unconditional surrender. The conventional bombs were causing all kinds of problems to the Desert planet people.

Then things started going wrong. In the south, all of a sudden, there were Jowfoondas that were disappearing without a trace. Almost 30% of the Jowfoonda forces had vanished and they could not blame the disappearances on the natives because those people were *all* in chains. In the northeast, the natives were suddenly free because the manacles and chains were missing. The Jowfoondas might have chased them down, however, their power weapons were no longer operational.

Yambagin Cho, Shalashak found that he was missing several key attack officers. They had vanished off of the ship and from areas of the continent with no explanation as to how or why…or where. New promotions were occurring in order to replace the needed leaders, however, a lot of the new leaders were disappearing as well…and there was no way, at this time, to obtain any new reinforcements.

Shalashak had to obtain a resounding victory on the planet in order to maintain the fear on the planet and sanity on the ship. He called in the newly promoted Vidimgombo, Lak-Lak. {You've got to attack the four city area in the northwest. If you have to lay waste to one or more of the cities…DO IT! We have got to get the planet under control and let them know that we're not going to put up with any talk of insurrection or insubordination on the part of the local trash. Do I make myself clear}?

Lak-Lak saluted. {It will be done! We will own all four cities, before today's sunset in that area, or all four cities will be in ruins}.

Shalashak saluted back. {Good}!

Lak-Lak left the Attack Coordination Room and headed for the hangar bay. He, like most of the personnel on board, was rather worried about the entire situation, however, he wanted to be a major part of getting things back under control. That would make his situation stronger and keep his promotion from being temporary to permanent.

He took one of the slide tubes to the hangar. He hit the floor hard and tumbled. When he got up he saw that all ninety-two fighter ships (that were still intact) were at the ready, each with their pilot standing by, except the one that he was going to use to lead the attack.

He patched his hand-held communicator through the public address system. {I'm not going to stand on any ceremony, I'm just going to say…get in your fighters and let's go. The glory of the Empire calls for all of you to do your duty}.

All of the pilots got in their fighters, waiting for the launch command. Little did they know there were eighty-nine Owlamites who were also manning the fighters as well. Three of the fighters were left without an Owlamite for one of the devious parts of the plan.

There were Owlamites, who were currently wearing space suits, they had borrowed from the Jowfoonda supply area, watching as yellow suited Jowfoondas strapped the pilots into the fighters. There were Owlamites, who were currently wearing space suits, they had borrowed from the Jowfoonda supply area, watching as yellow suited Jowfoondas went through the steps of depressurizing the hangar bay and opening the giant doors in the bow of the space ship. There were Owlamites, who were currently wearing space suits, they had borrowed from the Jowfoonda supply area, watching as blue suited Jowfoondas did the final steps, outside the fighters, for launching the attack.

There were eighty-nine Owlamites sitting in the cockpit with the fighter pilots, watching to see exactly how a takeoff, attack and landing would be accomplished.

Officer Grade 3, Sankiki was the ranking individual of all of the personnel in the fighters. "**Okay, all of you who are in the fighters – remember there are three of the fighters that we've painted orange. The orange paint is in Spy dimension, so the *bimyocks* can't see it. If you're in one of the orange fighters…get out now and get to a fighter that doesn't have an Owlamite in it. Do any of the three orange fighters have an Owlamite in them**?" She waited for a response and heard nothing. "**Remember that when their high muckity-muck calls for a testing of the guns…the three orange ships are going to have a tragic accident. Any questions**?" Once again she waited for a response. "**We've watched them do this before and we've all had lessons in their language. Make sure you know what you're doing before you do any…funny things with the Jowfoonda pilot. We may have to let a lot of them survive the day…but that's one of the crazy things about war. Are there any questions**?" Again there were no responses. "**Let's urinate on the Jowfoonda Empire today**!"

Lak-Lak gave the order and his was the first fighter to

launch. The other ships were all launched in a very short time. All of the ships gathered up into formations of five ships, with Lak-Lak leading the charge with a partner fighter on his port side. He did a dive toward the Desert planet. {All ships, engage your weaponry and prepare to knock the local trash into submission}.

Soolchakan was in fighter number fifty-nine. He watched the pilot go about all of the steps in arming the guns. He had seen this at least seven times before and was able to recite the order in which all of the switches were engaged. He had to remember that this was important and could not allow himself to be bored with the repetition. He had to *know* the procedures.

The formation of fighters headed down into the atmosphere of the planet. There were several of the pilots who giggled and smirked as they saw the four cities below, just waiting to be blown to rubble by the powerful pulse weapons of the Jowfoonda Empire. They were flying almost directly straight down in order to get to the targets as quickly as possible.

Lak-Lak got back on the radio. {Flights 1 through 4, take the southern city. Flights 5 through 9, take the central city. Flights 10 through 13, take the northwest city and Flights 14 through 18, take the northeast city. I'll be doing a little shooting of my own, but mostly I'll be watching you. Take out the biggest buildings first. The more rubble that rains down on the trash…the quicker we'll get this thing over with}. He watched his altimeter. {All Flights…break off for your targets…NOW}!

The ninety ships made their turns, heading for their assigned city. Lak-Lak leveled off and listed his ship slightly towards port in order to get a good look at the sight that was about to unfold before him. His Aide flew in a parallel path. {Don't wait for the order. Once you're in position…open fire and show no mercy to the trash}. Lak-Lak chuckled to himself. He started looking for something that he wanted to personally destroy.

Soolchakan was in Flight number 12, ship number 59. He looked around to see if any of the orange fighters were with his Flight. He was disappointed when he saw nothing but the white and silver fighters all around him.

Flight 5 was the first on in position to fire. They swooped down and opened fire on a group of tall buildings in the heart of the city. They opened fire…and nothing happened to the buildings. The five ships had planned on blasting the tops off of the buildings and then flying over them with some continuous shooting. Instead, they all had to do a hard emergency diversion in order to keep from slamming into the undamaged buildings. The plan by the Owlamites had worked perfectly. The guns were in Ghost dimension – so were the power beams that they were shooting. The Jowfoondas could see the beam, however, there was no damage being done to anything…in Desert dimension.

Flight 6 followed closely behind and came up with the same confusing results.

Soon Lak-Lak was hearing from all of the Flight Commanders that the power beams were not causing any damage to any of the structures in any of the cities. The ships were flying around making a lot of noise. Some of the windows in the buildings were damaged by sonic booms, however, that was the *only* damage in any of the four cities.

{This is Honroodo, Pyondyoo! Flight Commander of Flight 15. We're currently flying over an unpopulated area of the city. Our power beams...aren't even hitting the ground! We've made four strafing runs...in a large area of dirt. There is NO scorching...of the ground...no dirt flying up...and no damage... at all}.

Lak-Lak was horrified at the reports. He rammed the throttle in his ship and aimed the nose at one of the largest structures in the central city. {I'm coming down to see for myself! All Flights... stand by}! He flew down and made a strafing run across the top of a building. He saw no smoke or debris flying anywhere. He made a quick turnaround and flew over the building again. He was irritated and confused at the sight of...no damage.

{All Flights, this is Vidimgombo, Lak-Lak. All ships head up to an altitude of forty-five *kistoo* and go back to the Ispododokodor}. He clenched his teeth and called on the radio again. {Yambagin Cho, Shalashak...I'm requesting that you jettison all refuse from the Ispododokodor and give us some targets to shoot at. Something is dreadfully wrong here. Our guns are totally ineffective against...anything on the planet. We can't even hit the *ground*}.

Shalashak was sitting there with his teeth clenched as well. {Vidimgombo Lak-Lak, I understand! I am ordering all of the starboard trash bins to be emptied into space. That should give you a lot of *somethings* to shoot at...and try to figure out what's going on}. He grunted in frustration. {Navigator, once they've finished with the jettisoning, pull hard to port! We're going to get out of their way and let them shoot}.

The navigator responded. A supply officer called out that the jettison of the junk was complete. The navigator hit the button and the ship veered to port.

{Navigator, get us three *kistoo* away from the junk field and hard to starboard. I need to see what happens when they fire on the junk}.

The navigator watched his monitor, then pulled the ship hard to starboard at the proper interval and kept the ship at a parallel course that followed the junk field.

Lak-Lak called out to the pilots. {Get into line formation. We'll each have an attack at the debris and try to figure out what's going on. See if any of our guns are destroying anything in this place}.

Sitting in the main conference room, Owlamite Command Staff was listening to all of the information that was being relayed to them by Officer Leader, Hrombisk.

Hadathoo got a little impatient. **"What's the report on the three target fighters? Is anyone ready to give them a big surprise?"**

"This is Officer Grade 5, Kongee of Team 4899. I'm directly behind one of the orange ships in fighter number 77. As soon as the *bimyocks* start their strafing runs at the junk, I'll hit the ship with everything that this fighter has."

"**This is Officer Grade 5, Twiliysk of Team 1339. I'm directly behind one of the target ships as well. It will get strafed.**"

"**This is Officer Grade 5, Kwykod of Team 3239.**" He chuckled to himself. "**As those two ladies said…as soon as they start their attack on the junk…all three target ships are dead. I've got the third one in my sights right now.**"

Hadathoo smiled. "**Thank you.**"

Lak-Lak pulled up to the level of the debris field and headed for it. He got his sights on a rather large piece of junk, aimed and fired. He saw his beam score a direct hit on the piece… go directly through it…and cause it no damage. He let off of the trigger with his mouth hanging wide open and his antennae wriggling in a wild manner. {I…hit it…but…no damage}! He shook his head. {All Flights…attack in numbered order…in line formation}. He veered hard to his starboard in order to get away from the debris and find a suitable place to observe the other ships from. {Flight one…attack}!

Flight 1, with ships numbered 8, 26, 33, 40 and 41, all lined up. They all zeroed in on some of the debris. The Flight Commander gave the order to fire. All five ships opened fire with all guns…and nothing was destroyed.

Lak-Lak growled in frustration. {Flight 2…attack}!

Flight 2 had the same empty results.

Flight 3 had the same empty results.

Flights 4, 5, 6, 7 and 8 had the same empty results.

Flight 9 was getting ready for their run. Twiliysk was in ship 51 which was directly behind one of the orange ships. As soon as Flight 9 got into formation behind Flight 8, she hopped her entire fighter into the Desert dimension, pulled the trigger on all guns and ship 22 of Flight 8 was obliterated in a fiery explosion. Ship 10 was on the port side of 22, ship 61 was starboard. Both of these ships received a bit of shrapnel damage as 22 blew up.

Immediately after the guns had fired on ship 51, the Jowfoonda pilot shut down all of the weaponry while all kinds of strange sounds of panic came out of his mouth. {This is Vilvak Third…Ooshgoo…ship 51…my…guns…malfunctioned and…fired on the ship ahead of me…I've…shut down all weapons on the ship}.

{This is Honroodo, Biyok…Commander of Flight 8! Ship number 22…totally destroyed…pilot lost! Suggest ship 51 get back to the hangar and get the weapons checked}!

Lak-Lak growled. {That's not a suggestion…that's a command! Ship 51…to the hanger bay…NOW}!

At that moment, Kongee in ship number 77 giggled as she hopped her entire ship into Desert and fired on a ship that was orange in Flight 10. Ship number 91 suffered a direct hit and was obliterated. Ship number 70 on the port side was damaged and ship number 112 on the starboard side was damaged.

{This is Vilvak Second, Yod-Yod! My guns just malfunctioned as well! I just hit…one of the ships in Flight 10! I'm shutting down all weapons. I'm…headed for the hangar…to check the ship}.

Lak-Lak was sitting in his ship letting out a high-pitched buzz of some kind with his teeth and fists clenched tight. Sankiki was in his ship and had to cover her ears.

Flights 12 and 13 fired on the debris field with the same baffling results.

Soolchakan was sitting in fighter number 59. He felt a little deprived over the fact that he had not been able to fire on any of the orange ships. As soon as the pilot of his ship was finished firing on debris, Soolchakan goosed the throttle slightly and the ship lurched into the debris field...and collided with a piece of junk. He snickered as the Jowfoonda let out a little squawk...that sounded more like a belch.

{This is Vilvak Second, Dossdowbo! I...just hit one of the pieces of debris. I think...I sustained some damage to my ship. The throttle...jammed...somehow and...that's when the collision occurred...and...}.

Lak-Lak growled. {Vilvak Second, Dossdowbo...land your ship in the hangar! Give the report to the maintenance personnel so they can figure out what went wrong. I don't need a full report now. GO LAND}!

Dossdowbo sat there making a few strange noises as his antennae were wriggling madly all over the place. {Yes...Sir... landing...immediately}.

Flights 14, 15 and 16 fired on the debris with no damage to the junk.

In Flight 17, ship number 76, Kwykod grinned as he pulled the trigger on the orange ship number 48 from Flight 16. Another ship obliterated and two more ships damaged.

Another distraught Jowfoonda pilot called in: {This is Vilvak Second, Bot! My guns just malfunctioned as well…and… the fighter directly ahead of me…was destroyed}.

Shalashak stood up from his Command seat on the Bridge. {ALL SHIPS, SHUT DOWN YOUR WEAPONS AT THIS TIME! ALL SHIPS, LAND, NOW! MAINTENANCE PERSONNEL, GET TO WORK ON THOSE POWER WEAPONS, NOW! I WANT A FULL REPORT ON WHAT JUST HAPPENED… BEFORE ANYONE GETS ANY SLEEP}!

The Owlamite Command Staff were all laughing. Their dirty little plot had worked. The Jowfoonda were, once again, showing the Owlamites how to launch, fly, attack and land the fighters. The Owlamites were learning all kinds of new things about the Jowfoonda space craft and the Jowfoonda were coming up with even more baffling conundrums to consider in this strange dimension. The plan worked except for the fact that they were not able to put the mother ship into maintenance mode.

Shalashak had ordered that the entire maintenance section should be looking over the three ships that had pulled the trigger and the one ship that had collided with junk. He also ordered the Science section of the crew to devote all of their attention as to why they could not even hit dirt on the planet below with their power weapons.

The maintenance checks on the ships took three days. The Maintenance section came up with absolutely nothing out of the ordinary. The Science section took almost eight days and could come up with nothing but theories. The reports from the pilots who had blasted their comrades were being closely scrutinized during that time. The pilots were being interrogated with some rather vicious zeal.

Finally, all sections said that they were ready – or as ready as they could be with the information given to them. Yambagin Cho, Shalashak took his place at the head of the conference table. The Executive Officer, Yalkaska, Shikshoy was to the right of the Yambagin Cho. Vidimgombo Lak-Lak sat next to Shikshoy.

The Kooz personnel were sitting on the left side of the Yambagin Cho. The Koozgofon placed his gong on the table. The Kooztoyso and the Koozyast both placed their speaking sticks on the table. The Koozloomon stood behind the trio.

All of the section Commanders came in and sat at the table. Communications, Maintenance, Medical, Military, Science, Security, Supply and Weapons.

The four defendants were brought in and had to sit against the back wall facing the conference table.

The science and maintenance personnel, who had been investigating the fighters and the strange occurrences, were standing against the wall behind the Section Chiefs.

Shalashak looked around at all of the Jowfoondas in the room. {We are here to determine exactly what happened on *Sizgothok* Day. There were some strange phenomenon and some deaths. How do we respond to the phenomenon and were those deaths really accidents? That is why we are here}. He picked up a pad and perused it. {Tomontain, Ijbisko, the head of the Science Division will report first}.

Ijbisko stood up. {The argument as to why our power weapons did not work against the buildings and people of the planet can be explained with phenomenon that has proven itself a few times...the laws of physics changes in different dimensions. Something that works a certain way in one dimension...has a different result in another dimension. Food that is nutritious in one dimension...can become deadly toxic in another. We...however, have come across a different conundrum. When our fighters fired on the debris field...once again, nothing was damaged. That would mean...normally...that our power weapon is useless in this dimension. But...we have the three fighters that were fired on...and blown up. If the debris field could not be damaged... why were the fighters destroyed? The only answer to this is that there is some quality, which we have not yet isolated, about the fighters...that allowed the power weapons to work. Nothing in the debris field had a power unit, of any type...that was working. The fighters were powered up. The answer has to be in the engines or other working mechanisms in the fighters...that makes them helpless against attack by power weapons...in this dimension}.

The Koozgofon held up his stick and lit it up. {What about the planet? Don't they have some power units of some type working there? Why didn't the power weapons work against that}? He shut his stick off and laid it down.

Ijbisko shrugged. {That is a power source...that is OF this

dimension. Nothing that was fired on, that is *of* this dimension… was damaged}.

The Koozgofon grunted and stroked his chin in thought.

Shalashak cocked his head to the side. {Could we possibly adjust our weapons…to something where…we use a power source…OF this dimension}?

Ijbisko sighed. {That thought has occurred to us and we're looking into it. The problem there is…it might only take five *winsa*…or it could take as long as fifty *klinjiy* to perfect that sort of thing. We have no way of knowing…until we can complete some experiments along that line}.

Shalashak hung his head and groaned. {We don't have that kind of time}.

Sankiki leaned over to Bonarain. "What did he say? *Winsa*? *Klinjiy*? Whuzzat?"

Bonarain shrugged. "They're time measurements. A… *winsa*…is one of their days. From what I can understand of it… their *winsa* is about 8% longer than one of our days. That's why it doesn't seem to translate…in what we're understanding. The *klinjiy* is their year. It is about 17% longer than our year."

Sankiki shook her head. "So…why did the words… translate earlier…but not now?"

Bonarain shrugged again. "All I can think of…is that they're being a bit more technical now than they were before. Something about…terminology or vernacular or dialect that just… doesn't seem to be the same."

Sankiki nodded (still somewhat unsatisfied). "Thanks."

Shalashak looked up. {That means that…the only way we can obtain a power weapon in this dimension…is to reinvent our power weapons}.

Ijbisko nodded. {I'm afraid that is the only option available to us. Other than that, we'll have to use conventional projectile weapons}.

Tomontain, Quorig, head of the Military stood up. {That's impossible! If we have to use projectile weapons…we're outnumbered over 180,000 to 1 by the indigenous trash. We couldn't possibly hope to gain victory against those odds…without power weapons}. He sat down, shook his head and huffed.

Shalashak nodded. {What would you need…to build a power weapon in this dimension…that would function in this dimension}?

Ijbisko cleared his throat. {We would need to obtain some of the things they use for their electrical sources. Unfortunately, we cannot obtain it…unless we do so by force and…then we'd have to battle against them with conventional weapons…in order to get what we need or desire}.

{And we'd have to pay a heavy price}, said Quorig.

Soolchakan sighed. "Would we have to be the ones who stop them from obtaining any…power source?"

Sankiki chuckled. "Of course."

"I thought so," he said bitterly.

Shalashak did not look happy as well. He shook his head several times before looking back up at Ijbisko. {Thank you for the report. Who's next}?

Tomontain, Chijjer, the Chief of Maintenance stood up. {I have the report on the fighters and the...alleged malfunctioning of the guns. Thirty personnel have gone over the three ships that... pulled the trigger on our own. No one has been able to find anything wrong with any of the fighters. The only way that those guns could have possibly gone off...is if the pilot *purposely* aimed and fired. We've found no malfunction in any of them nor have we found anything in the flight recorder that shows any form of a computer error. All three...purposely aimed and fired at the unfortunate victims}. He let the information sink in for a few moments. {The other case, where Vilvak Second, Dossdowbo, negligently ran into a piece of debris...it was just that – negligence. Once again, at least thirty mechanics and technicians have gone over the ship and the flight recorder. There is absolutely no sign of any malfunction, mechanically or in the computer. All four fighters were in perfect working order when the incidents occurred. The only possible conclusion is pilot error...or just plain stupidity}.

Shalashak sat there with his shoulders hunched down. The antennae on his head were wriggling in a wild manner. They suddenly stopped wiggling. {Is there any reason why we should not put the three pilots on trial for murder and/or insurrection}?

Tomontain, Atahatha, the Chief of Medical, stood up. {Yes, Sir, there is. We've given all four of the pilots in question a thorough mental and physical examination. We even used truth drugs. The four pilots in question...did not remember doing the deeds that caused the deaths of three of their fellow pilots and also caused the damage to several other fighters}.

Shalashak stood up. {Are you telling me that someone can get away with murder just by saying they don't REMEMBER}? He seemed furious.

Atahatha shook his head. {No, Sir, that's not what I'm saying. Vilvak Second, Dossdowbo had some kind of mental relapse and even under the influence of truth drugs, he does *not* remember accelerating into the debris field. The other three pilots – Vilvak Third, Ooshgoo, Vilvak Second, Yod-Yod and Vilvak Second, Bot...none of them remember arming and firing...ever under truth drugs. Something did happen to all four of the pilots. If Yambagin Cho, Shalashak remembers...your own edict...that we keep a close watch and examination of any...actions that seem untoward or unusual...this is it. The insanity, be it temporary or permanent, apparently did happen...to all four of these pilots. If they had consciously committed the acts that they're accused of...we would've obtained a full confession from them...when they were under the influence of the truth drugs. We received no such confession from any of them. What that tells us...is that the insanity that was found in our home dimension...has somehow seeped into this dimension and we are in just as much danger from that phenomenon...here...as we were there}.

Shalashak hung his head. {We have fighter pilots...who are having a temporary attack of dementia...they end up shooting another pilot...or damaging their craft. After the incident...they remember nothing...because of some sort of brain fadeout...is that what you're telling me}?

Atahatha nodded. {That is an accurate assessment of the situation, Sir. This area…is proving itself…to be very dangerous to our mental health}.

Shalashak gave a deep sigh. {How long…do you think it is…before we all go insane}?

Atahatha scoffed. {There's absolutely no way to tell… with any form of accuracy. Each individual IS an individual and therefore must be treated *individually*! To try to categorize each one of us…as to when this one or that one will slip into…either temporary or permanent dementia…impossible to predict…with any accuracy or competency. The only thing that I can tell you… with any competency is that the indigenous inhabitants, in both dimensions…the ones who have not gone insane have survived. We would have to do a full examination of the survivors and watch for the insane ones…that could take quite a long time…and…by then…all of the Jowfoonda in the area…might be lost}.

Shalashak sat there with his head hung low and his antennae sagging. {This area has…proven itself…too dangerous for us to attempt any further claim…for the Empire, on it. In this dimension and…in our own dimension…the area…reeks of insanity. We don't know what's causing it…and it would be… too expensive in the cost of Jowfoonda lives in order to try to combat it. We must leave this area…and find a place that's…more suitable. The problem there is…we are in another dimension and…we have no way of warning our own people in our home dimension. Hopefully…because of the complete disappearance of a Conquering Vessel…with no sign of how or why…they'll get the hint and not follow us…to oblivion}. He sighed and shook his head. {We'll have to leave this place and find somewhere…more suitable to our life and capability…and some day in the future, find out how we got here and how to get back to our home dimension. We must start charting…an entire new…universe…and find a new home…to establish new weaponry in order to conquer. We…are alone in this endeavor. Prepare the ship to depart this area. Get all of the long range scanners…checking…in any direction…in order to find a new home…where we *can* survive}. He stood up. {You have your orders. This meeting is adjourned}.

Tomontain Chijjer stood up. {Yambagin Cho, Shalashak! Before we depart, we need to do a little more troubleshooting. This is the only way that we can depend on the ship. We need to put the entire ship in maintenance mode…and check all systems. I'd hate to go to star-speed and…suddenly find out that there's an unknown problem…minor or major}.

Shalashak nodded. {How long should that take}?

{No more than four *winsa*, Sir}.

{Get it done…and let's get out of here}.

Sankiki stood up. "That's it! You were able to take some of those handheld devices…while they were in that mode…and get rid of the self-destruct systems in them. They're going to do it to the entire ship. Get as many personnel on this contraption as we can…get all of the passwords that can be obtained…and then we can get rid of all of the self-destruct devices." She grinned. "Then…this ship…will be ours…and we can do anything with it that we desire."

In a very short time, all Owlamites were aboard the

Ispododokodor, watching and obtaining passwords, command functions, maintenance functions and many other useful tidbits of information that would help them learn the ship. Once they had full knowledge of the ship…there were now over 61,000 new deposits into Jahong's Death.

And they renamed the ship – *Owlam the First*.

8

Hadathoo sat there chuckling. "I really wonder about the mentality of those Jowfoondas. They had conquered most of the Desert Dimension planet…using hand held conventional weapons and conventional bombs. When their fighter ships had problems, all of a sudden they panicked about that…and were ready to turn around and run. Why didn't they…consider using the hand held weapons…in those four cities?"

Shyshee shrugged. "That's a very good question. I think they were more worried about the…local dementia…than any form of weapons malfunction."

Hoynama smiled at Hadathoo. "Would you believe that we've finally broken into the logbooks of that…Yambango… Chalk…Shaky-shake…or whatever his rank…and name was? We can listen to all of his lamentations and ravings about the planet… and the dementia…and dimensional shifts."

Hadathoo shrugged. "I think that, unless it's important, we only need to listen to some of the highlights. There's a lot of it that could be redundant and therefore a waste of time."

Hoynama nodded. "I'll get some of the Aides, from all of our Teams, working on that."

Till looked around somewhat confused. "I heard you say

that they used their power weapons in all of the smaller cities, towns and villages…actually…they didn't. I checked on a few of the log entries, that were not password protected, by some of the lower ranking personnel and…they had some of the fighters fly overhead, making a lot of noise and they put on a light show with the hand held weapons. They never really did any damage with the power weapons. That was why they didn't have any faith in that weaponry."

Hadathoo sat there with his mouth hanging open. "They… simply…scared the *piddleeyanks* out of the citizenry…of an entire planet into submission…with…noise…and hot air."

Till smiled and nodded. "Yes, Sir. That's what happened."

Beemella scoffed. "That means…the technology of Desert planet is…*not* as sophisticated as we originally thought. If it had been…they wouldn't have given up so easily. They might've actually fought back and the Jowfoondas would've found out earlier…that their toys didn't work."

Till chuckled. "Actually…they do work. We just shut them off…at the right time."

Hadathoo groaned and shook his head. "How ironic. They used conventional weapons to rescue their people. They used conventional weapons to conquer most of the planet. That hid the fact that they had power weapons. They wanted to hide that fact until they were ready to do the most damage to the large cities that they could inflict on them. That was when we struck… and stopped them from doing anything."

"I just wonder if we're really going to be able to use any of

this new technology," said Antrong. "We've got the ship intact...
minus those *chokwad* self-destruct devices but, do we really know
how to use it...and keep up the maintenance on all of this stuff?"

Wymini snickered. "Do you remember that...one of the
fighter ships collided with a piece of that junk?"

Antrong sighed. "Yes, I heard about that collision...so
what."

"It was Officer, Soolchakan of Team 7016 that caused the
collision." Wymini had to clear her throat to keep from laughing.
"I found out that his Team member, Officer, Kiyalee...you know,
the one who still has a fully functional 161...she already fixed the
damage on that fighter. It's fully functional now...as well."

Yamananee looked shocked. "Has he taken it out and
tested it yet?"

Wymini nodded with a big grin. "It seems that this Officer,
Kiyalee...can fix just about anything mechanical. It is working as
it should be."

Hoynama shrugged. "Why not? She's had a full year to
pour over all of those manuals that she pulled out of the engine
maintenance area. I'll bet she could fix just about anything on that
ship."

Hadathoo sat there with a grin on his face. "Are you telling
me...that everything on that ship...is fully functional?"

Till looked up from a report that he was looking at.
"Absolutely, Sir! Between Officer, Kiyalee and all of those Teams
that were assigned to study physics...we've got a good bunch of

people who can keep that thing running…for a long time."

Hadathoo nodded thoughtfully. "How many of the fighters do we have?"

Till frowned. "In the hangar bay…we have 107 working fighters…and three of the transport ships…why?"

Hadathoo nodded again. "The Jowfoonda ship…is far more sophisticated than anything that the Algothons have…isn't it?"

Till shrugged. "Absolutely! Again…why?"

Hadathoo started drawing a circle on the table with his finger. "For over two and a half centuries…we've allowed the Algothons to live…because we were trying to learn something… anything…that we could from them." He stopped drawing his imaginary circle. He looked up with an evil grin. "We now have some incredible firepower with that ship. We could get rid of the Algothons if we really wanted to."

Shyshee cleared her throat. "Do you not want to learn anything more from the Algothons?"

He leaned back in his chair and clasped his hands across his chest. "We can't learn anything…from the Algothons…that is as sophisticated as… *Owlam the First*…can we?" He looked around at a group of frowns. "I think it's time to get rid of the Algothons."

Deelka was horrified. "You mean…just…wipe them out?"

Antrong scoffed. "YES! How many times…how many

times has Officer Leader, Ota reported to us that those *bimyocks* are trying to build the firestorm weapons again?"

Yamananee clicked her tongue. "Not only the weapons, but the rockets to carry them all over the planet again. This is a new generation of Heyyah in that city. All of the ones who did that first launch and saw the horrid results...are long dead. This new bunch...thinks that they can build a (ahem) safer weapon."

Hadathoo closed his eyes and shook his head. "Twenty Teams we've had watching them...for all these years...and...what we're learning about the Algothons is that *they* haven't learned a thing. They still want to conquer through destruction...just like the Jowfoondas. I think that it's about time we brought those twenty Teams back to do something more constructive...for the city of Owlam. We use our new ship and eradicate the entire city of Algothon and all of its technology. We get rid of that bunch... once and for all."

Beemella grimaced. "But, Sir...what will the rest of the world think? What will they do to us...when they find out that it was us using an outworlder space ship to destroy the Algothons?"

Hadathoo raised his eyebrows. "How is anyone going to find out? Are you going to tell them? I'm not!" He looked around the table. "It has been just over a year since the Jowfoondas attacked the whole planet. Is there anyone else, on this planet, who knows about a bunch of...strangers...from another planet?"

Everyone on the staff shook their heads.

Hadathoo grinned. "So, we attack from the sky, Algothon is destroyed...and no one else but us...knows how or why."

"That's vicious," said Hoynama.

"That's necessary," said Antrong.

Till glanced around the table and then at Hadathoo. "When do you want it set up?"

Hadathoo gave an evil chuckle. "As soon as possible."

Till and all of the computer personnel were on the space ship entering the coordinates for the attack on Algothon.

Hadathoo looked at all of the activity going on with all those computer people on the Bridge. "What's taking so long?"

Till looked up. "Sir, you did say that you wanted Algothon...ONLY. If we don't get specific, we could devastate a much larger area. The weapons are very nasty to anything they hit. They're not picky, they're destructive."

"Yeah...uh...I was just thinking...how deep down...will the damage be?"

"Do you mean...how many of the underground levels will be demolished?"

"Yes! Exactly what I meant."

"According to what I'm seeing, it could destroy the first four levels."

"Don't they have...seventeen...sub-levels?"

"Yes, Sir."

"Should we...maybe...empty some of those underground vaults...that is if there is anything we want to keep?"

Till shrugged and smiled. "Only if there's something there that we want to keep. Otherwise, we can destroy the top levels, landmark the lower ones and Jump down there any time we want to."

Hadathoo nodded thoughtfully. "That's what I thought." He cleared his throat. "How much longer are you going to be...in setting this thing up?"

Till shook his head. "At least five days."

Hadathoo grinned. He made a mental call-out to all Owlamites...except the ones watching the Teltermak on Satroco Isle and the ones doing the programming on the space ship. The order was for them to get down to the first six levels of Algothon and empty all of the vaults. Get any usable equipment to a lower level or get it to the gorge. Landmark the lower levels and fill them with all kinds of goodies and plunder. He sat back in the Commander's chair on the Bridge. "We have five days to get all of that accomplished."

The plundering was finished in three days. The people of Algothon were all rather perturbed over the fact that massive amounts of equipment were disappearing from the underground vaults and they had no idea who was stealing it or how they were getting it out of Algothon. There were also massive amounts of equipment and wealth disappearing from the surface area. The Prominent Investigators were ready to start drugging the entire city, again, in order to find out who, what, where, when, why...and especially HOW.

The day finally arrived. Till walked up to Hadathoo. "We're ready to get rid of the Algothon threat once and for all... as soon as the orbit gets us to the optimum position for total destruction."

Hadathoo nodded. "Are there any of those *bimyocks* in the lower sections of the underground?"

Till shrugged. "As far as we know, there're at least 2,500 of them down there doing some inventory on what's still in the vaults. They're trying to figure out how things got moved around."

Hadathoo sighed. "We can take care of them...later. For now, let's get on with this mess. Algothon will never be a threat to Owlam...or anyone else...again." He glanced around the Bridge. "Commence firing...when ready. Don't wait for an order."

Till nodded. "Yes, Sir." He looked at the console. "Would you like to be the one who pulls the trigger?"

Hadathoo hung his head. "Why not? I'm the one who gave the order. If I don't have the guts to follow through...I can't really expect anyone else to follow me." He stood up. "Yes, I'll be the one who starts it." He walked to the weapons console. "What do I do?"

Till pointed at the keyboard. "We've programmed it so that all you do is hit these three keys, one at a time, and the ships pulse beams will start up."

"Then what?"

"Then…it'll do what it has been programmed to do… destroy Algothon…and nothing else."

"Let me know when."

Till pointed at a chronometer on the main viewing screen. "That's your countdown, Sir. When it hits zero…hit the keys.. and…that will be the end of Algothon."

Hadathoo looked at the countdown and thought that he should feel some kind of guilt over the fact that he was going to annihilate over 30,000,000 Heyyah. For some strange reason, he had no feelings at all. What he was about to do was completely necessary and therefore no guilt. He had to stop the destroyers.

The countdown hit zero and he tapped the three keys. The lights on the Bridge dimmed as the ship used most of the power available, to fire the destructive pulse beams at Algothon. The count was now going up. At ten, the count stopped, pulse beams stopped and the lights on the Bridge went back to normal.

Hadathoo looked at Till a little startled. "What happened?"

"It's done," said Till sadly. "Algothon…is gone. Everything that was inside the walls…and the walls…all gone."

Hadathoo closed his eyes and scratched his head. "HOLD ON! It took you…over six days…to set it up…and…only ten heartbeats…for the complete devastation of the city?"

"Yes, Sir."

"If it only took…ten heartbeats…to destroy the city, why did it take six days to set it up?"

"Sir, you did say…that you wanted it to be…precise. You wanted to destroy Algothon and nothing else. It took five and a half days to set the exact measurements of the location, in order to carry out your order…Sir."

Hadathoo hung his head. "When I said…precise…I didn't mean…to the most minute *nano*-taja. I meant…that I wanted to see Algothon destroyed but…not very much of the countryside damaged. You took me…a little too literally." He shook his head. "Well if you had to misunderstand my exact meaning at least it was in a way that didn't completely ravage the entire continent."

Till cleared his throat nervously. "I'm glad that you're not upset. I did do it…in the clearest manner…from what I understood." He did a little fiddling with some dials. The view screen changed and showed the location of destruction. "There is all that's left of Algothon. Nothing but four enormous round pits of beige dust. The dust goes about eighty-five taja deep. That means that the top four subterranean levels are dust as well."

Hadathoo sighed. "Levels five through seventeen…are still intact?"

"Yes, Sir. They're intact and so is any Algothon citizen that was down there doing inventory at the time."

Hadathoo growled. "Get…as many Teams as necessary… and get rid of the rest of the Algothon citizens. I said that I wanted them all eradicated and I meant it."

Two hundred Teams went into the lower levels under the dust pits and tossed 2,519 Algothon citizens into other dimensions to their deaths. The ultimate punishment for Algothon was over.

There was nothing left of the city or any of the inhabitants. There would be no more Algothons attempting to conquer the planet… ever again.

After that horrid deed was done, Team 7016 went to the Bridge of the space ship to talk to Hadathoo.

Soolchakan smiled at Hadathoo. "Sir, if I may…I would like to request something that seems…a little unusual."

Hadathoo scoffed. "After some of the *h'oolyach* that your Team has pulled, I can't think of one thing that you could come up with that'd be unusual." He shook his head, looked off to the side and scoffed again. "What is it?"

Soolchakan looked off to the side nervously. "Before you became the *Voice of Power*, there was another one before you, I don't remember which one, but…it was stated that we would not be allowed to search out any…new dimensions…until we had some kind of protection…from…the unknown."

Hadathoo narrowed his eyes. "I think I know where you're headed, but go ahead and continue."

"Yes, Sir…thank you, Sir. With this ship…uh… *Owlam the First*…we now have the protection that we need…in order to go to some of these other dimensions…and take a good look…in safety."

Hadathoo pondered for a moment. "What gave you the idea to try this?"

"Well, Sir, when we sent the mother ship into Desert...in orbit...we found out that we'd been looking at a very small portion of a complete planet. The ship, in outer space in this dimension... was in outer space in that dimension...and we were able to see the entire planet. So...now we know...that Desert...is NOT just one little desert...it is a desert on a planet, in a star system, in an entirely different dimension that...just happens to be in the exact same place as Hardooth is...in this dimension. Suppose...that Jahong's Death...is another dimension, just like this one, but... there's not a planet...in this spot. Jahong hopped...into outer space in that dimension...and that's what killed him. It wasn't something...that we can't see, it was just that he hopped into outer space...and all of the enemies that we've thrown in there all... suffered the same fate."

Hadathoo's eyes and mouth were wide open in wonder. "That could mean that the one we call...Shogoot's Search... is not an entire dimension of liquid acid...it's just possibly...a lake of acid...on a planet...in another dimension...that is another universe as well." He shook his head and chuckled. "Incredible!"

"Yes, Sir...so if we could take the mother ship...and hop it into some of the other dimensions...that we haven't been able to search...we could find out...just exactly what is there and how we could utilize it."

Hadathoo snapped back to a sense of reality. "No! I will not allow the mother ship to be used for the hopping. You can... take a fighter...or two." He nodded with a satisfied look on his face. "Yes, you can use a couple of the little fighters...keep in constant contact and do the exploration there. If it is possible to take the mother ship there…we'll do it…if we have a real need to do some grand explorations." He smiled at Soolchakan. "Yes… just the fighters."

Soolchakan smiled back. "Thank you, Sir."

Kiyalee climbed into one of the fighters. She scowled at Soolchakan. "You're crazy! Why'd you get us in on this?"

He climbed in the cockpit of a fighter. "I thought that it'd be interesting."

Chyning huffed. "Interesting! Right! You wanna kill yourself like Jahong did."

"No," he said sternly. "We have the space ship around us. This thing is capable of flying in outer space, so that means that we should be able to survive going to these other dimensions without having to worry about safety."

Bonarain shook her head. "I hope you both survive. Chyning and I will be here to listen in on what's going on…and I hope…that everything turns out okay."

Kiyalee grunted. "You hope? I got a bulletin for ya…I HOPE!" She began the start-up procedure for the fighter. "I don't give a *chokwad* about what you hope."

Soolchakan began his start-up. Since both fighters were making an abysmal amount of noise in their start-up, he decided to communicate telepathically. "**Where shall we start**?"

Kiyalee snorted. "**How about going back home and**

have a good steaming hot mug of kwatha."

Bonarain snickered. **"As I recall, Beasties is one of the easiest to get to. Why don't you start with that one**?"

"Good as any," thought Soolchakan. **"As soon as we're airborne, we'll go to Ghost and then to Beasties**."

Kiyalee sat there with her eyes closed, trying to understand what he meant. **"Why do we have to go to Ghost? What's wrong with just…hopping**?"

"Suppose we end up in another part of the planet. Suppose the planet is not exactly aligned with Hardooth. We could end up in the middle of the planet and…I don't want to think of what could happen."

Kiyalee huffed. **"That actually makes sense**."

They had finished the start-up. Soolchakan looked over at Kiyalee as he closed his canopy. **"Let's go**."

She snarled and bared her teeth at him.

The two fighters lifted off and headed out of the hangar in the mother ship. Bonarain hit the switch to close the big doors. Instead of re-pressurizing the entire hangar area, Bonarain and Chyning Jumped to the Fighter Control Bridge in order to listen in on their Team members.

"Okay…to Ghost dimension," thought Soolchakan.

Kiyalee just huffed.

They hopped to Ghost.

"**Now to Beasties**."

They made the hop to Beasties.

"**Oh...that's...incredible**," thought Kiyalee. "**I never dreamed that it could look like that**."

Soolchakan chuckled. "**Enjoy the view. That's the place that you discovered. Even though it looks a lot like Hardooth...the land masses are different and...I don't see...any...cities. Do you?**"

Kiyalee looked everywhere. "**I don't see any either**."

"**Let's orbit around to the other side of the planet. If there are any small towns or villages...there should be some lights on...somewhere...if there's a town**."

"**Wait! What's that?**"

"**Uh...what is...*what*?**"

"**Right there...in the water!**"

"**WE'RE LOOKING AT A PLANET 35 KILOTAJA BELOW US! Most of what I'm looking at is water. Where in the water are we looking?**"

"**In the north...western area! That...island...it's...moving!**"

Bonarain was listening in on the mental communications. She looked at Chyning in shock. "How could...an *island*... move?"

Chyning held her hands up as in surrender. "Don't ask me,

I'm sitting next to you. They're the ones in Beasties."

Soolchakan looked in frustration for anything that was moving. An island? How could an island move? Then he saw something that was very large, in the water and it *was* moving. **"Let's go...down a little. Take it down to ten kilotaja and...get a better look at this...moving island."**

The two of them flew their fighters down inside the atmosphere. They kept their eyes on the gargantuan moving object. As they got closer the thing looked even bigger than before.

Soolchakan laughed. **"Do you remember that huge brown beast that ate the giant pink sand snake?"**

"How could I forget?"

"We're looking at the thing...right now."

Kiyalee shook her head. **"Oh *h'oolyach*! Are the sensors in this ship...set to our form of measurements?"**

He snickered. **"They sure are."**

"That big brown beast...its neck alone...is two and a half kilotaja in length."

Bonarain looked at Chyning in shock, however she had a smile on her face. **"Hey, Kiyalee...give us a few more bits of description on that thing."**

Kiyalee circled around the creature. **"The head...is... at least thirty taja in length. Like I said...the neck is two and a half kilotaja. From above...the body looks round. It has four flippers...two on each side...each one is one** and a half kilotaja in length. The body is four kilotaja long...and three kilotaja wide. It has a tail...that's...four kilotaja in length. That thing is...."

"It is definitely the top of the food chain on this planet," sent Soolchakan. "Okay, we've had a better look at the thing. Let's get some altitude and check the other side of the planet. I don't think that anyone would live on any coast...anywhere on this planet. The big pink sand snake and that big brown beast...I don't see how anything could live here...without having to hide from those two monsters."

Kiyalee scoffed. "The fishing industry would sure suffer badly."

Bonarain turned to Chyning. "I'm gonna have to go there...and get a look at that thing...one of these days."

Chyning huffed. "ONLY...from outer space, my dear."

Soolchakan and Kiyalee regained the altitude and flew around to the other side of the planet. They started looking for any sign of lights in the current dark side of the planet.

"I see one," sent Kiyalee. "Look over there...in the southern hemisphere. There's a big light there."

Soolchakan sighed. "It's a forest fire. It's burning a big area and it's completely out of control...because there's no one there to fight the fire."

"Oh...you're right. It is...just a big fire," sent Kiyalee sadly. "I don't think that there's much more we can do here. Where do we go next?"

Soolchakan sniffed. "**What's the next one on the list...as far as easiest to get to?**"

"**That would be the Water Dimension,**" sent Bonarain.

Soolchakan grunted to himself. "Water," he said. "Oh well." "**Let's gain a lot more altitude before we go there. It'll give us a good look, especially if it's another planet.**"

"**Lead the way,**" sent Kiyalee.

They both turned their noses up, directly away from the Beasties planet. He watched his altimeter as they were flying up. No matter how many times he saw it he was amazed at the speed these things could fly...with seemingly so little effort.

"**At 100 kilotaja, we stop and hop.**"

"**Right...almost there.**"

They leveled off at 100.

"**Let's go...now.**"

Kiyalee started laughing. "**Well whaddaya know? It's just another planet. Apparently we always hopped right into the middle of that big ocean.**"

"**Yeah, and the reason that our victims drowned... it was right in the middle and...it looks like it was probably more than 2,000 kilotaja to the nearest beach. Not much chance of survival there, is there.**"

"**Nope! Do we check for intelligent life here?**"

"**We don't need to** *check*. **Can't you see those coastlines? I see a lot of harbor cities and it looks like a lot of industry in those places**."

"**The cities are big, but...the ships aren't**." Kiyalee snickered. "**I don't think these people have discovered electricity yet**."

"**I agree. All those ships...and they're all the type that depend on the wind. I don't see any form of electrical device anywhere**."

Bonarain frowned. "**How can you be so sure? Aren't you 100 kilotaja away from the planet**?"

Soolchakan growled. "**Don't forget...these ships are small but they do have a magnification device...where we can do a quick look at certain things**."

Bonarain turned red as Chyning sat there giggling.

Kiyalee licked her lips. "**What' next**?"

Chyning giggled again. "**Have fun with this one...it's the bug dimension. Kiniski's Search...remember**?"

"**Oh yuck**," sent Kiyalee!

"**No...hop**," sent Soolchakan.

They hopped to the bug dimension. They saw no lights on this planet and went down inside the atmosphere for a quick search.

"**Oh yuck for real**," sent Kiyalee! "**There's a

continent…and…I don't see anything on it…but bugs. It looks like…4,000 kilotaja from east to west and 3,000 kilotaja from north to south. Coast to coast bugs… everywhere! They're doing nothing but…eating each other."

Soolchakan snickered. "There's a few islands out there that look like they're inhabitable, but…with all those bugs controlling the uh…six large continents… it ain't worth trying to live here. At least not until there is some major bug extermination accomplished." He sighed as he looked at the planet full of insects. "What's next on the list?"

Bonarain pursed her lips and looked off to the side. "It… is…Jahong's Death. That's the next one…in order."

Soolchakan sat there with his eyes closed for a few moments. "Okay. Jahong's Death! Let's get out of the atmosphere of this planet and then…we'll see what is… there." He swallowed hard. "You ready?"

"No, but we gotta do it anyway."

"Let's hop."

And they did.

Kiyalee looked up, left, right and over her shoulder. "Uh… there's…nothing here! Absolutely nothing! I don't see…anything. I don't even see any stars…anywhere."

Soolchakan frowned as he checked his sensors. "I'm detecting…some organic matter. It's about twenty kilotaja...beneath us."

Kiyalee was a little startled. She checked her sensors. **"You're right. There is some...organic matter...a LOT of it! Where'd all of that stuff come from...when there's no planets?"**

"Turn you nose down towards the stuff and... maybe we can get a better visual and...make some sense out of it."

"Okay, I'm turning my nose down and...WHAT?!"

Bonarain jumped. **"What's the matter? What happened?"**

Soolchakan shook his head. **"There is a star. ONE star. One great big star...and nothing else but this strange organic matter that's just...slowly floating towards the star."**

"I can't get a fix on the star," said Kiyalee angrily. **"I can see the *chokwad* thing but...it just isn't showing up...on my sensors."**

Soolchakan grunted. **"Go long range on your sensors. That star is a lot further away than you think."**

Kiyalee scoffed. **"Okay, I'll check it and...wait...uh... that thing is over...oh that's impossible! According to this...that star is...over 35 light years away...but...it looks like...it's close to us."**

Soolchakan gave her a helpless chuckle. **"That should**

tell you how big that thing is. It IS…over 35 light years away…but it looks close by because it IS that big."

Kiyalee squawked. "But…if the thing is that big… that would mean that the circumference…would be measured…in light years…*as well*."

Soolchakan shook his head. "Yup! The circumference, the diameter and the radius…all would be measured in light years. That thing is…incalculably large. Over 35 light years away and yet it looks like it's closer to us… than our star – Holgotho – is to Hardooth."

Kiyalee let out a loud breath. "And it's the only star in this entire dimension."

Bonarain looked at Chyning with wonder. "I've got to go *there*, one of these days, and take a look."

Chyning nodded wide-eyed in awe. "I agree."

Soolchakan turned back to his short range sensors. "So what is this crazy organic matter that's floating around? OH MY CONSCIENCE!"

Kiyalee was surprised by his sudden outburst. "What's the matter?"

He growled. "That…organic matter…it's…all of the…Cacktash and Perfor…and Jowfoonda…and everyone else that we've thrown into Jahong's Death. That's all of those bodies…that blew up from the sudden change in pressure. We're looking at all of the exploded blood, guts and bones of everyone that we tossed in here."

Kiyalee felt nauseous. **"Let's get out of here. I feel sick. What's next**?"

Chyning giggled. **"The next hardest dimension on the list is Spy.**"

"Don't need that one," snarled Soolchakan. **"What's next**?"

Chyning giggled again. **"Jump!**"

Kiyalee snarled this time. **"Which one is next, and if you say Ghost, I'll smack you!**"

Bonarain cleared her throat and broke in. **"Shogoot's Search. Be careful because that one was liquid acid.**"

Soolchakan sighed. **"Let's get out, about 1,000 kilotaja. Put these crazy…electromagnetic shields on maximum.**"

Kiyalee nodded. **"Okay.**"

They moved out to the distance that he called for and hopped.

Kiyalee's jaw dropped. **"Wow! That is…one big planet.**"

Bonarain felt like she wanted to be there and see all of this, however, Hadathoo had stated that someone had to stay behind and monitor the progress. She knew that once everything had been established as "safe" inside one of the newly acquired spacecraft, that she would be able to explore all she wanted. "**Why did you go out 1,000 kilotaja? How big is the planet? What do you see**?"

Soolchakan growled. "**ONE AT A TIME! First of all… it is a *big* planet. I decided that I didn't want to be too close to that acid…no matter how good these shields are. According to the sensors, this planet has an equator that is…nine times the size of Hardooth. I see a large planet…that is further away from its star than Hardooth is from Holgotho. According to what we're seeing…this is a dead planet…that is covered in all kinds of deadly chemicals and volcanoes. It looks like…when we tossed some enemy into Shogoot's Search…we were in close proximity to a large lake of concentrated liquid acid.**"

Kiyalee let her breath out. "**It looks like this one is the seventh planet…in a star system that has eleven planets.**"

Bonarain nodded as she listened. "**Does it look like there's a planet that can be inhabited**?"

Soolchakan shrugged. "**If anyone else wants to come back here and explore that possibility…they're welcome to do so. Right now, all we're doing is doing a quick "check and go". What's next on the list**?"

Bonarain cleared her throat. "**Stink.**"

Kiyalee huffed. "**Should we go out further**?"

"**No**," he sent. "**Just hold your breath…and hop.**"

Kiyalee gasped. "**If…you like…orange and yellow… you'll love the look of this planet. From pole to pole… it's just streaks of orange and yellow. It's…uh…the twenty-second planet…in a star system of…WHAT… FORTY-SIX PLANETS? That sure is one greedy star**."

Soolchakan snickered. "**Look at the size of the star. It's clearly fifteen times the size of Holgotho.**"

"**Yeah, I guess it can afford to be greedy.**"

"**I don't see anything that differentiates solid from liquid.**" He shook his head. "**I'd say…that what we see…is mostly gas.**"

"**How odd**," sent Chyning in a churlish manner. "**A planet that stinks, is mainly gas.**"

Soolchakan yawned. "**What's next?**"

Bonarain looked at the list. "**Quagando's Search.**"

After they hopped and did a cursory look, Kiyalee snickered. "**Shall we do a spin and roll?**"

Soolchakan sighed. "**Why not?**"

Bonarain frowned. "**What do you see?**"

"**Nuthin',**" sent Kiyalee. "**We're in the middle of a great big universe…and we're not close to any star system…anywhere.**"

Soolchakan looked at his screen. "**According to long range scanners, the closest…object is…about ten light** years from us and it's a...what the *chogo* is a rogue asteroid?"

Bonarain thought for a moment. "I think that a rogue asteroid is probably one that's not orbiting some planet or star. It's just...free floating, screaming the way along, out in space."

Soolchakan chuckled. "That could cause some problems."

Kiyalee scratched her chin. "Nothing much to look at here. What's next?"

Chyning started giggling.

Bonarain gave her an admonishing glare. "The next one is Observation. After that, you have Atasini's Search... this one came back as an unknown liquid poison."

Soolchakan huffed. "Sounds like another dead planet. Let's get away from here and look back for a planet."

"No objection here," sent Kiyalee.

They hopped. They looked at their screens as the scanners did a quick job of looking over the planet.

"It is another dead planet all right," sent Soolchakan. "It is also smaller than Hardooth. The equator shows about 1500 kilotaja smaller."

"All this thing has, is two big oceans of that nasty poison and land masses with no vegetation," sent Kiyalee.

Soolchakan laughed and shook his head. "**It is also the one and only planet that's orbiting this particular star. Everything else that's in orbit...too small to even have an atmosphere or gravity.**"

Bonarain nodded. "**The next one is Sleemata's Search. Everything we sent there got very wet...and drowned. Maybe it's another planet and we dumped everyone into a big ocean.**"

"**Could be,**" sent Soolchakan. He sighed. "**This is getting a little boring. Now that we have a clue about some of these things, it doesn't have the aura of danger or mystery anymore.**"

Kiyalee scoffed. "**Is that a problem?**"

Soolchakan smiled. "**Let's hop.**" After the hop, he nodded as he looked down on the planet. "**It is another planet. According to the scanners it is...very similar to Hardooth in size and atmosphere. There are four continents... thousands of islands of various sizes and looks like there's three major oceans.**"

Kiyalee sniffed. "**I'm not seeing any cities...or towns. All I see on the land masses is...vegetation and...some insect life. I got birds on one continent. Other than that...no sentient life.**"

Bonarain made some annotations. "**The next one is Forest.**"

Soolchakan smiled. "**We didn't see much of that**

from the land. I can hardly wait until we see it from the air. Let's hop."

Kiyalee laughed. "It's a forest all right. There's more land mass than there is ocean. The oceans...are more like large rivers between the continents."

"Check that other thing on your scanners," sent Soolchakan. "There may not be much on the top...look at the depth of those waterways."

Kiyalee gasped. "Is that...for real?"

"If you don't believe it, run it again," sent Soolchakan mirthfully.

Bonarain wanted to strangle them. "WHAT!? What are you talking about?"

Soolchakan snickered. "According to the scanners... that the Jowfoonda (ahem) gave us, the deepest spot, in any of the oceans on Hardooth, is 9.754 kilotaja. Here on this planet...the shallowest waterway that I can find is...19.886 kilotaja."

"They may have small surfaces, but they run awful deep," sent Kiyalee.

"Lots and lots of birds, bugs and fish. I don't see any mammals, reptiles or...cities or towns," sent Soolchakan.

Bonarain leaned back in her chair and stretched. "The next one is Illa's Search."

They hopped to Illa's Search where they found themselves in another outer space area, far from any star system.

"**The next one is Imyaya's Search. The only thing that was found there was...more poison**," sent Bonarain. "**You think maybe it's another planet...that is uninhabitable**?"

Soolchakan licked his lips. "**We'll know when we get there**."

After the hop, Kiyalee grunted. "**Another large planet...with nothing attractive at all**."

Soolchakan aimed his sensors directly at a large whirlwind that was just north of the equator. "**This planet is...three times the size of Hardooth. It also is showing that most of the ground and liquid...and atmosphere is highly toxic. I'm also seeing one of those giant whirlwinds...that could probably swallow up all of North Chilamte. The eye is 18 kilotaja in width, the circular winds go out...over 2,000 kilotaja and...is that for real**?"

Kiyalee sat there wide-eyed looking at her sensors. "**The wind speed...on the outer fringe...of that whirlwind... over 5,000 kilotaja...gusting to 5,800...that's incredible**."

Bonarain smiled. "**Not much that we could do there, is there? The next one is...Ninka's Death! That's the place...where that really hot fire comes from**."

"**We're going to hold off on that one...for now. I've got a theory about that one...and I need to talk** to Hadathoo about it before anyone goes there," sent Soolchakan.

Chyning pursed her lips. "**Would you care to enlighten us on…your theory?**"

Soolchakan sighed. "**You'll hear it when I talk to Hadathoo. What's next on the list?**"

The next two – Tywhee's Search and Atsi's Death – turned out to be two more universes where there location put them absolutely nowhere near any star system. The next one was Chaya's Search. This was another poison planet with nothing that they needed. Next on the list was "Desert". They were, by now, very familiar with this one. Ghost was the next one on the list.

Kiyalee groaned. "**How many more are left? They weren't joking when they said that each one of these was harder to hop to. I'm getting *really* tired.**"

Bonarain clenched her teeth. She knew that they had been doing a great deal of hopping and knew that it was going to wear them down. "**There's only four more on the list. Can you last that long?**"

Kiyalee growled. "**The four that are the hardest to get to!**" She sighed. "**I'll try.**"

The next three - Kiymee's Search, Naka's Search and Sesqua's Search - were once again nothing but an outer space area that was not close to any star system.

"**All right,**" send Bonarain. "**This is the last one on the list. Yoyee's Search. All we know…it's another one**

that consists of a solid poison, *unknown* solid poison."

Yoyee's Search turned out to be just another useless poisonous planet, in a star system of six useless planets.

Soolchakan and Kiyalee hopped back to Home. They landed their fighters and both crawled out of the cockpits and nearly fell down from being so exhausted from all of those hops.

Bonarain stood there with her head cocked to the side. "Hadathoo wants this report as soon as we're finished. We're not finished…because we never looked at Ninka's Death. When are you going to let us in on this secret?"

Soolchakan was leaning against the fighter to prop himself up. "As soon as I get enough strength back…to go to the Command Conference room…and talk to Hadathoo."

Bonarain was a little disgusted. She turned to Chyning. "They're completely spent. Why don't you and I do the Jumping for them…to the conference room?"

Chyning nodded, took hold of Kiyalee and vanished.

Bonarain sniffed as she walked over to Soolchakan. "Looks like I get you." She took hold of him and Jumped them both to headquarters.

Hadathoo and the others looked over the list of what had been found.

"Very interesting," said Hadathoo with a smile. "It turns out that…when you have the proper protection…you can go anywhere."

Shyshee snickered. "All this time we've been worrying about all of the enemy bodies that we were throwing into Jahong's Death...and all this time...there's nothing there...but one... absolutely gigantic star. Amazing."

Antrong looked up. "What about Ninka's Death? I see here that...you didn't go there. Why?"

"Because of a theory I have, Sir," said Soolchakan.

Hadathoo scratched his nose. "Care to share that thought with us?" He smiled.

Soolchakan smiled through his exhaustion. "No problem, Sir. As you know, when we sent something there...and we had a rope tied to it, the rope got burned up...and the fire was abnormally hot."

"I'm aware of that," said Hadathoo in a dull manner.

Soolchakan smiled again. "If you look, Sir, on the list, there were several...other-dimensional areas where...there is a planet...in the exact same location as Hardooth. There are other dimensions...where there's nothing. My thought, Sir...is that in Ninka's Death...at the precise same location of Hardooth...there is a...star. That is why the fire burns through the dimensional barrier...and why it is so infernally hot."

Hadathoo nodded. "So why didn't you check on that?"

"Sir...even in Ghost...or Spy...I don't think that the fighters could've taken that kind of heat."

Beemella scoffed. "You could've flown out a ways to avoid that heat."

Soolchakan shrugged. "The fighters don't have that kind of range. They can fly short distances...but then have to come back to the mother ship in order to get their batteries recharged." He sniffed. "A scout ship...on the other hand...does have the range. If we take a scout ship...go out about...100,000,000 kilotaja from Hardooth, turn around and zero in on the exact location of Hardooth and then hop to Ninka's Death...I think that my theory will prove correct."

Hadathoo looked at Till and smiled. "You like playing with those spacecraft. You're the one who discovered that ship... initially. Would you like to be the one to...carry out the experiment that he's talking about?"

Till smiled and nodded. "Absolutely, Sir. The theory is sound...the way he describes it. The thought that...another dimension...the size of the universe...is nothing but fire...I don't believe it. But the middle of a star...that's believable."

Hadathoo chuckled. "All right Team 7016. Are you up to participating in the experiment?"

Soolchakan sighed. "As long as someone else does the hopping. I'm very tired."

"Same here...Sir," said Kiyalee.

Hadathoo nodded. "I'm sure that we can find a few other Teams who are willing to hop a scout ship...into Ninka's Death."

Till smiled. "Starting with my Team 31." He looked

around the table. "Anyone else want to join us?"

Wymini chuckled. "Why not? I'm in…along with my Team 36."

Scout ship number 4 separated from the mother ship. The only ones on board were Teams 31, 36 and 7016.

Till and Wymini were standing next to the Commander's chair on the Bridge. They were frowning back at their Team members. None of the Team members wanted to be in on this rather risky maneuver.

Till's Team members, Ababi, Hoodeefa and Choychata all glared back angrily at him for volunteering them for this mission.

Wymini's Team members, Officer Grade 5, Poroth, Officer Grade 6, Yiltakazi and Officer Grade 7, Afa-Im had the same angry looks.

Till decided to ignore all of the angry looks. "Officer, Soolchakan, you've had some experience flying a Jowfoonda fighter - is this thing any different?"

"Like night and day," huffed Soolchakan as he looked over the navigational panel.

Poroth came over and looked at the panel. "All kinds of things that you have to keep track of, aren't there?"

Soolchakan glanced at him. "Amazing isn't it?"

"So how did they do it?"

"Practice, practice, practice," chuckled Soolchakan.

Ababi folded her arms in anger. "Why don't we get those computer experts in here to fly the thing? Didn't they fly it over Algothon…when we evaporated that city?"

"No," said Till. "They simply allowed the thing to continue orbiting Hardooth."

Ababi scowled and turned around shaking her head.

Bonarain looked at the panel. "It's really not that difficult. Look at how it's labeled: Pitch, yaw, roll, turn, climb, descend, speed…be it regular or…light speed."

Choychata huffed. "If you can make it out so easily, why don't you fly this *chogo* thing?"

Bonarain shrugged and sat down. She started activating the commands and everyone could feel vibrations in the floor of the ship.

She looked around smiling. "Okay, which direction do we want to go?"

Till shrugged. "Head for the planet…Rogoth. That's as good as any place to go right now."

Wymini frowned. "He originally said that we need to go about 100,000,000 kilotaja away from Hardooth…to avoid being inside a star. Is Rogoth far enough?"

Bonarain fed in the coordinates and looked things over. "More than enough. We'll be able to get a good look at Rogoth and see what happens when we hop."

"Okay," said Wymini. "So set the course and let's go... using that...light speed."

Bonarain hit a few more things on the panel and nothing happened. She looked at a written message that scrolled across a readout on the console. She read it and huffed. "This silly machine won't let us. The readout shows uh...too dangerous to go to light speed...inside a star system. We have to go outside of the star system in order for us to use it. We're going to have to use the normal engines...in order to get the necessary distance."

Till snarled. "How long will that take?"

Bonarain did some calculating and squawked in surprise. "According to this...at maximum...on the regular engines...it'll take eighty-one days to get there."

Till hung his head. "Oh no...that's much too long."

Wymini shook her head. "We've got to figure out something better."

Choychata scoffed at them. "Why don't we just Jump this thing to Rogoth?"

Soolchakan sneered at her. "You got a landmark on Rogoth?"

Choychata opened her mouth to say something, then closed her mouth and eyes and turned away as she cleared her throat.

"I didn't think so," said Soolchakan patronizingly.

Ababi spoke to Soolchakan in an equally demeaning manner. "So have you got a better way of doing it?"

Soolchakan smiled. "Pitch the nose of the ship up 90 degrees and move away from the system in a perpendicular direction until we *can* use the light speed." He turned to Bonarain. "Will that do it?"

Bonarain cocked her head to the side. "We'd be out of the system faster."

"So let's try it," said Wymini.

Bonarain fed in the new coordinates. They all felt the ship move. They could tell it was moving, however none of them could tell which way or how it was moving. Bonarain kept on watching the messages that were scrolling. After several moments moving with the regular engines she got an all clear from the computer.

She giggled. "Here we go!" She hit the command button for light speed.

Once again everyone on board knew that something had happened. It did not take very long, however, they were all glancing around at each other with a great deal of apprehension.

"Uh...we're there," said Bonarain.

Till's jaw dropped. "Already!?"

Bonarain nodded. "That light speed...gets you where you wanna go...REAL quick."

"No joke," said Wymini...with her hand over her heart and a look of shock on her face.

"Now," said Bonarain. "I'm going to mark the exact spot of where Hardooth is. We can't see it from here...unless we go to extreme magnification. Once we make the hop to Ninka's Death, if that mark is inside a star…we'll know that Soolchakan was right." She punched in a few things on the console. A small block appeared on the main view-screen. "That's Hardooth," she said.

Till smiled. "All right people…are we ready to hop…to Ninka's Death?"

The response was a group of grumbles and mumbling.

Wymini smiled. "First…why don't we go into Ghost? We can hop to Ninka's Death in Ghost…and if it is nothing but fire… we should be safe from it…I hope."

"All right," said Till. "Let's hop this big bucket into Ghost."

Everyone concentrated on the hop and the ship was now in the other dimension. There was still a lot of apprehension on the faces of the present Owlamites.

Till got all of them in a circle. "We're going to do this. Everyone get ready. I will call it." He looked at all of their faces. "Ready…NOW!"

There were several gasps as the hopped. They all looked around with fear and some trepidation on their faces.

Bonarain looked at the scrolling messages and let out a loud breath. "Soolchakan you *bimyock*…you were right."

Everyone else looked at the view-screen. A large star was in the middle of the screen and the block that gave Hardooth's exact location was right in the upper part of the star.

Ababi looked at the block. "It looks...from here like it is in that star. Are you sure that it is not...just in front of the star, from our viewing angle?"

Bonarain looked at the telemetry. "According to what we have here...this side of Hardooth is located...895 kilotaja inside the chromosphere of that star. The rest of our planet is further in... completely engulfed by the star. THAT is why that fire burned so hot and...for some reason was able to cross the dimensional lines. The temperature inside a star is...incredible." She turned to Till. "Ninka's Death is safe to go to...as long as we're at least 100,000,000 kilotaja away from Hardooth...preferably away from the star."

Till stood there nodding with a big grin on his face. His expression changed to a frown. "Uh...what is the...computer doing?"

Bonarain looked up at the view-screen and then back to the console. "Counting."

"Counting...what?"

"It's counting the planets that are orbiting this star."

Wymini's jaw dropped. "But...it's...over fifty...and still going."

Bonarain snickered. "I know. It's amazing."

Everyone watched as the count went higher and higher. It finally stopped at ninety-four.

Till was leaning against the Commander's chair. His

mouth was hanging open. "There are...ninety-four...planets...in this one...star system?"

Bonarain grinned at him. "Yes, Sir."

Wymini shook her head. "One of these days we may have to come back here and inventory all of them. See if any of them are...inhabitable."

Soolchakan snickered. "Yes, Sir." Then he looked confused. "Any particular reason you want to inventory this star system...Sir?"

She sighed. "We already had to move once. We might need to manufacture another refuge...in a different dimension."

9

They took all of the data collected from Ninka's Death. The Command Staff, for the most part, was enraptured by this new information. Now they knew that they could search out, discover and travel to other dimensions, without the fear they had gone through before. With the space ship, they had the protection needed to be able to go to these dimensions safely...for the most part.

Hadathoo leaned back in his chair with a satisfied smile on his face. "I'm so glad that Officer, Soolchakan was correct in his theory. A lot of the...unknown...is now known. We're going to have to do some more exploring, because...I feel that there are more dimensions out there...we have yet to discover."

Antrong nodded. "Yes, but we still have this...problem... here at home. The others on North Chilamte...in this area they have now designated...Paselter...they're still trying to force us into joining their coalition in order to make the country stronger. The longer we hold out...the worse things will get."

Hoynama hung her head. "Why don't we just disappear altogether? We have the gorge. We have a space ship. We have our...dimension shifting capability. There are hundreds... no thousands of places that we could go...where we won't be bothered into joining...others who...will want to take advantage of our capabilities...militarily."

Hadathoo sighed. "First things first. I understand your concern. I'm concerned with it as well. We all are. Before we... drop off of the face of the planet...I would like to have a few alternatives as far as where we go. So...along that line...I'm going to make a *Voice of Power* decision." He cleared his throat. "To all Owlamites, everywhere. This is Hadathoo speaking. The ban on looking for new dimensions is permanently lifted. You may look for them, but you may not go there...yet. We have obtained a space ship, whereby we can go to these other dimensions safely. If you think that you have discovered a new one...let the Command Staff know and we will utilize our space ship...*Owlam the First*...to go there and find out if we can continue to go there safely. Do not try to go there by yourself." He stopped talking and cleared his throat several times again. "Do you think that'll get a nice search going?"

Till chuckled. "Without a doubt."

Wymini hung her head. "I'm already getting some mental communications about some new unexplored dimensions...from Team 7016."

Hadathoo groaned. "We're going to have to start calling them by numbers. If we don't...we're going to have at least twenty or thirty that are...called...either Soolchakan's, Bonarain's, Kiyalee's or Chyning's...goodies." He looked at Wymini in a forlorn manner. "Have they said...how many they're talking about?"

Wymini giggled. "So far...at least three."

Antrong groaned. "Three…already?"

Yamananee shrugged. "Why don't you let them use a couple of those little fighter craft again? Couldn't hurt…could it?"

Hadathoo pondered for a moment. "No, it couldn't. Let them know that they have the use of a couple of fighters…but we want a full report on what they find."

Wymini smiled. "Of course."

Deelka chuckled nervously. "Uh…Team 7016 isn't the only Team that's done some exploring. I've received a mental communication as well…from two other Teams. It seems that they've found something…worth exploring."

Hadathoo smiled. "Keeps them busy. Keeps all of us learning…about all kinds of new things around us."

Yamananee frowned. "Sir, I just got a request…from Doctor Shurmook. He wants to get into the computer…on *Owlam the First*…and look for…any kind of pharmaceuticals that he can locate in there."

Hadathoo shrugged with a smile. "Why not? Get him to the computer…with one of the computer experts…and let him have all kinds of fun."

Beemella smiled. "Shurmook isn't the only doctor who wants to get in there."

Hadathoo sighed. "Tell all doctors…they can have all the time they want looking for whatever they want in that computer."

Till chuckled. "There are sixteen doctors…and there are already twelve of them on the ship."

"Good!" said Hadathoo. "We might get something that we can use…something like the *Tuzine*. It may even be better than the *Tuzine*…who knows?"

Shyshee rolled her eyes. "Now all sixteen doctors are on the ship. Most of the nurses are as well."

Hadathoo just sat there chuckling while shaking his head.

The doctors got on board *Owlam the First* and started digging for anything they could find. They were flabbergasted when they could not find any antibiotic medications. They had to look into the anatomy of the Jowfoonda for the answer to that puzzle. It was found that the Jowfoonda were naturally immune to bacteria…any form of bacteria, therefore they had no need for a cure of any type.

What the doctors did find - five different types of antivirus medications. This got their full attention. They knew that if they could introduce an antivirus to Hardooth, that medication would be even more valuable than *Tuzine* and even harder for anyone to duplicate because it came from the spaceship and not anything on the planet.

They started digging even deeper into the Jowfoonda archives for anything that they could find on these drugs. What did they cure? Why did they need five different types? Was there any drawback as far as using this medication? What do you do in case of an allergic reaction? They had several questions they needed to answer before unleashing these things on Hardooth.

The doctors also found a new way to take care of broken bones. The thing they did not like about this procedure was that it had been designed to work on Jowfoonda. Would it work on… anyone else? The procedure was similar, however it required use of some of the drugs and electronic gadgets in order to work. They wondered if they would have the opportunity to use it on anyone…without raising suspicions.

Because of the fact that they might have to do a great deal of hopping in order to find out about the new dimensions, the Command Staff meeting began on scout ship number one. It had been separated from the mother ship and was currently floating in space just two kilotaja away from the mother ship. Before they went to the hopping, there were a few other things that they wanted to discuss first.

Hadathoo threw the document over his shoulder in disgust. "The peoples of Paselter are demanding that we either join them or leave them. They are making it an ultimatum. No more debates. After all this time…can't they just leave us alone?"

Antrong looked a little puzzled. "All this…time? It has only been four years since you took over…and…well…they…are getting demanding."

Hoynama shook her head. "They can demand all they want. We still can't afford to give up our secrets. We especially can't give up the secret that we can read their minds. It could cause…incredible problems."

Deelka huffed. "How could they possible kick us out… and expect us to go? That ultimatum…is nonsense."

Till sighed. "They could cause us all kinds of immeasurable grief. They could cut off all kinds of trade and…surround us and…not let us go anywhere."

Deelka laughed. "We can go anywhere we want. How could they stop us?"

"That would mean that we have to give away our capability of Jumping and hopping to other dimensions," said Hadathoo sadly.

"We always have the gorge," said Hoynama with a shrug.

"It seems that we've got a few more places that we could go," said Hadathoo. "Have you taken a look at this list? In just one year…since we allowed our people to start looking for other dimensions…twenty-seven new dimensions…that we didn't know about before."

Shyshee sat there with a sour look on her face. "Yeah! Twenty-seven new dimensions…and…Team 7016 found seventeen of them." She shook her head. "How do they get so… lucky?" He grunted in exasperation.

Hadathoo growled. "With that teaching capability that Officer, Bonarain has, I don't think I'd call it luck. I think that… she is capable of anything…and that Team has a strong advantage because of her."

Till picked up the list. "So what all do we have? According to the list, there are nine star systems...that are relatively close to us...in these other dimensions. That gives us more places that we could go...if push comes to shove."

Hadathoo looked around grimly. "No matter how hard we get pushed...this planet is our home. I have no intention of leaving...this planet. We may have to spend the rest of our lives in the gorge...but I, for one, am NOT going to leave this planet."

All of the Command Staff nodded in agreement.

"All right," said Hadathoo in a haughty satisfied manner. "What about these new dimensions?"

Shyshee waved her hands. "Sir, it's not so much the dimensions...but the number of them. Each one has a different... imagery...that we use in order to go there. We have nine primaries that everyone is used to. There are sixteen that we now know how to get there safely...should we find the need. Now...there are twenty-seven more. How...are we ever going to be able to remember...nine plus sixteen plus twenty-seven...which equals *fifty-two*! Very soon...there could be even more."

Hadathoo smiled. He cleared his throat. "To all Owlamites, everywhere...from this day forth...whenever you are given a new imagery...to a new dimension...you will take each one to heart and you will memorize them. You will NOT forget them. We have our original nine and that was easy. Sixteen were there that we knew of and did not use...now an additional twenty-seven. It will be done! Memorize them all and never forget them." He cleared his throat again. "And that includes me."

Shyshee sat there staring with her eyes wide open. She turned only her eyes to Hadathoo and smiled weakly. She cleared her throat and leaned back in her chair.

Hadathoo chuckled. He looked down at the list. "Who is first?"

Wymini snickered. "Since it is Team 7016 that has seventeen new dimensions to show…we decided to get them out of the way first. Not to mention the fact that…Officer, Bonarain is on that Team and can make it all clear…for everyone else."

Hadathoo nodded. "Sounds good. Bring in Team 7016."

Yoytay ushered them in.

Soolchakan bowed his head slightly. "Sirs, I am here to report to you that I personally have discovered five new dimensions. The first one…we can only see outer space. There is no star system…within thirty-three light years of our position."

Antrong frowned. "What is the advantage of this one?"

Soolchakan smiled. "Because, if you are in one of the space ships…and have to run from…oh say another space ship… this one is easier to reach than Beasties."

Antrong nodded politely.

"Begin," said Hadathoo with a smile.

Soolchakan started sending the imagery. The members of the Command Staff received it and also sent it to all other Owlamites. The scout ship was hopped to the new dimension.

Hadathoo looked up at the view-screen. "I don't see anything different...that should tell us that we're in a different dimension."

Officer Grade 3, Sankiki of Team 254 interjected. "We do have proof, Sir. If you look at the monitor...to the side of the main view-screen, it shows a...frequency that is being recorded here."

Hadathoo shook his head. "Which means...what?"

She smiled. "Each different dimension has its own frequency. When we go to a different one...that frequency is registered in the computer. The computer also starts mapping all of the stars that can be seen...within 200 light years."

Antrong frowned. "Is 200 light years the limit of the computer?"

"No, Sir, we're just limiting it now...because there are billions, possibly trillions, of stars in each dimension...for the most part...and that would take up an incredible amount of space on the hard drive. Unless you want to do a full exploration of each dimension...it's best to hold it to 200 light years."

"Excellent point," said Hadathoo emphatically. "Now...is there anything more to see in this dimension...at this time?"

Sankiki aimed the pointer at a specific star. "That one there...is the closest one to us. It is 33 light years away."

"So we call this dimension...*Soolchakan 1*," said Hadathoo. He sniffed. "Did you have more...than one?"

"Yes, Sir," said Soolchakan. "The next one has a star

system…that's very close."

"Oh, good," said Hadathoo happily. "We get to see something other than stars in the far distance."

Sankiki raised her hand slightly. "Sir, if you keep your eyes on that monitor, you'll see how the frequency changes when we…hop."

Hadathoo nodded. "Sounds good." He turned to Soolchakan. "The…imagery?"

Soolchakan started concentrating again. The new imagery was sent to all and distributed.

Hadathoo watched the monitor and raised his eyebrows slightly as the wiggly lines on the monitor abruptly changed in a radical manner. He looked up at the main view-screen. "Where's this…star system?"

Sankiki smiled. "Sir, we have to move the nose of the ship…down 47 degrees and slightly to port in order to see it." She turned to her other Team members and signaled them to change the angle they were viewing."

The star system came into view on the screen.

"Oh, lovely," said Hoynama. "What all do we have here… and how long would it take to get there?"

Soolchakan cleared his throat. "According to all of the information the computer can give us, if we use the light speed capabilities of this ship…at the slowest of the light speeds, it would take about a quarter of a day to get there. According to long range scanners, the system has eight planets. Not one of them is inhabitable, but, there is a wealth of raw minerals…should we need to obtain them."

Hadathoo nodded. "So…dimension…*Soolchakan 2*…has no life of any type, but we could get raw ore…if we need or want it."

"At any time, Sir," said Soolchakan with a smile.

Hadathoo nodded. "Do you have another one?"

"Yes, Sir," said Soolchakan. He closed his eyes and started sending the imagery.

Hadathoo's shoulders sagged and his mouth fell open. "We are looking at…infinity times a million." He scoffed. "Each dimension…is a new universe…that stretches on into infinity. The amount of outer space…out there…is…unbelievable."

Soolchakan smiled. "Yes, Sir, it is. This particular dimension…I guess you'll be calling *Soolchakan 3*…the closest star system in this one is nineteen light years away."

Hadathoo nodded. "Anything else special here?"

"No, Sir," said Soolchakan.

Hadathoo nodded again. "Next!"

Soolchakan sent the imagery. "This one…*Soolchakan 4*… the closest star system is 56 light years away."

Till snickered. "Not very neighborly are they?"

The entire Command Staff chuckled.

Soolchakan cleared his throat. "The next one...I guess we're calling it: *Soolchakan 5*, is harder than Kiymee's Search. It's not as hard as Naka's Search...but it is hard." He closed his eyes and sent the imagery.

Several of the Staff sat there rubbing their foreheads after the hop.

"That could be a brain-buster," said Deelka. "Is there any use in this one?"

Sankiki pointed out two star systems. "These two systems are approximately seventeen light years away."

Hadathoo frowned at her. "How much difference in time... to get to each one?"

She smiled. "According to the computer...if we headed for either one at the maximum light speed...the difference is negligible."

Hadathoo looked at Soolchakan. "Any more...from you?"

"No, Sir," said Soolchakan with a smile. "Those are the five that I discovered. Now, it's Bonarain's turn."

Bonarain stepped forward smiling.

Hadathoo looked at her sternly. "Do you have any dimension that's gonna give us a brain cramp like *Soolchakan 5*?"

Bonarain giggled. "No, Sir. I've discovered four...and none of them are a brain cramp...like *Soolchakan 5*."

Hadathoo chuckled. "Hallelujah! I still want a mug of

kwatha before we continue."

Yoytay had to get the rest of Team 24 to serve everyone mugs of kwatha before they could continue.

Bonarain finally got the chance and started sending the imagery for *Bonarain 1*.

Hadathoo let out a sigh with a smile. "That one was easy. It seemed easier than *Soolchakan 1*."

Bonarain chuckled. "No, Sir, it is…slightly harder than *Soolchakan 1*…but not much harder."

Sankiki pointed to a star. "That one is the closest in this dimension. It's 41 light years away."

Hadathoo nodded. "Anything else here?"

"No, Sir," said Bonarain.

"Next!"

Sankiki pointed to a star. "*Bonarain 2* is another one where the closest star is 16 light years away."

Sankiki pointed to a star. "*Bonarain 3* is another one where the closest star is 85 light years away."

"*Bonarain 4* has a star system that is very close," said Sankiki. "There are eleven planets and one is inhabitable. The inhabitable planet has vegetation, water, reptiles, amphibians, fish, mollusks and insects.

Hadathoo looked around. "Next?"

Kiyalee walked up smiling. "I found five more…no brain busters."

Hadathoo smiled. "Good."

"*Kiyalee 1* has a close star system…just two planets that are nothing but rock," Said Sankiki.

Sankiki pointed to a star. "*Kiyalee 2* is another one where the closest star is 25 light years away."

Sankiki pointed to a star. "*Kiyalee 3* is another one where the closest star is 36 light years away."

Sankiki pointed to a star. "*Kiyalee 4* is another one where the closest star is 44 light years away."

"*Kiyalee 5* has a close star system," said Sankiki. "There are ten planets. One is slightly inhabitable…if you don't mind extremely hot weather. This planet is about 800,000 kilotaja closer to the star and as a result…the temperatures are much hotter than here. The equatorial area is intolerable…unless you're there at night. All we've found so far…is vegetation."

Chyning stepped forward. "I found three dimensions."

Sankiki had her Team change the pitch of the ship. The view-screen showed a very large dark planet. "This planet…here in *Chyning 1*…is a rogue dead planet. It is 29 light years away from any star. It appears to have some liquid on it, but we can't tell what it is because…all of it is frozen solid and…not being anywhere near any star, it will remain that way for…a very long time.

Sankiki pointed to a star. "*Chyning 2* is another one where the closest star is 38 light years away."

Chyning giggled. "Get ready for a major brain cramp." She started sending the imagery.

Almost everyone in the room groaned or moaned and went limp in their chairs.

She giggled again. "This one…*Chyning 3*…is even harder than Yoyee's Search."

Antrong looked up. "Really?" he said sarcastically. "I would've never guessed."

Beemella and Deelka just gave her a nasty look and grunted.

Sankiki pointed to a star. "*Chyning 3* is another one where the closest star is 46 light years away."

Hadathoo shook his head. "Do we have any more…brain busters like…*Chyning 3* coming up?"

Sankiki chuckled. "No, Sir. The toughest one left…was found by Officer Grade 7, Eematoss of Team 6559. The one she found is a little less tough than Chaya's Search."

Hadathoo shook his head again. "No more today. After that…slap in the head from *Chyning 3*…I think we could all use a little rest…before we take on the other ten dimensions. We're adjourned until tomorrow."

Hadathoo called the meeting to order, with the other personnel who had discovered a new dimension. "We'll go in Team number order. So…who is first?"

A man stepped forward. "I'm Officer Grade 4, Bodge, of Team 90. I discovered a new dimension that has a star system close by."

"All right," said Hadathoo with a nod. "Give us some imagery."

Bodge started sending. All of the people on the scout ship watched the view-screen.

Hoynama frowned. "Where's this star system?"

Sankiki turned to her Team member. "Turn 110 degrees to port."

As the ship completed the turn, the star system came into view.

Sankiki pointed to a planet. "This is the outer most planet of this system. There are eleven planets in this system and two of them might be inhabitable. We haven't done enough research on them to be able to tell yet."

Hadathoo nodded. "Okay, *Bodge 1* has possibilities. Anything else about this dimension?"

"No, Sir," said Sankiki. "Other than this system, the closest one is 37 light years away."

"All right," said Hadathoo. "Who is next?"

A woman stepped up. "I'm Nurse Neeleekee of Team 255. I discovered another dimension with a system that's even closer."

Hadathoo shook his head and chuckled. "I wonder if the Algothon knew what that abominable thing would do to us... would they have launched? We have so many new things we're finding and the Algothons got nothing."

Everyone in the room pondered that thought in their own way.

Hadathoo smiled. "The imagery, please."

Neeleekee closed her eyes and started sending.

Sankiki walked up to the view-screen. "As you can see, we are in the middle of this system. It consists of sixteen planets. The fifth planet is inhabited, by a sentient species...and they have the capability of space travel." She pointed to a moving object. "That is one of their larger freight carrying vessels. It's even larger than *Owlam the First*."

Hadathoo nodded. "So for the current time...we leave them alone and that way we avoid any conflict with them."

Antrong frowned. "Should we try to contact them?"

Hadathoo clenched his teeth in thought. He shook his head with a worried look. "I don't like the idea of having to explain... to someone else that we have this dimension shifting talent. If those people are...war like...they may try to exploit us. Observe first – then act...one way or another."

Till nodded. "I agree. We have no idea what they might

do."

Hadathoo cleared his throat. "That's *Neeleekee 1*. What's next?"

Another woman stepped forward. "I'm Officer Grade 7, Avana of Team 476. I'm afraid that there's nothing special about the dimension that I discovered."'

Hadathoo shrugged. "Nevertheless, send us the imagery."

Avana closed her eyes and sent.

Sankiki pointed to a star. "This is the closest system in *Avana 1*. It is 22 light years away."

Hadathoo nodded. "Who's next?"

A man stepped forward. "I am Officer Grade 4, Bonlosk of Team 519. Mine is a little different. We had to get into the Jowfoonda archives to even find a name for this situation. They called it a nebula." He started sending the imagery.

Several of the Staff grunted as they had to work a little harder with this one than they had with the first three.

Hoynama gasped. "What…is that?"

Sankiki smiled. "It is nothing more than a great deal of space dust or haze. It's quite colorful, but has no useful purpose… other than being used as a navigational guide."

Deelka snickered. "How could you use…a cloud…as a guide?"

"Because it really doesn't alter that much," said Sankiki.

"You know where it is and that helps you determine where you are…in relation to the nebula." She smiled. "Other than that, the closest system in *Bonlosk 1*, is 29 light years away."

Hadathoo frowned. "Why haven't we seen…any other nebulas…before?"

"We haven't looked at them, Sir," said Sankiki. "There are many others…in several of the known and newly discovered dimensions. The difference here…we hopped right into the middle of this one."

Hadathoo chuckled. "Interesting!" He sighed. "Who's next?"

A woman came forward. "I'm Officer Grade 5, Amtosha of Team 1007. Here is my imagery." She closed her eyes.

Hadathoo scoffed. "That one is almost effortless… especially after that last one."

Sankiki chuckled. "Yes, Sir. This one, *Amtosha 1*, has a nebula off to the right, as you can see. That nebula is rather close…comparatively speaking. The closest system here is 35 light years away."

Antrong snickered. "Proof positive that there are other nebulas."

Hadathoo smiled. "Yes, we now have visual evidence of that…for all. Next?"

Another woman came forward. "My name is Officer Grade 7, Unmeena of Team 2821. I wish I had something special to report…but I don't. Here's the imagery."

Sankiki pointed to a star. "This is the closest system in *Unmeena 1*. It's 49 light years away."

The next to come forward was a man. "I am Officer Grade 6, Zhorgon of Team 3779. My discovery is very easy to get to." He sent the imagery.

"That was rather easy," said Hadathoo. He frowned. "The screen…looks a little fuller…than the other dimensions."

"Yes, Sir," said Sankiki. "This dimension has a lot of stars that are within 200 light years. Unfortunately, the closest one, in *Zhorgon 1*, is 16 light years away."

Hadathoo nodded. "Next?"

A woman stepped up. "I'm Officer Grade 7, Siysay, also of Team 3779. My dimension has a system that's close." She sent the imagery.

Sankiki had her Team turn the ship. "This system, in *Siysay 1*, has eleven planets. There are three…that are possibly inhabitable, but, we're going to have to do some close checking on them to make sure."

A woman came forward. "I am Officer Grade 6, Lawsing of Team 4079. I've discovered another dimension that has a close star system." She sent the imagery.

Again, Sankiki had the ship turned. "Here's the system in *Lawsing 1*. It has nine planets…four of which are immense. So far, we haven't seen anything that is inhabitable."

Hadathoo nodded. "How many are left?"

"Just one," said Sankiki with a grin. "But get ready."

Hadathoo narrowed his eyes. "For what?"

A woman stepped forward. "I'm Officer Grade 7 Eematoss of Team 6559. The dimension that I've discovered…is a brain cramp to get to. It also has something that we never expected to see…but it's there." She closed her eyes and started sending.

Hadathoo shook his head. "Okay it was a jolt. It's not as hard as Desert or Ghost though. Now…what's so unique?"

Sankiki chuckled. "First of all, the closest star in *Eematoss 1*, is an incredibly large star. It's not near as big as the one in Jahong's Death, but it is…*big*! It's so big that there are forty-one planets orbiting it…and…" She pointed to a spot on the screen. "…you can see a smaller star is orbiting this larger one."

Numerous jaws and shoulders dropped.

Sankiki turned to the Staff with a smile. "The smaller star…that is in orbit…is just a little bit larger than *our* star." She looked back at the screen. "There are possibly two inhabitable planets in this system."

Hadathoo shook his head and smiled. "The possibilities are endless…so far."

Sankiki smiled. "And growing. I've heard rumors…from a few others that they're looking for other dimensions. Some say they…might have found something. We now have fifty-two dimensions…and it could easily grow."

Till chuckled. "Infinity times a million."

Hadathoo grunted in agreement, then chuckled. "Infinity times *infinity*!"

Antrong was chewing on something as he looked around the conference table. "We can't keep putting it off. One of these days, we're going to have to give the people...the citizens of Paselter, a firm answer. Are we going to join, and give away all of our secrets, or are we going to run to the gorge and hide for who knows how long?"

Beemella scoffed. "What's to stop the people of High Country, in South Chilamte, from demanding that we join them?"

"They still don't know that we're there," said Yamananee. "We've kept it a good secret and we're the only ones who've gone down inside that gorge."

Till was drumming his fingers. "Someone tried to build a bridge across the gorge, near where we live. We made them give up when we kept collapsing the thing. They went somewhere else to build their bridge."

"Far away from us," chuckled Hoynama.

Shyshee sniffed. "If we disappear, who is going to continue making *Tuzine* for the world? If we disappear and then suddenly reappear in a century or two, they might be a little upset over not having the wonder drug."

Hadathoo sighed. "The only way to disappear and not have

anyone look for us, is to give the secret of the *Tuzine* to somebody else."

"Who," said Wymini with a furtive glance?

"I suggest the Kalash," said Hadathoo.

Beemella looked around. "Anyone else got a suggestion? Or do we go with that?"

There was a long silence as everyone pondered. To give up the *Tuzine* was a big enough decision. The new anti-virus medications that the doctors had found might have to go with it.

Hadathoo sighed. "Let's go home and think on it for a day or two. Consider any alternatives and then we'll come back and make a decision. I don't want this to be a quick do-it-now thing. I want everyone to think about it. See if there is a better suggestion somewhere in our minds."

They all departed silently.

Two days later they reconvened. There was a rather melancholy attitude at the conference table.

Hadathoo sniffed. "Rather than telling anyone to do it, I'm going to ask for a vote. We'll vote on the idea of giving the secret of the *Tuzine* to a friend. We'll also vote on disappearing." He swallowed hard. "Does anyone wish to discuss either issue before we vote?"

Antrong cleared his throat. "Let's just vote and see if there is any impasse."

Hadathoo nodded in agreement. "All those who vote to give the *Tuzine* to an ally, raise your hand."

Eight hands went up. Beemella sat there sadly staring down at her clasped hands.

Hadathoo sighed. "Do you have a problem, Beemella?"

Beemella looked up. "For centuries we've protected this precious secret. Now, we're just going to…give it away." She wiped a tear from her cheek. "Can we put a stipulation on it…that if anyone lets the Teltermak know the secret…we'll come back and strike with a vengeance?"

"I think we can do that," said Hadathoo softly. "I think… we'll also tell them why we don't want the Teltermak to get the secret."

All of the Staff nodded in agreement.

"To the other issue," said Hadathoo. "All who vote to do a permanent move to the gorge…by all…raise your hand."

Eight hands went up. Shyshee looked around a little perturbed. She huffed and raised her hand.

Hadathoo shook his head looking somewhat frustrated. "Is there a problem?"

Shyshee glanced around at all the other faces. "All of the centuries that Owlamites have fought to keep our city and now we're just gonna leave. It seems like we've been totally defeated."

"Not really," said Deelka with a smile. "We still have an entire city here. It's just hidden in Spy dimension. You can come back here…any time and be nostalgic."

Shyshee huffed. "You're right. I should be thinking… about all of us. Protect all of us in any way that we can."

"So it is settled," said Hadathoo. "Before we make the final Jump to the gorge…is there any more business that we should take care of today?"

Wymini chuckled. "Would you believe that…Team 7016 has reported finding six more dimensions? They'd like to give us the information."

Hadathoo hung his head. He shook his head and started laughing. He looked up. "Why not? Bring em in."

Sankiki pointed to a star. "*Soolchakan 6* is another one where the closest star is 29 light years away."

Sankiki pointed to a system. "*Soolchakan 7* has a star system close by that has eight planets. One of them is possibly inhabitable."

Sankiki pointed to a star. "*Bonarain 5* is another one where the closest star is 44 light years away."

Sankiki pointed to a star. "*Chyning 4* is another one where the closest star is 36 light years away."

Sankiki pointed to a star. "*Chyning 5* is another one where the closest star is 33 light years away."

Sankiki pointed to a star. "*Chyning 6* is another one where the closest star is 103 light years away."

Hadathoo looked at the new information. "Is there anything else?"

Till raised a hand. "Yes, Sir. All of this time…we've been looking at and for other dimensions. What's wrong with looking at our own? We have the Jow…uh… *Owlam the First*. Why don't we go take a look at some of our own planets? Let's see if there's something in this system we can utilize. We still have the Jowfoonda archives and they took a look at the planets. Why not us? We, at least, live here."

Hadathoo smiled. "Why don't you take care of that then, Officer, Till?"

"I'd love to," said Till. "Just as long as I get to take our specialists at discovery with me…Team 7016."

Soolchakan shrugged. "I don't have a problem with that. I've been a little curious about some of the other planets as well. This'll give us a chance to give all of them a good look over and see what's really there."

"Sounds good," said Bonarain.

Kiyalee sighed. She gave Soolchakan and Bonarain a dirty look. She shrugged. "Why not?"

Chyning stood there akimbo. "I'll go…as long as the kwatha is made from the real stuff."

Till smiled. "I'd like to take a few of the computer and physics Teams with me as well."

"By all means," said Hadathoo. He stood up. "Let's inform every one of the move. I'll take care of…the gift of *Tuzine* to the Kalash, myself."

Hadathoo hopped into Spy and then Jumped into the office of the First Leader of the Kalash. He stood there waiting until the business at hand was concluded. Dynolok of the Great Wall sat down at his desk, after shooing all of the others from the meeting out. He leaned back in his chair and took several deep, controlled breaths. He closed his eyes. At that moment, Hadathoo hopped back into Home dimension.

"Good afternoon," said Hadathoo quietly.

Dynolok nearly jumped out of his boots. He was sitting in his chair looking up at Hadathoo in shock. "I…didn't hear…you being announced."

Hadathoo shook his head sadly. "I wasn't announced. I snuck in. I wanted to talk to you in private…about a certain matter."

Dynolok looked suspicious. "What is so private – between us – that you had to sneak in?"

"It's about that unification. We Owlamites are just…not joiners. As friendly as the Kalash and others on this continent have been…we just cannot give up our independence."

"Then you'd stand alone in any battle."

"We've been alone for centuries."

"This'll hurt your trade. We, and others, who are citizens of Paselter might not let people of other lands in to trade for *Tuzine*. This could cause all kinds of problems for us."

Hadathoo nodded sadly. "That is why we're going to give up the *Tuzine* and leave."

Dynolok stood up. "You can't stop making the drug! Too many peoples depend on it. What do you think that people are going to say about you if you just…quit?"

Hadathoo placed a small binder on Dynolok's desk. "That is why we're going to give the secret of *Tuzine*…to the Kalash."

Dynolok fell back into his seat with his eyes and mouth wide open. Hadathoo calmly laid the binder on the desk and pushed it closer to Dynolok. He sat there trying to say something, however, nothing came out.

Hadathoo took a step back. "It's all in there. Everything you need to know about the plants and herbs used to make the drug. The only stipulation that we have on it…don't ever let the Teltermak know the secret of manufacturing *Tuzine*. They want to have complete control of it. Don't let them know anything."

Dynolok picked up the binder and opened it. He read the ingredients. "That's why it was so elusive!" He chuckled. "Only certain parts of the plants are used."

"Yes," said Hadathoo softly. "Using other parts of the plants destroys the drug."

Dynolok turned a few more pages. "What's this…I can't even try to pronounce it?"

Hadathoo chuckled. "I can't pronounce it either. The doctors said it very carefully several times. I still don't know what they said."

Dynolok nodded. "Okay…so what is it?"

"What *Tuzine* is to bacteria, that drug has the same healing quality against any virus."

Dynolok's jaw fell open again. "An…antivirus…that's just as powerful as *Tuzine*?"

Hadathoo nodded and smiled.

"And…you're giving it to us?"

"Yes."

"For…what?"

"Because of your friendship. We're leaving so that we won't be a burden to you or any of the citizens of Paselter. People are used to coming here for the *Tuzine* so we see no reason to make anyone change that habit. So we will say…goodbye…and just disappear."

"But you don't have to do that." Dynolok looked around as if he wanted to say something to change Hadathoo's mind. He looked down at the binder, flipping a few pages as he did.

While Dynolok's mind was on the binder, Hadathoo simply hopped to Spy.

Dynolok looked up and opened his mouth. His expression went to something dull normal as he looked around in stunned surprise. He called out to Hadathoo several times and walked around in the office trying to find his visitor. He spun around in one place several times, making all kinds of strange huffing noises. He grunted and walked to the door of the office. He swung the door open and looked at the four Aides in the reception area. "Where'd he go?"

The two men and two women all stood up looking very confused.

One of the women finally conjure up enough courage to speak. "Where did…who go…Sir?"

Dynolok clenched his teeth. "Hadathoo…the leader of the Owlamites! He was just in my office."

One of the men shrugged. "He didn't come through here, Sir. Neither coming nor going."

Dynolok looked at all of the faces and saw nothing but the same confusion that he was feeling. He looked down at the small binder in his hand. He opened it and flipped through the pages again. He looked back up at the four confused Aides. "Someone… call the chemists…and the doctors. I have something here…I'd like to have them look at."

One of the women picked up a communicator and started punching a code in on it.

Dynolok went back to his office feeling rather confused and somewhat ill at ease. How had that man entered this office – and exited – without any of those four seeing him? Very strange… very irritating. Maybe that rumor about teleporting was true… maybe.

10

Many of the Owlamites were rather perturbed at having to give up the city of Owlam, the *Tuzine* and the newly discovered antivirus medications. They accepted it. One, because the *Voice of Power* had ordered it. Two, all realized that the dimension shifting and the mind reading capability could cause them no end of grief from friend and foe alike. Until further notice, they would live all of their lives in the gorge.

The only explorations that were going to be allowed, at first, would be to find out about their own solar system. The computers in the Jowfoonda archives were a wealth of information, however, there were a few things in there they wanted to see in order to believe what was written there.

For any of the Owlamites who were feeling any fear of traveling in space to the other planets, they found that in the Jump dimension, distance really did not mean a thing. If they were on the ship and it was orbiting a planet over one hundred million kilotaja away, they could still Jump back to their apartment and then back to the ship without any problems.

The first thing they did was go to the inner planets. Malitay was closest to their sun Holgotho. It was a planet that had nothing on it that they could see they needed. Not only that, it was so close to Holgotho that the surface temperature, even on the back side of the planet was incredibly hot. The only thing they thought they might possibly need from here was lead. There was lead, in liquid form, all over the place on the side that faced Holgotho.

Krog was not much better. It was cooler, but not by much. It was just a great big round rock.

Olotoosh was different than the other two in that it had a satellite. The small moon was nothing but a crater scarred rock. There was nothing there other than rock and dirt. The planet had several types of liquids flowing around, however they were all toxic and useless.

Next, of course was home – Hardooth. The only thing that was any form of a mystery to them was their moons. They explored the larger moon, Zhagool, first. It appeared to be just about the same thing as the moon orbiting Olotoosh. The only difference was that it was about 8,500 kilotaja larger in circumference. The smaller moon, Niygool was also larger than the Olotoosh moon, however not by much.

Both moons were a bit of a disappointment, until someone noticed that there was some kind of building on the back side of Zhagool. A close inspection of this building showed it was a structure that had been placed there by the Jowfoonda. There were currently six of the bug-faced creatures, still alive, who were trying desperately to repair their communication devices and get in touch with anyone outside of this star system. The structure, as a whole, was hopped into Jahong's Death and no one thought anything more about it.

The next planet out was Bygloto. It had one moon as well.

It was another planet that had large areas of liquids that were all toxic. The moon was not any different than the moon orbiting Olotoosh.

When they got to Chabayo, they were all gawking, open mouthed, in awe. When they read the Jowfoonda entries on the planet and saw the term: Gas Giant, it meant nothing – until they actually saw the planet. The size alone was awesome. The fact that there were 49 satellites orbiting the big giant was another thing that made them drop their jaws. They could not take their eyes off of the big cloud of gas surrounding – who knows what? The northern hemisphere was several different shades of green. The southern hemisphere had some yellow stripes and some red stripes. Even though the giant was spinning eight times faster than Hardooth in its rotation the colors never merged, even though it was nothing but gas. They could not really understand how or why, the colors never merged. They stayed constant in their part of the huge gas cloud.

As they looked at all of the data that was coming in, they found that there were actually four of the satellite planets that were large enough they had an atmosphere. The sensors showed that all four had a rather toxic environment (not to mention that they were extremely cold), so there was no point in making any further attempt at exploring them.

Two of the smaller moons were being constantly pulled about by the gravity of the giant and the gravity of the other moons. As a result, the crust of these two smaller moons was being cracked and corrupted in many ways and there were volcanic eruptions all over those two moons.

In the same orbit as Chabayo, there were the running twins – Ragath and Rogoth. These two planets were on the other side of the star. In order to get to them quickly, they had to fly north of their star system until the ship would allow star speed. What could have taken over 160 days at regular maximum drive, was turned into less than a quarter of one day by doing the northern arc.

They first went to Ragath, the one being chased. Again they were staring at another gas giant. This one was different shades of yellow from top to bottom, with the exception of a dark blue band at the equator. Again, this planet rotated eight times faster than Hardooth. This giant had only twelve moons. Only one was large enough to have an atmosphere and it had an equator that was 16,510 kilotaja in circumference. None of the other eleven had a circumference greater than 9,000 kilotaja.

After confirming all of the Jowfoonda data, they headed for the chaser: Rogoth. They were all a little skeptical about some of the data that had been gathered on this gas giant – 452 moons? That sounded absolutely ridiculous. They should be slamming into each other and creating all kinds of havoc in their orbits. Once they arrived at Rogoth, they saw that the information was true. There were 452 orbiting satellites. The main reason that they were *not* slamming into each other was because of some kind of orderly orbiting around the gas giant. All of the ones that were close were flying around so fast that you could see them move. They were orbiting the giant at least three times per day and all staying in their set orbit. The ones that were further away from the planet were moving slower and were staying in their orbits as well. Not one of the satellites was over 7,000 kilotaja at the equator.

This gas giant was different shades of blue. At the top it was dark. As you looked further south, the blue shades became lighter until the south pole was almost the same color as the Hardooth sky on a clear day. This one rotated over nine times faster than Hardooth.

Onward to the next orbital path where there were two more gas giants. They went to Dilhazass first. This was another one that rotated about eight times faster than Hardooth. It had bands of different widths from top to bottom. They were either blue, red or yellow. Again they did not mix.

This one had 16 moons. Fifteen of them had an atmosphere, however not much of one. All were toxic, containing mainly ammonia, carbon dioxide and methane. The sixteenth moon was in a very erratic orbit as it was being pulled around by the giant and all fifteen of the other satellites. Miraculously, somehow, it never hit anything.

They did another arc upwards in order to get to the other gas giant in the seventh orbital path. Weeloow was the last giant they had to survey. It was almost identical to Dilhazass in coloration of the bands. This one had 31 orbiting satellites and there was nothing very striking about any of them.

The next planet was Makatindi. This planet was very boring, considering the colorations they had seen on the five gas giants. The only thing that they found fascinating about this planet was the fact that there were numerous rivers of liquid nitrogen all over the planet. The moons looked very much like Zhagool and

Niygool – nothing special at all.

The next planet was Bri. Here the sensors went crazy in the evaluations of the mineral wealth of this very large planet.

Till sat in the command seat frowning at what he was seeing. "What is molybdenum?"

One of the members of the physicist Teams, Officer Grade 5, Azza, was looking over the data. She turned to him. "Sir, that's one of several kinds of steel."

Till nodded. "All right, and what is that tungsten?"

"That's another form of steel. Both of them are good kinds of steel."

Till cleared his throat as he looked over the list. "Is that… platinum…is that another kind of steel?"

"No, Sir," said Officer Grade 6, Yoodyoom. He was looking at another list of different types of minerals. "Platinum is probably the highest quality of the precious metals."

Till was taken aback. "What's so flaming precious about it?"

Yoodyoom put his list down. "When we use metals to make our electronic wiring, the better the metal, the better the current and the better the electronically controlled machine runs. Copper works fine, silver is better, gold works even better than that. Platinum tops them all."

Till sat there nodding. "Do we use platinum in any of our electronic toys?"

Officer Grade 3, Hodrock chuckled. "We've been looking at the Jowfoonda archives and according to what they discovered – in this system – virtually all of the platinum is on Bri. According to what they found on Hardooth, there isn't enough platinum to make a ball the size of your fist…on the entire planet. Here on Bri, as you can see, there's a vein of the mineral that could improve all of our equipment…if we take some of it back with us and smelt it into wires."

Till shrugged. "So let's get a big sample of it and take it back home."

Officer Grade 7, Queequima shook her head. "Sir, we're on one of the scout ships. We can't get a sufficient amount on this ship. It doesn't have the storage capacity of the mother ship. We need to get the mother ship out here if we plan to get a decent amount of platinum."

Till leaned back in the chair. "Fine. Let's get…some kind of sample right now, so we have something to show for this expedition and get someone working on improving our equipment."

Queequima looked pale. "How…would we do that, Sir?"

Soolchakan chuckled. "We've got those space suits. All we need to do is put one on, go into Ghost, get down there on the planet and snatch some of it out…and Jump back here to the ship. It's not that big of a problem."

Till smiled at Soolchakan. "Go ahead."

Chyning sat there giggling when she heard that.

Soolchakan looked at her and cleared his throat. "I think that we'll get a much better amount if two of us go."

Chyning stopped giggling and stuck her tongue out at Soolchakan.

The two of them got into space suits, Jumped down to the surface of the planet and went into Ghost. They were given mental communication as to where to go to find the purest part of the vein. Both of them grabbed two fistfuls and then Jumped back to the ship. Once back on the ship, the specimens had to be left alone for a while. They had been inside the planet for countless eons and were extremely cold.

Till looked at the four specimens. He turned back to the physicists who were looking at their consoles. "Are we about finished cataloging all of the minerals?"

Queequima shrugged without looking back. "The Jowfoonda did all of that. We're just confirming it. We've got all of the cataloging that we need…including the fact that the larger moon has a few very good veins of mineral ore as well."

Till raised his eyebrows. "What about the small moon?"

"It's just a big round rock," said Queequima."

Till nodded. "Then let's go find Afkoth."

The planet in the tenth orbit was useless unless you wanted a virtually unending supply of sulfur, frozen methane or frozen ammonia. The five moons had nothing that was useful either.

The last planet, Denhahbon, was way out. They could

barely see Holgotho on the monitor from where they were currently located. Denhahbon was nothing but one great ball of frozen toxic liquids with 250 large chunks of debris orbiting it. There were no moons at all.

Till shook his head. "The only use for this planet would be…a sentinel out in space, watching for another intruder like the Jowfoonda. Of course that would only be useful if the intruder comes from the direction that Denhahbon currently happens to be located." He sighed. "Have we got everything cataloged and looked at?"

Officer Leader, Hrombisk shrugged. "It's not that exciting is it? The only planet that we found…a lot of use for was Bri."

Till nodded. "At least we found something. Let's get back to Hardooth and I'll give the Command Staff a full briefing."

Hrombisk stretched. "Do you think that we'll find anything useful in any of the other dimensions that we've discovered so far?"

Till chuckled. "We already found some useful plants in forest. We brought some of those trees and plants here and re-vegetated our planet. Maybe we can find something else useful. You never know, until you try. It'd be nice to find something else we can use." He sighed. "In the meanwhile, let's get all of this data back to the Command Staff. I'm sure they'd like to know some of this."

"Especially the platinum," said Hrombisk.

Hadathoo looked over the list. "Malitay has an abundance of lead. Have we ever been short of lead?" He looked around the table.

"There were a few stories," said Antrong. "But those were from a long, long time ago. Ever since we developed the pulse weapons, we've never been lacking for lead. It's just never been that high a priority...to find another source."

Yamananee frowned. "Do we really need it?"

"It's always nice to know where things are...even if you don't need them," said Shyshee.

Hadathoo chuckled. "Yes, I like to know where things are." He looked back at the list. "Krog...is nothing but a great rock!"

Till shrugged. "If there are any usable minerals, they're too deep for the sensors to locate."

Antrong shook his head. "Olotoosh and Bygloto are covered with all kinds of toxic liquids. Not much use there. We always have the Teltermak if we want something toxic."

Everyone got a laugh out of that.

Hadathoo went back to the list. "Chabayo is a gas *giant*. Is it really that big?"

Till shook his head and shrugged. "Sir, you really have to see it to believe it. All five – Chabayo, Ragath, Rogoth, Dilhazass and Weeloow – all are giants and that's why they have so many satellites and none of them are really that crowded...even the 452 moons of Rogoth."

"This seems silly," said Hoynama. "The gas giants all seem to have the same colors – even though they're completely different planets."

"Not so silly," said Deelka. "Look at the colors. Mainly blue, red and yellow with an occasional green. Just your basic colors. All other colors are mixtures of the three basic, with green being one of the easiest colors to make by mixing blue and yellow."

Hoynama shook her head. "Why haven't they all mixed together, especially if they're whirling in their rotation at eight to nine times as fast as Hardooth? It seems to me they should have mixed a long time ago and all of them would be brown."

"Strange phenomenon that I can't explain," said Till.

Hadathoo chuckled. "Hoynama, if you're really that interested, why don't you start a study group to find out?"

She shook her head. "I'm not that interested, just fascinated and confused."

Hadathoo gave her a patronizing glance. "Okay, so Makatindi, Afkoth and Denhahbon are all useless. This thing about Bri though…a wealth of minerals that we could possibly use." He frowned. "This stuff – platinum. Are we sure that it could live up to what the Jowfoonda claim…in their reports?"

"We checked a lot of the components on the scout ship as we were coming back, Sir," said Hrombisk. "Many of their really highly sophisticated pieces of equipment do have platinum wiring in them."

Deelka perked up. "Why don't we have that Officer, Kiyalee start making some of this platinum wiring and see what it can do?"

Kiyalee clenched her teeth and fists when she heard that.

"No," said Hadathoo. "I think that someone else needs to be doing some of the work. After they've manufactured some wire, then give it to Kiyalee and others who are good with their hands and see if they can do something with it."

Kiyalee sighed, looked up and silently mouthed the words: Thank you.

Beemella looked at Hadathoo helplessly. "Like…who?"

Hadathoo smiled. "Teams 1150 and 1151, come to the Command Staff conference room immediately."

A few moments later, the two Teams were being ushered in to an already rather crowded conference room.

"Team 1150, introduce yourselves," said Hadathoo.

A woman stepped forward. "I'm Officer Grade 3, Andatam, Team Leader. I have here: Officer Grade 5, Sososkom, Officer Grade 6, Bithyati and Officer Grade 7, Okotami."

Hadathoo nodded. "Team 1151, introduce yourselves."

Another woman stepped forward. "I'm Officer Grade 3, Seequeta, Team Leader. My Team consists of: Officer Grade 5, Veedia, Officer Grade 6, Tongtom and Officer Grade 7, Issooa."

Hadathoo smiled. "Team 1150 and 1151, from this day

forward your primary interest will lie in manufacturing. If you need any guidance in this task, consult the Algothon archives. I'm sure that they have some kind of guidance in there. Once you've accomplished the task of turning this...platinum ore into useful wires, give that wiring to Officer, Kiyalee and see if she can do any more adjustments on our 459's with this platinum wiring that will make them even stronger." He leaned back clearing his throat. "Any questions?"

All of the members of 1150 and 1151 shook their heads.

"Good!" said Hadathoo with a smile. "You're dismissed to begin your new endeavor. Let's pray that it helps all of us."

Teams 1150 and 1151 simply vanished.

Hadathoo looked around. "Is there any other business that we should discuss at this time?"

Till smiled. "We've discovered a few new dimensions, Sir. We've been doing some exploring of our own star system, why shouldn't we do the same with the other dimensions?"

Hadathoo looked up pondering. "Only the ones that have a star system that's close by...at this time. I don't want our people being scattered all over some other dimension or dimensions. Ours is big enough at this time. Again - explore only those that are close by." He looked around the table. "Are there any objections to that, or suggestions?" He heard nothing. "All right, Officer, Till, you have your guidance."

Till smiled. "Thank you, Sir."

Bonarain looked at her Teammates. "Here we go again."

Chyning grunted. "Maybe we should move all of our possessions onto that scout ship number 4. We seem to be spending an inordinate amount of time there."

"No," said Kiyalee flatly. "They still don't have any decent kwatha on that ship…unless we supply it."

Soolchakan sighed. "So supply some kwatha…at least for us."

The expedition got started.

Till was looking at the list. "Which dimension is the first one with a close star system?" He looked around. "I don't care if we have a full report from that little expedition that Team 7016 took. I want to do a thorough scan of any close star system."

Officer Grade 4, Quonbaya, Team Leader for Science Team 214 checked the list. "Obviously, Sir, that would be *Kiyalee 1*. Other than Home, there're very few that're easier to get to and this one has a small star system with only two planets."

"All right," said Till. "Let's hop to that one."

Once they were in *Kiyalee 1*, they found the two planets very quickly. They established orbit around the planet furthest from the star and started scanning for anything that was down there on the planet.

Bonarain, meanwhile, was looking over the roster of personnel on this exploration mission. "Okay, we've got a

Command Team, two of the Physicist Teams and…Team 153?
What are they?"

Soolchakan looked at the list. "That's Officer Grade 3,
Eeleeg. He was the one who was constantly looking below the
surface and blowing up the Teltermak tunnels."

Bonarain nodded. "Okay, so he can blow up a tunnel. Big
deal."

"He can FIND tunnels," said Chyning.

Bonarain shrugged. "Well if they think he's needed…
what can I say?" She looked back at the list. "Team 196 –
they were one of the Teams that did a lot of experimenting with
plants. I guess their expertise could come in handy. Team 214
general sciences, Teams 221 and 222 Medical, Teams 256 and 257
computer operators, Team 989?" She looked up. "Isn't that one
of the Teams that we had to fight…for our home?"

Soolchakan snickered. "Team 989 are the fighting
specialists. Officer Grade 5, Honn is currently the top ranked
fighter in all of Owlam."

Kiyalee looked up. "But you knocked the *h'oolyach* out of
him…didn't you?"

Soolchakan chuckled. "Yes, and you beat the snot out of
Shaffani in that little melee."

Bonarain sighed. "Okay – fighters." She went back to the
list. "Team 1002 and 1003 computer repair personnel, Team 2002
is one of the shipwright Teams."

Chyning giggled. "Yeah! Team 2002 with Officer Moonta."

Kiyalee started looking around at everybody. "Has she ever been able to get over being seasick?"

Chyning was laughing harder. "No, she's over there…with a bucket in her lap and her face is the loveliest shade of green."

Bonarain grunted in disgust at Chyning. "That poor thing is in misery." She huffed. "I wouldn't call that shade of green lovely."

"Oh well," said Soolchakan. "For some reason she just can't get over her motion sickness."

Bonarain continued: "Team 2790 is…construction?" She shrugged. "Why not?" She shook her head. "Team 3784 is a bunch of architects. Then…there's just a bunch of Teams…that have no real specialty or designation."

Kiyalee looked slightly interested. "Like who?"

Bonarain frowned. "Teams 6005, 6015, 6112, 6177, 6489, 6863, 7011, 7012, 7013…and us."

Soolchakan grunted. "Workers! Just general laborers… until Hadathoo assigns us some specialty using the *Voice of Power*. Whatever the specialty Teams need help with, we're supposed to render assistance."

Kiyalee folded her arms across her chest. "Well I'm not fetching kwatha for anybody other than my Team. If they want that kind of laborer, they can do it themselves."

Soolchakan sighed. "Don't etch that statement in granite… yet."

After doing full scans on both planets in the star system, Till sat there looking disgusted. "Two huge planets…and there's nothing but rock!"

Officer Grade 4, Oona of the physicist Team 2495 shook her head. "Two planets that are larger at the equator than Hardooth by over 30,000 kilotaja and they have nothing to show for it. Yes, both planets are nothing but rock. They both have an atmosphere, but they consist of nothing but hydrogen, helium, nitrogen, carbon monoxide and carbon dioxide. If we ever need those gases, we'll know where to come to get them."

Till turned to Hrombisk. "What's the next one on the list?"

Hrombisk smiled. "That would be 'Beasties,' Sir."

"No point in going there, is there?"

Hrombisk smiled. "On the contrary – that initial exploration found that there were eight planets in that star system. When they did that speedy exploration, they didn't check any of the other planets. They did do a little bit more exploration of the 'Beasties' planet, but none of the others in the system."

Till nodded. "Okay, so we've got seven other planets in that system to look at."

"Yes, Sir."

"Let's hop!"

After four days of scanning the other seven planets, Till was sitting there looking disgusted again. "Planet number one…a big hot rock. Planet number two is also hot, has no liquids of any sort but it has a lot of dust storms and as a result we can't seem to find out what the mineral content is. Planet number three: Beasties itself. Planet number four is another dry arid, but cold, planet. Planet number five is a gas giant with thirty-five nondescript satellites. Planet number six is covered with…where the *chokwad* does all of this *ammonia* come from? A planet that's got an equator of 91,700 kilotaja and the only liquid that we can find on it is ammonia." He shook his head. "Planet number seven is covered with liquid nitrogen, liquid methane and…surprise, surprise, frozen ammonia. Planet eight is another big rock covered with frozen ammonia." He dropped the list. "What's next?"

Oona looked up. "Sir, that would be what we called the Water dimension. There is an inhabited planet among nine planets. Again, it was just a quick check and count on that system."

Till nodded. "Now, we go do a full check on that system… let's hop."

Planet number one was another one close to the star and could only be labeled with the "hot rock" designation.

They began their orbit around planet number 2. Till frowned as he looked at the warning going across the screen. "What's that warning all about?"

Oona made a strange sound as she looked it up. "According to readings on Hardooth, the atmospheric pressure at sea level…is 15. The reading on this planet is over 500. If we tried to go inside the atmosphere on this planet, we'd be crushed."

Till grunted. "Then I suggest we don't go inside the atmosphere of this thing. Can we get anything else other than that?"

"No, Sir," said Oona.

Till shrugged. "On to the next one."

After a full day of scanning the report was done. Planet #3 was a hot arid place that had no liquids, few minerals and dust storms with speeds over 1,000 kilotaja.

"What's the story on planet #4?"

Oona looked at her information. "It's what we originally called the Water Dimension. It is an inhabitable planet that has a sentient species. They have yet to discover electricity, so their ships are still controlled by the wind and they have nothing but antique machinery. The planet has one satellite…that is nothing but rock."

"Okay," said Till. "On to the next one."

Planet number 5 was a gas giant with 16 satellites.

Till frowned as he looked at the view-screen. "Why is this…planet…flat on the top and bottom…and bulging in the middle?"

Oona snickered. "It's because of the speed. They all seem to rotate at such a fantastic speed…this one rotates 6.5 times faster than Hardooth. Seeing as how it's moving so much faster and the radius of the planet is about 40,000 kilotaja longer, the outer gases have to move at incredible speeds. Otherwise…it would be round."

Till nodded. "Is there anything special about any of its moons?"

"No, Sir, nothing."

"Okay, on to the next planet."

As they approached the planet, everyone was looking at it in wonder.

Till was the first one to ask. "What…is that phenomenon?"

"The Jowfoonda called it…*rings*, Sir," said Oona while she was still transfixed on the sight. "It is…multi-billions of…small objects that are…circling the gas giant…in perfect formation."

Till chuckled. "Perfect…and perfectly beautiful."

"It also has 12 satellites," said Oona.

Till scoffed. "Who cares? Those…*rings*…I just don't…" He trailed off with his mouth hanging open. He had a look of child-like wonder in his eyes.

Oona looked up at Till and snickered. "There's nothing else here of interest. Shall we go on to the next planet?"

Till sighed. "Might as well. I doubt if we'll find anything… quite as amazing as those rings though."

Bonarain turned to Soolchakan. "Do you remember seeing anything like those rings?"

Soolchakan simply shook his head.

Planet #7 was a very large planet with a strong gravitational pull. The only thing that they could find here was that it had a toxic atmosphere.

Planet #8 was another gas giant with 15 satellites.

Planet #9 was unlike other planets in that it was not completely round. It looked as if a huge portion of the northern hemisphere had been somehow cut away. The only satellites here were several hundred asteroids.

Till stretched. "What's our next hop?"

Oona looked at her list. "That would be *Soolchakan 7*, Sir."

Till was taken by surprise. "7? Did you say 7? I thought that there were only 5 that had been discovered...by him...since that ban was lifted."

Oona smiled. "Yes, Sir. However, since the last time there was a count and this exploration began...Team 7016 discovered about 5 or 6 more dimensions."

Till huffed. "It figures that *they* would. Okay...let's hop."

Soolchakan 7 consisted of six planets. Three useless planets and three more gas giants with a total of 45 satellites.

The next dimension was *Bugs*, or *Kiniski's Search*. Seven planets, four planets of no use at all, the Bug planet, one gas giant and one rather large planet with a great deal of mineral wealth.

The next one they searched was in *Soolchakan 2*. There were eight planets (not inhabitable), three of which had an abundance of minerals. There were two gas giants with thirty satellites – nine of those satellites also had a wealth of raw minerals.

The next dimension was labeled: *Lawsing 1*.

Till chuckled. "A dimension that's not named for anyone in Team 7016? Amazing!" He looked off to the side with a stupid grin. "Absolutely amazing!"

Oona chuckled. "Officer, Lawsing is on Team 4079."

"Well congratulate her for finding it before anyone on Team 7016 did."

In this dimension there were nine planets, most of them massive. The really large ones had an immense amount of mineral wealth, however, because of their gravitational pull, it was almost impossible to get any of the minerals off of the planets – without some kind of better or improved technology.

Doctor Kazkim of the Medical Team 221 came forward. "Sir, this next dimension was discovered by Nurse Neeleekee of the Medical Team 255."

Till nodded. "Is she with us today?"

"No, Sir, she isn't."

Till grunted. "Pity. She should be."

Oona looked at her pad. "This particular star system has 16 planets. The fifth planet is inhabited by a sentient race, who have the capability of space travel."

Till cleared his throat and readjusted himself in the Command seat. "How far have they gone?"

"We'll see as we explore," she said. "The best thing to do right now is maintain ourselves in Spy."

"Right, because we really don't know their attitude."

The first two planets closest to the star are basically boiling hot globes. The third planet has a toxic atmosphere, however, the people of the fifth planet have colonized the satellite of the third planet. The fourth planet has a crushing atmospheric pressure and the two satellites are not very accommodating either. The fifth planet has a moon that has been colonized as well. The sixth planet is a gas giant with twenty-two satellites, three of which have been colonized. Planet seven is a large planet with strong gravity and toxic environment, with three moons – that are colonized. Planet eight is a gas giant with thirty-six satellites, four are colonized. Planet nine is another large toxic planet with two satellites – both colonized. Planet ten is nothing but a cold dead useless rock. Planet eleven is a gas giant with only three satellites – one colonized. Planets twelve and thirteen are both large toxic planets with no satellites. Planet fourteen is a gas giant with twenty-six satellites - four of them colonized. Planet fifteen is a giant planet with heavy gravity and a toxic environment. Planet sixteen is a gas giant with twenty-five satellites – five of them are colonized.

Till looked at all of the data that had been gathered. "It appears that they've been at this…off-world colonization for some time. Several moons have been colonized and are thriving. Is there any sign that…they've traveled outside of their star system?"

One of Till's Aides, Hoodeefa shook her head. "So far, Sir, we haven't seen anything coming or going…beyond the sixteenth planet."

Till nodded. "Have we seen anything that labels them as conquerors?"

"Not yet," said Eeleeg. "We still haven't been able to crack their language or writing."

Till turned to Bonarain and smiled. "Do you think that you might do something here?"

Bonarain gave him a strained smile. "I'd have to spend some time with them, Sir."

Till nodded. "We'll talk about that later…after we have all of the close star systems explored."

Soolchakan shook his head. "Sir, even if they do want to be conquerors…they're in a different dimension. The only way that they could pose a threat to us…is if they obtain dimension shifting capabilities."

Till smiled. "THAT is why I want to know if they're conquerors. If they're just explorers…we might greet them. If they want to enslave us…we may just have to do the same thing to them…that we did to the Jowfoonda."

Soolchakan shrugged. "Yes, Sir."

Till sat back. "What's the next dimension?"

Oona looked up. "That would be *Bodge 1*, Sir."

Till nodded. "Who is…Bodge?"

"He's a member of Team 90, Sir."

"Okay, let's go."

Bodge 1 was a star system with eleven planets. The two closest to the star were again, nothing but boiling hot globes. They were given the designation of "hot rock". The third planet might have been inhabitable if it had not been so hot. The fourth planet showed that it could be very hospitable. There was no sentient race. There was an abundance of mammals, reptiles, birds, fish, mollusks, and insects. The fifth planet was a miniature planet that barely had an environment and was extremely cold. The sixth, seventh and eighth planets were all gas giants with a total of sixty-four satellites. The seventh planet was also a planet that had rings around it. The ninth was a large planet with a toxic environment and three satellites. The tenth planet was nothing but a cold dead globe. The eleventh planet was a little larger than Hardooth that had one satellite, however it had no atmosphere.

Till smiled. "Good! One possible planet there. No one to complain if we go there and…explore on the ground." He nodded happily. "What's the next dimension?"

"That would be *Shogoot's Search*," said Oona.

This star system of eleven planets turned up nothing that they could use. Three of the planets were hot rocks. Three were cold rocks. Three planets were too toxic to think about and the other two were gas giants with some 56 satellites.

Next they went to *Siysay 1*. The initial glance had shown

three possible planets that were inhabitable. The three possibilities turned out to be rather depressing. Two of them were too close to the star and as a result, even though they had a nitrogen/oxygen atmosphere, the water was mainly steam and vapor. The third was a little too far away and was in constant winter. Other than that the planets were either too hot, too toxic, too cold or gas giants.

Next on the list was an old friend: Stink! They had seen 46 planets in this system. Other than the Stink planet, there were eight hot rocks, thirteen with toxic environments, sixteen cold dead rocks and three gas giants with 104 satellites. Nothing that could be used.

Next was *Bonarain 4*. There were two hot rocks, five cold dead rocks, one toxic planet, one giant planet with a giant gravity, one gas giant with 25 satellites and one planet with a nitrogen/ oxygen atmosphere. The good planet had no sentient life. The only things they found were reptiles, amphibians, fish, mollusks and insects.

Next was *Sleemata's Search*. This one had two hot rocks, two cold dead rocks, two gas giants with 50 satellites, a toxic planet, a giant planet and the one they had originally called: Underwater. This planet had living fish, amphibians, mollusks, insects and arachnids.

On to *Tinani's Search* or Forest. Three hot rocks, nine cold dead rocks, three gas giants with 64 satellites…and the Forest planet. This was the one with large continents and very deep waterways. The only life was birds, fish and insects.

Imyaya's Search was next. Originally all that had been

known of this one was that there was an unknown solid poison. Now, they found three hot rocks, two cold dead rocks, two gas giants with 52 satellites, the poison planet and one with a sentient species. These people were in a pre-industrial age with very few machines and no electricity.

Kiyalee 5 was their next destination. It had three hot rocks, four cold dead rocks, two gas giants with 53 satellites and an inhabitable planet with only birds, fish, mollusks and insects.

Next was *Nirka's Death* – the one with 94 planets. There were sixteen planets that were all close and nothing but hot rocks. Sixty-six of the mix were useless cold rocks. There were eight gas giants with a total of 276 satellites of their own. One large planet with a very toxic environment. There were three planets that were almost in the exact same orbit. They were almost equally spaced in this orbit. One of the three had nothing but vegetation on it. One had vegetation with mammals, reptiles, birds, fish, mollusks, insects and arachnids – no sentient life. The third had a sentient species that had just discovered metals and the forge. They had swords and axes as weapons. The only projectile weapon they had was the spear. They were very warlike and ambitious conquerors. The Owlamites on the ship decided that they did not have to worry about this species for several centuries.

The next one was *Eematoss 1*. This was the one that had a giant star. It was so large, there was a smaller star orbiting this one in the fourteenth orbit. There were three planets that were orbiting the smaller star as it orbited the giant. The smaller star had one hot rock, one cold rock and one inhabitable planet with mammals, fish, mollusks, insects and arachnids. Orbiting the big one (other than the small star with its three planets), there were seven hot rocks, twenty cold dead rocks, six gas giants, three toxic planets and one that was inhabitable with mammals, reptiles, fish, mollusks, insects and arachnids – no sentient life.

Next they went to *Chaya's Search*. Four hot rocks, one cold dead rock, one gas giant and the initial "liquid" poison planet that had been discovered first.

On to the Desert Dimension. There they found three hot rocks, three gas giants with 80 satellites, one very large planet with a toxic environment, one cold dead rock, and of course, the Desert planet itself. The Owlamites wondered, when these people did not have indoor plumbing or electricity, why did they have buildings that were as high as fifteen floors. They must have one long nasty sewage chute in each tall building.

The last dimension in their quest was Yoyee's Search. This one was rather depressing because it was a star system with six planets full of nothing but toxins – solid, liquid and gas.

After two years of searching the known dimensions with close star systems, they took their report back to Hadathoo and the Command Staff.

While the Command Staff poured over all of the new information about the different systems, Kiyalee was greeted by Officer Grade 3, Andatam of the manufacturing Team 1150. She was given eight coils of platinum wire. Each one was a different diameter, according to the information they had received about the different sized wires used in the 459's. She graciously accepted the wires and went back to apartment 12-562 in order to look over the schematics and see what could be done with this new experimental platinum wiring.

Kiyalee was sitting at a table in the big dining room with all of the spools in front of her. She had a 459 and all of the charts, graphs, schematic, diagrams, tools and other whatnots on another table. She sighed as she opened up the main schematic and started checking on which wire should be installed where.

Bonarain came up to Kiyalee with a steaming hot mug of kwatha. "I thought you might need this right now."

Kiyalee sighed again and took the mug. "Thank you," she said quietly. "I did need…something." She looked at the first page of the schematic as she stirred the kwatha.

Soolchakan watched as Kiyalee was perusing her schematic. "I wonder how long it's going to take to get that done."

Bonarain shrugged. "As long as it takes. The cannons work now. I'm not worried about what it will take to…improve them…if it does improve them."

Hadathoo was getting bored reading about the different systems that were close by in the other dimensions. "So many… useless planets. So many gas giants. So many planets that are close to their stars and are constantly getting cooked as a result. Still…in all of that we find seventeen planets that are inhabitable… or inhabited."

Till nodded. "And only one of them where they have space travel capability. We don't know if they're going to be conquerors or just explorers…yet."

Antrong frowned. "Why don't we know that yet?"

Till smiled. "We didn't go there to do that much exploration on one species. Besides, they're in a different dimension. Right now, there's virtually no chance at all that they pose any danger to us."

Hoynama was a little indignant. "Didn't you have that Officer, Bonarain with you? Why didn't she do some mind reading and translation of their language…so that we WOULD know?"

Till glared at her. "Again…we didn't go there for that. And again…they are in a different dimension. Right now, Officer, Bonarain is working with Officer, Kiyalee on that upgrade of the 459 cannons. I don't really see that any translation of a species from a different dimension as alarming at all. Don't make such a big fuss over it. If this was a species in Home dimension that was on the verge of attacking us, I'd worry…but not until then."

Three days later, Soolchakan reported to the Command Staff, that Kiyalee had finished the platinum wiring on three of the big cannons.

Shyshee pursed her lips. "Do we take them to Desert dimension and test them again?"

"I don't think so, Sir," said Soolchakan.

Hadathoo looked a little indignant. "Oh…and why?"

Soolchakan shrugged. "Sir, we now know that it is an

inhabited planet. What we need to do is choose a target, with nothing in between that we could fire at without hurting anybody's feelings…or lives."

Beemella scoffed. "All right, what do you suggest should be this target?"

Soolchakan smiled. "Zhagool."

Hadathoo's jaw dropped. "That's…just over 1.45 million kilotaja away from here. How do you intend to check on the accuracy…or possible damage?"

Soolchakan smile was even larger. "We have someone firing the cannon from here. We have someone else, in Ghost or Spy dimension, in fighters on the surface of Zhagool. When the cannon is fired, we look to see if it hit, where it hit and if it did any damage. Hitting Zhagool shouldn't hurt anyone's feelings at all."

Hadathoo looked around the table. "Who wants to set this experiment up?"

"I will," said Yamananee. "I remember how a 459 shot an Algothon satellite right out of the air…that was way up there in outer space. I'd like to see if it can hit Zhagool from here."

Hadathoo leaned back in his chair. "You got it."

"Thank you, Sir," said Yamananee with a smile.

Six cannons were positioned at the top of the gorge, pointing up into the sky. They were going to wait until nightfall to do the experiment when the two moons would be in full glory and easy targets. They had to keep someone on guard up there the entire day, making sure that no Heyyah came walking along who could notice something strange going on when they fired the cannons.

As the sun started setting, Soolchakan, Chyning and two of Yamananee's Team, Officer Grade 6, Oreesk and Officer Grade 6, Quanda climbed into four fighters. They were given pictures of specific places on Zhagool to use as landmarks in order to Jump the fighters to Zhagool without using up any of their power in the engines. One by one they Jumped to their spot on Zhagool.

Chyning looked around the desolate landscape of the moon. **"Hey, Soolchakan, how come we keep ending up on these silly buggy rides**?"

He chuckled. **"Because we're being honored with these tasks. They know our history and that we've completed all of our assigned tasks in a way that was beneficial to all of Owlam."**

Chyning let out a disgusted grunt. **"I wish that they'd quit honoring *us* so much."**

He just sat there snickering.

Yamananee surveyed that area with binoculars. **"Everyone who is on the ground here...if you're not firing one of the cannons, keep an eye out for anyone who might see our light show and come over here to investigate. I don't see anyone...but that doesn't mean that no one is there."**

"This is Officer Grade 5, Bathki of Team 7005. Don't worry, Sir, we'll keep our eyes open."

"This is Officer Grade 5, Sonjanimi of Team 7007. What do we do if we do see anyone? Are we going to get rid of them...or what?"

Yamananee clenched her teeth. "No fatalities if it can be helped. We might just go ahead and confuse them, but I don't want any killing unless it is absolutely necessary for our survival."

Oreesk and Quanda sent a mental message that they were in position.

Yamananee nodded. "Just a little while longer. Wait until Holgotho disappears completely over the horizon."

Oreesk looked around from his position. "Better hurry it up. We only have one day of air in these silly little contraptions."

"No you don't," sent Kiyalee. "If you check, right behind your left elbow, I put two oxygen bottles in each one of the fighters in order to give you more air."

Soolchakan chuckled. 'Always the innovator, that one,' he thought.

The last rays of Holgotho were finally gone. The only light was coming from the two full moons as they were high in the sky. Everyone prepared for the test.

Yamananee looked around her. "First, we're going

to fire the three cannons that haven't been changed. I want to see if there is any chance that they could hit Zhagool...before the platinum. Then we'll fire the three modified cannons."

Bonarain, Kiyalee and Officer Grade 5, Shondana from Yamananee's Team got into position with the three unmodified guns.

Yamananee sighed. "**Get ready for anything. You on Zhagool, look for the beams.**" She nodded. "Open fire."

Three bright red beams came from the cannons aimed at Zhagool. They held the triggers down in order to make sure that the personnel on the moon could see them.

"**I've got one,**" sent Oreesk.

"**I've got one,**" sent Soolchakan.

"**I see the third one,**" sent Quanda.

Chyning just grunted.

The three moved closer to where the beams were hitting Zhagool. The fact that the beams were so fast that they were already showing on Zhagool, 1.45 million kilotaja from Hardooth was something that amazed everyone involved in the experiment... except Chyning, who just sat in her fighter brooding. With the thick gloves on, she could not even look at her fingernails.

Soolchakan reached his beam first. "**It looks as if the dirt is vibrating. It seems to be bouncing around inside the beam. The beam itself, is about 10 taja in diameter.**"

Oreesk reached his beam. "**Confirmed. It looks like the dirt is dancing. I don't see anything getting damaged, but the dirt is definitely being disturbed**."

Quanda finally checked in. "**This is interesting. No damage but the dirt is definitely moving around**."

Yamananee was standing there snickering. "**Confirm – you are actually seeing the beams hit…Zhagool…1.45 million kilotaja away**."

"**Yes**," sent Oreesk. "**The beams are here, they are 10 to 12 taja in diameter, at this point, and the dirt IS dancing**."

"**All right then**," sent Yamananee. "**Cease firing and now we'll test the newly modified ones**."

The three women let go of the triggers and all three rubbed their hands for a few moments.

"Holding that trigger gets a little tiring," said Kiyalee.

Yamananee gave Kiyalee a patronizing glare. She turned to Shondana. "It couldn't be that bad…could it?"

Shondana stared back in a dull manner as she rubbed some feeling back into her hands. She said nothing. She just walked over to one of the modified cannons and got into position.

Bonarain and Kiyalee both walked over to their modified cannons while giving Yamananee the same nasty 'return' glare.

Yamananee huffed. "All right, all right! So it can be fatiguing." She sighed. "**Are we all ready for the next test?**"

The four on Zhagool called in that they were ready. All three women on Hardooth who were still rubbing some feeling into their hands…said no.

Yamananee sat down. "Let me know when you're ready."

Officer Grade 7, Falfa of Team 7005 pointed to the south. "What is that?"

Bathki raised her binoculars. "Oh, *h'oolyach*! It's a campfire." She turned to Yamananee. "We may have company… in a little while."

Yamananee sighed. "Can't be helped. If there is somebody who comes over here from that fire…grab hold and Jump them back to the fire. Hopefully there aren't too many of them and it'll be rather difficult for them to explain how they…got Jumped… back to their campfire."

Bathki let out a sharp quick growl. "There're two men… coming this way…from that campfire."

Yamananee hung her head. "Everybody, hop everything into Spy. If those two get all the way over here…Jump them back to their fire."

Bathki turned to her Teammates. "Widzidom, Pintay…get ready to Jump those two."

All of the equipment was hopped and all of the personnel hopped. They watched the two men come closer.

"I swear it was over here…in this area," said the tall man.

"It *was* somewhere over here," said the short one.

The tall one stopped and looked around. "Could it have been some hallucination?"

The short one shook his head. "Hallucinations can only be seen by one person…usually someone who's crazy. We both saw it. That ain't hallucination."

Widzidom walked up to his victim. He chose the tall one. Pintay smiled as she walked up to the short one.

Yamananee stood there with her hands clasped at her waist. **"Make sure that you get them at the same instance."**

"Call it," sent Widzidom.

Yamananee nodded. **"Ready? Now!"**

Suddenly both of the Heyyah men were standing back at the campfire, looking away from where the beams had originated. Both men were standing there frozen with wide open eyes and mouths. They knew it was their fire because of the large bird being cooked over the fire. Both made some strange noises, trying to say something, however, neither one could articulate anything that could be understood.

Bathki appeared at the campfire in Spy. **"Widzidom, come back and help keep watch again. Pintay, keep an eye on these two *bimyocks*."**

The tall one looked at the short one with terror in his eyes. "What…happened?"

"I…don't know! I don't think…I wanna know," stammered the short one.

The tall one wiped some sweat from his forehead. "Let's… just forget about this. No one…would believe us…anyway."

"Yeah…forget about it." The short one went to sit down by the fire. "What if it happens…again?"

"If *what* happens again?"

"Oh…nuthin'."

'Good thought process,' thought Pintay as she chuckled.

Yamananee turned back to the shooters. "**Everyone on Hardooth, back to Home dimension now. Are you ready now**?"

All three of them nodded.

"**Okay, you four on Zhagool, we're ready now. Watch for the beams**." Yamananee took one more glance at the campfire area. "**Ready? Now!**"

Pintay laughed out loud as the two Heyyah men turned away from the bright red beams, with their eyes clenched shut and whimpering.

Chyning was startled as one of the beams hit very close to her. "**That beam…it…the *chogo* thing just blew a hole in Zhagool! It's still…digging! There's so much flying dust! I can't see anything but dust!**"

Oreesk called in. "**I've got the same thing near me! You've actually blown a hole in Zhagool's surface!**"

"**I've got the third one in my sights**," sent Quanda.

"It's kicking up a huge dust cloud."

"**Cease fire**," sent Yamananee. "**Are you saying that the beams are…in reality…destroying something…at that distance**?"

"**Yes**," sent Chyning. "**There's a great big cloud of dust. It doesn't look like it's going to settle…very soon**."

"**Same thing here, Sir**," sent Oreesk. "**A lot of dirt just…hanging in the…well I can't call it air…there is no air here on Zhagool**." He chuckled nervously. "**It's just very, very slowly drifting back down to the surface. Some of it was blasted…about fifty taja in the…uh…above the surface**."

"**Same thing here**," sent Quanda. "**Big, big dust cloud that is just lingering up there**."

Yamananee was staring at Zhagool. She turned back to the personnel in her area. "All right, let's get all of this equipment back down below. "**Pintay, forget about those two and let's disappear. The four of you on Zhagool, wait until the dust settles and then measure any…hole…or crater that resulted from our test**."

Oreesk sat there in the fighter looking around somewhat disgusted. "**How are we supposed to measure the… resulting mark on Zhagool? Did anyone bring a tape measure**?"

"**I did**," sent Soolchakan. "**I'm moving to Chyning right now. When we finish her…blemish, I'll come over**

to you two and we can measure yours." He flew his fighter over to Chyning.

She was still staring at the big dust cloud in shock. It appeared that the cloud was settling faster than they thought. This was a relief because they would not have to spend too much time doing nothing but watching descending dirt.

Chyning glared at Soolchakan through the clear canopies of the fighters. "**How are we supposed to measure the... blemish**?"

He sighed. "**Put that helmet on, screw it down and go on oxygen from the suit. Get out of your fighter, I'll give you one end of the tape measure and you go to the other side of the blemish...or to the bottom of the hole and we measure**."

"**And what if it's a hole that's...over fifteen taja. How am I supposed to get out**?"

He sighed in frustration. "**You landmark your fighter and Jump back to it from the bottom of the hole**."

Chyning shook her head in disgust. She pulled the helmet from behind her, brought it down and sealed it. She went on backpack oxygen and waited until the last few bits of the cloud finally settled. She raised her eyebrows in surprise. "**It is a hole**!"

Soolchakan snickered. "**It most certainly is**."

The two of them opened their canopies and climbed out of the fighters. Chyning turned and landmarked her fighter, using a large rock nearby as an additional aid. She walked over to where Soolchakan was already shining a light down the hole.

Chyning swallowed. "**That ain't no small hole**."

"**I can see that**," sent Soolchakan. He held up the tape measure. "**You get hold of one end and the first thing we'll measure is the diameter of the hole**."

Chyning took the end of the tape and walked around to the other side. They both knelt down to get the tape in the correct places.

Soolchakan looked back up, towards Hardooth. "**Bonarain, are you ready**?"

Bonarain smiled. "**There are several of us in this conference room waiting, with pen in hand, for the information**."

Soolchakan checked the tape. "**Diameter is four and a half taja**."

Chyning shook her head. "**Now you want me to drop down there…when we can't even see the bottom**."

Soolchakan sighed. "**Remember that this is 1/5 gravity. You shouldn't have to worry about any nasty bump at the bottom**."

Chyning looked at him. She mouthed the words: "I hate you." She pulled her arms close to her body and jumped into the hole. She was relieved that the lower gravity made the fall a very slow one. She looked up. She grunted in disgust because all she could see was the forward edge of the helmet. It did not allow one to look up and see anything without leaning back. She just sighed and accepted the inevitable. She was able to slow her descent even more by occasionally spreading her legs and scraping the walls with her feet...until she finally hit bottom. **"I'm here...at the bottom."**

Soolchakan looked at the measurement so far. **"Can you squat down to put it ON the bottom?"**

"Its pitch black down here! I can't see a thing."

"What about your helmet light?"

"It's not working."

Back on Hardooth, Kiyalee looked up surprised. "It's not?" She made an annotation on her paperwork about a faulty helmet light.

"Okay, just make your best guess at getting the end of the tape somewhere around your nose level. We'll add your, nose to the ground, length later."

Soolchakan looked at the tape. **"36.3 taja up here. Add her height, from the nose down, and it comes to about 41.5 taja deep."**

Yamananee clenched her teeth. **"I don't want 'ABOUT'! I want some precise measurements."**

Soolchakan groaned. **"OH COME ON! We just fired a 459 across 1.45 million kilotaja of outer space and blew a hole in Zhagool. Now you want that hole measured** down to the smallest *micro*-taja? Get serious! If the shot was fired from only 5 taja away, I could see the measurement with a microtaja. But after *1.45 MILLION KILOTAJA*…why do we have to be so *chokwad* precise?"

Yamananee flushed. She rubbed her mouth several times and sniffed. "**41.5 taja is acceptable**." She looked off to the side and cleared her throat. "**Which gun dug that hole**?"

Soolchakan hung his head. "**You must be joking. If you wanted to know which cannon blasted which hole, you should have fired each one individually, not all at the same time**."

Yamananee flushed again and clenched her eyes shut. "**Please go and measure another hole**."

Soolchakan shook his head. "**Yes, Sir**." He tried not to sound too sarcastic.

The hole where Oreesk was, turned out to be the same 4.5 taja in diameter. This hole was 44.5 taja deep. The hole that Quanda had found was 4.5 taja in diameter and 40 taja deep.

Hadathoo read the report from Yamananee. "It seems that these platinum wires have…made an already deadly weapon… even more…destructive." He leaned back in his chair and shook his head. "I certainly wouldn't want to be on the wrong end of a 459."

Antrong looked up. "According to Officer, Kiyalee, if we give her the computer repair personnel, they can have every 459 upgraded in about 20 days."

Hoynama stroked her chin. "Could we do the same thing… with a 456…or the pulse pistols…and rifles?"

Till shrugged. "I don't see why we couldn't."

Hadathoo snickered. "It sounds as if we need to go back to Bri and get some more of this platinum."

Everyone nodded in agreement.

11

For the next 305 years, the Owlamites hid in the gorge while looking for more new dimensions. They gave up trying to name each dimension after the discoverer of the dimension. All that did was confuse. They, instead, kept a log of who did discover that specific dimension and numbered each and every one, 1 through 239, according to how difficult it was to get to that specific dimension. When Hadathoo asked who it was that had numbered them and how they were able to number each one accordingly, he was told that it was the physicists who had come up with a formula in determining difficulty. The physicists showed Hadathoo a five page equation on how to determine where each one should fall in line numerically, Hadathoo decided he did not really need to know how they determined it, he would just accept their word as to which ones were numbered where.

The naming system had been even more complicated by the fact that Soolchakan had eventually discovered fourteen different dimensions. He did not find them in numerical order. Bonarain had finally discovered ten – not in numerical order. Kiyalee had eight new ones and Chyning ended up with ten – none of them in numerical order. The only other personnel who discovered more than one dimension were: Officer Grade 5, Amtosha of Team 1007, Officer Grade 6, Zhorgon of Team 3779, Officer Grade 6, Lawsing of Team 4079 and Officer Grade 7, Eematoss of Team

6559. Each of these individuals discovered two each.

They ended up with 186 dimensions where they were not close to a star system. 27 dimensions had a close star system with an inhabitable planet. 20 dimensions had a star system with no usable planets (including Stink). Other than Home dimension they had five utility dimensions which were Spy, Jump, Observation, Ghost…and Stink. A total of 239 including Home.

The gorge was called the divider gorge by the Heyyah who lived in this place that they had named "High Country". It was called High Country because it was a very high plateau and all the way around the country it was nothing but high cliffs. There were very few breaks in the cliff where someone could just walk up or down without the aid of mountain climbing equipment. On the north, east and west the country was surrounded by ocean. On the southern border there were two other countries: Joktel and Peegruch.

There had been a few attempts by someone in Joktel to get up the cliffs and take some of High Country. Their main problem was the fact that they never could get enough personnel up on top of the cliffs to gain any strong hold up there (mainly because the Owlamites did a lot of sabotage to the attempts by the enemies).

There were four attempts from the northern part, by way of the ocean through cuts in the cliffs. This was stopped because it was just too expensive to resupply anyone who was up on top of the cliffs…and for some very strange reason, the invaders kept falling back down off of the cliffs (pushed by Owlamites of course, however, they never knew that fact).

There were two attempts to invade from the west, however, they failed for the same reason as the invasion attempts from the north. There were never any attempts from the east because the surf conditions did not allow any ship to get close enough and any landing craft would have been slammed up against the cliffs (plus for some very odd reason it always smelled like raw sewage in the central part of that area).

The Teams that had been spying on Algothon were now being utilized to spy on the Teltermak and the Axswain. These two races still seemed to pose a threat to the safety and survival of the Owlamites, however, the later still could not figure out why they were as heavily desired as slaves. The Teltermak had gone out of their way to exterminate other races they felt threatened by, why did they want to keep the Owlamites alive as slaves when they did not enslave anyone else...just murdered them? The Owlamites kept the two races separated, on their islands, as much as possible.

The Kalash on North Chilamte were becoming extremely wealthy by manufacturing and distributing the powerful cure-all drugs that had been dropped in their laps by Owlam. They still did not understand why they had received this boon from a people who had mysteriously vanished. They kept a few annotations in their archives that if the Owlamites ever returned, they would be sure to ask a few questions.

All of the Owlamite weaponry had been upgraded with platinum wiring and now, the Owlamites had some of the most devastating weaponry that had ever existed. They kept it all stored in secret, however, they were ready to pull it out and use it against any enemy that reached the gorge. That enemy would never know what hit them and there would be no one left to tell the story of how they had been defeated…by an army they could not even see.

In the 311th year of Hadathoo's tenure, which was the 576th year since the firestorm weapons had altered the people of Hardooth into different species, Master Officer, Till, once again, sounded the klaxon in regards to invaders from outer space.

Officer, Bonarain was one of the first ones notified, much to her chagrin (in the bathtub), in order for her to make an attempt at reading minds and comprehending a completely alien language.

All Owlamites and their equipment (including the *Owlam the First*) went to Spy dimension until further notice. All Owlamites went to Spy dimension and waited to hear what these new invaders were like.

On board the *Owlam the First*, they separated the scout ship #1 from the mother ship. They were going to use the scout to do the job intended for it and scout this new extraterrestrial race. Since they could not make the thing go to light speed inside a star system, they once again had to go up out of the system and arc over to where the new "unfamiliar" was located - currently mapping out the mineral wealth on the planet Bri.

Hadathoo looked at the location of the foreigners. "More greedy *bimyocks* that're going after our mineral wealth," he muttered.

Till nodded. "All the more reason to stop them…especially if they're coming as conquerors."

Antrong turned to Bonarain. "Are you getting anything yet?"

Bonarain smiled nervously. "Uh...Sir...I...don't even know...what I'm looking for...or at...yet. What am I supposed to be receiving?"

Hoynama looked at Hadathoo while pondering. "Sir, is it wise to have all of the Master Officers on board...at this time? What happens if this new enemy just happens to take this ship out? The Supreme Officer and all of the Master Officers are taken out in one blast."

Hadathoo sighed. "We don't even know if they're hostile... yet. They may just be some curious explorers. You do have to admit that Bri is a jaw-dropping curiosity to all who come here. It is one planet that has more mineral wealth than any inhabitable planet, that we know of."

Hoynama huffed. "I suppose you're right. I still feel very uneasy about this."

Hadathoo smiled at her. "That is why we're investigating in the Spy dimension."

Shyshee snickered. "Don't you mean...dimension number 53?"

Hadathoo's shoulders sagged. "Forgive me...old habits die hard."

Hoynama giggled. She turned away, loudly clearing her throat, and tried to get back to being serious.

Bonarain was still sitting there wondering exactly why she had to be the one to do this. Why was no one else able to attempt a mind reading on this foreign race?

The ship slowed to conventional speed as the light engines disengaged. At first they did not see the foreign ship. Then it came around Bri on an equatorial orbit.

"That monster is bigger than the one we swiped from the Jowfoondas," said Antrong.

"Yes," said Shyshee. "It doesn't have any scout ships attached to the sides like our ship does though."

The ship was at least five kilotaja in length. It was silvery in color with many lights scattered from one end to the other. It consisted of one, very large, central cylinder with two smaller cylinders on the sides. There was one large bulge in the top of the central cylinder, near the front. The main guess of all the Owlamites was that the bulge was where the main Bridge was located.

Antrong again turned to Bonarain. "You need to Jump inside there and start your language reconnaissance."

Bonarain scoffed at him. "HOW? I haven't seen any *inside* of that thing. I have no landmarks to go to. What am I supposed to do, just Jump and pray?"

Hadathoo snarled. "Does anyone have any constructive ideas?"

Soolchakan cleared his throat. "Yes, Sir. We currently have six of the fighters on board this ship. Take a fighter over there, in Spy…er…53 and do some initial explorations. While there, get a landmark, bring the fighter back and then do the Jump."

"Excellent idea," said Antrong. "I suggest that Team 7016 take four of the fighters and perform this initial exploration."

Chyning gave Soolchakan a nasty glare. "We're being honored again," she said in a truculent manner.

Soolchakan just shrugged.

The four of them grudgingly headed for the bay where the fighters were currently parked. None of them were in any great hurry to get there and start performing this "initial exploration" of the foreign ship. They arrived in the bay and found five women and one man waiting there with the space suits that Team 7016 always used…when needed.

Soolchakan frowned as he looked at the suits. He looked up at the six people. "Who are you?"

One of them smiled. "I'm Officer Grade 5, Oolsena." She pointed at the other two. "This is Officer Grade 6, Zayza and Officer Grade 7, Yeenfa." She turned back, still smiling. "We're the Aides of Master Officer, Antrong. He told us to be ready in here with your spacesuits and help you put them on."

Another woman came up. "You know us, don't you?"

Bonarain nodded. "Yes, you're Shondana, Oreesk and Quanda from Yamananee's Team."

Soolchakan looked at his three Teammates and shook his head in disgust. "Sounds like we've been set up."

Chyning blew a raspberry. "Yuh think?"

The ones who were there held up the spacesuits in order to assist Team 7016 in getting ready.

Chyning yanked her suit out of the hands of Oolsena and walked away. "I know how to get dressed by myself," she snarled.

Oolsena was taken aback. "You don't have to be so snippy about it."

Chyning glared back at her. "When I've been set up, don't talk to me about being snippy." She started stepping into the suit.

Zayza walked up to Chyning. "You need help with these things. That's what we're here for."

Chyning looked at Zayza with nothing but hate in her eyes. "If I need any help, I'll get it from Bonarain or Kiyalee. Now... GET AWAY FROM ME!" She stepped in the suit while still glaring angrily at Zayza.

Soolchakan, Bonarain and Kiyalee graciously accepted the help from the sextet that were in the bay. Bonarain and Kiyalee then went to assist Chyning with all of the zipping, buttoning and snapping that was required in order to make the suit airtight.

There were four of the six fighters that were sitting there with their canopies raised. Chyning walked up to one of the open fighters, looked inside and shook her head. She turned around. "Hey, Kiyalee...your helmet is already installed in this one."

Bonarain walked up to another opened one and checked. "Soolchakan, this one is yours," she said dully.

Shondana walked up to Soolchakan. "What's the matter with you four? We came here to assist you and you're treating us like we did something nasty to you. Why?"

Soolchakan got right in her face. "Because your boss, Antrong, set us up. I'm getting tired of being his play-toy. I guess his mommy didn't give him enough toys when he was growing up and he's decided to play with us...and I'm getting *very* tired of it. Every time something comes up, he's more than willing to volunteer us – Team 7016 – for the dirtiest and the most dangerous jobs. Why are we being nasty to you? GUESS!" He turned around and climbed into the fighter."

Shondana snarled back at him after he turned away. "I'm not part of Antrong's Team. I'm part of Yamananee's Team."

Soolchakan just shook his head.

Bonarain glared at her. "Antrong is the Sector 1 Commander. Yamananee is the Sector 1 *Vice* Commander. WE are members of Sector 4. Why is he volunteering members of Sector 4 for the dirty jobs, when he should be volunteering you or any other member of Sector 1 for this *h'oolyach*?"

Kiyalee chuckled. "It really gets you when you realize that, of the four Master Officers, Antrong is third in line, as far as rank is concerned. Hoynama and Shyshee both outrank him...yet he acts like *he's* the big *h'oolyach*."

The six outside the fighters went to assist in the final strapping in. Chyning glared at them and closed her canopy. When the others saw her canopy shut, the other three canopies all closed very quickly. The six that were standing outside of the fighters all shook their heads and despondently walked away.

Soolchakan looked around the bay. **"Let's hop to Observation and get out of this big bucket."**

Chyning snickered. **"Don't you mean 108**?"

Soolchakan chuckled. **"I suppose I do. Is everybody ready**?"

The three women all sent a yes. All four hopped to Observation (108) and they fired up their engines. They turned their noses towards the foreign ship and slowly made their way towards it.

The comparison had been misleading. The size of the planet Bri was not a good comparison in determining how large this new ship was. As they got closer their sensors were gathering more accurate information and they found out that this new ship was 8.2 kilotaja in length not 5. The central cylinder was 1.7 kilotaja in diameter and the two outer cylinders were each .8 kilotaja. Soolchakan sent the correct data back to the personnel on scout ship #1…who now were rather embarrassed as to why they had not checked their sensors to begin with.

Bonarain surveyed the large ship. **"Where should we try first**?"

Soolchakan sighed. **"Let's try the closest part. This side cylinder that we're coming up to."**

Kiyalee frowned. **"Don't you want to check that bulge up top…and see if it IS the Bridge**?"

"**Let's get inside first.   Then we'll look at the different parts**," sent Soolchakan.

Bonarain sent: "**We've got to catch up to their speed, or all we're going to do is fly through that big thing.**"

"**I know**," sent Soolchakan.   "**I'm just wondering which part would be the best place to enter.**"

Kiyalee huffed.   "**Does it really make that much difference…yet**?"

Chyning just shook her head.   "**Do you feel honored yet**?"

The four of them got in a line where they were paralleling the port side cylinder.

"**Go on inside when you feel comfortable with matching their speed**," sent Soolchakan.

Antrong was getting impatient.   "**JUST GO INSIDE!**"

Chyning clenched her teeth.   "**You're not out here, so SHUT UP!**"

Antrong turned to Hadathoo looking rather angry.   "When they come back I'm going to…"

"You're gonna to shut up," snapped Hadathoo!   "Like she said, *you* are not out there. They're trying a tricky maneuver they've never done before, and they don't need any distraction." Hadathoo leaned towards Antrong. "So…SHUT UP!"

Antrong sat there with his mouth hanging open. He sat

down looking totally angered and embarrassed.

Chyning was the first to go in. She flew in and turned slightly to avoid any collision with any of her other Teammates. She looked at the personnel that were running around in a massive bay that stretched from bow to stern. **"THESE ALIENS, THEY'RE STICKS!"**

Soolchakan was the next one to fly into the bay. He was frowning as he flew through the side of the cylinder and his expression changed to surprise when he looked at the foreigners. **"They...are sticks."**

Bonarain and Kiyalee both entered about the same time. They were just as shocked when they saw the inhabitants of the big ship.

Bonarain shook her head. **"Are those the...aliens? They couldn't be! Those things have to be...some kind of mechanical helper."**

Chyning scoffed. **"What kind of...mechanical worker would need clothing...and a helmet?"**

Hadathoo was getting a little curious now. **"What are you talking about? What do they look like?"**

"I'll send you the data," sent Soolchakan. He started a full organic scan on the – whatever it is – that was closest to him.

Everyone on scout ship #1 turned their full attention to their monitors as the data came in. It is male. He is 8.2 taja in height. .4 taja in width at the waist and .6 taja in width at the shoulders. The skin is dark yellow. Biped, that walks upright with arms and opposable thumbs on hands with three fingers and the thumb. The legs are 33% of his height. Each arm is 4 taja in length and .2 taja in circumference. His head seems to be the same dimensions as his waist, .4 taja across and .2 taja deep. He has one eye in the top middle part of his head. He has a respiration system that is similar to Heyyah, with no visible nose. He has a gastrointestinal system that is also similar to Heyyah with only a slit for a mouth. He has a double set of genitals. One set of testicles has nothing but male sperm, the other has nothing but female sperm. There were jaws dropping all over the Bridge of scout ship #1.

Shyshee was the first to find her voice. "That *doovoft* can choose the gender of his children. All he has to do…is choose which penis he…" She looked up somewhat confused as to what she wanted to say next.

Hoynama chuckled. "It takes all of the surprise out of wondering what the child is going to be, doesn't it?"

Hadathoo groaned. "Can we concentrate on something other than his…genitalia?"

Antrong looked up and sniffed. "**Do they all look like that**?"

"**No**," sent Chyning sarcastically. "**They're all different. Some of them are aquatic and they've got a pool for them to swim in. The ones that don't swim are urinating in the pool. It looks hilarious looking at a male who's peeing with two streams**."

"**ENOUGH**!" sent Hadathoo. He scoffed as he looked at Antrong. "That has got to be one of, if not the MOST, incredibly *stupid* questions I've ever heard in my life."

Antrong sat there red faced with his eyes and mouth clenched shut.

Chyning sat there in the fighter grumbling and thinking all kinds of really nasty thoughts about Antrong.

Soolchakan was looking around the big bay. "**I don't think they're here for any peaceful reasons. This bay… is a hangar bay for…I have no idea, how many small fighter ships**."

Hoynama raised her eyebrows in thought. "**Is there a chance that we could take those fighters and use them for ourselves**?"

Kiyalee laughed out loud. "**I don't see how! They'd require massive modifications. The cockpit is designed for these…*sticks*. I don't think I could get more than… my leg in there. Getting my entire body in there… impossible!**"

Antrong broke in. "**Officer, Bonarain, can you read their minds**?"

Bonarain sat there with her teeth clenched. "**I was trying to do just that…and then some *bimyock* interrupted me**."

Hadathoo growled at Antrong. "Until *further* notice… SHUT UP! And I mean mentally as well! All you've done so far is muddy the water."

Antrong's face turned even redder. Hoynama and Shyshee sat there giggling which did not help Antrong's ego at the moment.

Bonarain listened for a response. "**Can I try to do some mind reading without being interrupted now**?"

Hadathoo scowled at Antrong. "**Go ahead, Officer, Bonarain. I guarantee that you won't be interrupted again...by anybody**." He glared at Antrong.

Bonarain smiled. "**Thank you, Sir**." She closed her eyes and laid her head back as she tried to concentrate on the imagery for mind reading and translation. She opened her eyes and looked directly at one of the sticks. She started getting something from him. It was starting to come through when she felt her fighter move. She looked to her left startled.

Soolchakan was standing next to her fighter smiling. "**You're ship started sinking through the floor. May I suggest putting the landing pads in Home dimension**?"

She smiled back and made the hop of the landing pads. The fighter stabilized in the way it was sitting in the bay. She went back to the mind reading.

Till looked up at Hadathoo. "How long should we wait?"

Hadathoo smiled and made himself comfortable in the Command chair. "Until she is finished. This is only the second time this has been done and I don't expect it to be instantaneous."

Till nodded. "Good point."

Antrong still sat there brooding.

Bonarain shook her head and huffed. "I don't believe this." She looked at her Teammates. **"We need to look at the rest of the ship. I'm not believing what...I'm picking up."**

Soolchakan raised his eyebrows. **"Any place in particular that you want to go?"**

Bonarain shrugged. **"Let's go take a look at the Bridge."**

Soolchakan turned to Kiyalee. **"Why don't you go look for the engines. Chyning...just...explore...randomly."**

They all hopped their fighter landing pads into Observation and headed out to the different parts of the ship. Soolchakan and Bonarain flew outside of the ship and headed for the bulge on top near the front. They flew through the skin and into a large open area where there were numerous "sticks" sitting at different work stations pulling on numerous wires that hung from the ceiling.

Soolchakan watched a few of them messing with the hanging wires for a few moments. **"They sure like playing with their ceiling decorations."**

Bonarain shook her head. **"Those aren't decorations. Those hanging wires are their...computer keypads."**

Soolchakan looked at her as if she were crazy. **"WHAT**?!"

She shook her head and shrugged. **"All those...crazy hanging wires are their keypads to their computer system."**

They landed their fighters and hopped the landing pads into

Home. They got out of the fighters and started walking around the Bridge. Soolchakan stopped and watched with fascination as one of the sticks was reaching up and pulling on different hanging wires. As it pulled on different ones, there was a monitor in front of the stick where different symbols were appearing as if the creature was typing.

He looked up to get a good close look at the hanging "keyboard" these people were using. The ceiling was about 9.5 taja high. The wires were hanging down in square clusters. He counted one of the groups and came up with 18 x 6 which came out to 108 in each cluster. The gray wires hung down about 3 taja. At the bottom end of each wire was a tiny cylindrical light. Each of the 108 lights in each cluster was different. In each cluster that was not currently in use, all of the lights were white. A few clusters, that were not in use had been raised so that they were hanging down only about one taja and the lights were off.

Then he noticed that the colored lights were not the same at each station. At one station, the light on the left front end was dark green. At the next station is was red. At a third station it was purple. Now he was getting even more confused. He decided to ask Bonarain if she knew anything about this conundrum.

He looked for Bonarain. She was aimlessly wandering around the Bridge looking around in every direction with exasperation on her face as if she were lost.

He sniffed. "What's the matter?"

She looked at him and huffed. "Where's the Commander's chair? There's all kinds of work stations…but I can't find the

Commander."

Soolchakan did a full circle as he was looking for some kind of Command seat…or at least someone who looked like they were in charge, but not doing anything. He turned back to Bonarain and chuckled nervously. "Good question."

"They've got to have some head *bimyock*…in here… somewhere!"

"Aren't you listening to them…talking…and figuring it out from there?"

"Can't you hear them?"

He grunted. "All I hear is a bunch of buzzing."

She hung her head. She looked up. "Don't you know how to do the mind reading and translation?"

He shook his head helplessly. "No."

She blew her breath out in exasperation and started walking slowly towards him as if she were going to some punishment.

He cleared his throat. "Can you…give it to me…I mean force feed it…without knocking yourself out?"

She sighed. "As long as I don't have to give it go Kiyalee and Chyning…*today*…I can. I can do it once a day, without knocking myself out."

She was finally standing directly in front of him. They both shrugged and put their foreheads together. He felt numerous groups of information coming into his head. He did not immediately try to comprehend each one individually, he just accepted them as they came. Suddenly Bonarain collapsed against him.

He caught her as she fell. He felt a little out of breath. "I thought...you weren't gonna be knocked out."

She looked up at him as if she were dizzy. "I'm...awake. I...didn't say that I wouldn't be...affected. I just said it wouldn't... incapacitate me. Just let me get my bearings." She held onto him breathing rather heavily.

He held her up and looked around. He could understand the sticks now. The buzzing sound was their way of talking. Before it had been nothing but a monotone buzzing. Now, it was clear articulation of words.

She pushed away from him. "Okay, let me go."

He let go with one arm. She wobbled a little. He kept hold of her until she stopped her unsteady movements. "Are you sure that you're okay now?"

She pulled away completely. She rubbed her eyes. "Yes, I'm good. Now, let's see if we can find out who is in charge of this big bucket and...where the Command station is located."

Both of them began wandering around the big room. They could see there were dozens of work stations and most of them were manned with one of the sticks. No one was standing over anyone giving orders. Each station was being worked without any supervision.

Bonarain scratched her head. "Where're the women?"

Soolchakan shook his head. "From the pornographic images I'm seeing in the heads of some of these sticks…I don't think that there are any women on the Bridge. I think that…this society is rather male oriented."

She looked as if she had something in her mouth that tasted very bad. "I think you're right."

He stopped at one of the stations with curiosity eating away at him. Before she had force fed him, he had no idea what was on the monitor. Now, he could read it. The stick that was currently at this station was making special annotations about the vast wealth of minerals on Bri. This stick was paying very special attention to two elements that Soolchakan had never heard of. He made a mental note to check the Jowfoonda archives and see if they had anything like this in their encyclopedia of elemental information.

Bonarain huffed. "Are you still looking for the Command area?"

He looked up a little surprised. "Uh…yeah. I…uh…was just thinking…the view-screen…look at it."

She sighed. "I can see it…what's your point?"

"Wouldn't the Commander be seated in a position where… he has a centralized view…of the view-screen?"

She nodded. "That would make sense."

He moved slightly to his right. "Okay…now…I am standing directly in front of the center of the view-screen. The Command chair…has to be somewhere along this line."

She shook her head. "Okay...where?"

He looked behind him and saw nothing but work stations. He started moving towards the view-screen, looking at all of the work stations as he moved. He was less than ten taja from the screen when he noticed a railing. He walked forward to the railing leaned over and looked down. "I found it!"

Bonarain looked over where he was standing. "You found what?"

He turned to her and pointed down over the railing. "The head *doovoft* is down here."

She looked at him incredulously and came running over to the railing. She looked down.

The Command area was very small. There were six steps leading down to it on either side of a small box area that was no more than five taja across. There were three seats down there, facing the screen, each one was about .9 taja in width.

Soolchakan shook his head. "They certainly don't need much room, do they?"

Bonarain said nothing. She was standing there with her eyes closed. He realized that she was reading their minds. He shrugged and started intruding on their thoughts. After a few moments, they both stopped mind reading and looked at each other.

"Let's get out of here," he said flatly.

She nodded. "I don't like what I just heard," she said

gravely.

They headed back to their fighters.

He jumped in his fighter. **"Kiyalee, Chyning...where are you?"**

Kiyalee responded first. **"I'm inspecting the engines like you said...what'd you think I was doing?"**

"Are you finished?"

"Yeah, why?"

"Go back to the scout ship...now. Chyning... where are you?"

"Exploring and counting."

"Find anything that we might need to know?"

"Both of the side cylinders are hangars for their small fighters. There are fighters on both sides of the cylinders. From front to rear there are 250 in each line. That's 1,000 fighters on this thing. They've also got some larger ships that look like troop transports. There are 20 troop transports."

Soolchakan sighed. **"Yup! This is an invasion vessel. They're doing specific mapping of all of the planets. They already know that Hardooth is inhabited and they're planning an invasion."**

Chyning shook her head. **"My, what a surprise,"** she sent cynically.

After they landed on the scout ship, it was Jumped back to Hardooth. The Command Staff headed for the conference room to get a full briefing from Team 7016.

Bonarain started the briefing. "These people are called… Zizzikinza. They're conquerors. They…have no qualms about enslaving other races. You have two choices: Be a slave or die. Right now, they're mapping the other planets, looking for any form of any element or mineral ore that they can exploit. They'd use us as slave labor to dig for all of it, and they're heartless in the way they treat their slaves."

Hadathoo leaned forward. "Do we have any idea how long it'll take them to map out Bri…and then continue on?"

She shrugged. "The thoroughness that they're… performing, they're inventorying the planet Bri, down to the last speck of dirt. If we could get into their computer system, we'd know exactly how much everything on that planet weighs, down to the slightest amount. How long will that type of inventory take? I don't know, but they've been at it for at least thirteen days…and they're still working."

Shyshee shrugged. "There's five gas giants, with several orbiting moons…that gives us a little time to think this thing through."

Hadathoo frowned. "What's the possibility of taking over this ship the same way we got one from the Jowfoondas?"

Bonarain shook her head. "I don't see how. Their computer

system…is so complicated that…it would take years of practice before we could figure it out."

Antrong scowled at her. "Are you saying that our computer personnel are incapable of figuring out their computers?"

"Given enough time, no I don't think it'd be a problem. The problem here is that we don't have that kind of time. I'm not trying to say that they can't…eventually figure it out, I'm saying that we don't have the time to try figuring it out before they get here."

Antrong turned to Hadathoo. "I'd like to get the opinion of the computer experts before I'll believe that we're that helpless."

Hadathoo gave Antrong a dirty look. He turned to Bonarain. "Why don't you get with Officers, Sankiki and Tula? Jump them up to the Zizz…what did you call them?"

"Zizzikinza, Sir."

"Yes, thank you. Take those two up to that ship and see what they say."

"Yes, Sir." She vanished.

Hadathoo cleared his throat and sniffed. "Officer, Kiyalee, what can you tell us about this ships engines?"

She shrugged. "Sir, I heard that the laws of physics are the laws of physics. One light speed engine is very similar to another light speed engine. After seeing the engines on that Zizzikinza ship and comparing it to *Owlam the First*…they're so similar that it's not worth talking about, Sir."

Hadathoo nodded. "Then we could take that ship and use it like we do *Owlam the First*."

"No, Sir. Not without some major modifications all over the ship."

Antrong scoffed. "Why are you so pessimistic? What could be the problem?"

Kiyalee was ready to knock Antrong out. "Sir, I am not being pessimistic, I am being realistic. The Zizzikinza designed the corridors, the work stations, the doors, the rooms…the entire ship according to their body style. You saw the report on that one we analyzed. The widest part of his body was his shoulders. Zero point six taja…at the shoulders. Your head is wider than that. We'd have to rebuild the entire inner part of the ship. Widen the corridors, widen the doors, widen all of the work stations, widen the toilets, widen the sinks, widen all of the furniture, widen the beds…everything would have to be widened. It'd be a monumental task."

Before Antrong could admonish her again, Shyshee spoke up. "How wide are the corridors…at this time?"

Kiyalee calmed a little in answering Shyshee. "Sir, the corridors – all of the corridors that I saw – are just a little over two taja wide."

Shyshee nodded. "The doors?"

Kiyalee scoffed. "Just a little less than one taja."

Hoynama was ready to ask a question, however, Bonarain reappeared in the conference room with Sankiki and Tula in tow.

She glared at Antrong.

"Ask them now!" said Bonarain. "I took them to the ship and they've seen the computer system. Ask them...Sir!" When she said the word "Sir" she snarled it at Antrong.

Antrong ignored Bonarain. "Officer, Sankiki, what do you have to say about this...allegedly difficult computer system?"

Sankiki shrugged. "If you want me to figure that thing out...in a few days...forget it! I've never seen anything like that in my life. I wouldn't even know where to begin."

Antrong looked worried now. "Officer, Tula, what say you?"

Tula scoffed. "She doesn't know where to begin? I've got a bulletin for you. I don't even know how to start, let alone where to start."

Antrong glared at the two women. "Has Officer, Bonarain given the two of you a dose of pessimism as well?"

Tula angrily stormed around the table to Antrong's position with her teeth clenched. She grabbed hold of Antrong by his right ear and before he could let out a yelp, the two of them vanished.

Hoynama stood up. "Where did she take him?"

Bonarain stood there with a big grin. "I'd say that she took him to the Zizzikinza ship...to show him what they're up against."

Wymini leaned forward. "Is it really that crazy?"

Bonarain's smile got bigger. "Why don't you let that

smart-alec Antrong answer that question when he gets back?"

Wymini looked at Antrong's chair and smiled helplessly. A few moments later Tula reappeared in the conference room next to Antrong's chair and there was a loud thump as Antrong hit the floor.

Tula looked down at Antrong. "Oops! I missed!" She walked away from his seat and back to the end of the conference table. She folded her arms and turned back to glare at Antrong as he got up and got resituated in his chair.

Antrong looked around – red faced again. "I...uh... think..." He looked down at the table. "I...suggest...that everyone on the Command Staff...should go there and take a look at this...highly irregular...computer system that they have."

Hadathoo clasped his hands on the table. "Any particular reason why we should?"

Antrong cleared his throat. "When I saw the initial report...I couldn't believe what I was reading. Now that I've seen the...thing...it is an...accurate description. But I still think that... all of us...should take a look at that...system...at least once."

Hadathoo sniffed. He looked at Sankiki and Tula. "I'm hearing all kinds of things about this system. I think we do need to know a little more about it." He smiled. "Since they are doing some...very time consuming inventories of the planets and all mineral content...it'll be...maybe a few months...before they get here. If you two could take your Teams and...study their computers and how they use them...I think that a study like that would be a lot better than any snap decisions."

Sankiki looked at Tula and shrugged. "I don't think it'd hurt to take a longer look…do you?"

Tula shrugged. "I suppose so. If we're not being rushed… very much, I'd like to see if I could figure out…some of that silly thing."

Hadathoo smiled. "Good. I'm not going to tell you to take the ship over, I just want to know what you can find out. Any feasible scenario will help. If it is not feasible…we send the whole thing to Jahong's Death…and let them attack…the remains of the Jowfoonda."

Sankiki and Tula both nodded and smiled. They then disappeared.

Hadathoo smiled at Antrong. "See how much easier it is with a civil tongue in your head?"

Antrong just blushed.

Hadathoo looked up. "Officer, Chyning, you haven't reported yet."

Chyning stepped forward with a sour look on her face. "All of the work is done by the men - all of the technical work that is. The women are all in a central area where they do nothing but domestic stuff. It appears that they have a multi-generational ship…either that or those families are here for colonization. The women have babies, cook, clean and are nothing but housewives." She shook her head. "I think…while I was there…that I saw one of those…Zizzys being born. They laid the mother down on her stomach…and just peeled the newborn off of her back." She cleared her throat. "At least that's what it looked like to me."

Hoynama nodded. "You saw these…narrow corridors?"

Chyning snickered. "Boy did I. There are 32 levels in the central cylinder. There are thousands of kilotajas of corridors on all levels…and most of them are about two taja wide. Then there are side passages where the corridors are…" She looked up while pondering. "…I'd say a little less than one taja wide. The doors, the bathtubs, the beds…everything in that ship is designed for those skinny sticks. If anyone else tries to take that ship over… you'll get stuck somewhere in some narrow corridor…while they get away in a slot somewhere. Once you're stuck…you are now an easy target."

Shyshee smiled at Soolchakan. "Do you have anything else to add?"

Soolchakan shrugged. "It's a very narrow minded society. The men rule, the women obey. The only ones that the women can boss around are the slaves. They have a massive fighting capability in those side cylinders. They also have the capability of landing a large invasion force. I don't know what kind of weaponry they have, but I'll wager that it is probably some kind of powerful pulse weapon. The fact that they're planning on taking our home world…with just one attack ship…they probably do have some pretty nasty weapons…and tactics." He pursed his lips. "I personally heard the Commander and the Executive Officer talking about setting up for an invasion of Hardooth as soon as possible. Their estimate on when, is…39 *kikakay*…whatever that is."

Till grunted. "Too soon for us to study them in great detail."

Hadathoo nodded. "I think I want to see this...pull-string computer. I will take the advice of Antrong and go see that thing for myself. I'm not ordering any of the other members of the Command Staff to go look, however, if you want to...go ahead. Officer Soolchakan, would you mind Jumping me onto the main Bridge and showing me around?"

Soolchakan smiled. "With pleasure, Sir." He cleared his throat. "Sir, before I do that, I have another piece of information that the Staff needs to know about." He shuffled his feet a little. "I was reading one of the monitors as...one of the Zizzikinzas was entering information. He mentioned two elements that I have never heard of. I checked the Algothon archives and the Jowfoonda archives. I found one in the Algothon, I found both in Jowfoonda. They're called: Uranium and cobalt. The Algothons used uranium to make their firestorm weapons. It is the *main* ingredient. The cobalt...according to the Jowfoondas, is also used to make a firestorm weapon, however, according to what I was reading, the cobalt makes a much more *powerful* firestorm weapon." He cleared his throat. "If the Algothons had obtained cobalt for their weapons...Owlam would have been totally obliterated. The Zizzikinzas are planning on mining all of the cobalt from Bri...and using it for their purposes of conquering."

Everyone on the Staff looked a little stunned.

"We must obtain these...elements," said Hadathoo. "We must find them and...keep anyone from using them against us... no matter what the cost."

12

After three months, the Zizzikinza were now orbiting the gas giant Chabayo, analyzing its 49 satellites. The Owlamites knew that after Chabayo there was only the planet Bygloto between the Zizzikinzas and Hardooth. All 20 of the specially assigned computer operators and all 16 of the computer repair personnel had been going over the intrusive ship, attempting to find out anything that they could about the complicated computer system.

By now, Bonarain had been able to force feed the language of the Zizzikinzas to some fifty different Owlamites. Many of the ones who had learned this language were doing their best to pass on the information, however, none of them were quite as adept at teaching as Bonarain.

Sankiki and Tula were once again standing in front of the Command Staff.

"I don't see any shortcut way around it," said Sankiki glumly. "They made the system…completely tamper proof."

Tula looked rather defeated. "I agree."

Hadathoo nodded. "What is this…tamper proof way that you're talking about?"

Sankiki pursed her lips. She looked at Tula. "Do you want to tell them?"

Tula smiled. "You *are* the ranking one."

Sankiki wrinkled her nose. She turned back to the Staff. "When one of those…Sticks…goes up to start working on the computer, they put their hand on a big button. At first we thought that this button was…just a start button. It is *not*! It is a DNA sensor. In order for us to be able to use their computers, we would have to feed our DNA into their computer, make it accept us and then…we'd have to program our specific pattern…but first we'd have to be able to get in." She took a deep breath. "When I say – pattern – I mean…the way the lights are arranged. Each one of those hanging wires has a tubular light at the very bottom. It's about .2 taja long and it is capable of a tremendous variation in color display. You arrange the colors, according to your preference…and YOU have to remember your pattern. Now, let's say that you, Supreme Officer, Hadathoo, are being trained on that computer. A teacher will start the tutorial, which is also a programming application. Say that you want the first string on the far left, front to be your "save" string. You want your save string to be green. That is what is programmed in…for you. You want the next string to the immediate right to be your "scroll up" string. You want your scroll up string to be light yellow. Now you have two of them done. The next one to the right, you want that to be your "scroll down" string and you want it to be dark yellow. That is what is programmed into those three strings…for you. Now… Master Officer, Hoynama, let's say you're being trained as well. The string that Hadathoo wanted as his save string, you want, on your string cluster, that string is to be the space button and you want it to be pink. That is what is programmed in for you. The next one to it, you want it to be your backspace string and you want it to be lavender. Again that is what is programmed for you and no one else will have the same system. This way, no matter who is using which work station, once your DNA is sensed by the computer, only YOUR pattern will come up on those strings and no one else can read your pattern, because everyone has their own pattern and the odds of two different "Sticks" making the same exact pattern...impossible. If someone tries to sabotage anything...the computer can specify, without error, who did it, according to the DNA and the pattern used in the strings...and we have yet to figure out how to get ourselves in or even obtain a password. The only way that we can get any information from them is to read what is on the monitor as they...yank strings."

Tula interjected. "The only way to fool the DNA button is to figure out the pattern of one of the Sticks, kill him and use an amputated hand to fool the sensor. That could take months, if not years to learn his pattern, and those *doovofts* are just about ready to start their inventory on Bygloto with its one orbiting satellite. Next is us. We don't have years or months. I don't even know how many days we have before they're here at Hardooth. We have to figure out some way of...terminating them...now."

"We have to stop them...from getting to Hardooth." Hadathoo looked glum. "It seems that the only way we can do that...is total destruction of that ship." He looked around. "Unless someone can come up with a better suggestion."

Antrong sighed. "We can't go for any...face to face. They

outnumber our fighters almost 10 to 1.'"

"We, also, have never seen them in action," said Hoynama. "We don't know what their fighters, or the mother ship, are capable of. They could annihilate our home planet before we even realize what is going on."

"We have a way of testing their capability," said Shyshee. "It won't be that much of a risk…because they won't know where it came from."

Antrong scoffed. "Really? How?"

Shyshee gave Antrong an indignant glare. "We have ten fighters attack that ship while still orbiting Bygloto. They attack, from Spy or Observation…hit and run. We then watch the reaction of those "Stick" people."

"Good idea," said Antrong. "Get that Team 7016 on it."

"That's only four people," said Hadathoo. "Who are the other six?"

Antrong smiled. "We don't really need ten. Four should do."

"I disagree," said Hadathoo. "If they only see some silly little token attack, they might just ignore it all together. We *will* have ten."

Antrong shrugged. "Then get Team 7014 and 7015 involved as well."

The twelve members of the three Teams were instantly summoned. There were three of them that had to be pulled out of a bathtub and still had some very wet hair.

Soolchakan was one of the wet-haired ones. "Who came up with this scheme, Sir?"

Antrong glared at Soolchakan. "I came up with it! What's your problem?"

Soolchakan scoffed. He turned to Shyshee. "Sir, you are the Sector 4 Commander. Why do you let him push you around like this?"

Shyshee flushed. "Because he outranks me! Any more stupid questions?"

Soolchakan's jaw dropped. "SIR…when was the last time you checked the rank list? Antrong does NOT outrank you."

Everybody at the conference table started checking the list in the computer. Hadathoo's eyebrows went up. He turned to Antrong and cleared his throat. Till turned away from his monitor snickering.

Shyshee stood up with her teeth clenched and red-face mad. "I DO outrank YOU! I have ALWAYS outranked you. All this time you've been pulling rank on ME…and YOU are the subordinate."

Hoynama was almost as angry as Shyshee. "Shyshee outranks you…and I outrank Shyshee. You…you piece of *h'oolyach*…are number 4 in the rank line. I can't count the number of times you've pulled rank on me and…you were totally in the wrong you…you…SUBORDINATE!"

Shyshee leaned closer to Antrong. "From now on, SUBORDINATE, you will ask, IN ADVANCE, if you wish to use any Sector 4 personnel."

Hoynama leaned closer as well. "From now on, SUBORDINATE, you will give a written request, if you want to borrow any Sector 3 personnel."

Shyshee looked up. "Written request…that's a good idea." She glared at him again. "Did you hear that…SUBORDINATE?"

Till was fighting hard to keep from laughing out loud.

Hadathoo looked up from his monitor. "My, my, my. I think that it would do us all some good to make sure that we memorize who is where in the chain of command." He looked back down at the monitor. "Me – Hadathoo – number 1. Number 2 is Hoynama. Number 3 is Shyshee. Number 4 is…" He cleared his throat as he gave Antrong an indignant glare. "…Antrong. Number 5 is Till. Number 6 is Yamananee. Number 7 is Beemella. Number 8 is Deelka and number 9 is Wymini." He smiled. "Any questions?" He looked around expectantly. "No? Good! Now that that mess is settled…Master Officer, Shyshee, what is your suggestion?"

Shyshee gave Antrong another nasty glare. She turned to Hadathoo and smiled. She turned to Soolchakan. "Officer, Soolchakan, do you have any suggestions?"

Soolchakan grinned. "Yes, Sir. I suggest that the personnel who have to do this…experiment…come from Sector 1."

Shyshee nodded. "Any suggestions as to whom?"

Soolchakan snickered. "Teams 6432, 6433 and 6434."

Shyshee nodded again. "Any reason why you chose those three Teams?"

Soolchakan cleared his throat and smiled. "They're all Sector 1 Teams."

Shyshee opened her mouth in mock surprise. "Why that's a wonderful reason." She turned to Antrong. "If you have any objections…I don't want to hear it." She turned to Hadathoo and smiled. "Would you be so kind as to summon Teams 6432, 6433 and 6434, Sir?"

Now there were twelve more personnel in the conference room. Seven of them had been pulled out of bathtubs and one was wearing nothing but a robe and dripping wet.

Hadathoo gave Antrong a side glance. He turned to the twelve newcomers. "Please introduce yourselves."

A woman stepped forward. "Sir, I am Officer Grade 5, Sipitoy, Team Leader of Team 6432. These are my Team members." She pointed at them as she introduced them. "Officer Grade 6, Shkeej, Officer Grade 7, Iymiy and Officer Grade 7, Fisika."

Another woman stepped forward. "Sir, my name is Officer Grade 5, Oonooa. I am the Team Leader for Team 6433. My Team members are Officer Grade 6, Apa-Ay, Officer Grade 7, Kignoss and Officer Grade 7, Ezzatani."

A man stepped forward. "Sir, my name is Officer Grade 5, Rolgosh, Team Leader, Team 6434. My Team members are Officer Grade 6, Zinsing, Officer Grade 7, Naskah and Officer

Grade 7, Yeeyooa."

Hadathoo leaned back in his chair. "We are going to test the defensive capabilities of this Zizzikinza ship that has invaded our star system. Ten of you will be flying the fighters that we... obtained from the Jowfoonda. The other two will be observing what happens. Now...which of you will be the observers?"

Sipitoy smiled helplessly. "I thought...Sir...that it was supposed to be Sector 4 personnel that do things like that."

"Not any more," said Shyshee angrily.

Sipitoy swallowed and tried to smile again. "All right... Sir. What exactly are we to do?"

Hadathoo leaned forward and clasped his hands together on the conference table. "You will take ten fighters, you will hop your guns into Home dimension and attack the ship...at random places. We will watch what happens. If you feel that your life is threatened by any...counter attack...hop your entire fighter ship back into Spy and wait for further orders."

Sipitoy frowned. "Sir, uh...who is going to be flying and who is going to be watching?"

"Is there no rank structure in your Team?"

"Yes, Sir there is, but...who are the two observers going to be?"

Hadathoo shook his head. "You're the ranking one on your Team, you make the decision."

Sipitoy looked at the other eleven. "I'm the ranking one of

all of us. I'm going to be a watcher."

Oonooa smirked. "Since I'm the second ranking of all of us, I decide that I'm going to be a watcher as well."

"See how easy it is when you make a decision according to rank?" said Hadathoo with a smile. "Now, the two watchers will be Jumped to the Zizzikinza ship. One of you will be on the ship's Bridge, the other will be in the fighter bay…on the side of the ship that is attacked."

"I'm on the Bridge," said Sipitoy flatly.

"Good." Hadathoo turned to Oonooa. "You will probably need a spacesuit."

Oonooa had a nauseous smile. "Yes, Sir."

Soolchakan stood there smiling. He leaned over toward Bonarain. "**This may be fun to watch**."

Bonarain did not change her expression. "**I was just thinking the same thing**."

Kiyalee elbowed Soolchakan. "**Should we have our fighters ready**?"

He grinned. "**Have you finished the modifications**?"

Kiyalee gave him an evil grin. "**Of course I did. Now, should we have our fighters ready**?"

He looked at her patronizingly. "**What do you think**?"

Kiyalee giggled. "**I'll go warm them up**." She vanished.

The three Teams went to the hangar bay in the bottom of the ship. They were led to ten fighters and helped into space suits and then into the fighters.

Rolgosh noticed that Team 7016 was there, also dressed in spacesuits. "Officer, Soolchakan, why are you wearing those spacesuits? Are you going with us?"

Soolchakan smiled. "No, we're not going with you. We're here to help with any instructions that you may need. When you get ready to launch, the entire hangar bay is depressurized so we will need the suits in order to survive."

Sipitoy and Oonooa were standing there looking a little lost.

Sipitoy swallowed hard. "I've never been to the Zizzinkin...whatever it is...spaceship. How am I supposed to get there?"

Bonarain rolled her eyes, grabbed Sipitoy and Jumped her to the Zizzikinza main Bridge. She sniffed. "Any more problems, my dear?"

Sipitoy looked around confused. "I...can't understand them. What am I supposed to tell the Command Staff?"

Bonarain pointed and smiled. "Watch that main view-screen and tell the Command Staff what the Zizzikinzas are watching."

Back on the *Owlam the First*, Oonooa was looking a little worried. "Is she coming back to take me to that...hangar bay...on the other ship?"

Chyning sighed. She grabbed Oonooa and Jumped her to the other ship. "Here you are dearie. This is where you watch their reaction. I suggest if they scramble for their fighters, you make sure that your helmet is on correctly."

Oonooa looked half panicked. "Can you...help me... make sure it's on...correctly?"

Chyning assured her that everything was in place and that she was perfectly safe.

Oonooa took a quick glance around the bay. "What do I do?"

Chyning hung her head. "If these Sticks do anything, you report it to the Command Staff."

Oonooa smiled. "Okay."

Chyning vanished.

Now that all four of Team 7016 was back on board the *Owlam the First*, Soolchakan, Bonarain and Chyning went to one of the offices in the hangar area. Kiyalee was still performing the preflight on the fighters. The trio, in the office, sat down in front of a monitor that was tuned in to watch what was about to happen in space.

The hangar bay was depressurized and the ten fighters took off. Several of them wobbled a little as they slowly flew out of the bay. Once they were all clear of the *Owlam the First*, they all started heading towards the Zizzikinza ship...in no particular order or formation.

Soolchakan leaned back in his chair and put his head back. "Oh, help."

Bonarain snickered. "For who?"

He scoffed. "All of us."

Rolgosh was the ranking one in the fighters. "**What should we do? Should we get into...two formations of five or...one of ten or...two of three and one of four...?**"

Hadathoo groaned. "**Just get in one line, side by side by side...and try not to shoot each other down. When you get a little closer, open fire.**" He gave Antrong a nasty look. "Are all of your Sector 1 personnel this inexperienced?" He snarled. "I think that we need to get a LOT of the Sector 1 personnel more involved so that they can get some training that they've been deprived of...because someone kept on volunteering the other Sectors for all of the work."

Antrong looked away red-faced - again.

The ten ships all started getting into parallel flight - for the most part. Their unsteady flight continued.

Soolchakan could not take it any more. "**Separate yourselves a little...before you crash into each other.**"

Hoynama watched the screen. "They are *very* inexperienced...aren't they," she said facetiously.

"Very," said Shyshee. "My personnel are much better at it. They know what they're doing."

Bonarain sat there feeling a little glum. "Can we watch

this from the screens in our fighters?"

Soolchakan turned to her. "Yes…why?"

"I think that we should be ready…now!"

Soolchakan nodded. "Let's get our helmets on."

The ten fighters continued closing in on the Zizzikinzas. Hadathoo hung his head. He looked up exasperated. "**Open fire already**!"

All ten fighters opened up with conventional, pulse and torpedo weapons.

Till desperately tried to keep from laughing. "Full array, what a concept. Why not? It'll give those Zizzys something to think about."

"Hey, look!" said Beemella. "There's…some kind of distortion where the pulse beams are hitting…something that's surrounding the spaceship."

They watched as each beam made some strange rippling distortions. Then the torpedoes hit. There was a momentary explosion, followed by a larger rippling and then nothing. As each one of the conventional bullets struck the protective force-field, each one caused a momentary distortion-ripple and then back to normal.

Hadathoo growled. "**Cease fire! Hop your entire ship back into Spy and head back to the *Owlam the First*. We've seen what happens on the outside…what's going on inside**?"

"This is Sipitoy on the Bridge. The main view-screen switched from looking at Bygloto to looking for... whoever is firing on them. There's a general...agitation here on the Bridge. They're all very interested in what fired on them. They now...seem a little more agitated over the fact that they can't find the attackers. The view-screen is...changing colors...I think that they're looking...for any kind of...distortion...from where the projectiles were coming from."

Hadathoo hit the table with his fist. "Get someone over there who understands that Zizzy language."

Antrong finally looked up with some confidence. "Officer Sankiki...she does."

Hadathoo did not hesitate. **"Officer, Sankiki, get over to the Zizzy Bridge...now. We need someone over there who understands those Sticks."**

Sankiki huffed in irritation and made the Jump. She arrived and ascertained what was going on. The Ship Commander was not in his lower-level seat. He was shouting orders to different personnel as they were still attempting to find the attackers. **"Sir, the Zizzys are looking for their attackers. They're using infrared and several other types of photo-sensitive things...that I have no clue about. As Sipitoy said, the screen is changing color rapidly as they try to broaden their search. They've even got some kind of thing that followed the bullets and torpedoes back to their origin. They're very frustrated over the fact that they can't find** anything, but they're not giving up."

"**This is Oonooa in the hangar bay. It looks like they're scrambling some of their fighters. Some but not all. It looks like 40 of them...at least 40 from the port bay. Yeah, they've depressurized the bay and the 40 are taking off**."

Hadathoo nodded. "**Okay, Teams 6432, 6433 and 6434, the ones in the fighters...return to our bay... without crashing anything. Sankiki, Sipitoy and Oonooa, maintain your position...for the moment**." He looked back up at the screen. "Okay, what've we got?"

Till was watching the screen carefully. "There come the 40 fighters from the starboard bay. It doesn't look like they're launching anything from the port bay."

Hoynama was confused. "Why are they now...circling in that area?"

Till snickered. "That's the exact spot where our fighters first opened fire. That is the origin point of the weapons that were used against them."

"**This is Sankiki, Sir. They can't find anything so they're recalling those fighters. They're getting ready to break orbit and go on to Hardooth. They're saying that since Hardooth is the only inhabited planet, the shooters had to originate from there and they're going to go to Hardooth to hunt down and find the culprits...even if they have to destroy the entire planet...with nuclear weapons. They're outraged over being attacked**."

Hoynama turned pale. "Nuclear weapons? That's what the Jowfoonda called the firestorm weapons."

Soolchakan growled. "**Let's go!**"

Bonarain looked to the front of the bay. "**We can't... they've closed the doors.**"

Soolchakan looked at the door area angrily. "**Let's Jump out of here and go attack.**"

Chyning scoffed. "**How? You saw what happened. We can't shoot through their electromagnetic defense shield.**"

"**Those weapons were in Home. Right now, we're in Spy. We'll fly through the barrier in Spy and then open fire.**"

Chyning giggled. "**Oh. Sounds good.**"

Soolchakan looked around. "**So, let's go to Observation and Jump!**"

All four fighters Jumped below the *Owlam the First*. They turned their noses towards the Zizzikinza ship and blasted off at full power.

Bonarain looked around. "**Do you think we've passed our fighters yet?**"

Soolchakan grunted in disgust. "**I don't know. We've been using isolated communications and no one else knows what we're doing. We're going to have to let everyone else in on our party before we attack.**"

"**Why**?" sent Chyning. "**Do they really need to know**?"

Soolchakan shook his head. "**We've got three of our people on that ship right now. We need to let them know to get off…now**."

Chyning shook her head. 'Yeah, I guess so,' she thought.

Bonarain looked around. "**Should we hop to Spy and look for them**?"

"**No**," sent Soolchakan. "**We may end up colliding with them**."

Kiyalee shook her head. "**That'd end our party REAL quick**."

Soolchakan sighed and called out with a general sending. "**Soolchakan to Hadathoo…Sir, where are our ten fighters**?"

Hadathoo was momentarily taken aback. "**Uh…they're… currently bouncing and wobbling around the door to the hangar bay. All ten of them. Someone closed the door behind them**."

Soolchakan smiled. "**Thank you, Sir. Okay, Team 7016…hop to Spy and let's go attack**."

Hadathoo looked at Shyshee in total confusion. Shyshee was just as confused.

"**Attack WHAT? You saw what happened. How're you gonna get through that barrier**?" asked Hadathoo.

"The same way I've always gotten through the barrier...in Spy dimension!"

Hadathoo was now even more confused. "Till, have you found them?"

Till was adjusting several buttons. "Yes, Sir, I found them...but...there's something very confusing. They've... somehow...modified their fighters."

Hadathoo raised his eyebrows. "Modified? How?"

Till turned up the magnification. "Let me...zoom in on them...and..."

Hoynama was the first one to see it. "They've mounted a 459 cannon on each one of those fighters."

Deelka scoffed. "How can you fire a 459...from inside that closed cockpit?"

Till laughed. "They're canopies are open. They've got their full spacesuits on. They can fire the cannon without having to worry about breathing."

Antrong looked baffled. "Do they think that the 459 can break that defensive barrier?"

Hadathoo shrugged. "I don't know. Let's see what that Team does." He leaned closer to Antrong. "Let's see what that *experienced* Team does." He cleared his throat. "If we get out of this alive, there are a lot of Teams in Sector 1 who're going to be getting some very *intensive* training."

Shyshee was a little miffed over not being briefed on any

form of an attempted attack by 7016. "**Officer, Soolchakan… what are you doing? Why wasn't I briefed on any plan of yours**?"

Soolchakan grimaced. "**Sorry, Sir, but when I heard they were headed for Hardooth to attack immediately, I didn't have time to brief you…we had to act…NOW!**"

Chyning giggled and sent an isolated message. "**You lying *chokwad*! You thought this up three days ago.**"

Soolchakan isolated his thoughts. "**Shut up or we'll all be disciplined for insubordination.**"

"**I'm shutting up,**" sent Chyning.

Soolchakan went back to general sending. "**Kiyalee, head for the engines. Chyning head for the starboard hangar bay, Bonarain, go to the port hangar bay. I'm headed for the main Bridge. Is there anyone still on the Zizzikinza Bridge**?"

"**Yes!**" sent Sankiki. "**And I'm not alone!**"

Soolchakan grunted in disgust. "**Get out of there, because I'm about to turn that Bridge into total *h'oolyach*!**"

"**I'm Jumping to my home, right now!**" sent Sankiki.

"**Me too,**" sent Sipitoy.

Oonooa called in from the hangar bay. "**I'm still in the hangar bay, should I get out of here as well**?"

Soolchakan snickered. **"We're about to turn that ship into wreckage - what do you think?"**

"I'm Jumping to my home," sent Oonooa.

Soolchakan looked at the rear of the ship. **"Kiyalee, can you foul those engines by yourself or do you need help?"**

Kiyalee laughed. **"Fouling an engine is easy. It's one of the *easiest* things that you can do. I'll knock em all out without any problem."**

Hadathoo was surprised. **"How many engines are there?"**

Kiyalee shrugged. **"One light speed engine and four conventional engines."**

Hadathoo bit his lip. **"Take out that light speed engine first. I don't want them speeding away to Hardooth."**

Kiyalee clenched her teeth. 'What'd you think I was gonna do, you *bimyock*,' she thought. **"Better get away from the ship. I don't know what happens when a light speed engine blows up."**

Soolchakan clenched his teeth. **"Team, let's go to Observation. Tell us when you're going to...what are you going to do?"**

Kiyalee shrugged. **"I'm going to shoot a torpedo into the engine room. They keep on bellyaching about keeping the seal intact. A torpedo blowing up in there** should bust up just about anything that resembles a seal."

Soolchakan sniffed. **"Tell us when."**

Kiyalee took a breath to calm herself. **"I'm gonna shoot the torpedo and hop to dimension number 2 after I fire. I don't wanna be in this engine room when that thing goes off...I'm gonna be in a different dimension. I'll come back closer to the *Owlam the First*."**

"Okay, tell us when."

Kiyalee sucked her breath in. **"NOW!"** She pulled the trigger to launch the torpedo and hopped.

Every Owlamite that was watching was amazed as they saw approximately 1.5 kilotaja of the rear of the ship disappear in a fiery explosion. The ship made a violent turn to the left as it lost its entire rear end and started spinning out of control. It rotated six times and then suddenly the crew stabilized the badly damaged ship.

Kiyalee had hopped back and was now speeding back towards the Zizzikinza ship.

Hadathoo stood up. **"How were they able to regain control of that thing?"**

Kiyalee answered. **"Experience and four conventional engines."**

Soolchakan snickered. **"Are you going to take care of those conventional engines now?"**

"Yeah, that's a lot simpler and I'm not afraid of those explosions."

Soolchakan smiled. "Okay, Bonarain, Kiyalee, get to your places and start wreaking havoc. We want to stop them here...or at least cripple that thing."

Bonarain called in. "I'm inside the port hangar bay. I'm about to start my havoc." She reached up and pulled the trigger on the 459 and held it down. She slowly spun her fighter in a 360 degree turn. Suddenly she was looking down into outer space. "What happened? What'd I do?"

Hadathoo was sitting there staring in stunned silence.

Shyshee was the first to get her senses back. "You just cut the bottom off of the entire port cylinder. There's debris falling out of it everywhere. I think you made a BIG mess."

Kiyalee was having fun slicing through the four conventional engines with her 459. She made gaping round holes as she moved the cannon in a circular pattern. Any of the ship's crew that got in the way were cut in half. After disabling all four engines with some massive fatal damage, she looked around at all of the panic she had created. She hopped the end of the barrel back into Spy. She turned the nose of her ship up. She hopped the two torpedoes into Home and launched them at the upper hull. There was now a hole in the top of the ship and everything in the main engine room started flying out the hole.

Chyning did not know what Bonarain had done. On her side she just started taking pot-shots at any fighter that was trying to take off. Realizing that 500 fighters could take a while to individually blast, she turned her cannon to the outer hull and cut a hole that was approximately twelve taja round. Anything and everything that was not tied down was sucked out of the hole, including a few unmanned fighters, as the entire bay suffered rapid decompression. Now, with none of the pilots able to get to their fighters, it was easier to destroy the fighters in their parking spots, as well as the troop transports.

Soolchakan had brought his fighter into the Main Bridge. He heard the ship's Commander calling out orders that all three of the Auxiliary Bridges needed to be manned. He groaned in disgust. It was bad enough that he did not think about one Auxiliary. Now, to hear that there were three spares was rather irritating. He shook his head. No time to worry about something like that. Any ship that did not have one single working engine was not going anywhere soon.

He started listening to some of the chatter that was coming into the Bridge on the communication devices. Several sections were reporting hull breaches, with massive damage to the ship and massive loss of life. He calmly hopped one of his torpedoes into Home and fired it directly at the view-screen. He figured that it was going to make another hull breach here – it did not. He was shocked to see the screen shatter and the wall behind it – revealing several rooms behind the screen that were offices of some type. He huffed, reached up to the 459 and was ready to cut a huge hole in the hull, where the screen had once been. For some reason though, the Bridge did not suffer rapid decompression.

He was surprised to see all of the Zizzikinzas start rising

up off of the floor. They were now, swimming in the air. He sat there in shock, not able to figure out what was going on. Then he heard the Commander holler something about turning the artificial gravity back on. His jaw dropped. He had never thought about this phenomenon before. They had the capability of creating gravity artificially. He wondered if they had the same system on the *Owlam the First*. He giggled as he watched many of them floating around, not able to control any of their movement. Their arms and legs were flailing about wildly as they tried to catch hold of anything.

He noticed that there was a tremendous drawback to losing their artificial gravity. None of the computer string clusters were now hanging down in any organized fashion. They were all just tangled masses like some of the masses of seaweed that he had seen at some of the beaches he had explored.

He shrugged as he decided to put them out of their misery. He pulled the trigger on the 459 and opened up a ten taja wide hole in the hull in the front of the Main Bridge. He watched as there were several who tried to hang on to a railing, however, once all of the oxygen was gone, they quickly suffocated and gently floated away from their handhold.

Then everything fell to the floor. He grunted in annoyance. Someone in one of the Auxiliary Bridges had turned the gravity back on. Some of the Sticks, somewhere on this ship, still had some control of their badly incapacitated vessel.

Hadathoo made a call to all Owlamites. "**All Owlamites, except for the ones spying on the Teltermak and the**

Axswain, come to the *Owlam the First* NOW! Those Sticks are jumping ship in escape pods. I don't want any of those *doovofts* making it to Hardooth...alive! Everybody get here with any weapon that you can get your hands on. There's hundreds of those escape pods...running from the ship!"

Soolchakan groaned. "It's always something," he muttered dejectedly. He hopped the end of his 459 barrel back into Spy and flew out of the wreckage. He saw dozens of small orbs launching out of the hull of the ship. He hopped his cannon barrel back into Home. A short sweeping burst quickly cut six of the escaping pods in half and some six dozen Sticks were now floating, deceased, in space.

Bonarain, Kiyalee and Chyning were shooting escape pods as well. After several hundred of the pods had been destroyed they stopped coming out of the mother ship. Either they realized that to escape was death, or they had run out of escape pods, or any crew that was left was more interested in trying to save the big ship and was going to stay no matter what happened.

Owlam the First had hopped back to Home dimension and all of the guns on it were used to destroy escape pods. After half a day, they had destroyed every single pod that had been launched. Now they could turn their attention back to finishing the initial job of destroying that Zizzikinza ship.

Soolchakan was stunned. The crippled ship was not as crippled as they thought. It was moving away from Bygloto. With no power, the gravitational pull of the planet should have attracted the ship. The aft piece that had been cut off was moving slowly, almost imperceptibly, towards the planet. Most of the debris field was moving along with the large chunk.

Hadathoo looked at the monitor. **"Team 7016, you may land your fighters in the hangar bay."**

Soolchakan could not believe what he had heard. **"Sir, that ship is still able to move! Why aren't we going all out to destroy it?"**

Hadathoo chuckled. **"I am informed by the physicists that at its present speed, it could take between one year and one and a half years to get to Hardooth. If they're planning on trying to settle on the only inhabitable planet in this system, we have that much time to figure out a way to completely stop them. Right now, I want all fighters landed, so that we can look at the aftermath and start figuring out what we did and what else we need to do."**

Soolchakan shrugged. **"Team 7016, you heard the man...let's land."**

After retrieving all of the fighters (including the ones from Teams 6432, 6433 and 6434, the *Owlam the First* was hopped back into Spy. The Owlam ship was flying a very slow parallel course with the badly damaged Zizzikinza ship.

The Command Staff spent most of the morning reading the reports on the attack. It should not have taken that long, however, each one of the Staff read all of the reports at least twice.

"Interesting thing, this artificial gravity," said Hoynama. She looked at a footnote. "According to our physicists, this ship has that same kind of...scientific achievement."

Deelka snickered. "All the time, I thought that it was just something normal. I didn't realize that they had to put something in the ship...amazing!"

"I still like that attack plan," said Hadathoo. "Go to Spy, get inside and attack from the inside. It's sneaky and deceitful, but, it saves a lot of Owlam lives while maximizing the destruction of the enemy and their equipment...and they have no way of defending against that sort of thing."

Shyshee sighed. "It's a shame that we can't use any of their equipment or technology. Everything is too skinny or beyond our capability to understand because of that horrible security system they have in place."

Till looked up from the reports. "Do we still have someone over there keeping an eye on them? I mean...somehow, they are able to move their ship, even after we demolished all of their engines. How are they able to propel and control their ship?"

Wymini scoffed. "Don't worry. We've got at least 40 mechanics over there making sure that they can't fix their conventional engines. The Zizzys already gave up on their light speed engine, because they said that...something leaked away in the breach and they don't have the capability of replacing it... without a *lot* of help."

Hadathoo gave Antrong a nasty glare. "Meanwhile, your Sector 1 personnel need to start doing some serious training. The way they handled that initial experimental attack on the Zizzys was…at best – pathetic." He chuckled. "Maybe you were right, we should have had the Sector 4 personnel take care of the problem… because they, at least, know how to fly a fighter."

Antrong hung his head and had that familiar red tint to his face.

"Get Officer Leader, Hrombisk over here," said Shyshee. "Maybe he and all of his physicist friends can figure out how they're propelling that ship…with a shipload of dead engines."

"Good idea," said Hadathoo.

Four months later, Hrombisk was in the conference room ready to give an explanation.

"From what we can determine, from their chatter, is that this slow propulsion system is based on magnets," said Hrombisk. "It is simply a matter of pointing the end of the magnet at Bygloto that repels and pointing the end of the magnet at Hardooth that attracts. They don't really have much control of the speed, unless they shut the thing off. No matter how strong the attraction or repulsion, they still cannot go much faster than what they've achieved already." He shrugged. "They're making their way to Hardooth, in order to survive. I don't know if they really do plan on any conquest, because I and my colleagues have been looking at the science. If you want to know any military intelligence, you'll have to talk to your data collecting spy."

Hadathoo frowned. "Who was given that task?"

Hoynama did not look up from the written report. "Officer Leader, Dimatsee."

Hadathoo looked around without moving his head. "Is she here?"

Yoytay stepped forward. "Yes, Sir, she is."

"Well…bring her in."

Yoytay stepped out the door. She came back in a few moments later ushering Dimatsee into the conference room.

Hadathoo stood up smiling. "Welcome Officer Leader, Dimatsee. I hope that you can give us some good news." He motioned for her to take a seat and sat down himself.

Dimatsee sat down. "Sirs, thank you for seeing me. I have total assurance that the Zizzys do plan on going to Hardooth and…conquering. Right now, though, they have some serious problems along that line. Until they get to Hardooth and establish a controlled orbit, they have to use 98% of their current power for three things: One, the propulsion system. Two, the defensive electromagnetic shields. Three, life support. They have very little power for certain things like…manufacturing new weapons or repairing that port hangar bay. They were able to patch the starboard hangar, but they only have thirteen partially operational fighters. They only have one good troop transport and three others that are questionable."

"Why haven't you disabled those ships?" asked Hoynama.

Dimatsee smiled. "There's plenty of time for that. According to the physicists, it will take at least seven more months for them to get to Hardooth."

Beemella sat there scratching her chin. "Are they aware of us?"

"Oh, yes, Sir, most definitely they are aware of the *Owlam the First*. They did see it when the ship was hopped to Home and blasted all of the escape pods. They initially tried to use infra-red and a few other types of lenses to find us again, but they haven't been able to. The reason that they are continuing to Hardooth… they don't have any choice in the matter. Their ship is too crippled to make any attempt at any other inhabitable planet…in any system."

Yamananee put her report down. "How do we plan on stopping them altogether? Are we going to take our cannons and just chop that thing to pieces or are we going to hop the whole thing into Jahong's Death?"

Hadathoo smiled. "As Officer, Dimatsee stated – we have at least seven months to make that decision. Let's all ponder the thought and at a future meeting…we'll decide what to do then."

Six months later, they could see Hardooth from the ship without any magnification on the view-screen. The ranking physicist addressed the Command Staff with two other Officer Leaders at his side.

Hrombisk introduced the other two Officer Leaders. "Sirs,

this is Officer Leader, Mippa of Team 42 and Officer Leader, Nantasa of Team 47." The two women bowed slightly as each one was introduced. "You did give orders that the personnel of Sector 1 were to receive more training, especially in taking off, and landing of the fighters. While practicing their flying skills with the fighters, we tried an experiment. In this experiment, both of these Teams flew their fighters to the rear of the crippled Zizzy ship. They all slowly went up to the edge of the defensive shield of the Zizzy ship and started pushing. When you go up to it slowly, you can do this without damaging any of our craft. We were actually able to accelerate the movement of the enemy ship."

Antrong scoffed. "So you're helping the enemy get to Hardooth faster. How is this good news?"

"Sir, we were able to accelerate it and steer it as well, which means that we have full control of the ship. We can move it where we want to move it."

Antrong rolled his eyes. "So we can steer it, so what! We want to destroy the thing. Not…lead it around the system, playing with it like it were some bath toy."

"Sir, my point is that since we can control the speed and direction of that thing, we don't have to dump it in another dimension. If any of the other ships of the Zizzys decides to come here, they won't know what happened to their friends and that will not stop them from trying their own attempt at conquest. We were able to accomplish this with just eight fighters. Now, if, instead of eight fighters, we use eight scout ships, we could accelerate the thing to quite a greater speed…and crash it, nose first, into the back side of Niygool."

Hadathoo frowned. "Why would we want to do that?"

"Sir, if their friends come along and find one of their ships has been splattered all over Niygool, this would probably give them pause. They would wonder what happened. They would have a mystery on their hands that could distract them and give us more time to ambush a second attack ship."

Hoynama cocked her head to the side. "It'd be a monument to the defeated. They'd have to investigate what happened... especially if it was one of their own."

Antrong shook his head. "No, I can't abide by that. We already made the decision that we are going to dump them into Jahong's Death."

Hrombisk hung his head for a moment. He sighed. He looked back up. "Sir, if we just...dump them...into dimension number 45, they are still alive and active. Suppose that they are one day able to fix their ship and figure out a way to do their own dimension hopping. They could come back and wreak havoc on us. If, however, we slam the ship into the back side of Niygool and guarantee 100% fatalities of those on board, there would be no witnesses as to what happened and the new ones would also not be able to find any ship logs by which they could find accurate information because we would also pulverize and destroy all computer logs. The new ones would have to investigate and that would give us more time to...have fun...at our leisure...if you will."

Antrong shook his head. "I really don't like it."

"I do," said Hadathoo. "Leaving evidence that their ship met with a fatal accident and left nothing behind to tell the newcomers what happened...that could give us an advantage, either of having them distracted or possibly chasing them off altogether."

"I agree," said Hoynama. "It'd be a sign to any other invader. Something is wrong here. Do they really want to try conquest when an attack ship lies in ruins on a moon?"

"I like the plan," said Shyshee. "Where I have a problem... how fast can we get it going and are we assured that the destruction would be total?"

Hrombisk shrugged. "How fast can we get it going? We don't know until we try. Are we assured that the destruction would be total? No! However, after the ship has been crashed into the back side of Niygool, we could have several personnel go there and look for any usable computer items...and destroy or corrupt them completely."

Till cleared his throat. "You keep on saying the back side of Niygool...why Niygool and why the back side?"

Hrombisk smiled. "Zhagool rotates at least four times per orbit. With a good telescope, we have always been able to see all of Zhagool. Niygool always has the same face to Hardooth. If we crash the thing on Zhagool, someone with a good telescope could see it and now there would be others on Hardooth who would be asking a lot of strange questions. If we crash it on the back side of Niygool, only *we* know it is there and no one else on Hardooth is any the wiser and there are no uneasy questions...by anybody on

Hardooth."

Hadathoo nodded. "It IS a good idea. I like it. Is there any other discussion or question…or argument?"

Wymini looked confused. "What about the Sticks on that Zizzy ship right now? Don't you think that they may attempt to prevent our little escapade from occurring? Won't they be able to use that…magnetic drive to stop us…or themselves?"

Hrombisk shook his head. "We can sabotage most of their systems right now, including the magnetic drive. We can have them absolutely helpless in half a day. They won't even know that they're accelerating until someone looks out a window and sees Niygool coming closer at a very rapid rate."

Antrong sat there pondering a little longer. He finally turned to Hadathoo and shrugged. "Why not? If nothing else, it'll be a learning experience for all of us. Leaving a mess on Niygool for any other intruder…who knows what kind of distraction…or fear they'd experience?" He nodded. "So, who is going to fly which scout ships?"

Hadathoo stood up. "Let's get some Teams back on *Owlam the First* and those scout ships and…begin our experimental escapade."

The only change to the plan was that all eleven of the scout ships would be used. They decided to use forty of the fighters as well. This would give all kinds of personnel all kinds of training in this new attack format and the more that knew how to do it, the better for all. Four of the scout ships were approximately one third of the way back from the front, surrounding the enemy ship. Four more scout ships were two thirds of the way back surrounding it as well. The other three scout ships were directly in the rear doing nothing but pushing. The forty fighters were to take positions where they could and assist in steering – if necessary. All ships were in Spy, with a small portion of them in Home so that they could push on that defensive barrier.

Once all of them were in position, Hadathoo sat in the Command chair on the *Owlam the First*, getting ready to watch the spectacle. "Hrombisk, this is your plan, go ahead and get things started."

"Yes, Sir." Hrombisk took a deep breath. "**Step one… destroy all three Auxiliary Bridges. Report in once that's accomplished**."

A few well-placed hand-held bombs and all three Bridges were badly disabled. The saboteurs reported in.

Hrombisk nodded. "**All ships, assume your assigned positions**."

After all ships reported in the order was given. The massive wreckage was being moved easier than they initially thought it would be to move. They started moving faster and faster. There were a few times that they had to make a slight course adjustment, however that turned out to be no problem at all.

The only real problem that occurred that they had not foreseen was the fact that the scout ships were capable of flying faster than the fighters and at a certain point all of the fighters had to break off and head back to the mother ship because they could not keep up.

A call came in from the lead scout ships. **"Hrombisk, there are a lot of smaller craters that are coming in to focus. How long do we keep pushing?"**

Hrombisk chuckled. **"All ships break away and let the momentum carry them into Niygool. If the Zizzys are able to somehow stop their forward motion...we can always try it again."**

All of the scout ships pulled away from the Zizzikinza ship and slowed to a stop. The big Zizzikinza ship continued on at the same speed without slowing. When it impacted on Niygool there was a tremendous fire that was snuffed out almost immediately by the void of outer space. There was a massive dust cloud and large amounts of wreckage that flew several hundred kilotaja because of the lower gravity of Niygool.

Hadathoo nodded. **"People of Owlam. It works! We have a new tactic that we can use against any enemy."**

13

236 years after defeating the Zizzikinza invasion, the Owlamites started becoming somewhat complacent. They had learned to utilize the long range scanners supplied by the Jowfoonda and they allowed the scanners to go on automatic in order to keep from having to do the job themselves. In time, some of them forgot to check on the automatic scanners and no one noticed that some of the scanners were malfunctioning.

548 years into the tenure of Hadathoo and 843 years after the firestorm weapons had done their damage, the Owlamites and Hardooth were attacked – by another Zizzikinza ship. It was not a minor attack. Officer Leader, Ota reported that the Teltermak were attacked by some invader from the sky. Officer Leader, Boneech reported that the Axswain were attacked from the sky. There were Teams all over the world that were exploring places that they had never been before and they reported attacks from the sky. The last ones also reported Owlam fatalities.

Senior Officer, Deelka started calling out to all of the Command Staff. There was no response from Hadathoo. There was no response from Hoynama. There was no response from Shyshee. There was no response from Antrong. She finally received a response from Till. Till informed her that he was currently with Beemella and Wymini. It appeared that those were the only four, of the Command Staff, that were still alive.

Till was now trying to assess the situation while pondering the fact that once again an attack had occurred and most of the Command Staff was dead as a result. He ordered everyone into Spy dimension and onto the *Owlam the First* to try and see who this invader from the sky would turn out to be. As soon as all of the Owlamites were aboard their aging spacecraft, they saw a fully intact Zizzikinza ship with fighters still being launched from the side cylinders.

Till clenched his teeth in anger. He got on the ship's communicator system. "All personnel who are totally proficient in flying our fighters, get out there and slice that Stick ship to pieces. After you've done that, kill all of their fighters and any escape pods that you happen to see flying around."

Soolchakan smiled at his three Teammates. "Shall we attack that thing the same way that we did the other one?"

Chyning gave him an evil smile. "It worked once, we'll do it again."

Soolchakan immediately sent the message to Till. "**Master Officer, Till, this is Team 7016. Let us take care of the mother ship and tell everyone else to do the mopping up after we dissect the big one.**"

Till did not take long thinking about it. "**All Owlamites... back away from the mother ship and let 7016 do their damage. They killed that last one, so I figure they can do it again. Once they've killed it, you all start working on fighters and escape pods. Try not to use your 459**

cannons, as you may damage each other. Now, let's get these marauders!"

Once again, Team 7016 took off from the *Owlam the First* and went into their attack formation against a Zizzikinza ship. Soolchakan to the Main Bridge, Bonarain to the port hangar bay, Kiyalee to the engines and Chyning to the starboard hangar bay.

Bonarain was the first to arrive at her destination. She did the same tactic as before. She opened fire with her 459 and held the trigger as she spun around. The results were the same as before. Everything that was in the way of the beam was cut in half and the entire bottom of the port cylinder fell away from the ship. Since her beam was also entering the big central cylinder, she ended up doing some massive damage inside the ship itself.

Kiyalee flew into the area with the light speed engine and decided to try something different. This time she did a quick shot near the top of the large containment area of the engine. This broke all of the attachments at the top and made the entire thing lean over dangerously. She then fired a quick shot near the bottom. This put everyone in the area in a panic as several loud alarms went off. They jettisoned the interior portion of the engine. A few moments later there was a violent explosion that made the entire ship shake and start spinning out of control. They were able to regain control a few moments later with the conventional engines. Now Kiyalee went after those engines as she started drilling some fatal holes in each one. In a very short time, the ship was crippled and they had to start using their magnetic engines.

Chyning decided to try a different tactic as well. She

flew to the bow of the starboard cylinder and opened fire with a sustained blast as she flew lengthwise along the cylinder. Before she reached the stern of the starboard cylinder the entire right side started tearing away from the mother ship. The amount of debris flying around was immense.

Soolchakan flew into the Bridge. He tried to listen to what was going on. After listening for a few moments he sent a new message: **"Start doing a side-to-side chop job on this big ship. Slice off sections of it. They're saying they can't control any form of a landing, even if they do get through the atmosphere safely. If a ship this size hits the land or water, it'll cause all kinds of catastrophe on the surface of the planet and then this planet won't be worth holding onto for at least another...I don't know what they're time measurement is, but they said...250... of something before they could inhabit. All three of you, head to the port side so that you don't crossfire on each other. Remember that I'm still in the Main Bridge."**

The three women headed that way. Once they could see each other they took up positions and started cutting sections off of the end of the big ship. Several times while they were cutting, each one had to hop their barrels back into Spy because some curious Zizzikinza fighters were attempting to find the origin of the deadly beams that were killing their ship.

After seeing most of the power go completely out in the Main Bridge, Soolchakan opened fire and cut a mammoth hole in the starboard side of the Bridge. He watched as most of the Bridge crew got sucked out the hole by rapid decompression. He hopped his barrel back into Spy and flew out of the ship to join his teammates in the slice-and-dice of the big ship.

There were several hundred escape pods that were shooting out of hundreds of orifices in the big ship. They headed for Hardooth. As soon as they had successfully achieved an entry into the atmosphere, over one hundred Owlamites in Jowfoonda fighters were cutting the strings to their parachutes and the escape pods were now plummeting in an uncontrolled free fall into the South Seyap Ocean. Several Zizzy fighters were attempting to defend the escape pods, however, they did not know what or where to shoot at anything and ended up getting shot down themselves.

As the big chunks of the demolished space ship started entering the atmosphere, there were numerous indigenous races on Hardooth who got to see quite a light show as the majority of the ship burned up on entry.

In that short amount of time, the Zizzikinza ship was reduced from a finely tuned attack machine with a full crew of dedicated conquerors, to nothing but debris full of mangled and incinerated bodies.

Soolchakan sent a new message: **"The Sticks on the Main Bridge made a call to…someone else. They said that they were receiving catastrophic and fatal damage and that the other ships needed to respond immediately. I think we need to check our long range scanners…and our entire star system. There may be more of those *doovofts*…close by."**

Till nodded. **"All of the computer people…get out**

there and do some checking on our equipment and do some reconnaissance as well. We might have some more nasty surprises out there - somewhere!"

Sankiki turned on all of the scanners on the *Owlam the First*. She set it to scan any place in the star system for any kind of spaceship. It did not take long to get a response. She groaned as she looked at the monitor. "**Sir! There are six more of those Zizzikinza ships…orbiting Rogoth. It appears as if they're breaking orbit and heading this way.**"

Till gritted his teeth. "**All fighters that aren't shooting down enemies inside the atmosphere, start heading to Rogoth.**"

Now it was Soolchakan's turn to clench his teeth. "**Sir! The fighters don't have that kind of range. We have to land them on the mother ship and have it take us out there.**"

Till clenched his eyes and fists. "**All right! Land on the mother ship and let's get ready to meet those monsters out there.**"

Oonooa smiled as she headed for the mother ship. "**Sir… out there we won't have to worry about the direction that we fire our new 459 cannons. We shouldn't have to worry about hitting anything on Hardooth, once we've passed Bygloto.**"

Till gave a sigh of relief. "**Thank the Great Maker for that.**"

They Jumped their ship and met the six Zizzikinza ships almost eighty million kilotaja from Rogoth. All 111 of the working Owlam fighters simply hopped to Observation and departed the big ship without much ado.

Till did not bother with the ship to ship communication. **"All fighters – that system that was used on the first Zizzy ship…do it out here. Side-to-side filet job all six of those *chokwad* ships before any of them realize that someone is attacking any of them. There are six of them and 111 fighters. That makes seventeen per Zizzy ship with three left over. Get into position before any of them have a clue. Call in when we're all in position."**

Kiyalee did her own sending: **"Get near the stern area. Their main light-speed drive is in the very end. Hit that before they can go to light-speed. Then all they'll have left is the conventional engines. We can take our time with those. After we've crippled all of their engines, we can take our sweet time doing the rest of the chopping."**

Till sat there nodding. **"I agree. Do it that way!"**

Soolchakan and Bonarain were doing a fly-by as they counted the fighters in place.

Kiyalee did her own fly-by, giving instructions to the last three in each formation as to their exact needed location… as well as a safe distance. After having been very close to two explosions of light-speed engines, she also gave instruction that at the first sign of the ship lurching or bucking or jumping, take your

entire ship back to Observation, including the barrel of the guns…
otherwise *you* might become a casualty of the explosion as well.

As soon as Soolchakan and Bonarain called in that all
108 fighters were in position, Till gave the order to fire. 108
supercharged 459 beams started cutting through the hulls of
the enemy ships. It was only three heartbeats later that all six
Zizzikinza ships did an unusual jerking motion and all of the
Owlam fighters were back in Observation. Two heartbeats later,
all six experienced massive explosions in the stern. Two ships
experienced cascade explosions that totally obliterated their entire
ship. There were several dozen Owlam fighters who backed off
very quickly, seeing as how they were caught in the blast area of
the ship that they were firing on.

One of the big ships started moving away in a somewhat
controlled manner. The other three just drifted helplessly.

Kiyalee scowled as she saw the one moving. She headed
directly for it, hopped her barrel into Home and opened fire on the
area of the conventional engines. In less than four heartbeats, that
ship was now floating helplessly.

Someone in one of the fighters called in: **"What do we
do now?"**

Kiyalee answered: **"Start chopping the remains of
the big ships. Some of them may still have that magnetic
drive and they just might try to get to Hardooth. We
have to stop them here."**

Hrombisk did a sending: **"If we stop all forms of their
propulsion here, all of the debris will eventually drift**

into the interior of Rogoth. All of them will be lost in the gravity and gas of Rogoth and we won't have to worry about them again."

Another call came in from the fighters: "**What makes you think they won't ever come back again**?"

Till chuckle. "**Because they're sending out a distress call. We've already translated it and it seems that they're invoking some deity and saying that it is the will of that deity that they stay away from this star system. The cripples are also saying that they're going to make an attempt at getting out of the system. They're going to attempt a rendezvous at...9908 by 1667 by 4429. If they're not at that point in...56...whatever that time measurement they're using, then they're all dead. Let's make sure that no one makes that rendezvous.**"

Soolchakan sighed. "**Are you saying that you want us to continue chopping and make sure that they never get any repairs done**?"

Till leaned back in the Command chair. "**We're going to make sure that any ally of theirs does not get any first hand story of what happened here. They're going to get a bunch of panicked radio communications and find no survivors...or debris. Hopefully that'll discourage any further attempts at another Zizzikinza attack against us.**"

The chopping attack and hunt for any escape pods or courageous fighters continued for almost two days. When they were finished, they all simply watched as they could see some of the debris going back to Rogoth because of the gravitational pull of the giant. Numerous stops in the *Owlam the First* had to be done to replace depleted 459 power packs.

There were several who asked why they could not push the pieces into the gas giant, the same way they had crashed the first ship on that moon. Hrombisk explained that since they had completely destroyed all of the power capabilities of the new ships, they no longer had their electromagnetic shields surrounding their pieces. When the original had been pushed into the moon, the electromagnetic shielding of both the scout ships and the victim were on. It was like one rubber ball pushing another. Since they only had their own shielding, he did not think that it could withstand the force of pushing all of that debris into the gas giant. It was rather difficult for anyone without physics training to argue with his educated findings.

Now that they saw that there were no ships, small or large, from the enemy that were moving under their own power, the Owlamites departed the scene of the massacre and went home…to count their own casualties.

Another unhappy roll call had to be done. Hadathoo's entire Team had been wiped out so Till had to call on someone who was experienced at the roll call. Officer Grade 3, Nayna and Officer Grade 4, Akantini were pulled from the new Teams they had been assigned to because they were the most experienced at calling the roll. Till's Aides, Officer Grade 3, Ababi, Officer Grade

6, Hoodeefa and Officer Grade 7, Choychata watched carefully as Nayna and Akantini performed the gloomy task.

Once it was firmly established that Hadathoo, Hoynama, Shyshee, Antrong and Yamananee were all dead, along with all of their Teams, Till was now the *Voice of Power* and had to establish a new Command Staff.

Till was now the Supreme Commander. Senior Officer, Beemella had been the Sector 2 Vice Commander – now promoted to Master Officer and Sector 2 Commander. Senior Officer, Deelka had been the Sector 3 Vice Commander – now promoted to Master Officer and Sector 3 Commander. Senior Officer, Wymini had been the Sector 4 Vice Commander – now promoted to Master Officer and Sector 4 Commander.

Officer Leader, Skalix of Team 37 was promoted to Master Officer and became the Sector 1 Commander. Officer Leader, Dimatsee of Team 39 was promoted to Senior Officer and became the Sector 1 Vice Commander. Officer Leader, Anbrom was promoted to Senior Officer and became the Sector 2 Vice Commander. Officer Leader, Jeejow was promoted to Senior Officer and became the Sector 4 Vice Commander. Officer Leader, Mippa was promoted to Senior Officer and became the Sector 3 Vice Commander.

Till also made sure that all eight of his Staff members memorized the list as to who had rank over whom. He did not want to see another mess like the one that had been created by Antrong. It was very unprofessional. By rank: Till, Beemella, Deelka, Wymini, Skalix, Dimatsee, Anbrom, Jeejow and finally

Mippa. He made his senior Aide, Ababi give each one of them a form that said that they understood the order and if there were any arguments caused by anyone…that person might very quickly be demoted.

Nayna and Akantini finally finished the roll call. Ninety-four Teams had been killed. Thirty-nine other Teams had lost one or more members. 102 men and 323 women died in the second (and what they hoped was the last) Zizzikinza attack. In an attempt to get all remaining Teams back to four members, several had to be split up and go to other Teams. When the final new tally was done, there were two Teams – 4700 and 5783 – that unlike all other Teams consisted of two men and two women. All other Teams had four members, one man and three women.

Till now had to create a new law stating that the long range sensors would be checked and maintained regularly. Another surprise attack would not be tolerated.

While doing their maintenance checks on the sensors, there were also checks on the debris field around Rogoth. It took three months for all of the Zizzikinza debris to disappear in the gas that was whirling around the in the giant.

There was a new discovery that surprised the Owlamites. All of the Kalash people they had been acquainted with were now deceased. It seemed that the average life span of a Kalash (since the firestorm weapons went off) was around 600 years. The Rahanan-Sar lived an average of 350 years. The Saraff-Or still had a few people that were alive that remembered the firestorm weapon, however, most of them were very old. The T'Mor had a life span of about 800 years, so all of the ones that had been rescued were dead, however, the new ones still told the magnificent saga of how the Owlam people had executed a full rescue and assisted in the devastation of the nasty Sodle. The Cowpa had a life span of around 550 years so all of the old ones were dead. The Towtoo had a life span of around 700 years. All of the old ones were dead. The only ones who were still there and not really showing age (that much) were the pink-haired Argaman-Or.

The Owlamites started looking at each other very critically for any gray hair or wrinkles or anything that showed any sign of being elderly. 843 years after the firestorm attack and not one Owlamite had died from old age or disease. The 2,600 plus Owlamites who had died had all been killed in battle. Not one, so far, from anything else. It made them wonder about their true longevity.

221 years later, when a Team was out performing preventive maintenance on one of the long range scanners, they observed a large spaceship entering the star system. They immediately abandoned their task and Jumped back to Hardooth to report what had happened.

Once again the Owlamites had to begin the reconnaissance of a new invader. This new ship looked as if it had been thrown together by someone with absolutely no sense of organization. Whoever did it, knew there would be no form of friction in the void of space, so they did not concern themselves with superfluous things like aerodynamics. There was one very large box that had numerous connections between it and several other sections of the ship. Some of these other sections were smaller boxes. Some were round or oval or crescents and even a few cylinders. There were a few that had no real shape, just parts that had been randomly thrown together.

Bonarain had done her best to train others on how to perform the mindreading and translation imagery, however, the only ones who seemed to get it were her own Team members. Everyone said that it was because she liked her Team better or it was because she was able to practice on them more than others and therefore, they had no argument in saying that they did not get it.

Team 7016 was once again "honored" to be the lead Team in flying into the new ship and attempting to determine language, intent and layout of this new alien ship. Considering the accidental way in which this "thing" was thrown together, it took nearly a full day to finally find either the Main Bridge (or A Bridge) or the Main Engine Room.

Soolchakan got rather close to one of the inhabitants of this flying maze and prepared to turn the biosensors on. Before he turned it on, he mentally sent a physical description. "Tall and hairy. This one appears to be somewhere between 11 and 12 taja in height. Gender is impossible to determine because of all that long thick white hair. I've seen several of them and none of them appear to be wearing clothing. They have different colored belts. I don't know yet, whether the belt signifies rank or section or…

fashion."

He sighed and turned the biosensor on. He read as the sensor examined the creature. 11.2 taja in height. Female reproductive organs, currently between menstrual cycles. He looked the creature over several times in regards to the fact that he was looking at a gargantuan female. The sensors continued the scan. 7.2 taja in circumference at the waist and 8.1 taja in circumference at the shoulder. Skin color difficult to determine because creature is extremely hirsute. Totally covered with white hair. Biped that walks upright with arms and opposable thumbs on hands with seven fingers and the thumb. The legs are 31% of the overall height. Each arm is 7.1 taja in length. Respiratory, circulatory and gastrointestinal system very similar to Heyyah anatomy.

Everyone else on the mother ship all stood there gawking when they saw the height.

Till finally broke the ice. "11.2 taja in height and 8.1 taja in circumference at the shoulder. I don't think we'll have to worry about any skinny corridors for these beasts."

Kiyalee found the engine room. She sighed with boredom as she saw the light-speed engine. **"The laws of physics is the laws of physics. The light speed engine here…very similar to the ones on *Owlam the First* and the Zizzy ships. The conventional engines are much the same as well. I don't think that we're gonna learn anything new here…not with these engines.**"

In going around the different parts of the ship, they

discovered that the male and female were all pretty much the same in appearance. All of these adult aliens were between 10 and 12 taja in height.

Bonarain entered a section of the ship and started her mindreading translation act. She sat there for several moments before she found someone who was relaxed and simply doing his normal chores for the day. The translations started kicking in. Every few moments he would look up and ogle one of the females. Bonarain was baffled as to why the male considered the way her hair appeared between her shoulder blades. She just continued listening for anything that she could get from him. It became boring and repetitive as he kept on staring at the hair in the middle of his target's back. Bonarain now had a little bit of a working knowledge of the language so she switched to another target. There had to be something else to think about other than the hair on someone's back - WRONG. This male was ogling the same female for the exact same reason. She snarled in frustration and went on to another.

Soolchakan was not as adept as Bonarain when it came to the translation thing. He concentrated on a certain female for a long time before the language finally came through. She was a very vindictive individual who was planning on doing something very nasty to a certain male if he did not leave her alone. Once all of the language came through, he decided to go check on another one of these people and he pitied the poor slob who crossed that female. The new one he found was an immature male who was very upset over the fact that he was forced to do any work at all. Soolchakan sat there listening to the complaints just to make sure that he was getting all of the language and syntax down pat.

After listening to all the lust that she could stand, Bonarain called out to the Team and said that it was time for a meeting. **"We need to get together and trade notes on these people."**

Soolchakan hung his head. **"Where?"**

"I agree," sent Kiyalee. **"I have no idea where I am on this thing. I'm in the engine room...but I have no idea where any of you are...in relation to where I am."**

Chyning sent a perplexed message as well. **"I'm kinda lost on this flying nightmare. I don't see any...form of organization in this thing."**

Bonarain sighed. **"I've flown outside of the hull... in the portion that I was in. It...looks like a...quarter of a globe. Can any of you see a shape like that...from where you are?"** She held her position waiting for the others to find her.

Chyning pulled up next to Bonarain. **"Have you ever seen anything that was manufactured...that is so disorganized...on purpose?"**

Bonarain just shook her head.

Kiyalee arrived at the gathering point. **"Someone needs to be jailed for manufacturing this mess."**

Soolchakan was growling to himself. **"Where are you? I can't find a thing in this...twisted labyrinth."**

Chyning giggled. **"What...you haven't found us**

yet?'"

He clenched his teeth. "**If I had found you, I'd be there**." He headed for the outer perimeter of the mess and started orbiting it slowly.

Finally there was a call. "**I see you**," sent Bonarain.

He looked around even more frustrated. "**WHERE**?!"

Bonarain chuckled as she gave the instructions. "**Point the nose of your ship, 90 degrees down**."

He made the adjustment. "**Okay, I see you**." He flew to the rendezvous point. "**Okay, what did you need or want?**"

"**Now that we've all seen a part of this...muddled mess, let's compare notes on what we've found...and where**," send Bonarain.

They flew into the "quarter globe", landed their fighters and got out.

Bonarain held her hands out as if she were giving a tour. "This area is for salvaging any pieces or parts that they're able to...salvage or recycle. There's not a whole lot to talk about other than that – in this area."

Chyning grunted. "I was in a kitchen – disgusting! Blech!" She shuddered.

Kiyalee frowned. "What's so disgusting about a kitchen?"

Chyning shuddered. "They like to eat fresh meat. They have live animals in there and they're...cutting them up."

Soolchakan shrugged. "Okay, so they're carnivores...so what?"

Chyning gave him a disgusted look. "They don't have any stoves," she said slowly.

Bonarain's jaw dropped. "RAW? They eat their meat... raw?"

Kiyalee looked nauseous. "You could have gone a century or two without saying that."

"Okay," said Soolchakan. "Let's get to something useful. I've discovered that each one of the pieces of this...confusing mess...can break away and be an independent ship by itself. Each one has an engine section, each one has a Bridge. What we need to find is the Main Bridge...that controls this entire...mess."

Bonarain looked concerned. "How many *pieces* are there?"

Chyning checked the monitor in her cockpit. "According to the picture that I see, there's, at the very least, 25 different pieces."

Kiyalee looked a little hopeful. "How about the biggest box section? Has anyone checked that?"

"I did," said Soolchakan. "It seems to be nothing more than the living quarters for all of these...has anyone figured out what these hairy beasts call themselves?"

Bonarain chuckled. "Are you ready?" She looked at each of their faces. "They call themselves: Chokchakchok!"

Kiyalee looked at her dully. "You can't *possibly* be serious."

Bonarain nodded with a big grin.

Chyning shook her head. "That's insane. Who'd call themselves something like that?"

Soolchakan sighed. "Someone who has been calling themselves that name…all of their lives. Let's just call them… Choks…just to save time…and syllables." He huffed. "And we still don't know where the Main Bridge is yet."

"Also," said Kiyalee. "How do they break apart?"

"Those…great big round poles…that connect the pieces…are retractable hallways from one piece to another," said Soolchakan. "When someone is going to break away, they just disconnect, pull the things in…and fly…wherever."

"Hold it," said Bonarain. "I'll ask." She walked up in front of one of the Chokchakchok as he was walking along carrying a large crate. She gave him a full blast of mental control. The big Chok stopped walking and dropped the crate. It shattered when it hit the floor and he stood there looking a little stunned.

While maintaining control, she pointed at a wall to her right. "Over there…is a main listing…of all of…the sections and rooms."

Soolchakan, Kiyalee and Chyning went to investigate the listing.

Chyning scoffed. "Is the print small enough?"

"No wonder we didn't see it," said Kiyalee.

Soolchakan looked it over. "All right, I found the guide to the Main Bridge. All it says after that is…1-1-1-1. WHAT DOES THAT *H'OOLYACH* MEAN!?"

Bonarain was still controlling and questioning. "It means…Section 1, Level 1, Corridor 1, Room 1."

Soolchakan snarled. He glared back at Bonarain. "Which one of these pieces of…flying chunks…is Section 1?"

Bonarain sighed. "He doesn't know."

Kiyalee waved the big Chok off. "Let him go for now. We'll figure it out later."

As soon as Bonarain broke off the mental control, the big Chok let out a blood curdling scream and fell on his back. When he dropped the crate it had landed on his feet and, in all probability, broke, shattered or crushed every bone in his feet and he did not know or feel it until she mentally released him. He was screaming so loudly that the Owlamites could not hear each other talking.

Chyning walked away giggling. "**Fussy, isn't he**?"

Soolchakan shook his head. "**Let's get back to the *Owlam the First* and give the Staff a report on this h'oolyach**!"

"**We've got nothing to report**," complained Kiyalee.

"**We can report what little we've found and why**," sent Soolchakan.

Till still felt a little uncomfortable sitting at the end of the conference table. He had been in another chair for so long that it had been his place. Now, the one where Hadathoo had always been just did not feel right. He knew, though, that he must accept it and carry on with the ones that were here. "Officer, Soolchakan, you say that there is not much to report. Why do we need to be here if there is so…little to report?"

Soolchakan smiled. "Sir, there is very little to report because that ship is…a very complicated maze. It is a collection of smaller ships that are hooked together. We can't seem to find anything because of this maze."

Beemella scoffed. "Why didn't you destroy it? If it is that big a problem, just blast the thing like you did the Zizzikinza ships."

Soolchakan held his hands up. "Please, Sirs, before you voice any questions, please hear me out." He lowered his hands. "Yes, we could have started blasting the thing with our big powerful 459 cannons. If we did…we learn nothing. If…however, we were to hop that entire mess…into Dimension 45 and get rid of all the inhabitants, once we've figured out their language and computer system…now we have the whole thing to ourselves and that gives us a much newer ship than the *Owlam the First*. Remember, Sirs, that our acquired ship is not getting any newer. There have been a few repairs where the mechanics have had to machine some of the parts necessary to keep the thing flying. If we get a new ship, we have a new computer, we have a new set of weapons, we have a new system…we have a new set of long range scanners and we could also possibly have a new set of one-man fighter ships."

Till leaned forward. "What is the advantage of stranding it in Jahong's Death?"

"Sir, there's nothing there for them to conquer. We have all kinds of time to study it and they have no one to shoot at or conquer. If we do find out that they are just some curious explorers, we can always hop them back…outside of the system. If we find out that they are conquerors…we get rid of them and we still have the ship."

"What if they blow it up?" Deelka folded her arms. "What do we learn then?"

"We then learn that they are scared easily and are prone to suicide." He smiled and shrugged. "And if they blow themselves up in Dimension 45…they won't contaminate our system with any debris field."

Skalix chuckled. "What happens if the Zizzikinza people are stubborn and try again? Should we hop their ships into 45 as well?"

Soolchakan smiled. "Think of all of that equipment that was lost when we did nothing but demolish that entire Zizzikinza fleet. Tula and Sankiki both stated they would need…possibly years, to learn that complicated computer system. We hop the Zizzikinza ship into 45, evict all of the indigenous personnel and the ship is ours to study…for however long we wish."

Wymini shook her head. "Before we condemn these new

people to 45, I'd like to know whether or not they're coming as conquerors."

"They are," said Bonarain. "I got a little more than just their language, alphabet and some idiosyncrasies. Between the lustful thoughts of those two men, they were thinking of how... once they were able to obtain some property and slaves on our planet, they would be rich and they would be able to awe that female that they kept ogling."

"I think they may be the type who...kill and eat their slaves," said Chyning. "I remember how...some of the animals... that they had in that kitchen...looked like some kind of bipedal creature. I didn't think to read their minds, but...they could have been a member of an intelligent race that was taken prisoner somewhere else." She shuddered. "They don't have any knives in their kitchen. They just rip the animals...or whatever those creatures are...apart with their bare hands. They don't have any ovens or stoves. They eat raw meat and...well, like I said they just rip it apart...and eat."

Jeejow nodded. "Okay, we put all of these ships in 45. We study the personnel on board...until we either send them on their way or kill them. We now have all of their technology and property. What happens if we find...firestorm weapons on any of these ships?"

Soolchakan chuckled. "We store them. If we send them off to the Sun, we might end up doing damage to the Sun. If we blow them up somewhere else, we could contaminate someplace else for...who knows how long?"

Till cleared his throat. "We...store them...where?"

Soolchakan smiled. "Zhagool."

"That's ridiculous," said Mippa. "Store them on a moon with no atmosphere where they would stand out like a beacon at night for any marauder to come along and steal?"

Soolchakan shook his head and hands. "No, Sir, not out in the open. We could make underground vaults, the same way we made these apartments here in the walls of the gorge. We put them in vaults, far underground, and no one knows that they are there but us. If one of them should...accidentally...detonate...what'll be destroyed? It'll blow a big hole in Zhagool. Who gets hurt?"

Till nodded. "Interesting points. Something of that magnitude...I remember my predecessors suggesting that the Staff go home and contemplate these ideas for a few days. I understand, at the speed that the aliens are going, it'll be over two months before they...uh, what did you call them?"

Bonarain smiled. "They call themselves: Chokchakchok. We were calling them Chok for short."

Till stroked his chin. "I think I'll follow that suggestion immediately. Anyway, as we've been told, it'll be over two months before they get here. We can hold the decision on that major hop until then."

Soolchakan bowed slightly. "Sirs, thank you for your time."

Till gave a cordial nod. "Thank you for your suggestions."

Wymini snickered. "I don't need two days. I'm all in favor of all of his suggestions and it's going to take a very strong argument to make me change my mind."

"Same here," said Mippa.

After Team 7016 walked out of the conference room, Soolchakan turned to his Teammates. **"That'll give us some extra time to find that** *chokwad* **Main Bridge."**

"And a lot of other things," sent Bonarain.

Kiyalee gave a deceitful grin. **"Then let's get out there and see what we can get away with."**

"I like that idea the best," sent Chyning with a greedy grin.

Team 7016 headed to their specially modified fighters and Jumped to the Chok ship. They spent half of a day looking for anything that resembled a Bridge and came up empty. There was a lot of background noise so in order to be able communicate with each other, they had to use the mental communication.

Finally Bonarain called out. **"I've got an idea that should work."**

Soolchakan looked around helplessly. **"I'm ready for just about anything. What's the idea?"**

"Let's see if we can find one of these *Wathoot Fovoks* **who does know where the Main Bridge is. Start reading a few minds and ask some questions."**

Soolchakan sighed. **"Won't hurt to try."**

They went to a highly traveled corridor and started checking all of the Choks that were wandering around there.

Finally Kiyalee perked up. "**I found one…she's a Bridge Officer**."

Chyning ran over to Kiyalee. "**What color is her sash**?"

Kiyalee pointed. "**See for yourself - white**."

Bonarain groaned. "**I thought that white was a kitchen aide**."

"**Apparently not**," sent Chyning. "**Can you make her lead us to the Main Bridge…now**?"

Kiyalee wiggled her eyebrows. "**That's where she's headed right now. I won't have to *make* her do anything**."

Soolchakan breathed a sigh of relief. "**Get back in your fighter and we'll follow her that way**."

Chyning scoffed. "**Why should we follow her that way**?"

"**Because if we leave the fighters here, in this maze, we may never find *them* again**."

Chyning chuckled nervously. "**I didn't think of that**."

Kiyalee looked at the crowd around the area. "**How are we going to be able to keep an eye on her…there's too many of these hairballs**."

Soolchakan groaned. "**How many of them are wearing a white sash**?"

Kiyalee turned red and Chyning just sat there giggling.

Bonarain looked around at some of the other big hairy beasts that seemed to be wandering around aimlessly. **"Just for laughs – did you get her name?"**

"You don't wanna know," sent Kiyalee.

"Yes, I do," Bonarain shot back.

"Then you read her mind and get her name," snapped Kiyalee.

Bonarain focused on her and read her mind looking for the name. After she got it she broke the connection. **"You're right...I didn't want to know. What are you calling her?"**

"Thick Head," sent Kiyalee flatly.

Chyning was now laughing harder.

"Thick Head sounds quite a bit like the first two syllables of her name," sent Bonarain.

Soolchakan sighed. **"You noticed that as well, I see."**

"Let's just follow her and find that wretched Bridge," sent Bonarain.

They followed the big female through two sections of the ship. One thing they noticed that was peculiar was the fact that whenever someone was in one of the sections, the artificial gravity was on. When they were going through the connecting hallways, there was no gravity and each of the Choks had to pull themselves along on all kinds of railings provided in the tunnels. When you got to the end of one of the tunnels, you had better be ready to set your feet in the correct direction otherwise you were in for a rather rude and/or painful surprise.

Thick Head plodded along through two more sections until she turned to the tunnel leading to one of the smallest parts of the giant puzzle. Each time she turned into one of the non-gravitational tunnels, Soolchakan went to the outside in order to keep track of where they were in the maze. When she turned to that last tunnel, he was rather irked, wondering why she was going there. Then she got there. It was the Main Bridge.

Soolchakan sat there in his fighter muttering. **"Of all the h'oolyach! I passed by this section...I don't know how many times...because I figured that it couldn't possibly be the Main Bridge."**

"What's so special about it?" send Chyning.

"It's *only* the smallest of all of the sections in this huge mess," sent Soolchakan bitterly.

The three women, at first, did not believe him. Each one of them flew outside of the hull to investigate for themselves and found that he was telling the truth. The Main Bridge was absolutely the smallest of all of the pieces in this giant network of jumbled pieces. Plus, everyone who was working on the Main Bridge was wearing white sashes. Some of them were a bright pure white while others were different shades of off-white. After doing a little of some scattered mind reading, they found that the brighter and more pure white ones were the ranking ones.

Now they were able to landmark a few places, in and

around, the Main Bridge. Now they were able to obtain a few passwords and some other symbols and an illustrated map of the entire network of attached pieces.

As they continued to read minds, they were increasingly confused as to why the male Choks considered a certain place in the top, middle of the back to be so sexy.

They listened in on numerous conversations and minds. The Choks were definitely planning on conquering Hardooth. Soolchakan relayed the intentions of the Choks back to Till and the rest of the Command Staff. Till ordered 100 Teams aboard the Chok ship to make sure that there were enough Owlamites on board who could execute the hop to Dimension #45.

The hop was done on command and the Chokchakchok immediately went to red alert and prepared to an attack from sources unknown. They remained on high alert for two days while attempting to figure out where they were and how they got there. They did try to get some readings on that one and only star in #45, however, they were not able to get any better readings than the Owlamites had obtained with the Jowfoonda sensors.

With the 100 Teams on board, the Owlamites were able to find out a lot of things about the Choks a lot faster. They found that the Choks had a very large arsenal of firestorm weapons. The architects that were manufacturing vaults on Zhagool hastened their pace in accomplishing the task. They found out how many weapons there were and did a few calculations on how many could fit in each vault. When there were six of the vaults ready, they gave the word and the Owlamites started "moving" the firestorm weapons to the new underground areas on Zhagool.

The thefts were noticed immediately by the Command Staff of the Choks, however, they were baffled as to how the weapons were disappearing right in front of their faces and they could do nothing about the thefts.

After one year of studying the Choks and their ship, the Choks themselves were hopped into Dimensions #2, #3, #4 or #5. Now the Owlamites had obtained *Owlam the Second*. They figured that they were a little bit better prepared for any enemy that came along with two spaceships.

14

One of the first things that was found, when the Owlamites started digging into the Chokchakchok archives was they had a certain blood enemy, who should be destroyed on sight, a race called the Zizzikinza. There were four other races of enemy that were found, however, nothing much about their description or capabilities. Some, at first, thought that maybe the Choks should have been befriended because of their hatred for the Zizzys. Once it was brought up, that both races were hardcore conquerors who did not want any allies, just slaves, they did not feel so bad about eliminating the Choks that had been on this giant maze of a ship.

They were able to get into all of the systems on this new ship and upgrade just about everything they needed in their home in the gorge with all kinds of new technologies. They were able to obtain more of the platinum from Bri and do all kinds of things with their old equipment. They mined a rather large amount of gold, silver, copper and some of the other metals from Bri and did quite a few upgrades with all of that material (even though the large amount that they took was trifling compared to how much was actually on Bri.

What was the most frustrating part of the Chok ship was learning where each section was located. Memorizing those locations and being able to go to that specific place when they needed to be there – without Jumping. The memorization process took another three months.

One of the best results of all of this new technology was that they were able to install all kinds of tiny little cameras and listening devices in the homes of the Teltermak and the Axswain. They were able to keep an eye on them without being there. Now, they could do what the majority of the survivors of the firestorm weapon had been trained to do – watch - from a protected and isolated location so as to not endanger any of their own.

It was finally decided that once they had obtained all of the information and useful equipment from any of the sections of the Chok maze, each part that had been picked clean would now be slammed into the back side of Niygool. Most of the pieces were slammed into Niygool using the older parts of the Chok ship as a target. They did not want to spread it out too far. The crashed ships could possibly be a distraction for any new invader coming into the system and give the Owlamites a little more time to prepare for any defensive act. That was their main hope. If there was another alien invasion, they would watch how these new invaders reacted and alter any plans accordingly. They left five pieces, of the Chok maze ship, floating aimlessly in Jahong's Death…just in case they wanted to use them again.

116 years later in the 341st year of Till's tenure, the klaxon went off again. Someone was invading the star system again – with a very large armada. According to the sensor readings, there were 42 ships orbiting Ragath and two ships orbiting Bri.

They once again pulled all of the Owlamites into Spy and onto the *Owlam the First.* They headed out to Ragath to find out who the invaders were. Once they arrived at Ragath there was a mutual groan of disgust. Once again the Zizzikinzas were invading. This time, however, they did not send any token force. This time there were 44 ships.

Team 7016 launched their fighters to do some initial investigating. What they were investigating was not quite clear to them. They had been on the Zizzy ships before. What could possibly be so special about this – other than the fact that there were 44 instead of just one or seven? They headed out to check and see if there were any differences in these ships. It had been several hundred years since the last Zizzy invasion and possibly these ships were upgraded.

Soolchakan brought the old information up for comparison. As they flew closer to the three lines of Zizzy ships that were orbiting Ragath he yawned as the sensors began gathering data. He looked at his screen in shock. The Zizzys had most definitely done some upgrading of their ships. The old had been 8.2 kilotaja in length - these were 9.7 kilotaja. The old had been 1.7 kilotaja in diameter - these were 2.9. The outer cylinders had been .8 kilotaja in diameter - these were 1.6.

Then they saw another ship come around Ragath. All four of Team 7016 dropped their jaws when they saw this one. Soolchakan switched his sensors to specifically scanning this monstrosity instead of general scans. This new one, which had to be the flagship, was 14.4 kilotaja in length. The central cylinder was 4.6 kilotaja in diameter. The outer cylinders were 2.2 kilotaja in diameter…all four of them.

Chyning was the first to do any mental message. "**Are you seeing what I'm seeing**?"

"**One big monster of a ship**," sent Kiyalee.

"**With more than four times the firepower**," sent Bonarain.

Soolchakan did not do any mental messages. He simply transmitted the findings to the Command Staff on the *Owlam the First*. He decided to wait for a response from them rather than make any hasty decisions of his own.

Beemella looked up from her screen. "I think these *bimyocks* mean business this time. We've made them lose eight ships…and I think they really want to enslave this system."

Till sighed. "Then we need to make it too expensive for them to obtain it. We have to make that entire armada disappear." He cleared his throat. "Get 100 Teams on all of the…regular ships. Hop them to 45. Get…150 Teams on that big one and hop it."

Deelka frowned. "What if that big one…what if there's more than one of them circling Ragath?"

Soolchakan heard them thinking. "**Sirs, you have open thoughts. If you want us to check on that big one…to see if it's the only…big one, we have a way of checking to make sure**."

Till chuckled. "**All right, do your check**."

Soolchakan snickered. "**Bonarain, start going around

Ragath. Head right. Chyning, start going around Ragath heading left. If you meet on the other side and don't see any more of the big ones, we'll know that there's only one."

Chyning had her nose a little out of joint. "**What're you and Kiyalee gonna be doing while we're doing our orbit?**"

"**Kiyalee is going to be checking the engines and I'll be checking the Main Bridge. Any more questions?**"

Chyning grunted angrily at herself. "**Bonarain...meet you on the other side.**"

Bonarain just snickered as she turned to a westerly orbit.

The check did not take very long. Bonarain and Chyning met on the other side without seeing another one of the giant ships. Chyning turned around and flew next to Bonarain going back around. She decided that if Bonarain had not seen another one, there was no point in her covering that area again. They went back to the big one to do a little spying on it.

Kiyalee flew into the big ship. She had to do a little searching because the engines were not in the area she thought they would be. When she finally did find them she just shook her head and chuckled. "**There's nothing like overkill. This ship has three light-speed engines. It has ten conventional ones. It appears they have to have all three of them running in order to obtain and maintain light speed. They're hooked up in line.**"

Soolchakan was in the Main Bridge area. **"They don't need much of a bigger Bridge. This one is not much bigger than any of the other ones that I saw. It still has those infernal hanging keyboards though**."

Till waited until all of the Command Staff had finished assigning Teams to the Zizzy ships for hopping. "Are we all ready?"

"We have all of these ships taken care of," said Wymini. "We need a little while longer for the scout ships to get to the ones at Bri and get enough on board for that hop."

A call came in. **"This is Officer Leader, Ota. We're here at Bri. Those thieving** *doovofts* **have already started mining ore off of the planet**."

Till snarled. **"Do you have all of the necessary personnel on the ships to perform the hop**?"

"Yes, Sir."

"Good! Let's hop the ships and go for the ground crews after the ships are gone."

"There might be a bit of a problem here, Sir," said Skalix. "The Choks and the Zizzys hate each other. We have Chok ships, or at least part of them, in 45 already. What happens to them…if we hop the Zizzys into 45 right on top of the Chok ship?"

Till smiled. "Since there aren't any Choks aboard the… pieces and since we've just about gutted them, I don't really see a problem if they attack an empty hulk."

"I don't like that," said Deelka. "Are you sure we've pulled everything out of that ship that we can use?"

Till shrugged. "What is still there in 45 has been floating around there for 19 years untouched. If we needed anything else on those pieces, we certainly don't need it very badly. Let's go ahead and let them waste a few shots on it. It might be fun to watch."

"Yes, Sir," said Deelka with a shrug. "Go ahead and tell the Teams when to perform the mass hop."

"Remind me," said Dimatsee. "Why do we want to keep these complicated computerized ships?"

"So our computer people have something to work with in figuring out the puzzle of those hanging keyboards," said Till. "If we take this entire armada intact, then our computer people will have all kinds of equipment that they can toy with in order to learn that complicated mess, and maybe we'll be able to improve some of our systems in the process. Plus, if we destroy a few computers in studying them, we still have numerous spares."

Dimatsee sighed. "Yes, Sir."

Till called out. **"Is everybody ready?"**

The ranking member of each group that was on board each ship called in that they were. Till gave the order for the mass hop and forty-four Zizzikinza ships were suddenly in 45 and every one of them went to full battle stations immediately. Over 20,000 fighters were launched when they saw the Chok remnants. The first fighters that got within range opened fire – until they saw that there was no return fire. Most of them orbited around the Chok remnants for a while. They were scanning the empty hulk. All the fighters returned to their home ship and the armada was in complete disarray trying to figure out where they were and how they got there.

All of the computer personnel were on board the giant flagship attempting to learn anything they could about the system. They could not find any stars except for the one and only mammoth star in 45. The only other mechanical thing they could find was the Chok ship (that had been picked clean of every usable item). They were able to detect a massive amount of organic matter. After examining some of it they determined that it consisted of Zizzikinza DNA, Chokchakchok DNA, Jowfoonda DNA and numerous others they did not recognize.

Kiyalee yawned because she had seen this system before and even though the ships were new and improved, the light speed engines were still the same. You do not change something like that unless you can prove that the change is an improvement. Anything else would only make something less efficient.

There were several hundred Owlamites who stayed on the Bridges of the Zizzy ships for some time attempting to figure out the job each of the Sticks as they sat there yanking the hanging cords. Trying to keep track of and follow the same Stick was very difficult because the Sticks were so similar that it was nearly impossible to tell them apart. At least with the Choks, they could see the difference in the colored belts that were worn. Here, there was very little difference.

After ten years of frustration, by both the Owlamites in trying to learn the complicated system and the Zizzikinzas in that they never could figure out where they were, the Owlamites finally tossed all of the Zizzikinza personnel into outer space. There was no point in keeping them.

After forty years of studying the Zizzikinza armada, there was a Staff meeting.

Tula, the ranking computer repair individual and Sankiki, the ranking computer operator, were there.

"We've tried," said Tula. "There's just no way around it. In order to learn their system, we'd have to have one of their instructors teaching us. The first step is having the computer analyze your DNA. If it is not Zizzy DNA, the computer won't accept it and we get nowhere."

"I hear what you're saying along that line," said Till. "Isn't there a way that you could reprogram the computer to accept Owlam DNA?"

Tula hung her head. She looked back up and sighed. "Before we could do that, we'd have to be able to get IN the system. We can't even do that unless one of the Sticks cooperated with us. That means that we would have had to have turned one of the instructors to our side, in order to betray their own." She shook her head. "Impossible!"

"They can't be controlled...like we were able to control the Choks," said Sankiki. "We tried on several of them...it only gave them a headache. They never cooperated with us at all."

"So you're saying that the Sticks are somewhat like the Teltermak," said Wymini. "We can read the minds of the Sticks, but we can't control them."

Sankiki shook her head. "We've had thousands of opportunities, with numerous Owlamites trying – nothing. We even tried two, three or four working together to control one Stick." She sighed. "Nothing worked. We cannot get in their system. They've made it completely tamperproof."

Till leaned back in his chair and huffed. "Is there anything in any of the ships that we can use?"

Tula shrugged. "Individual components, hull parts, wall parts, maybe a few other things to repair the ships that we have. Nothing major."

Skalix looked up. "Individual...components?"

Sankiki nodded. "A diode is a diode, a capacitor is a capacitor, a resistor is a resistor. The law of physics is the law of physics. Electricity can be controlled in a certain manner and the different components, no matter who makes them, will still perform the same function."

Till shook his head and shrugged. "Strip them and...let them just float towards that star. Obviously there's nothing else we can do. I wish that some of our engineers could have survived the firestorm weapon." He sighed. "All we have is watchers, farmers and a few doctors and nurses. We don't have any inventors who could work with that stuff or come up with new things. Everything we have...we had before the firestorm. All we can do is repair and...steal from somebody else. We're nothing but a bunch of observant thieves. Over twelve centuries and all of the inventions that we have we stole from someone else and had to watch how it works."

211 years later in the 592nd year of Till's tenure, the klaxon went off again. A groan was heard throughout each occupied apartment of the Owlamites. Four ships were entering the system.

When they turned the cameras on to get a look they saw ships that they were totally unfamiliar with in their configuration. All four were large triangles with a large dome on the top. Each side of the triangles was 2.4 kilotaja in length. The domes went up .7 kilotaja. The thickness of each triangle (without the dome), from top to bottom, was .65 kilotaja. They moved in formation towards Hardooth. They did not seem to have any interest in any of the other planets in the system. Either they already knew what was there or they were only interested in an inhabitable planet. There were numerous poles, probes and other paraphernalia sticking out of the front point of the ships. The Owlamites were not sure whether they were weapons or sensors. Then they saw a very unusual readout come up on their screens. The ships had no atmosphere inside – it was all liquid.

Wymini scoffed. "We're being invaded by FISH!?"

"Intelligent fish," said Beemella. "I don't think that anyone is just sending us some additions for our oceans. We've got enough strange fish as it is."

Deelka looked around smiling. "We still have to investigate them. See if they are conquerors or just…curious."

"We've never seen someone come out of the sky that's just curious," said Till despondently. "What makes you think that these are different?"

"We can always hope that there is someone out there who is only curious," said Deelka. "There can't possibly be that many that are…viciously ambitious."

"We *hope*," said Till with a smile. He leaned back and mentally sent a summons.

Soolchakan and the rest of Team 7016 was standing there in the conference room. "Why is it always us first, Sir?"

Till smiled. "Because no one seems to be as inventive as your Team when it comes to investigation. The four of you found more dimensions than any other ten Teams put together. Officer, Bonarain has an extraordinary talent for taking complicated things and simplifying them to where everyone understands them. You think faster on the run than anyone else. Officer, Kiyalee has a knack for mechanical things that no one else seems to have. Should I go on?"

"Yes, Sir," said Chyning. "I haven't heard you say anything nice about me."

Till cleared his throat and looked around nervously for a moment. "No one else can work with those three the way that you can. You're used to them and their idiosyncrasies. That is a big plus in your favor." He clasped his hands together on the table and smiled.

Chyning looked at Soolchakan as she turned around and

sent a private message. **"Was that *h'oolyach* supposed to be a compliment**?"

Soolchakan just shrugged and cleared his throat. "What are the orders, Sir?"

Till smiled. "The normal reconnaissance on this one may not be possible. You saw the information that…there is no air inside those ships, just liquid. This is very possibly some form of aquatic life that has beaten all other aquatics in intelligence…and space travel."

Soolchakan smiled. "Find out what we can and send the information back."

Bonarain stared at the ceiling. "Read their minds and get their language."

Kiyalee was staring blankly. "Investigate their power source."

Chyning was standing there with her arms folded. "Put up with the rest of my Team because no one else will have me and I'm the only one who can put up with them."

With Chyning's remark, Till flushed and looked sideways.

Chyning glared at Till with a sarcastic grin.

The coordinates of their current location showed they were coming in somewhere between Ragath and Rogoth. Team 7016 was going in first with Team 1137 close behind. Till was hoping to train other Teams on the tactics that 7016 used, so even though Officer Grade 3, Vooseea of Team 1137 outranked him, Soolchakan was in charge.

They found the four ships traveling along at a rather fast rate for being inside a star system. They were in a line formation. Soolchakan headed for the lead ship. All orders were the same. Soolchakan, followed by Vooseea, was looking for the Main Bridge. Kiyalee, followed by Officer Grade 6, Zhork, was looking for the engine room. Bonarain, followed by Officer Grade 5, Oditay, search areas in the starboard section. Chyning, followed by Officer Grade 7, Pelaheesha, started their search in the port area.

Soolchakan (as usual in Spy dimension) penetrated first. He went through the hull and shook his head in dismay. "**They ARE fish. Big long fish. They have a head that looks somewhat like Heyyah. They have a fish body with four arms. Two arms high above the head and two low below the head. They have a large dorsal fin, a smaller belly fin, two long, narrow side fins and a large tail fin. I have no way of determining gender without the sensors. The skin on the face is grayish-yellow. The arms are the same color. The side of the body is silvery. The fins are all somewhat transparent, but grayish in color. They look like they have two eyes on their face, with a BIG mouth and a mustache. I don't see a nose, but that doesn't surprise me because fish don't have noses, just gills. The heads are all bald – no hair or tendrils... or antennae. I'm turning on the sensors for some more specifics on this really big one that's close to me.**"

The sensors started sending readings to the scout ship. "Specimen appears to be close to *Lepomis* family of fish. Male. 13.8 taja in length. 5.3 taja in height. 1.1 taja in width.

"Looks like we may be in for more narrow corridors," sent Soolchakan. **"These fish are, just under, twice as wide as the Zizzys. Hopefully they need a wider corridor so that they can slither through without bumping fins...or anything else**."

The sensor continued. "Water breathing gills on either side of the neck. Two eyes that have special genetic coverings enabling them to see clearly underwater. Four arms, each one is 3.3 taja in length. Eight fingers with opposable thumb on all four hands. Circulatory and gastrointestinal system all similar toe *Lepomis* family of fish. Noted difference between *Lepomis* and specific specimen being scanned: Two orifices, both appearing to be mouths. Upper mouth is only .3 taja wide and is used for communication. Lower mouth is 2.2 taja wide and is used for eating."

Soolchakan cleared his throat. **"That lower mouth is definitely used for eating. There are bunches of small fish swimming around here and...big boy here just snapped one of them up...in his big, lower mouth. He didn't chew or even appear to swallow. He just snapped and...the little fish was gone. Meanwhile I can see his... upper slit of a mouth moving. I think he's talking to... another fish next to him. I'm now going to look for the Main Bridge**."

Bonarain called in. "**These people have a strange language. Their words are all rather long because they appear to have only one vowel sound. They call themselves the…***Doolood*. **The large grayish fish ARE the intelligent ones and they have numerous species of smaller fish swimming around here that they snap up as food. They eat whenever they see one of those smaller fish come close enough. I don't think that we're going to have near the problem with this bunch, as far as the computers go. The keyboards are long strips with only…eighty-one keys…in four rows. If we capture their ship and want to use their computers, we'll have to find a way that they can be used…out of the water.**" She sighed and shook her head. "**They are conquerors. They're coming here to take our planet. They're going to use us as either slaves…or food.**"

Kiyalee was the next one to call in. Her tone of thought was one where she was trying to keep from laughing. "**They're conventional engines are just like ours. They have a big problem. In order to keep the conventional engines running, they have huge oxygen tanks hooked up to them. Water in the combustion chamber won't allow combustion. They have to feed air to the engines to keep them running. Their light speed engines are much the same as others. Funny thing here is that they have to keep the light speed engine high and dry as well. I wonder how these people were ever able to develop anything like this, while living underwater. It'd be interesting to read their history.**"

"It would be interesting indeed," said Till.

Chyning finally sent in a report. **"They don't appear to have any fighters. What they have are...I guess... some kind of land crawler. It's big and bulky. It has six mechanical legs. It has...what appears to be some kind of pulse weapon sticking out...ten different places and directions on the sides. Each one is about 19 taja in length and 6 taja in width and...9 taja high. I don't think they can move very fast at all. They look so...awkward."**

Bonarain had completed the mind reading and translation. She sent the information to her Teammates, because they always received it without giving her a headache, now that they had each received a little bit of training and coaching on how to accept it.

Chyning shook her head. **"They are some kind of land crawler. They have some kind of small conventional engine in them that requires air in order to work. I think Kiyalee needs to come take a look at these things... in order to see if we could sabotage them without destroying them. I don't know whether or not we'd wanna keep them."**

"I haven't seen them yet," thought Kiyalee. **"But I can tell you that they are crawlers, from what I'm getting up here...in reading minds. They take these big ships down inside the atmosphere, land in the water and then deploy their attack crawlers. They've got some kind of pulse weapon on them that these fishies are awfully proud of."**

Oditay broke in. **"Sirs, I don't think that these... fishies...could survive in our oceans. I've examined the water here, with the sensors, and...the alkaline level is incredible. The water inside the spaceship has an alkaline level of 22.7. Our oceans would have to be modified...before they could survive outside of their ships."**

Till smiled. "Okay, we've got one weakness there. That's a good start."

Skalix snickered. "Knock the oxygen bottles off of the engines now...and they're stranded for a while...out there. If they do get here, all we have to do is knock the oxygen bottles off of the crawlers before they break the surface of the water and we'll knock them out as well."

"I wonder how they were ever able to conquer others... with those kind of weaknesses," said Mippa.

Till gave her an evil grin. "Because there were others who didn't know, in advance, that they were coming." He leaned back pondering. "Very possibly, also, they conquered peoples who were nowhere near as advanced."

"That second one...that's entirely probable," said Jeejow. "How could an aquatic race...conquer someone on the land and expect them to pay homage...unless they have total advantage in every way, shape and form?"

Till nodded his head as he closed his eyes. **"Officer, Kiyalee...what would it take to...sabotage their engines and strand them where they are for the time being?"**

Kiyalee just sat there in the fighter laughing uncontrollably.

"**Sirs, this is Officer, Zhork. I'm in a fighter next to Officer, Kiyalee and she…can't stop laughing. I don't know what her problem is…but…maybe as soon as she finishes her little fit of hysterical laughing we'll get an answer out of her. She apparently thinks that the question is…rather humorous**." He kept on looking at her, helplessly wondering just what could possibly be so funny.

It took a little while, however, she finally calmed. She looked over at Zhork. "**Have you ever heard such a stupid question in your life**?"

Zhork chuckled nervously. "**Supreme Officer, Till is still waiting for an answer to his question**."

Kiyalee took several controlled breaths. "**I'm sorry, Sir, but, sabotaging these engines will be the ultimate in simplicity. Someone else already said it. This kind of engine needs air, not water, to function. All we have to do is cut the air lines to the intake on all four engines and they will stop…very quickly…if not immediately from *literally* drowning out**."

Till flushed. "**All right, how many personnel will it take to cut off all of their engines simultaneously**?"

Kiyalee cleared her throat as she quickly assessed the situation. "**Four engines per ship, two air lines per engine, all it'll take is eight per ship. Cut all eight lines, per ship, at the same time and all sixteen engines should drown out, at the same time**."

Till looked around the conference table. "Thirty-two personnel. Let's get them in here, get them briefed and on the ships...as soon as possible. Since they're conquerors, we need to stop them at the earliest possible moment." He scoffed. "Stop them as far away from Hardooth as possible and we shouldn't have to worry about them damaging this planet...or us. If there are any more of their ships close by...they won't be able to figure out who stopped them out there...I hope."

Wymini shrugged. "The farther away from our home...the better the chance that they'll look elsewhere for the culprit."

Jeejow looked skeptical. "Shouldn't we hop them into...45 first? If we hop them out of here, then...once something catastrophic happens to their engines...they won't have any rescuers they can call on."

"Or, we can sabotage them here and find out how many others DO come to their rescue," said Beemella. "Either way, we will learn something about them."

"Or we can have it both ways," said Skalix. "We could hop two or three of them into 45 and sabotage what we leave here. If there are any others that're close by, I'm sure that they'd respond to the disappearance of three and the crippling of the one that remains."

Till nodded. "I like that. Only I think it should be two and two. Hop two and cripple two." He smiled. "Then we do what we do best – observe."

Deelka cleared her throat in a very loud manner. "Do we cripple the ones that we hop?"

Till snickered and shrugged. "Where are they gonna go?"

Anbrom smiled. "They could fly in one gigantic circle around that star."

They called Teams 6300, 6367, 6424, 6434, 6475, 6590, 6670, 6672, 6777, 6832, 6863, 6922, 6992 and 7001. These Teams were brought in to be trained on some of the tactics that Team 7016 had been using. Till had a bad feeling about the fact that Team 7016 was brought in on everything and everyone else seemed to be getting lazy by standing off to the side and just watching. He wanted to get more personnel involved – just in case.

Soolchakan tried to hide any sarcastic feelings over the fact that someone had finally decided to get others involved. Till was the ninth *Voice of Power* since the firestorm weapon had gone off and the first to really get serious about training others as useful secondary personnel. Chyning did not hide her feelings at all (which got admonishments from Soolchakan and Bonarain).

The fourteen Teams, along with Teams 7016 and 1137 headed to the Doolood ships, after getting the full briefing on what was going to be done. Two ships were to be hopped into Jahong's Death (45). After the hop was accomplished, all four were to have their conventional engines crippled. With the *Voice of Power* calling the moments of execution, the plan went through flawlessly.

They labeled the Doolood ships as 1, 2, 3 and 4. 1 and 2 were hopped and crippled, 3 and 4 were just crippled. All four of the Doolood ships instantly went to full alert and none of them had a clue as to what had just happened. Bonarain was the primary on reading minds in Home (1) Dimension on ship 3 and Kiyalee was on 4. Soolchakan was on 1 and Chyning was on 2. Team 7016 started watching the actions of (what appeared to be) the ship's Commanders on each ship.

One of the first things they discovered was that the conventional engines did more than just propel the ships. They were also the power behind one of the redundant tasks of circulating the water inside the ships. If the water was not circulating, it was not being oxygenated and the Doolood could end up suffocating from stagnated water. There was a scramble as numerous battery operated pumps were turned on in order maintain the circulation.

Soolchakan sent a message back to Till. "**Sir, apparently the oxygen in still water is tapped out faster than the oxygen in ambient air. It seems that every single room on the ship has one of the water pumps. It also seems that they're ready to sacrifice certain rooms. Some of the rooms are being abandoned and everyone is going into other rooms. One fish keeps a close eye on the pumps at all times, in order to keep each pumps going. They've got all of the mechanics working on getting those air lines cleared – RIGHT NOW.**"

Till listened intently to all of this. "**Officer, Kiyalee, how long do you think it'll take to get the things working again**?"

Kiyalee clenched her teeth in disgust. "**Sir, seeing as how we've never observed this before…HOW THE CHOKWAD SHOULD I KNOW**?!"

Till closed his eyes and flushed. Several of the Staff sat there snickering. He opened his eyes and gave them all a rather patronizing look.

Kiyalee continued. **"Sir, they'll be finished when they're finish. Other than that...I'm not even gonna hazard a guess."**

Till bit his lip. **"Thank you. Just keep watching and time them please...thank you."** He sighed. "I guess that once in a while, we all ask a very stupid question...whether we want to or not."

It took almost half the day for the Doolood to repair air lines and purge the water from the engines on one ship.

Chyning called in. **"Sir, ship number 2 has finally restored their engines to working condition. They're trying to contact the other ships, asking why they didn't get any help from them. They just noticed that they can't find two of the other ships and they just noticed that they're not in Home anymore."** She giggled. **"I don't know which discovery was the bigger surprise."**

Bonarain called in. **"Sir, ship number 3 is done with repairs. It looks as if they're just as surprised as ship number 2 about the turn of events."**

Soolchakan called in. **"Sir, ship number 1 is repaired and confusion is everywhere. They've discovered the big star of 45 and the...ahem...other matter that's floating towards the star. They're asking a lot of questions about the...turn of events. Right now they're** trying to find some answers."

Kiyalee sighed and shook her head. "**Sir, I may have to help these _bimyocks_ with the repairs. They've only got one engine's air lines repaired, but the engine itself is not purged of water and the ones working on the others are even more incompetent. I'll let you know...what happens...if or when something does happen.**"

Bonarain was observing some of the other activities on her ship. "**Sir, ship number three is moving closer to number 4. They are...extending some kind of...armature...of some kind, towards 4. It just attached to 4 and...it's some kind of...hallway...because some of the fishies from 3 are going, through it, to 4. I think that they're going over to assist with the repairs...I think.**"

Kiyalee scoffed. "**These _doovofts_ need all the help they can get. I sure wouldn't want any of them working on anything that I would need, especially if it was some kind of life support system.**"

Several more umbilical lines were stretched from ship 3 to 4 and several more Dooloods swam through them to assist in repairs to 4.

The Command personnel on ship 3 were desperately trying to determine what had happened to ships 1 and 2. From what the Owlamites were getting from the radio transmissions, ship number 2 had been the flagship of the four. The next highest ranking individual in the quartet was on ship number 4 and he was still swimming around on the only crippled ship.

While all of the activities were going on, Team 7016 was doing everything that they could to listen intently and pick up the language of the Doolood.

"**Sir, I was right**," sent Bonarain. "**They only have one vowel sound. It seems that the Commander of this minor armada...his rank is called...Chooloo Fooz. The second ranking man on ship 4 – his rank is Chooloo. They're griping at some...Ookoonyoo on ship 4 that hasn't finished the repairs and that Ookoonyoo is griping at some...Yoomyooyoo and a Yoomtoo about the repairs. I'll try and figure out...what is what. It's going to be REAL fun...with only one vowel sound to work with.**"

Chyning was trying to keep a straight face. "**Sir, I've got that...Chooloo Fooz on my ship. From what I'm hearing...a Chooloo Fooz is equivalent to an Officer Leader. That Chooloo is an Officer Grade 1.**"

Soolchakan called in. "**Sir, I've found a...rank structure guideline, of some kind. According to what I'm seeing...their Supreme Officer is called a Chooloo Koosoo. The Master Officer is a Chooloo Mootoo. The Senior Officer is a Chooloo Zhoo. The Officer Leader is a Chooloo Fooz. The Officer Grade 1 is a Chooloo. The Officer Grade 2 is an Ookoontoo. The Officer Grade 3 is an Ookoonvoo. The Officer Grade 4 is an Ookoonyoo. The Officer Grade 5 is an Oodoontoo, The Officer Grade 6 is an Oodoonvoo, and an Officer Grade 7 is an Oodoonyoo. Are you ready? The enlisted ranks...the**

E-9 is a Yoomyootoo. The E-8 is a Yoomyoovoo. The E-7 is a Yoomyooyoo. The E-6 is a Yoomtoo. The E-5 is a Yoomvoo. The E-4 is a Yoomyoo. The E-3 is a Too, the E-2 is a Voo and the E-1 is a Yoo. Have I confused you enough yet, Sir?"

Till flopped back in his chair snickering. "Ooh, ooh, ooh, ooh, ooh, ooh! This language is gonna be a HUGE load of laughs." He grabbed the table and pulled himself back up. He looked around at the whimsical looks on all of the faces of the Staff and Aides. "Whoot doo woo doo wooth thoos boonch?"

Deelka now looked confused. "What?"

Till cleared his throat. "What do we do with this bunch?" He grunted in disgust.

"We try to coomoonoocoot with them," said Anbrom.

Till gave him a condescending look. "No thank you," he said caustically.

Some time later, Kiyalee called in. **"Sir, they've finished the repairs on ship number 4...and...they just jettisoned the Officer who...did not get his personnel motivated or trained...or moving fast enough to get the repairs done...quickly. We have a big fish...out there floating around**."

The Command Staff all sat there looking at each other in shock.

Till slapped himself to wake up. **"What...no trial, no investigation or any kind of anything**?"

Kiyalee shook her head in despair. **"Sir, they just dumped him out of the ship with all of the ceremony of a bowel movement."**

Wymini swallowed hard. "I wonder how they'd treat a prisoner who committed a minor infraction."

Till shook his head. "If we can get into their computer system, we'll worry about that at a later time. Right now, what are they doing – the ones that are still in Home…about the ships that we hopped?"

Skalix shrugged. "Call Officer, Bonarain and find out."

Till did the mental communication.

Bonarain called in. **"Sir, right now, they're stationary in space and they're doing some wide sensor searches looking for the two missing ships. They're also sending information…to someone, somewhere about their situation."**

Soolchakan called in. **"Sir, the ships here did some of the wide scan searches and they found the gutted shells of the Zizzikinza ships that we dumped here – once we'd cleaned them out of anything usable. Right now, the two Doolood ships are carefully closing in on the Zizzy ships."**

"They don't seem to panic very much, do they," said Deelka. "They responded to the crisis rather rapidly and…if someone failed them…" She shook her head. "…rapid justice for failure."

"Let's give the two in 45 some help," said Till. **"Go ahead and hop the other two ships into 45. I don't want them sending out too many signals to any reinforcements. If any reinforcements come in here, I don't want them finding anything…except maybe that one floating fish. If there's no debris…that'll give them something to think about and give us more time to react if they do send others in here. Meanwhile, we observe the four in 45.**"

Wymini smiled. "For how long, Sir?"

"Until we're sure that we don't need any of the biologicals," he said flatly. "We dump them and keep the ships."

During the next year, three more, smaller Doolood ships entered the system, performing wide scan searches looking for their missing comrades. All three scout ships were joined with their colleagues and now there were seven Doolood ships in 45 for the Owlamites to study.

15

Four years later, the Owlamites had been able to extract a rather large amount of information from the Doolood computers. A lot of it was rather distorted because of the outlandish lack of vowels in the Doolood alphabet and language. According to the doctors, the reason they only had one vowel sound was because their mouths were incapable of the other vowels. They did have most of the consonants, so some of the guesswork was made easier, as far as what the Doolood were attempting to put in their archives.

Till was sitting there rather relaxed. "Okay, give us a history lesson on all of this *h'oolyach* that we got from those fishies."

Sankiki looked down at her report. "You understand, Sir, that it is not complete, due to some of the guesswork and a massive set of archive files."

Till smiled. "No matter what you tell us, it'll be considerably more than we've ever heard before...especially information outside of our system."

Sankiki smiled and looked around at all of the faces of the Staff. She picked up her pad. "It seems that there are six major players in a very large area of space out there. They are all constantly fighting each other for total dominance of this part of the galaxy. The Jowfoonda, the Zizzikinza, the Chokchakchok and the Doolood – we've met. There are two others listed in the Doolood archives…we're not sure what the proper pronunciation is, because the Doolood used their own translation – or spelling of the words. The Ookoo and the Moofootoon are the other two factions…and we've never met them. All six are battling each other and none will ally with any of the other. They all seem to think that they are THE absolute superior race and an alliance with an inferior race would only serve to weaken them considerably. This is one reason why we have only been visited by one race at a time. It happens to be the one who is in charge of *this*…sector of the galaxy…at that time."

"Very possibly, their non-alliance bigotry is something in our favor," said Skalix. "If they refuse to work together, we'll never have to face any two at the same time."

"We're seeing some of the politics of this part of the galaxy," said Till. "Some are conquerors and some are conquered. Four of the six are giving us a bunch of headaches. It is only fair that we give them some headaches right back."

Sankiki nodded. "Yes, Sir. We also discovered that, at one time or another, the Doolood have been able to get into other computer systems…" She turned red-faced. "…including the computer systems of the Zizzys! I'd sure like to know how they were able to bypass that *chogo* DNA program and extract information from them." She clenched her teeth and cleared her throat. "Anyway, we got some information from their archives that gives us exact locations of the home worlds of all six of the antagonists…as far as where each star system is located. I don't know if that's information that you want or need, but, we have it nonetheless."

Till chuckled. "Any information is helpful. You never know what you can do with it…at first. This is where planning comes in. What do we do later?"

Sankiki continued. "None of the six major hostiles has ever been able to conquer the home world of any of the others. They're constantly fighting over other star systems and the ebb and flow of battle makes those systems change hands constantly. No matter who gets the upper hand in one area, they lose systems in another area to one of the other factions."

Wymini scoffed. "If any two of them were to actually form an alliance and work together, they'd probably kick the *h'oolyach* out of all of the others rather quickly."

"Let's just hope they don't," said Till.

"All these centuries and they still won't try to make friends," said Mippa. "Even the dumbest of *doovofts* should realize that everyone needs a friend."

Jeejow looked down his nose at her. "Does that include us?"

Mippa sighed. "We did…at one time. Right now, though.. it's a little discouraging along that line. We may have to in the future, but…"

"We'll turn that corner when we get there," said Till. "Have we sufficiently scared anyone of the different factions…

yet?"

"Unfortunately it seems that we've made them all very curious," said Sankiki. "There's an annotation about the disappearance of over forty of the Zoozookoonzoo ships at one time. The Zizzys were here with that big armada and when we swiped the whole armada, the Doolood were out there watching things with some extremely long range scanners. They saw the armada disappear and they wanted to figure out what had happened. They thought that the armada was waiting here, hiding with some kind of invisibility device and was going to ambush the Doolood if they came into our system. It took them quite a while to conjure up the courage. They finally sent the four ships as bait. When the four ships disappeared, they sent in those little scout ships, that are apparently capable of speeds much faster than any of the other ships. When those ships disappeared as well…now the Doolood are watching this system very closely trying to figure out where over fifty space ships have vanished to, without a trace."

"Maybe we should have smashed a few more ships into Niygool," said Jeejow. "Or would that have made them even more curious?"

"Hopefully it scared them off," said Till. "If we haven't… things could get rough."

"We could make them all disappear and leave a bunch of bodies floating around Ragath and Rogoth," said Beemella. "That should make them fear this place a little bit more."

"Or make them even more curious," said Wymini. "According to what she's saying, one or more of those *bimyocks* has or has had us under constant surveillance. We may need to branch out...and find those ships...and do some damage out there."

Till hung his head. "And the possibilities and the decisions...a longer list of both, that we have to contemplate."

"I've got a possibility that might REALLY scare the *h'oolyach* out of them." said Dimatsee with an evil grin. "We hop all of the crew of one of those ships into Beasties, without any of their technology. We let them run from getting munched by those giant pink sand snakes for a while and then put some of the survivors back on their ship and send them out of here. They'll think that coming in here, not only makes their ships disappear, but any survivors of the disappearances have gone completely insane. That might make them think again before coming back."

"The only way that might work is...if the survivors number less than 5% of the total crew," said Skalix. "Otherwise you have too many witnesses."

"Wrong," said Till. "We have a planet called Bri. According to all of the readings, that planet has more mineral wealth...than any other place we've discovered so far. This...platinum! There's more platinum on Bri than all of the copper, silver, gold AND platinum on Hardooth. We'd have to gut the mineral supply there, to scare away even the greediest. Where would, or could, we put that much...heavy and precious metals?"

They all sat in silence for a while contemplating the latest comment.

Jeejow was the first to break the silence. "Officer, Sankiki,

I was wondering how were you able to deal with underwater computers. All of that stuff inside the Doolood ships is immersed, so, how were you able to get all of this information while swimming?"

Sankiki chuckled. "*That* is another mystery. How did the Doolood get all of their technology? The conventional engines need air to function. So they have air tanks feeding air into the intakes for the combustion chambers. The computers don't function underwater because all of the electricity going through the wires would be arcing all over the place. Alkaline water is a wonderful conductor, so the electricity would be arcing to anything and everything, including the probability of electrocuting the computer operator and repair crews. The water also has a high saline content, and that would make for even more arcing. The computers are kept out of the water with sealed, waterproof keyboards connected to them. The Jowfoonda, the Zizzikinza, the Chokchakchok and the Doolood are all baffled at why so many ships have vanished in this star system. We're baffled as to how a race that cannot survive out of the water, invented technology that can NOT survive *underwater*."

"They might have stolen it…just like we did," said Anbrom.

Sankiki huffed. "From who? How? There's no clue, in the Doolood archives as to when or how they got this technology, but…they still have it. If they did steal it…they haven't admitted the thefts in their archives."

Beemella was scratching her head. "If they can't get the

computers wet…how can they possibly repair them?"

"They have a sealed dry area," said Sankiki. "The computers are never submerged. If they need repair, they have these robotic devices that'll pull a malfunctioning computer out of its slot, move it, on a conveyer belt, to another dry room and with other robotic arms, they do all of the repair work. The fishies are in the water, controlling the arms and the computers always stay high and dry."

Anbrom's shoulders sagged. "More and more, I'm thinking that these Doolood are bigger thieves than we are. There's no way…that an aquatic creature…no matter how intelligent, could have possibly invented all of these things which can only exist in a dry environment, on their own. It defies logic."

"Maybe they have some amphibious cousins," said Mippa. "The amphibians invented this stuff…and the Dooloods just… took over."

"Either way, they still stole it from somebody," said Anbrom. "I can't see them doing this…without a LOT of help. Or as I said, they're bigger thieves than we are."

"Is there any way that we could ask them?" said Till. "It is their history, so they should be able to tell us something…unless we've eradicated all of them."

Sankiki started giggling. "You…don't know?"

Till looked at her suspiciously. "Don't…know…what?"

"The aquarium," snickered Sankiki.

All nine of the Staff were now looking at her in shock.

Till was a little angry. "What has been going on behind our backs?"

Sankiki now got a little apprehensive. "I thought you knew!" She looked a little frightened.

Till stood up. "WHAT AQUARIUM?!"

"Sir, the architects...built an aquarium...a very large aquarium...on the other side of the gorge," said Sankiki defensively. "I thought that all of you knew about it. We kept about fifty of them alive...and we kept their high alkaline water... and the pumps that move the water in their ships...were installed in there. The ones that are in there are madder than blazes at us. They won't talk, but we can still read their minds. Unfortunately, we didn't get any of the really good technicians in that aquarium, but we still have a bunch of them."

"Are they...procreating in that...tank?" said Wymini.

"I don't know," said Sankiki. "I don't think so, but you'll have to check with whoever it is that takes care of the thing... things...fish...aquarium...setup." She looked around and cleared her throat while trying to clear her mind. "Why?"

"Because as big as the adults are...it might get a little cramped in there," said Wymini.

Till waved at Wymini to stop. "The important question is – are we getting any good information on how to run those ships... and maybe dry them out for our use?"

Sankiki smiled. "That's already been done, Sir. There are several Teams practicing with them right now."

"Right now," said Till, "I think I'm going to go look at this aquarium. I'm also going to find out why no one told any of us about that tank…and the prisoners…prior to this meeting."

With a shrug, Sankiki smiled. "Yes, Sir. Good question."

Wymini turned to Till. "Are we going to adjourn here… and meet at the aquarium?"

Till just nodded.

Till stared through a glass barrier at the captured Dooloods that were swimming around in the massive tank. The Dooloods were swimming around close to the area where the pumps were moving the water. The small mouths of the Dooloods were not moving very much at all. The large mouths were rhythmically moving as they sucked water in to wash it over their gills.

"Sir, I am Officer Leader, Zoolkog. Team Leader of Team 55."

Till turned to the man standing next to him. "You're the one who is taking care of our…prisoners?"

"Yes, Sir. I've been informed…that for some silly reason… neither you nor anyone else on the Command Staff had been told of this aquarium. My apologies, Sir, for this…very unfortunate oversight."

Till nodded. "Why are we keeping prisoners from this

race...and not the others?"

Zoolkog snickered. "This bunch has no way of escaping. The bug-faces, the Choks and the Sticks could've attempted digging a tunnel and escape that way. Where would this bunch go...even if they did dig a tunnel? They can't swim in our oceans, the alkaline and saline levels are way too low for their species. They'd need to have some kind of technology, in order to escape from here and make a clean get-away." Zoolkog looked through the glass at the prisoners. "How?"

Till looked up as he saw some troubling of the surface of the water. Virtually all of the Dooloods headed for the area where the water had been troubled. "What's going on there?"

Zoolkog smiled. "Feeding time, Sir. We head out to the waters in the west coast of High Country and catch some...rather large eels...that're prevalent in that area. We drop the eels in the tank to feed our prisoners. They love the eels."

"How can you be so sure that they...LOVE...the eels?"

"Because we can read their minds. They like the eels and they've found that they need to attack and eat the things before the eels die...and rot."

"Why would the eels die...and rot, so quickly?"

"It's that alkaline content, Sir. Our oceans have an alkaline content around 7.9. The Alkaline content of the water that the Dooloods brought with them is 22.7."

Till nodded. "So, our indigenous eels can't take that high alkaline level."

"Precisely, Sir."

"Who does the fishing…for the eels?"

Zoolkog smiled. "I'm in Sector 1, Sir. I have assigned fifteen Teams to take turns doing the fishing for our prisoners… and us. It seems that those eels nearly wiped out the population of that colorful *Digacha* fish…that all of us like so much. By decreasing the population of the eels, the *Digacha* fish is coming back…and *we* have more food."

Till chuckled. "Do we feed the Dooloods any of the *Digacha* fish?"

Zoolkog snickered. "No, Sir. They don't like them."

"You get this from reading their minds?"

"Yes, Sir. Go ahead and take a shot at reading their minds for yourself."

Till picked a big one and concentrated on its mind. The big Doolood was looking directly back at Till and picturing himself physically and brutally tearing Till apart.

Zoolkog turned away snickering. "Not very friendly, are they."

Till shook his head. "How long were you planning on keeping them prisoner?"

Zoolkog shrugged. "We have no other place to put them. We decided to keep them until they all die off. Did you have something else in mind?"

"Are they doing any…procreating?"

"We got a bit of a conversation between several of them along that line. They were wondering if we wanted them to breed. Then one of the females said that she was glad that there was no… mooshoothookoo, otherwise they might just have to breed. We haven't found the translation of that word yet. If we do, and we can supply it, then we'll make a decision on possibly breeding them."

Till shook his head. "No! This is an intelligent race. They came from another planet…another star system. Even if we could breed them…why? I don't want any slaves and…I doubt that they'd put up with it. No. Let them all die off…in the natural course of time…unless they become a real headache."

"Yes, Sir."

"By the way…how many…exactly, are in this tank?"

"Fifty-two, Sir."

"Any way, you know of, to tell their age?"

"No, Sir…other than size. We're relatively sure that they keep growing, much like our ears. The longer they live the larger they are."

Till sighed. "Yes, I had forgotten about our ears. They grow so…slowly. But grow they do and I guess unless someone can come up with a better, or a more provable theory, size determines age." He reached up and felt the points on his ears.

Three years later a new report came in.

Tula stood there smiling as she addressed the Command Staff. "Sirs, we found out how the Doolood got into the Zizzikinza computers. It is…slightly complicated…no it is very complicated. None of us ever thought of that method, but…it works…according to what we're reading in the Doolood archives. If the Zizzys ever come back…we can take their ships and attempt to use their computers in whatever way we see fit. If it does work…we *will* own them."

Deelka cleared her throat loudly. "Is there any more information on these…Ookoo or Moofootoon creatures?"

Tula hung her head. "No, Sir. The only thing that we know is…they exist. According to the Doolood archives, those two haven't been much of a factor for…over 200 *oobyooskoo*… whatever that *h'oolyach* is."

Till frowned. "Haven't you been able to translate it?"

Tula shook her head. "Some things…just seem to not be translatable…due to the fact that they only have one lousy vowel sound. Many of them we have to guess at and with no real comparison…in most cases we're stumped. We're observers… not linguists."

"And we can only observe which one has the most control over this part of the galaxy…at this time," said Till bitterly.

Ninety-two years later, the last of the captured Dooloods died of old age. The Owlamites had been wondering about the life span of the aquatic race. This told them that the Dooloods were not one of the races that could last several centuries. The water in the tank was diluted, boiled and then poured into the ocean. They decided to think about what they were going to use that very large room for in the future.

781 years into the tenure of Till and 1,624 years after the firestorm weapons had done their damage, Hardooth was under attack again. This time, again, it was an unknown enemy. Once again it was an attack from outer space and there was no warning. There was more chaos as the Owlamites that were scattered all over the planet, exploring, spying and sight-seeing were reporting attacks – and fatalities. Once again, the members of the Command Staff had to perform a rapid roll call of the Staff to see who was still alive. Master Officers, Wymini and Skalix were alive. Senior Officer Jeejow was alive. Till, Beemella, Deelka, Dimatsee, Anbrom and Mippa were all silent – deadly silent. Six of the nine Command Staff had been killed in the surprise attack. Also, Wymini could not get any response from one of her Team – Officer Grade 6, Yiltakazi was silent as well.

Once again the depressing roll call would have to be accomplished...as soon as the attackers were identified and vanquished. All of the Owlamites were now in Spy (53) or Observation (108). All of the Teams that had fighters went to their ships. All others went to the captured ships. They took off into the space around Hardooth and discovered that all of the attacks were coming from twelve ships, the likes of which, they had never seen before. If it was one of the enemy they were familiar with, the design of their ships had changed dramatically.

One ship was marked for Bonarain to fly into and attempt her mind-reading/interpretation skills. She was still the only one who could comprehend an entire language in less than one day. Team 7016 flew into the ship with her to attempt a full reconnaissance on the enemy.

The ship was a series of three round discs that were stacked. The discs were thirty taja apart. The middle disc was 1.1 kilotaja in diameter. The top and bottom discs were .7 kilotaja in diameter. Each disc was 40 taja thick. There were twenty connections between the central and each of the outer discs. Each connection was a large cylinder that was eight taja in diameter – plenty of space to be a hallway of some type. All of the pulse beams that were coming out of the ship were originating from the central disc. There were at least ten places that the beams originated from in the front.

Soolchakan flew towards the central portion, to find out what he could locate there. **"Bonarain, you go to the top disc. Chyning to the bottom**."

Before he could send anything to Kiyalee, she sent a message. **"I know…find the engines. Don't worry, I'm on it**." She shook her head. 'This is getting extremely mundane,' she thought.

Soolchakan entered through in Spy (53). He found a large room full of…the inhabitants of the ship. He randomly picked one of the large, dark green reptilian creatures and turned his biosensor on. 9.9 taja in height. Female, egg laying reproductive organs normally associated with reptiles. Biped that walks upright.

Hands have two fingers and opposable thumb. Feet have three clawed toes. Respiratory, circulatory and gastrointestinal system very similar to Heyyah anatomy. All indications that creature is a carnivore. Large ball like tail that does not seem to have any noticeable use.

Bonarain broke in on the reading. "**I think we found the creatures that the Doolood called Ookoo. Only thing is…these reptiles call themselves: Iyka**."

Soolchakan shrugged. "**Is there anything useful where you are**?"

"**Yes**," sent Bonarain. "**I'm on the Main Bridge. Most of this top disc is the main and auxiliary Command centers. I'm going to continue reading some minds now**."

Chyning broke in. "**This bottom section is living quarters, along with a big sickbay, and a huge area of mud and water…where it looks like they store their eggs…and it *really* stinks**!"

Soolchakan nearly choked on his own spittle. 'Store their eggs? What a concept? Why couldn't she just say that they lay their eggs there?'

Kiyalee called in. "**There's nothing resembling a light speed engine in the top disc. There're two great big conventional engines though. Probably there… if they separate this one from the big one. I'm gonna check the center disc now**."

Soolchakan started looking around for anything that looked as if it were a weapons control array. He wanted to stop those destructive beams if he could – before they caused even more damage. He searched around the outer perimeter and found that each one of their pulse cannons was individually controlled by one of the Iyka Reptiles. He pulled out his pulse pistol, hopped the barrel to Home (1) and fired a quick burst at the head of one of the gunners. A small hole appeared from which green ichor came seeping out. The Iyka's arms went limp to the sides, he staggered a few steps to his right and then fell dead. Another Iyka noticed and immediately replaced the fallen comrade on the cannon. 'That didn't accomplish much,' thought Soolchakan.

"**I found the light speed engine**," sent Kiyalee. "**I'm gonna disable the thing. Don't worry, I'm not gonna blow it up, just break the seal.**"

Soolchakan noticed a flurry of activity and several of the reptiles growling and snarling at each other. Several others were growling into some kind of communication system.

Bonarain called out. "**When you disabled their light speed engine, it looks like you disabled their weaponry as well. There's a whole bunch of bellyaching on the Bridge about getting the thing back on line.**"

"**That's gonna take a while**," sent Kiyalee. "**I blew a hole in the main frame and they can't do anything until that hole is fixed. If or when they do fix it, I can still blast another hole...somewhere else. That ought to keep them dancing for a while.**"

Wymini had been listening to the sendings from Team 7016. **"Officer, Kiyalee! Give us some idea where that light speed engine is, so we can knock out the other ships. We need to stop them from shooting at us...as soon as possible."**

Soolchakan growled. **"Why don't we just hop all of these monsters into 45 and deal with them later. That should stop them from shooting at us."**

Wymini did not contemplate for long. **"Sounds good. Hop those *chogo* things to 45 and...we'll assess all of the damages here. Then we'll go smack those monsters for attacking us."**

It did not take very long to get several hundred, very angry, Owlamite Teams on the Iyka ships. All twelve ships were hopped into 45 in a very short time. All twelve of them got a hole punched in the framework of their light speed engines in order to give them all something to worry about – along with the fact that they were clueless as to their current location.

The new roll call was started immediately. Wymini wanted to know how badly they had been hurt. She had been fourth in command and now seemed to be number one. When it was confirmed that Till, Beemella and Deelka were all dead, that confirmed that Wymini was now the *Voice of Power*. She reluctantly assumed command as the Supreme Officer. She had to get a new Command Staff up and running as quickly as possible.

Master Officer, Skalix was unharmed and his status did not change. He was still the Sector 1 Commander. Senior Officer,

Jeejow was promoted to Master Officer and was switched from the Sector 4 Vice Commander to Sector 4 Commander.

Officer Leader, Yim was promoted to Master Officer and became the Sector 2 Commander. Officer Leader, Xadorm was promoted to Master Officer and became the Sector 3 Commander. Officer Leader, Nantasa was promoted to Senior Officer and Sector 1 Vice Commander. Officer Leader, Marbing was promoted to Senior Officer and Sector 2 Vice Commander. Officer Leader, Am-Sisa was promoted to Senior Officer and Sector 3 Vice Commander. Officer Leader, Inditam was promoted to Senior Officer and Sector 4 Vice Commander.

Wymini heard about, and did not want to see another fiasco like the one that Antrong had pulled, so she made the pecking order quite clear: Wymini, Skalix, Jeejow, Yim, Xadorm, Nantasa, Marbing, Am-Sisa and Inditam.

While the roll call continued, Wymini called an immediate meeting of the new Command Staff. She was a little upset over the sequence of events. "I want to know how these…Iyka…got through our surveillance. Why did we *not* know about them… until they were blasting the *h'oolyach* out of us?"

"Because we've been sitting here stagnating, while they've been aggressively improving their systems," said Skalix.

Wymini flopped down in her chair and looked at Skalix as if he was crazy. "WHAT?"

Skalix shrugged. "Think about it…all of those… technological pieces of equipment that we have out there…we stole from other races. We obtained them…several hundred years ago. How old is the *Owlam the First*? We've been relying on outdated equipment while the Iyka have been improving theirs. Technologically, we came to a screeching halt. Once we get into some of the logs of the ship commanders, they'll probably have some whimsical remark about minimal effort in sneaking past all of those...antiques."

Jeejow let out a frustrated growl. "We're going to have to go back to our original method of observations. We're going to have to put some cameras out there...and we're going to have to have eyes on them – our eyes – day and night, that long boring process of watching the sky for any other predator that wants to own us."

"Precisely," said Skalix. "All of the sensors in the galaxy will do us no good...if someone like those Iyka can sneak through, by sending some kind of a false reading through the things. We will be taken by surprise...over and over and over..."

"I get your point," said Wymini dejectedly. She sighed. "We're going to have to get somebody...doing some kind of manufacturing...quickly."

Yim chuckled. "Why don't we see what we can steal from these lizards first? Maybe we can just update from them...and attach our own cameras on their stuff." He looked around the table. "Unless someone else has a better idea."

Wymini nodded. "Let's talk about...thefts...after the roll call is complete...and we have an idea of what we've lost." She sniffled. "I've already done my own roll call...of my Team. I've lost one of mine." She cleared her throat several times. "Officer

Grade 6, Yiltakazi…is gone."

"I don't think you'll have to look very far for a replacement," said Xadorm. "On the roll call…Till is gone…along with two others of his Team. Officer Grade 7 Choychata is…without a Team. You're short one woman…and she's short a Team. Why don't you go ahead and take her?"

Wymini nodded sadly. "I'll wait until the roll call is over. I'll let her know of that decision then."

As different Teams answered roll call, they then went to 45 to study the new ships and learn what they could about a full takeover of all of them. The Iyka were a very belligerent bunch with no concept of surrender. They also had a hard time taking defeat. They were more angered by the fact that they had no idea where they were rather than the fact that all of their light speed engines had been sabotaged.

The only Team that bypassed the roll call was 7016. They were needed to mingle among the Iyka and get any passwords that they could for the computer system. Bonarain and Soolchakan were the only ones who could read, write or understand the language. Bonarain gave Kiyalee a force feed in order to get her up to date in order to find out more about the conventional engines. Chyning would simply have to wait until the next day. Then she could have fun wreaking havoc on the Iyka - as much fun as her vindictive little heart desired. Once Bonarain had accomplished a force feed on Chyning, she started doing a slow feed to all other Owlamites in 45.

The main target was the vessel that appeared to be the

flagship. Once Sankiki and Tula were updated on the Iyka language, and given a few passwords that Soolchakan had obtained, they went to work on the computer system. At first the computer was difficult because it was definitely more advanced than anything they had ever seen. Once they got in and started finding the differences they had an easier time with finding anything they wanted. They had to eliminate a few Iykas in order to get in without being bothered by the reptilian security personnel.

Kiyalee and a few other physicists and mechanics watched closely as the Iyka repaired the light speed engines. Once they were repaired, the Iyka now had the frustration of no targets to shoot at because they still had absolutely no idea where they were or how they got there.

The roll call was complete. 162 Teams had been wiped out before anyone realized that they were under attack. Thirteen other Teams lost one or more members. 167 men and 509 women were gone. The reassignment of the short Teams had to be accomplished again. Choychata being switched to Wymini's Team 36 was the first of several moves. When they were finished, there were two Teams that only had three members.

There were entries in every logbook of all twelve Iyka ships about how the guardian beacons had been bypassed. One of them got very specific in that he had checked the archives, in regards to equipment that was that old fashioned. He had found that his great-great grandparents had figured out a way to beat those antiques. A very disgusted Wymini gave the order to do anything and everything to upgrade, update and prepare for anything that might come their way.

Officer Grade 3, Toytay of Team 256 found several entries in the logbooks about a race that the Iyka called the Mufayton. She reported it as her best guess as to what the Doolood had called the Moofootoon. It was another ambitious conquering race that was listed as something along the lines of a headache equal to the Chokchakchok, Doolood, Jowfoonda and Zizzikinza. The thing that worried Toytay was that according to the information in the logs – the Mufayton were telepaths. That was the only description of the Mufayton in the logs. There was nothing in there that told what they, or their spaceships, looked like or the last time there had been a confrontation between the Iyka and the Mufayton.

The Command Staff all hung their heads in gloom. They all remembered too well what had happened in going against another telepathic race. Why did the only one, so far, of the six races that were the biggest subjugators in the area have to be telepaths? Why could they not have been one of the first? Now, the Owlamites would have to be even more vigilant in looking for a different design of any incoming spaceships.

Wymini decided that they needed to slam some more ships into the back side of Niygool. Make it even more "well known" that certain enemies that entered this star system had met a disastrous fate. That would give the newcomers a mystery to solve before they could accomplish any takeover. They also put the antique equipment on Niygool, in 53, so that they could see a new marauder, without them even trying to bypass the electric guardians.

Kiyalee found the method that the Iyka were using to route their pulse cannons through the light speed engines. It increased the devastating effects by 220% according to what she read. She hooked-up and re-routed a 459 cannon through light speed engines. She had help in hopping the Iyka ship back to dimension 1 and Jumping (68) to Rogoth. She tested the destructive capability of the 459 on one of the smallest of the 452 moons orbiting Rogoth. In less than five heartbeats it was total destruction. Now there are only 451 moons orbiting Rogoth. The large chunks of the destroyed moon fell out of orbit and were sucked into Rogoth by the strong gravity of the Gas Giant. Kiyalee swallowed hard as she realized that the 459 cannon was truly becoming some kind of *ultimate* weapon.

All of the Owlamites who were on board the Iyka ship when the moon got dissected, stood there in shock for quite a while as they watched the big chunks disappear in the gas. The monster 459 cannons were now even more powerful than any of them had ever dreamed possible. The firestorm weapons could destroy a city – the new 459 could destroy a planet. There were many mixed emotions among the Owlamites when they realized that they had that kind of devastating power in their hands.

While the Owlamites were going through and learning the Iyka computer system, Soolchakan found something that piqued his curiosity. He found a photograph album that had belonged to one of the latest victims of 45. There were several pictures of a large mound by a river. There were several of the Iyka people in the photograph in front of the mound. There was a large pole, decorated with painted carvings, next to an opening in the mound. He started concentrating on that pole and the exact location.

He got into his fighter, went to Jump (68) and closed his eyes, thinking of that pole as a landmark. He opened his eyes – and nearly gagged…from the smell. He was parked in the fighter - on the Iyka home planet, in front of an Iyka home. He hopped to Spy (53) to keep from having to put up with the atrocious smell of rotting vegetation, fungus and mold. He smiled as he realized that he had done something that none of the six antagonists had ever accomplished - he was on the home world of one of the… headaches. It was time to take the fight to them and let them suffer from some of the devastation. It was time to bring some more Owlamites here, possibly with a few firestorm weapons…and give them a taste of their own destruction…on their own planet. He started thinking about how this might be done…if they could find some landmark on the other five planets.

He traveled around the planet for almost half a day. He found several large cities and some very interesting manufacturing plants.

He Jumped back to Hardooth. He reported to the Command Staff and informed them of his trip. He had no idea how far he had gone, however, he had done it. The 68th dimension of Jump had turned out to be an incredible weapon. All they needed was one landmark on the home world of their foe and they could strike back at that specific home world.

Wymini looked around the conference table with an evil grin. "Do you have any concept of how badly we can hurt any enemy? We could attack their home world and leave them in a mess…at home."

Yim chuckled. "We could leave them some cryptic messages as well. We could tell them to leave our home world alone...or there'll be more counterattacks. We don't tell them which world it is, we just let them know that they'll pay dearly if they don't leave us alone." He leaned back snickering. "They won't have any idea who it is that is causing them no end to grief."

Nantasa shook her head. "But if they don't know who it is...who will they stop attacking?"

"They'd have to stop attacking everyone," said Marbing sarcastically.

"But they'll be in a quandary and won't know what to do," insisted Nantasa.

Wymini scoffed. "And the problem is....?"

Nantasa sat there stammering and waffling in an attempt to come up with an argument. She finally just hung her head and clasped her hands on the table.

Wymini looked up proudly at Soolchakan. "We all need to get into those archives of all of the headaches. We need to landmark something on their home planet and...give each of them a few firestorm weapons...the hard way."

"Uh...no!" said Xadorm. "That'll quickly use up our supply of firestorm weapons...won't it?"

"No, Sir," said Soolchakan pompously. "When I was on the Iyka home world, I found a manufacturing plant...for *their* firestorm weapons. We can use their own weapons against them. We can even set one of the nasty things off IN the firestorm weapon manufacturing plant." He grinned triumphantly.

Jeejow grinned right back. "That's one of the sneakiest and nastiest thing I've ever heard of. I love it!"

"So do I," said Am-Sisa gleefully.

Wymini giggled. "How soon could you do it, Officer, Soolchakan?"

He cleared his throat nervously. "Sir, I'd need one...or more...of the physicists there to...figure that out...uh...how to make that thing...operate."

Wymini leaned forward. She had a menacing look on her face. "You got it! However many you want...get it done." She held her hand out and looked at her fingernails. "It's time to hit them all back...hard. I'm tired of being a target to all of these monsters. It's time that we made them know what the victims feel like. Let's find a good landmark for all of those planets...and start...getting some revenge."

"I've already got it for one planet," said Soolchakan. "If I can get a photo from any of the other planets...I think I can do the same."

16

Chyning gave Soolchakan a dirty look. "**Are we being honored again**?"

Soolchakan did not bother looking back at her. "**Do you wanna stay here and train others in flying fighters or go to some foreign planets, purloin some of their wealth and then blast the *h'oolyach* out of them**?"

Chyning sighed and looked at Kiyalee who just giggled.

Bonarain was looking over the orders. "**How many of the physicists are we taking to the planet with us**?"

"***We* do some recon first and then *they* decide how many physicists we need for the job**," sent Soolchakan.

"**I wanna do some massive damage to those Zizzys first**," sent Chyning. "**Those *bimyocks* have caused us more trouble than any of the others**."

Soolchakan sighed. "**Again…not up to us**."

The four of them huddled together. Soolchakan was the one controlling the Jump. He concentrated on one of the big landmarks that he had seen on the Iyka home world. The four of them hopped to Spy. He held his breath and Jumped all four of them to Iyka.

The first thing that the women did was look around in a rather curious manner. There were not many concrete buildings in the city. The buildings were not very tall and made mainly of thick, caked mud.

"Take a look at this place in Home dimension," sent Soolchakan. **"That'll be something that you'll never forget."**

The three women hopped to Home and immediately let out a moan of disgust and hopped right back to Spy...holding their noses.

Bonarain glared at Soolchakan. "You *melafathan fovok*! This entire place stinks just like the inside of their ships."

Soolchakan just stood there snickering. "I just wanted you to know about that before you got surprised by anyone else. You now know that it stinks here. I haven't found any place on the planet that doesn't stink...unless you're over 1,000 kilotaja from any shore line." He sighed. "We all know how to Jump here. We may have to Jump a lot of the physicists here...in order for them to set up any firestorm weapons. We may have to Jump a lot of people here...in order to have all of the decisions made about the primary targets."

"In other words - get used to it," said Kiyalee dejectedly.

Soolchakan cleared his throat. "Yes. So each one of you choose your Jump point and landmark it."

Chyning huffed. **"Do we have to warn them...about the smell?"**

Soolchakan shrugged. "If you want, you can. If you don't...that's your choice."

Chyning and Kiyalee looked at each other and giggled.

Team 7016 Jumped back to Hardooth. They then shuttled the physicist Teams 85, 207, 435 and 1599 to Iyka. After all of those Jumps, they went back to their address at 12-562 in the gorge, somewhat exhausted and spent a night asleep.

The next day, 7016 was contacted by Sankiki. She told them she had a landmark on the Jowfoonda planet they should take a look at. They reluctantly went to the main computer center and studied the pictures. There were 18 pictures in the Jowfoonda archives that were all pictures of the same building from different angles. It was some kind of nerve center in the middle of the capitol city on Jowfoonda. Soolchakan sighed as he prepared for his next Jump.

They looked carefully at the structure, hopped to Spy and then Jumped. Now Team 7016 was on the Jowfoonda home planet. They were disgusted over that fact that the bug-eyed monsters were everywhere. They were also a little surprised to see other creatures on the planet as well – until they realized that the other creatures were being treated very harshly by any Jowfoonda whenever they came within three taja of a Jowfoonda citizen. These were enslaved races.

"Let's do what we came here to do," said Soolchakan flatly. "It'd be impossible to...find the home planet...of all these... others and get them back home. It may turn out that...the only way they'll be freed...is through death."

Bonarain closed her eyes and groaned. "I hate to think of killing the innocent with the guilty."

Soolchakan hung his head. "Do you want to have to go through the selection process for all of these...*others*?"

Bonarain looked around sadly and sniffled. "Like you said: Impossible!"

"They wouldn't know what to do if you did free them," said Kiyalee. "Look at that...skinny little...white skinned thing. I read her mind and...she's a third generation slave. She and her parents were born on this planet...in bondage. She doesn't know any other life...or language."

Chyning pointed at one of them. "That one...the one that almost looks like a Sodle...he's fourth generation slave."

Soolchakan groaned. "We don't need to read their minds. We need to find some targets for the firestorm weapon. Reading the minds of slaves won't help much."

"I think it will," said Bonarain. "Some of these slaves have thoughts of being taken into high security areas...where the Jowfoonda discuss classified information. They treat the slaves as furniture and talk freely among them. We could pick up all kinds of goodies from them."

Soolchakan sighed. "Fine! Kiyalee and Chyning, you start exploring and look for manufacturing plants, military training areas and other strategic targets. Bonarain, you see if you can pick up any more valuable intelligence information."

Several days of exploring the planet led to all kinds of

discoveries about easy targets for the Owlam plan. They Jumped back to Hardooth with the information.

Team 7016 stood in front of the Command Staff.

"I picked up sixteen new languages while I was on Jowfoonda," said Bonarain. "It seems that the first generation slaves still remember their original tongue. Any second, third or fourth generation slaves cannot comprehend any of their original language."

Wymini frowned. "Does this help us with any targeting information?"

Bonarain shrugged and smiled. "No, Sir, but it does give us something new. I once heard that any new information makes you more powerful."

Wymini nodded. "That's all good and fine, but what we're looking for is a way of weakening the Jowfoonda. Now, do we have a list of targets on Jowfoonda?"

Soolchakan smiled. "Oh, absolutely, Sir. I have a list. Kiyalee and Chyning each have a list as well. When the firestorm weapons are placed there...it'll make a big mess on the Jowfoonda home planet and weaken them considerably."

"Good," said Jeejow. "Give me a written copy of all of those targets. Once our physicists are finished with the targets on Iyka, they can set up Jowfoonda. Right now, the computer people have found an interesting landmark on the Chokchakchok planet. We want you to do recon on that planet for targets as well."

Chyning huffed. "Why can't someone else do some of this

reconnaissance?"

Inditam shook her head. "Because, unfortunately, no one else does as thorough a job as Team 7016. When we send you, we know that the task will be accomplished in a complete and totally professional way. You've established yourselves as the most dependable Team in all of Owlamite society."

Chyning sent an isolated message to her Team. "**Got any ideas on how we can screw this up**?"

Soolchakan and Bonarain just gave Chyning an angry glare. Chyning looked off to the side sulking.

Wymini cleared her throat. "Back to some old business… have the banners been completed yet?"

"Oh, yes," said Am-Sisa. "We have 225 of them done for the Iyka home world. It was a little tough, at first, considering their alphabet, but they're done and ready to be deployed after the bombs go off."

As Team 7016 departed the conference room, Chyning was a little confused. "**What banners are they talking about**?"

Bonarain answered. "**They're telling the Iyka people that if they ever attack our home planet again, we'll come back and the destruction will be total. We won't leave anything alive on their home world at all.**"

Chyning scoffed. "**But if we tell them to leave Hardooth alone, don't you think that they'll send ALL of their military might against us**?"

Soolchakan snickered. "**That is why we are using the term: Our Home World. We're not telling them who it is, we're just saying that it is someone they've attacked and is now fighting back. We're not going to specify anything**."

Chyning sniffed. "**Before I go see this…landmark on the Chok planet, I'm going to go get some good hot kwatha**."

Bonarain snickered. "**That's the best suggestion that you've had all day**."

Team 7016 Jumped to their apartment to cook up a batch of kwatha.

Officer Leader, Hrombisk reported in. "All 1,262 firestorm weapons are in place. All we need to do is activate them and…the Iyka will have absolutely no more manufacturing plants on their… very smelly…home planet."

Wymini nodded. "What is the possibility of making all of them go off at the same time?"

Hrombisk pondered for a few moments. "That'll be rather difficult…but we know that from the time the first one goes off till the time the last one goes off…shouldn't be more than seven to ten heartbeats."

"I don't see a problem with that," said Skalix. "Even if it were twenty to thirty heartbeats, that's still total devastation in an extremely short time."

"Yes, it's acceptable," said Wymini. "I just wish that... we didn't have to keep on demolishing...an entire race...just to survive."

"I wouldn't worry about that," said Xadorm. "It seems to me that they've got plenty of their race...cavorting around in outer space. We will hurt them badly...at home, but I don't think that we'll eradicate them. Either way, it might make them think again about plundering another planet...or an entire star system."

"As soon as all of the banners are in place...set off the bombs," said Wymini. "Make sure that someone is there to unfurl the banners...and then get right back here."

Hrombisk smiled. "Of course, Sir. It'll be done. I'll report back, as soon as the banners are deployed."

Team 7016 was looking around one of the larger cities on the Chokchakchok home planet. They were amazed at some of the differences in structures.

Kiyalee shook her head and scoffed. "An underground cave dwelling...right next to a building 45 floors high. Other places that look...like animal dwellings...all over the place and yet, there're all kinds of modern buildings...and transportation... and roads. They sure like diversity."

"I think that they're captured slaves live in those caves... when not on duty," said Soolchakan. "I haven't seen one single Chok come out, or go in, any of the caves. I see several different other races though. The Choks live only in the modern dwellings."

Bonarain was concentrating on a rather tall, gangly looking creature that was covered with long matted brown hair as he came out of one of the caves. She closed her eyes and went over each part of his mind and memory that she could find.

Soolchakan sighed. "Trying to pick up a new language there…with that…pile of nasty looking hair?"

Bonarain opened her eyes. "I already did. He's a first generation slave, captured from his home planet. He's a Pikitow… whatever that is. He was a scientist on his home planet…now he's a janitor. These lousy Choks have no respect for anybody. We could sure use some of his knowledge of chemistry."

"Nope," said Soolchakan. "We don't have time to save anybody. Let's go find some targets."

They spent the next two months circling the planet looking for plants that manufactured parts for the spacecraft and any firestorm weapon facility. They listed each along with their geographical location. After getting what they figured was enough they Jumped back to Hardooth.

They arrived in their apartment and found a woman sitting in the dining room. She was sitting at one of the tables reading something and eating some kwatha.

Soolchakan slowly walked up behind her. "Who are you?"

The woman yelped as she jumped up and spit some kwatha out of her mouth. She staggered backwards away from Soolchakan and tripped over a chair, ending up landing on her derriere. She closed her eyes and put her left hand over her heart. "You scared the *h'oolyach* out of me."

Soolchakan chuckled with an accusing smile on his face. "We scared *you*? Who are you and what are you doing in our apartment?"

She opened her eyes and looked up with a guilty grin. She got up. "I'm Officer Grade 5, Xa-Xa from Team 85. Hrombisk is my Team Leader. I was told to wait here...inside, by...Wymini and Hrombisk. I was told to wait for you...for when you came back from..." She frowned. "Where were you?"

"Finding targets on Chokchakchok," said Bonarain with her own look of suspicion.

Xa-Xa chuckled nervously. She went to the table and started cleaning up the mess that she had made when she spit her food. "We need...all of us...the physicists need your help. We need to know if there are any more landmarks that you can think of...on Iyka."

"We already reported all of that," said Chyning angrily. "And that better not be any of our supply of kwatha that you've been eating."

"Yes, you did," said Xa-Xa. "You...reported all kinds of landmarks on Iyka. The trouble is...we blew the *h'oolyach* out of all of them...with the firestorm weapons." She shrugged. "Now...we need to go back and...inspect some of the damage. The problem is...all of the landmarks that *we* know of...are now nothing but rubble...or craters. We can't...go back unless we have a landmark...that wasn't...blown away."

Soolchakan turned away laughing. He went to another table and sat at one of the chairs. He leaned on the table and just continued laughing. His three Teammates thought he was crazy at first. His laughter became infectious and soon the three women were laughing with him at the thought of what had occurred on Iyka.

He finally regained a little composure, wiped some tears from his eyes, looked up at Xa-Xa and shook his head. "You destroyed...ALL of them?"

Xa-Xa smiled and nodded. "Yeah, we blew them all away... everything that looked like a target...where they manufactured spaceships, weapons and any other thing that looked like they could use it against us."

"What about the banners?" Bonarain gave Xa-Xa an accusing look. "Didn't they unfurl those banners...and let the Iykas know that we did it in a retaliatory strike? Why can't you landmark the banners?"

Xa-Xa chuckled. "The...Iykas have some very nasty looking claws...and some very sharp teeth. The ones who were there...with the banners...saw the Iykas attack and...shred the banners...in a very fast, crazy and vindictive manner. You know... mob mentality. There are no banners left...that we can landmark. All of that's gone...as well. We've got...nothing."

Soolchakan looked at his Teammates. "Do any of you remember anything...that might not have looked like a military target...anywhere on that planet?" He turned back to Xa-Xa and frowned. "How many bombs did you set off?"

Xa-Xa shrugged. "1,262."

The three 7016 women now had to find a place to sit down – quickly.

Bonarain had her hands to her temples. "TWELVE HUNDRED…?"

Xa-Xa nodded. "1,262…yes. Anything that looked like a military target…was blown away…completely." She shrugged. "That took all of our landmarks…as well."

Kiyalee shook her head. "Even the Algothons didn't set off that many bombs. Look what it did to Hardooth!" Her shoulders sagged. "And you set off 1,262 bombs…on one planet…all at the same time?"

Another guilty grin from Xa-Xa. "That's why we can't find any landmarks."

Chyning sat there looking totally disgusted. "Why do you need to assess anything? If you can't find any of the landmarks… I'd say that you demolished everything."

Soolchakan shook his head. "I can't think of anything else to use as a landmark."

"Finish cleaning up your mess," said Bonarain flatly. "That table isn't going to clean itself up."

Chyning scowled at Xa-Xa. "That better not be kwatha from our supply."

Xa-Xa chuckled nervously as she continued cleaning. "No…that kwatha was from my supply in my apartment."

"What about that island," said Kiyalee? "Do you remember that...rather isolated island...in the western part of that big ocean? It was some kind of vacation resort. None of us put it on our list...because we didn't consider it...militarily significant. It just looked like the Iyka were there relaxing and having fun, sunning themselves."

Bonarain and Chyning just frowned.

Soolchakan stroked his chin. "You talking about that one where...there were huts that were built...out in the water on stilts...all along those long piers?"

"Oh, yeah," said Chyning. "It did look like a nice vacation area."

"I remember it now," said Bonarain. "It was the least foul smelling place on the whole planet."

Xa-Xa smiled expectantly. "Great! Could you check... and see if it's still there?"

Soolchakan stood up and stretched. "Tomorrow! We've been doing a lot of Jumping all over Chok...with our fighters. We're tired. If you want us to do another Jump and then Jump several of you...it'll have to wait until tomorrow."

Xa-Xa tried to protest.

"Finish cleaning up your mess...and leave," scolded Bonarain! "We'll report to the Command Staff...and your Team Leader...*tomorrow!*"

Team 7016 Jumped up to their bedrooms. Xa-Xa just

stood there scoffing helplessly. She looked back at the table and sighed. She finished cleaning up her mess, picked up her pad and vanished.

The next day, Team 7016 was in the conference room.

Wymini looked a little upset. "Why didn't you come here immediately with this information?"

Soolchakan was taken aback. "Are you in that big of a hurry to destroy all of these peoples?"

"No," said Wymini patronizingly. "We want to get someone there to assess the damage before they start doing any repairs. We'd like to know just exactly what happened."

Soolchakan looked up as if asking for some divine guidance. "You set off 1,262 firestorm weapons and you can't make an educated guess as to what happened? The whole planet is toxic. All of that residual energy that caused us so much trouble… it's everywhere on that planet."

"We'd like to see it…first hand," said Hrombisk.

"We've already been there," said Chyning. "We went to that resort area. Believe me, no one is doing any more frolicking. They're all very worried and panicking trying to get hold of anyone…back…home."

"Nevertheless," said Hrombisk. "That is the resort. We'd like to take a look at the rest of the planet."

Soolchakan hung his head. He scratched his forehead. He

looked up. "All right! Come on! I'll Jump you there."

Hrombisk smiled. "I and my Team." He signaled to someone off to his right. Three women came up to join him. Xa-Xa was one of them. Soolchakan joined in on a huddle to Jump them to Iyka.

Chyning hollered at Soolchakan before he could make the Jump. "Where are you going?"

Soolchakan was a little bewildered. "I'm taking them to that resort on Iyka! What do you mean…where am I going?"

Chyning huffed. "No! I mean, where in the resort? If I have to Jump a Team in there, I don't want to Jump in on top of you."

Soolchakan sighed and nodded. "Okay. I'm going to… Jump them to the far end of the south pier."

Bonarain nodded. "I'll Jump a Team to the central part of the south pier."

Kiyalee smiled. "I'll Jump a Team to the central part of the north pier."

Chyning shrugged. "I'll put a Team on the beach… between the piers."

Soolchakan smiled. "Is everyone happy now? Okay, all those who are going, hop to Spy. Then we'll Jump."

Soolchakan Jumped Team 85. Bonarain Jumped Team 207. Kiyalee Jumped Team 435. Chyning Jumped Team 1599. All four Teams got together on the beach.

"Now," said Soolchakan, "you have your landmark area. You can bring your own fighter craft here, do all of the flying you want. Do you need any of us to stay here?"

Hrombisk looked up at the dark clouds overhead. "No, I don't think so. We'll bring the other six Teams here...ourselves. Thank you for the guidance."

Team 7016 Jumped back to the conference room.

Wymini looked over the list that was supplied. There were quite a few places on Chokchakchok that appeared to be military targets. "They're going to set up the bombing of Jowfoonda first," she said. "Later on, we'll hit the Choks." She looked up and smiled. "How do you feel about...a reconnaissance of the Zizzikinza?"

All four of Team 7016 gave her a dull stare.

Soolchakan licked his lips and tried to think of something else – other than another recon trip. "Can we start...in a few days, Sir?"

Yim was a little perturbed. "Wouldn't you like to get it out of the way...now?"

"No, Sir," said Soolchakan. "We'd like to sit down and prop our feet up for a few days. The physicists have all kinds of targets that they can look forward to on Jowfoonda and Chokchakchok. Do they really need something...NOW...in regards to Zizzikinza?"

Wymini shook her head. "No, I guess not. Not right... NOW! Go ahead and go home and...enjoy some kwatha. Take a ten day rest and then…hit Zizzikinza."

Soolchakan smiled and all of Team 7016 vanished.

Wymini smiled. "Now, we just wait until the physicists get back from Iyka and we find out if we have to hit those *bimyocks* again."

Xadorm shock his head. "After 1,262 firestorm weapons, I doubt that there's anything left to hit on that planet."

Four days later, Soolchakan was reading the updates from the Command Staff on the computer. The three women came down to fix some lunch and saw him reading and shaking his head.

Bonarain slowly walked up to him. "What's so interesting?"

Soolchakan continued shaking his head. "It's not interesting. It's what I expected. Iyka…is no longer an inhabitable planet. They've come to the conclusion that 1,262 firestorm weapons was overkill." He looked off to the right with crossed eyes. "DUH!" He shook his head. "They were able to track some of those reptiles that were at the resort. Those Iyka were able to contact a nearby spaceship and got shuttled out of there." He scoffed. "Too late! Over one hundred of them and now all of them are showing signs of being affected by that residual energy. Over half of those are already dead and the rest are…" He shook his head again. "The shorelines are covered with dead fish. All kinds and all sizes of dead fish. There's no green vegetation. It's all…yellow or brown. If the planet…does come back to a point where…someone can inhabit the planet safely…it probably won't be for at least 500 years."

Kiyalee scoffed. "Are they gonna do the same to Jowfoonda?"

"Not my decision," said Soolchakan. He hung his head. "What a mess. We just demolished a conqueror. Maybe now, they'll feel the pain of what they've been doing to others…and take a hint."

Chyning headed for the kitchen. "As you said, it's not our decision and I'm still hungry."

Soolchakan started feeding some information into the computer.

Bonarain frowned. "What are you doing?"

"I'm telling them to set up their own secondary landmark on Jowfoonda and Chokchakchok. A landmark that they're not planning on blowing up. That way we won't have to come up with a secondary one for them."

"They should know that by now," said Kiyalee.

Soolchakan turned to her. "How many times has someone told you how to do something that you already knew how to do? If they can do it to me, I can do it to them. If they don't like it when I do it to them, they need to stop doing it to me."

"You don't have enough rank to hit someone back like that," said Bonarain. "You may catch all kinds of *h'oolyach* for saying that."

He grinned. "No, if they say that I shouldn't do it, then

I'll tell them that because of all the times it has been done to me, I thought that it was standard operating procedure for all. If they don't like it...they should stop it themselves. We've all been at this for over 1,600 years. By now, everyone should know their jobs. Unless they change some kind of procedure...I think that all of us know how to do our jobs."

After they finished eating, Bonarain got on the computer to look for other updates. "Look here," she said. "When they shuttled those...contaminated Iyka victims to the spacecraft, Wymini had some of our Owlamite spies get on board the Iyka ship. Now we're getting current updates on them...from them."

Chyning was still chewing on a mouthful of food, so she sent her comment: **"That's amazing! The Command Staff came up with something like that...and they're not** *honoring* **Team 7016 with that task!"**

Kiyalee scoffed. "They're already setting us up to go to Zizzikinza. That's how they honor us." She stirred through her kwatha looking for more tasty lumps.

Team 7016 was on the Zizzikinza home world. They did not like what they were seeing in regards to all of the different races that had been enslaved, however, this planet did not stink to high heaven like the Iyka planet had. The Jowfoonda planet had a bad smell as well, because the bug-faced monsters had their own stench. The big ape like Choks were not the type to bathe very often because they believed that their musk gave them some sex appeal. The Zizzikinzas were abnormally clean, in comparison to the others.

They spent a month searching the planet for military targets and headed back to Hardooth.

Upon arrival at apartment 12-562, Team 7016 found a new message about the Jowfoonda. The physicists had not done the overkill this time. They cut the number of firestorm weapons down to 350 and blew up most of the targets with a plethora of conventional bombs that were found locally. The devastation was vast and they still poisoned the atmosphere to a point where the planet would need at least two centuries to return to something that was inhabitable.

Once again, the survivors were shuttled off of the planet and there was an Owlamite spy Team on board one of the flagships of the enemy.

Chokchakchok was attacked next. They kept the firestorm weapon count at 350. They had to use a few 459 cannons to demolish several manufacturing plants because there were not enough conventional bombs on the Chok planet. The result was still the same. The planet was too toxic to live on for at least 200 years and another Owlamite spy Team was on a Chok ship.

Once they found a good landmark on the Doolood home planet, they determined that Team 7016 was going to need a very large amount of oxygen tanks in order to accomplish the recon mission on that planet. One of the scout ships from *Owlam the First* was placed at their disposal, in order to have enough oxygen bottles and the ability to recharge them.

When Team 7016 got home they read the attack report on

the Zizzikinza planet. Old information – 350 firestorm weapons and a combination of conventional bombs and some devastation with the 459 cannons. Also another Owlamite Team on a Zizzy flagship.

Team 7016 reported to the Command Staff.

"I don't think we want to use any firestorm weapons on the Doolood home planet," said Soolchakan. "This is an entirely different situation on that planet."

"That is not your decision to make," said Yim. "Who do you think you are?"

"I think I'm the one who went to Doolood and looked over the entire planet, any more stupid questions…Sir?" Soolchakan stood there glaring. "I don't think that a firestorm weapon will work there…because…how far do the firestorms go…underwater?"

Yim's expression changed from anger to confusion. He turned to Hrombisk. "How far…would those firestorms go… underwater?"

Hrombisk stood there looking as if he were having a panic attack. "I…don't know, Sir. We've never exploded one… underwater. We have no idea…what would happen."

Soolchakan smiled. "Are you ready to listen?"

Yim settled back in his chair. "I guess I don't have a choice."

Wymini tapped her fingers on the table several times. "Yes, we don't have a choice, because we haven't heard what

Team 7016 has to say yet. I agree that this one will probably have to be handled differently…because they are fish." She looked up at Soolchakan. "Please give your report."

Soolchakan bowed his head slightly. "Thank you, Sir. More and more, I'm thinking that every bit of technology that those fishies have…was stolen from somebody else. They have air-breathing slaves, who live on islands, who perform all of the manufacturing work. They make the engines, they make the computers, they make all of the parts to the spacecraft and they make the firestorm weapons. They make all of the parts and then turn them over to their masters."

"Hold on," said Skalix. "If they make the things, why don't they use them against their masters and escape?"

Kiyalee interjected. "On this island, they make the engine blocks. On another island they make the pistons. On another island they make the rocker arms. Once they make the pieces, they turn them over to the Doolood who now assemble the pieces."

Skalix leaned back. "All right, that makes a lot more sense, thank you for the clarification."

Soolchakan looked around to see if everyone was finished. "There are 650 large Doolood cities – all underwater. The land mass on their planet is only 15%. The underwater cities are surrounded by walls. Now these walls are nothing like the walls that we had around our cities. These walls are made of some kind of glass and they're all about 50 taja thick. They have an abundance of holes in them so water can flow through freely. Each city has a triple porous glass wall around the entire perimeter. The reason that they have the walls is because there are some sea monsters there that love dining on…anything swimming that is smaller than their mouth. The largest Doolood that we saw was about thirty taja in length and…even that one could be swallowed with ease…by some of the bigger sea monsters. The smaller sea monsters are not ashamed of biting pieces off, one at a time. The sea monsters are constantly patrolling along the outer perimeter of the glass walls, looking for some hole to get through, in order to feast on the Doolood. The cities are, for the most part, round. I would estimate that most of them are over 2,000 kilotaja in diameter. There are an abundance of small connector tubes, going from one city to another, which the sea monsters are not able to break."

"Nice tour," said Xadorm. "What's your point?"

"The best way to cause the Doolood no end of grief, on their own home planet, would be to get a few thousand Teams to Doolood…and hop all of the city walls into Ghost or Spy…or… wherever. This would allow the sea monsters in for a massive buffet and still cause the Doolood more problems than they can handle…on their own home planet. Since the water that they live in is so high in saline and alkaline content…they can't live anywhere else. Their primary goal would switch from conquering other planets to just attempting to survive on their own planet."

Hrombisk smiled. "We could steal all of their firestorm weapons and have them in reserve for any other actions that we want to take against…whomsoever."

Wymini nodded. "How long do you think it would take to set that up?"

"As long as it takes to get sufficient Teams to Doolood, in order to perform a massive hop of all of the walls," said Soolchakan with a shrug.

"Let's do it," said Wymini.

Four months later, the Doolood who were on the home planet, were in a total panic attempting to save their own skins from the sea monsters and some rather large eel-like creatures. The only ones who could escape the sea monsters were the ones who could swim up into the shallow waters. Once they were in the shallows, however, they were easy prey for the different peoples that were once their slaves. They were either eaten by the sea monsters or cooked over a fire by the ex-slaves. The eel-like creatures made short work of the Doolood eggs.

Twenty-seven Doolood spacecraft were in orbit at the time of the attack and attempted to come down and rescue as many of their people as possible. Then they were nearly incapable of lifting off again because of the sheer weight of all the refugees (and water). When they performed the rescues, they heard of several large banners that were being unfurled under the surface, in the former city areas, of the vast oceans of Doolood.

Now there were some Owlamite personnel on board the Doolood vessels as well.

"All right," said Wymini. "What are our spies reporting from the spaceships of all these *bimyocks*?"

Skalix looked at his pad. "The Iyka now have no home

planet at all. It's so toxic there, they can't land anything on the planet without special protection. According to our physicists, the planet is dead...for at least 500 years. Nothing can live there. We've had a few go back there to take a look...since, somehow, we seem to be immune to that residual energy that keeps on killing...everything...else. The aquatic creatures, big and small are floating around with no kind of carrion eater to get rid of them. All of the vegetation is dead...the water is polluted and...nothing can live there at all."

He looked back at his pad. "The Jowfoonda home planet is not much better off. The only vegetation on the planet that's still alive is on isolated islands. We've seen a lot of dead aquatic creatures on the shorelines of the continents that were hit. The same isolated islands don't seem to be having this problem. Any wild life, be it something that goes by land, sea or air, they're only able to survive near the isolated islands. Everything else is dead." He sat down.

Yim stood up. "I've got the report on the Zizzikinza home planet. The difference between the Zizzy planet and the Jowfoonda planet isn't worth mentioning. It's gonna be at least 200 years before they can go home to rebuild anything." He sat down.

Xadorm stood up. "Chokchakchok...same thing." He shook his head. "I hope that they've learned their lesson...all four of these peoples who keep attacking us...have now suffered immensely. It should stop them from conquering...I hope...for quite some time." He sat down.

Jeejow stood up. "Back to those…fishies. The planet has survived. The Doolood who were, and now are, in the spaceships can survive. They have to go back to their home planet and recycle the water in their ships, every now and then, in order to survive. The saline and alkaline content doesn't make it possible for them to steal water from any other planet." He sniffed. "Very unusual. Anyway, they're rather helpless, as far as conquering because they can't get their slaves to do much of anything for them. It was the slaves who were building everything and now…the ex-slaves are taking it easy. The only way that the Doolood can come back, is to rebuild those glass barriers to keep the big sea monsters out and then start rebuilding their underwater cities. Until they have that done, they can't control or conquer anybody. They're stuck in neutral for the time being."

Wymini nodded. "Has anyone been able to find out anything more on that race they call…Mufayton?"

Nantasa shook her head. "We've got our spies going through all of the archives on those enemy ships that we can find. The only things that we've been able to find out so far…is what we already knew. They're another ambitious race of arrogant conquerors and they're telepaths. We don't know where they are, what they look like or what they're doing…at this time."

Wymini sighed and nodded. "We all need to keep watching…and learning. We need to find out anything that we can about…all six of these races. If for no other reason than to keep them off of our backs."

17

Two years later there was a call from each one of the spy Teams on the ships of the outworld enemies. Something was happening that made them all call in.

Wymini called the meeting to order. "What's the big emergency? I hear that all of the spies are calling in and...I don': understand why they're all panicking."

"I don't think they're panicking," said Jeejow. "Something has happened that is just too big to be a coincidence."

Wymini sighed. "All right...if they're here, bring them in."

One of Wymini's Aides, Officer Grade 5, Poroth smiled. "There are five of the Team Leaders of the spy Teams here, Sir." He ushered in three women and two men.

Wymini huffed. "I don't remember all of you, so please introduce yourselves."

One of the women took a step forward. "I am Officer Grade 4, Toktaya. Team 500. I am the Team Leader for the two Teams spying on the Jowfoonda."

Another woman stepped forward. "I am Officer Grade 4, Soshoa. Team 502. I am the Team Leader for the two Teams spying on the Zizzys."

The third woman stepped forward. "I am Officer Grade 4, Roodeeska. Team 504. I am the Team Leader for the two Teams spying on the Choks."

One of the men stepped up. "I am Officer Grade 4, Xookooz. Team 506. I am the Team Leader for the two Teams spying on the Iyka."

The second man stepped up. "I am Officer Grade 4, Yokond. Team 508. I am the Team Leader for the two Teams that are trying to keep from drowning while spying on the Doolood."

Wymini nodded. "Okay, why are we here?"

Toktaya took another step forward. "As my colleagues will give witness to, we overheard the Jowfoonda getting some messages from…what is left of their high command. The flagship should rendezvous at a place called Oonta Kon Yeffan Kell. Initially this meant nothing, until I compared notes with these others."

Soshoa cleared her throat. "When I heard Toktaya say that…little mess…I was surprised to hear the Zizzikinza got the exact same message. They got it at almost the exact same time and…yes those four words: Oonta Kon Yeffan Kell."

Roodeeska stepped up. "Yes, I confirm that the Choks received that same message. Rendezvous at that point at a specific time."

Xookooz nodded. "The Iyka received the same message… at approximately the same time."

Yokond smiled. "I echo the same message for the Doolood."

Wymini was now looking concerned. "All five flagships… from five different blood enemies…all received the same message at the same time? You're telling me they could be going to some… peace conference?"

The five Team Leaders all nodded.

"What do we know about this…Oonta…Kom Yeefa… what?"

Toktaya repeated it. "Oonta Kon Yeffan Kell. We know nothing about it except all five flagships are heading for…what appears to be the exact same place…as fast as their light-speed engines can carry them." She looked at her comrades. "If the flagships of all five enemies are going to some conference…it could be very important…or it could be nothing. We all felt that we should inform you of the meeting…prior to it happening, just in case it is something."

Wymini nodded. "And of course you'll let us know…one way or another…if it is important."

"Oh, yes, Sir," said Toktaya. "At the earliest possible moment, we'll let you know."

"Right now," said Xookooz. "We estimate that they'll all be there…at current speed, in less than a day."

"Thank you," said Wymini. "Keep us informed."

The five spies saluted and vanished.

Xadorm looked a little concerned. "Could these…arrogant, conceited conquerors be forming an alliance?"

Wymini frowned. "If they are…it could be some real trouble."

"Only if they're aiming something at us," said Jeejow."

Toktaya looked out a window on the Jowfoonda ship she was on. She saw that the flagship was flying the lead position in a formation of four ships. She turned to a colleague. "Weren't they supposed to come to this conference…alone?"

Officer Grade 4, Dibroko of Team 501 nodded. "Maybe… they've got these coming along as a backup. Once they get to a certain point…the other three will…stop." He shrugged.

An alarm went off. Both of them grabbed a handrail. They were now used to that alarm. It was signaling that the ship was changing speeds and in some cases there was a rather hard jolt. If you were not holding on to a railing, you usually ended up on the floor. The jolt occurred and they saw that all four ships were slowing down considerably.

Toktaya snarled. "I need to be on the Bridge…find out what's going on."

"You left someone up there didn't you? Someone is always supposed to be on the Bridge…just in case of…anything."

"Yes," she said in disgust. **"Officer Joboshok, where are you**?"

He responded. **"I'm in the engine room where you left me."**

"Then who is on the Main Bridge?"

"This is Officer, Vavakaya. I'm on the Bridge. What did you need?"

"Why did we slow down?"

"The head *bimyock*, on this ship, is telling the others to wait here. He's telling the other ships to listen in and come in shooting if anything goes wrong."

"That means that we're close to that...silly named destination," said Dibroko.

Toktaya sighed. "We are. I wonder about the others."

Dibroko shrugged. "Call them and find out. You ARE the ranking one in all of this mess."

Toktaya made mental call to the other Team Leaders. Roodeeska called in that the Choks were already at the rendezvous point. Soshoa called in that the Zizzys were still headed to the point in a four ship formation. Xookooz called in that the Iyka were going to send in the Main Bridge of their ship. It was going to separate from the other part so that fewer lives would be in danger...if the worst happened. Yokond called in that the Doolood were grumbling about the situation, but they were on their way.

Toktaya scratched her head while thinking. **"Officer, Roodeeska, you say the Choks are already there...what kind of a rendezvous point is it? Is it a planet or...what?"**

"It appears to be a space station of some kind. It resembles a giant bell. The bell is...about 50 taja in height and about 40 taja in diameter. The Chok ship is just... sitting here...with the nose of the ship pointed at the bell. Neither one has made any kind of communication or...action...either way."

"It appears that we're going to be there very soon and...I guess we'll find out what's going to happen then."

Toktaya and Dibroko had to grab the rail again as the alarm went off and the ship lurched forward.

Xookooz called in that the Main Bridge of the Iyka ship was on the final leg to the meeting point.

Soshoa called in that the Zizzikinza were on the final leg.

Xookooz called in again. "We have company! Another ship just showed up. It...is nothing like I've ever seen before. I don't know what to make of it."

Toktaya frowned in thought. "Describe the silly thing."

"It is...a diamond-shape...that is laying flat. It is about fifty taja from top to bottom and each side is...about one kilotaja. The top of the diamond has... hundreds of...small and large spires sticking up...all different lengths and widths. It doesn't appear to have any...windows. I don't see any lights except for a row of green lights that go completely around the ship...and the lights are pulsating. Is it possible that...this ship

is from that one we haven't met yet? Could this be…
Mufayton?"

Toktaya grunted, slightly panicked over this new ship. "**If
it is, we may need that translator…Officer, Bonarain.
Somebody who is already at the rendezvous point…
go back to Hardooth and get her. We need her here…
NOW!**"

Xookooz sent back in a cheerful manner. "**That's taken
care of. We'll have her here shortly.**"

Bonarain was just finishing the washing of her neck and
hair. She was letting the hot water just stream down her body
as she stood there under a shower head. She thought she heard
someone in the room and turned her attention to…who ever.

"Excuse, me, but are you Officer, Bonarain?"

She pulled her head out of the water stream and looked at
a woman that she was not familiar with. "WHO ARE YOU?"

The woman clasped her hands under her chin and had a
desperate and guilty smile on her face. "I'm Officer Grade 7,
Quipiama of Team 506. We're currently spying on the Iyka."

"SO WHAT?"

"Well, we've just arrived at the rendezvous point…
where all of the flagships were called to go too and…a strange
ship showed up…and…maybe it might be the Mufayton and…
we need you…to translate…maybe…I don't know…but maybe."

She flushed as she tried to display an even bigger smile.

Bonarain glared back at her and clenched her teeth. "Get out…of…my…bathroom. I'm…in the middle of bathing. Get out until I'm finished."

"But we need you there…"

"GET OUT!"

Quipiama looked around fearfully and then quickly departed the room.

Bonarain leaned her head against the wall. "In the name of the Great Maker, why can't someone else do this *h'oolyach*? Why is it always me?" She took her sweet time doing an extra rinsing on the back of her neck. She sent a mental communication to the rest of her Team about this Quipiama and the rendezvous point. When she finally got out of the tub, and again, took her sweet time, drying off, she put her robe, wrapped a towel around her head on and headed for her bedroom.

Quipiama was standing there, not quite sure what to do with herself as she was getting some very nasty glares from Soolchakan, Kiyalee and Chyning.

Bonarain walked up to Quipiama. "They can't do it… without me?"

Quipiama smiled. "You're the best. Everyone knows that."

Bonarain pulled the towel from her head and – slowly - started drying her hair with the towel.

Quipiama cleared her throat. "We need to get there…

quickly."

Bonarain pointed to her Teammates. "Take one of them, so they can landmark it, and come back and get me."

Quipiama tried to sound assertive. "We need to…"

Bonarain got right in her face. "I'M GOING TO GET DRIED AND DRESSED! If they don't like that…I don't care." She walked off while still toweling her hair.

Chyning walked up to Quipiama and held out her hand. Quipiama sighed, took hold of Chyning's hand and the two of them vanished.

Soolchakan sniffed. "We'll be down in the dining room."

"Thank you," said Bonarain cordially.

As Soolchakan and Kiyalee were walking down the stairs Kiyalee snickered.

"As Chyning says…are we getting honored again?"

"I'm afraid so," muttered Soolchakan.

By the time they arrived in the dining room, Chyning was already back. She was downing a glass of fruit juice.

"That didn't take long," said Kiyalee.

"There's not that much to landmark on an Iyka ship," said Chyning. She placed her left hand on her stomach, turned her head, stuck her tongue out and belched. She looked into the glass. "That's some potent stuff. We need to make more of it."

Kiyalee giggled.

Bonarain finally made her way to the dining room. She looked at the pitcher of juice on the table and saw only three glasses. "Where's mine?"

Soolchakan waved a hand at the table. "Kiyalee made this mixture with those berries that I don't like. I'm the one not drinking it."

Bonarain nodded. Kiyalee poured a glass for Bonarain and handed it to her. Bonarain took a sip and looked up as she moved her tongue around testing the flavor. She nodded and drank half the glass. She was nodding again as she suddenly belched as well. She looked in shock at the glass.

Bonarain looked at Kiyalee suspiciously. "Did you put something else...other than those berries in this stuff?"

Kiyalee stood there giggling. "No, just the berries."

"Well it fights back."

Soolchakan sighed. "Are we ready?"

Bonarain and Kiyalee both shrugged. Chyning held her hands out to set up for the huddle Jump back to the Iyka ship. The four of them huddled together and Chyning did the Jump.

Team 7016 showed up at the rendezvous point. They were on the Main Bridge of the Iyka ship, looking out at the strange diamond-shaped ship and the bell-shaped space station in the middle.

Soolchakan shook his head and grunted in disgust. "How were we supposed to get over to that diamond ship? We have no landmarks and we can't see the inside of the ship in order to get a landmark?"

"We're going to have to go back home and get our fighters and then fly across," jeered Chyning.

"Sounds about right to me," muttered Kiyalee.

Team 7016 vanished. They got back to where they had parked their fighters, got into their spacesuits, then into the fighters. Soolchakan gave the signal and the four of them Jumped back to the area of the bell-shaped space station.

Soolchakan looked around at the total inactivity that was going on outside of the ships. **"Has anyone shuttled over to the bell...from any of the other ships yet?"**

"Nothing yet," sent Xookooz. **"They're all just sitting here...and staring at each other."**

Soolchakan shook his head and sniffed. **"Okay, Team 7016, let's go inside that...diamond...and take a look see. Bonarain to the port side, Kiyalee look for engines, Chyning to the starboard side...and I'm lookin' for the Bridge."**

They went to their assigned areas and entered the stationary ship.

Finding this Main Bridge was easier on this ship than it had ever been on any other. He saw at least forty stations that were manned by this new alien. The body appeared to be very comparable to the Heyyah body. The head, however, was like an upside down pyramid with four sides...and a set of eyes on all four sides. Only the front side had a mouth and what appeared to be a very pointed nose. The top of the semi-flat head appeared to have several lumps that were of various sizes. Looking around at the different inhabitants of this ship, he noticed that the skin went from a dark yellow to a medium brown. He aimed his biosensor at the individual that he guessed was the ship commander and turned it on.

Specimen appears to be somewhat similar to Heyyah, from the neck down. Hermaphrodite. Height 6.2 taja. 2.1 taja in circumference at the waist. 2.8 taja in circumference at the shoulders. Biped. Two hands with three fingers and opposable thumb. Legs are 25% of overall height. Respiratory, gastrointestinal and circulatory system all similar to Heyyah. Eight optical organs in the cranium.

He stared at the readout in shock. Hermaphrodite? Is that normal or...? He scanned five more of the creatures and they were all hermaphrodites. 'These people could have two of them copulate together...and both could walk away pregnant,' he thought. He did not hear any conversation. At first he figured that they were just all sitting quietly, waiting for something to happen – such as all of the invited guests finally showing up at this prearranged rendezvous point.

He tried reading the mind of the original creature that he had scanned and heard a jumbled mass of conversations going on. He stopped the mindreading and shook his head. He wondered if they were all that scatterbrained, or maybe they were able to concentrate on more than one thing at a time. He tried mindreading several others and got the same results. He decided to leave this mental manipulation to Bonarain. This one was a little too complicated for him – even with the practice he had and the coaching from Bonarain.

Kiyalee sent a message: **"These people aren't any different. Their light speed engine is almost the same and their conventional engines are almost the same. The differences are not worth talking about."**

While Kiyalee was sending her telepathic message, Soolchakan noticed that the pyramid headed aliens were getting very agitated. They were all checking their monitors and keying in all kinds of information on their computer system. As soon as she finished, they all stopped what they were doing and looked around as if they were lost.

Chyning snickered. **"This bunch has a big supply of firestorm weapons. They've also got a big supply of pulse guns and rifles."**

Once again, while Chyning was sending, the aliens were agitated. When she finished, they again looked around as if lost. Some of them continued doing fast typing on their keyboards. Every few moments they would look up and look around as if trying to find something floating in the air.

Chyning sent out again. **"Something is going on. They're all getting some pulse weapons out. It looks like...."**

Bonarain interrupted. **"STOP THE TELEPATHICS!"**

She picked up the microphone in her fighter. "Use the electric communications around these *bimyocks*."

Soolchakan grabbed his communicator with a huff. "What's going on? Why can't we use the mental stuff?"

"Because these Mufayton, yes this is the bunch that're called Mufayton, are picking up on our mental communications. They can and are hearing all of our mental communications." Bonarain almost sounded panicked. "Remember those nasty Cacktash. Remember what they did to us."

Soolchakan groaned. "If we can't use our mental communication, we're going to have to send all of our spies back for electric gadgets. That could make things very difficult for all of us."

Chyning broke in. "You'd better think of something quick. The Doolood ship is coming into view."

Soolchakan grunted in disgust. "I've got an idea. Let me test something first. We need to see what their range is."

Kiyalee scoffed. "How we gonna do that?"

"Kiyalee, you get to the Jowfoonda ship. Chyning, you get to the Zizzikinza ship. Bonarain, you stay where you are and see if you can keep reading them," said Soolchakan.

"I can read them," said Bonarain. "Loud and clear. I've already got the translation. That's how I know that they were reading us. They're trying to remember what was said so that they can use some crazy computer program to translate our language."

"Okay," said Soolchakan. "I'm going to the Chok ship. Now…Kiyalee, are you in place…with…whoever the Team Leader is there?"

"I'm here with Officer, Toktaya," said Kiyalee. "What do you want me to do?"

"Send a mental message to Bonarain."

"What message should I send?"

"COUNT!"

"Okay, don't get snippy! **One, two three, four, five.**" She got back on the communicator. "Bonarain, did they hear that?"

"No, they didn't," said Bonarain. "Maybe they do have very limited range."

Soolchakan nodded with some hope. "Chyning, who are you with?"

"I'm with Officer, Soshoa on the Zizzy ship."

"Good! Give Bonarain a slow count."

Chyning sighed. "**One, two, three, four, five.** Bonarain, did you get that?"

"Yes," said Bonarain. "Again, they didn't pick it up."

Soolchakan chuckled. "Okay, Bonarain, send a count to me."

"You're joking!"

"No, we're testing their capabilities."

Bonarain rolled her eyes and snarled. "Okay." She sniffed. **"One, two, three, four...OH *H'OOLYACH*!"**

Soolchakan felt a little panicky himself. "What happened?"

Bonarain came back in a small scared voice. "Four of them...looked directly at me...and now...they have some... kind of...hand held device...they're scanning...right where I'm standing...with those devices. Oh, *h'oolyach*, their eyes...they bulge out...when they're mad...or excited...or whatever they're feeling right now."

Soolchakan smiled. "Okay, now we know! They can hear our mental messages when we're on their ship, but not off of it. That helps."

Bonarain snarled. "HOW?"

"All personnel, this is Soolchakan with a plan to foul up the mental processes of this new nemesis. If these Mufayton and all of the others send some... representative to that bell ship...we go as well. When we're there, whoever is the spy on the Jowfoonda ship, go ahead and send some messages, back and forth, in the Jowfoonda language. Same for the Zizzys. When you go to the bell, send in the Zizzy language. Same for the Chok, same for the Iyka and same for the Doolood. When you send the messages, send isolated messages to each other only. That way, those Mufayton will think that everyone, now, has some kind of mental telepathy and it'll give them fits."

Xookooz shook his head. "**Officer, Soolchakan, you need to work in the department of dirty tricks**."

"**Thank you**," sent Soolchakan smugly.

Chyning giggled. "**Keep the enemy confused. That's always a good plan**."

"**It also looks as if we're gonna have to assign a new Team of spies to this new nemesis**," sent Toktaya. "**We're going to need to keep track of them as well**."

"**Don't worry**," send Soolchakan. "**I'm sure that the Command Staff is already working on that and my Team has already obtained some landmarks in that Mufayton ship**."

'Grunt for yourself,' thought Bonarain.

"**It looks as if they're getting ready to start their meeting**," sent Roodeeska. "**I can see shuttlecraft heading out of each one of the big ships**."

Toktaya snickered. "**Make sure that we have Officer, Soolchakan's little trick ready to confuse the newcomers**."

Soolchakan flew his fighter inside the bell-shaped ship. There was not very much in there. The largest room took up the entire top of the bell. It was obviously a conference room that contained nothing more than a hexagonal table with three chairs on five of the sides and a very large aquarium on the sixth. From the sizes of the chairs, it was not difficult to determine which side the skinny Zizzikinzas were going to be seated. It was also obvious which chairs were going to be used by the giant Choks.

Soolchakan landed his fighter directly in the middle of the table and shut his engine down. He sat there waiting to see what was going to happen. He turned a recorder on in his cockpit to get all of the fun.

Three Doolood came swimming into the aquarium and moved to three underwater microphones that were installed there. Officer Grade 4, Yokond came in and sat next to the aquarium. He had a woman from his Team standing next to him.

"This is my Teammate, Officer Grade 7, Nap," said Yokond. "She's going to work with me on your dirty little scheme."

Soolchakan just chuckled.

Three of the giant Choks walked in with Roodeeska and one of her Teammates. Next the Zizzikinzas walked in with Soshoa and a Teammate. The fourth group to come in were the Iyka with Xookooz and one of his Teammates. Soolchakan snickered as he saw the Choks and Zizzys cover their noses when the Iykas entered. The Mufayton came in with Kiyalee and Chyning following them. Last, the Jowfoonda contingency which included Toktaya and one of her Teammates.

Bonarain came into the conference room. She went to Chyning and whispered something in her ear. Chyning gave Bonarain a dirty look and vanished.

Bonarain looked at Soolchakan. "I'm going to listen to this stuff here. Chyning is going to monitor it in the Mufayton ship."

Soolchakan just nodded in approval and settled down to listen.

The central Mufayton stood up and was the first to speak. "What are we here for?" His voice was high and nasal sounding. He sat back down.

The central Zizzikinza stood up. "There is a problem in star system Ponsok Kon Yeffan Chood. I know that the Chokchakchok, the Jowfoonda, the Iyka and the Doolood have been there attempting conquest, but no one has lost as much as the Zizzikinza in attempting the conquest. No one has conquered it or even knows who, or what, we are up against. All that we know is that every ship that has entered that system…either disappeared without a trace, or was able to send out a distress call…and then disappear…without a trace."

The Mufaytons all let out a string of staccato sounding beeps (maybe it was their way of laughing). The central one spoke again. "It sounds as if your personnel are totally incompetent. Why do you keep attacking…if you can't win?"

Roodeeska sent to her Teammate: **"That smug *thwot* wouldn't be laughing if they'd lost a ship or two in that system**."

The response was immediate. All three Mufayton turned to look at the Choks and all of their eyes started bulging out.

Bonarain squawked in horror. "The bumps…on top of their heads…they're *moving*!"

"So they wiggle their bumps," said Soolchakan. "What of

it?"

"NO!" said Bonarain. "The bumps…are moving…from one place to another on the top of their head!"

"Oh, that's disgusting," said Kiyalee.

'O…kay,' thought Soolchakan. "I wonder what else we'll learn about these *doovofts*," he said.

The central Doolood got close to his microphone. "Thoo soom hooppooned wooth oos. Oovoory shoop coolled oon thoot thooy woore oondoor oottoock, froom oossooloonts thoot thooy cooldn't soo…oon oonoo soottoong. Oonfroo-rood, doogoonool, hoot sookoong, phoos oot oor oonoo oof thoo soottoogs. Whoovoor woos oottoockoong…thooy hoov oo vooroo noostoo oond poowoorfool ploosmoo boom thoot…ooroodoocootoos booyoond oonoothoong thoot woo hoov oovoor oomoogooned… oor oosed oogoonst ooch oothoor."

The Mufaytons staccato giggle again. "So you're attack ships are not any better than the Zizzikinzas. I repeat – why are we having this meeting?"

Now, there were snide remarks going mentally from all of the Owlamites present, in several languages, in regards to the comments by the Mufayton. The response by the Mufayton was that their eyes were practically hanging out of their sockets and the bumps were migrating all over the tops of their heads.

Kiyalee turned away, gagged, put her hand over her mouth and appeared to turn a little green.

"I still don't see the problem," said the Mufayton. "We

have not attacked this system and the rules specifically state that we do NOT go all out on any system unless all six of us have been defeated there. Since only you five...incompetents...have lost, why should we be bothered?"

The Jowfoonda had their antennae wiggling all over the place. "Because all of US have had our home worlds attacked as well. This system – Ponsok Kon Yeffan Chood – is the only one that could possibly have that kind of power! They attack from nowhere, they kill completely, they destroy totally...and...no one else has displayed this tactic or capability. My home world is... totally uninhabitable...for at least twelve generations. They made a radioactive disaster out of the entire planet."

The Zizzikinza banged his fists on the table. "The same with my planet. We don't dare go anywhere near it for at least sixteen generations...OUR *HOME* WORLD!"

"I repeat the statement," said the Chok. "Our world is dead...for at least twenty generations."

The Iyka shook his head grimly. "I fear that our world...is dead...forever."

The Doolood grabbed the microphone. "Thoo glooss boorroor wools. Thoo thoongs thoot took oon hoondrood fooftoo- soox goonoorootoons too boold woor doostooyood oon oone dooy. Oot wool took oot loost fooftoo goonoorootoons too roopoor thoo doomooge."

The Mufayton were not laughing now. "All five of your home planets...are destroyed...that completely?"

"Yes," said the Chok. "And again, this system is the only one that has shown that kind of attack or defense capability. It has to be them!"

The Iyka leaned back. "Of course, we could wait until they destroy your home world...and then either laugh at you... or ignore you completely. The choice of saving your home world from this destruction...is now. Are you with us...or do we collectively destroy you as well?"

Roodeeska sent a telepathic message to her Teammate. **"Maybe we should destroy the Mufayton home world anyway. I don't like the way that they're procrastinating."**

The Mufaytons looked at the Choks in shock. Their bumps started migrating around their heads again. Their eyes bulged momentarily and then sunk back in their heads. They looked at each other with their side eyes and did a few mental communications among themselves.

"The Mufayton people are always ready to assist in the destruction of a bad influence," said the Lead Mufayton. "There are enough opponents in this outer space. If it comes to the place where we have to collectively destroy a new problem, we are ready and we have 185 Battle Craft that we can put in the fight... immediately."

Kiyalee crossed her arms. "*H'oolyach*! They've got over 350. They just don't want these others to know how many they've got."

The Lead Chok grunted. "We have 176 that are ready for this fight."

"Woo hoov oon hoondrood ooghtoo-ooght," said the Doolood.

The Iyka looked around. "We can supply 197 ships."

"The Jowfoonda have 184 ships ready for this endeavor."

"The Zizzikinza Empire has been hurt badly by this pestilence. At this time, we can only supply 151 ships."

Soshoa shook her head. "That mendacious *doovoft* could supply 330."

"I hope that they're not talking about us," said Toktaya. "That's over 1,000 Battleships that would be coming at us."

The Mufayton nodded. "All right, just exactly which star system is it?"

The Chok Leader punched a few buttons on a keyboard in front of him.

Soolchakan was shocked as a three-dimensional hologram of the star system in question appeared, circling around his head. "Oh...*H'OOLYACH!*" He hung his head. "It is our system."

Xookooz snarled. "Are you sure?"

Soolchakan pointed at the holographic pictures floating around his head. "That right there is Ragath...and Rogoth. That one is Bri. And, of course...THAT...is Hardooth."

"We have to report this to the Command Staff...as soon as possible," said Toktaya.

"Of course," said Soolchakan. "Wait until those Mufaytons

are out of here, otherwise, they'll all know that…we know."

Yokond growled. "I hope that we come up with something…so I don't have to go back to swimming with those *chokwad* Dooloods."

"Let them disperse," said Toktaya. "Then…we go back to watching our charges and…Team 7016 goes back to the Command Staff and gives a full briefing."

"No," said Soolchakan. "We have to get someone in the Mufayton ship…in order to follow them. We need someone… now!"

Toktaya sighed. "I can spare Officer Grade 7, Pathsing, from my Team."

Soshoa nodded. "I'll give Officer Grade 7, Tabtaba."

"I'll give Officer Grade 7, Ullakama," said Roodeeska

"Officer Grade 7, Quipiama," said Xookooz.

"Four Grade 7's," said Soolchakan. "Which one is gonna be in charge?"

"I'll give Officer Grade 5, Amseska," said Yokond.

Amseska looked a little panicky. "If I can't communicate mentally…then how do I get in touch with…anybody?"

Soolchakan huffed. "Go to the Mufayton ship, landmark something, Jump back to Hardooth, grab some electric hand-held communicators and then Jump back."

Amseska smiled and turned red. "Sounds good."

Bonarain gave them a few pointers on the language of the Mufayton before the personnel went to that ship.

Everyone departed to go back to their specific spacecraft and prepare for the attack. Soolchakan decided that they should stay and look over that bell-shaped meeting place. It was a very strange situation where all six of these conquerors hate each other, however, they do have peaceful meetings at this particular spot in space.

The top floor was the meeting room. The floor beneath was some kind of cafeteria. It appeared to have some places to prepare food and eat. They compared the tables and some of the other things to the dining facilities that they had seen in the spacecraft of the antagonists. The bottom floor appeared to be some kind of waste disposal area. There did not seem to be anything else in this ship. It was a meeting place and nothing more. That was only one purpose behind this, very minor, space station. The only difference in any part of the ship was that one sixth of it was prepared for each one of the conquerors – including the fact that there was one sixth on each floor set up for the Doolood.

Soolchakan looked at his Team. "Are you ready?"

All three women nodded and the bell-shaped ship was hopped into dimension #45.

Chyning snickered. "Now, we're the only ones who know where this *chokwad* thing is. Do you think we should tell anybody else?"

"That can wait," said Soolchakan calmly. "It's really not important at this time…to anybody."

Team 7016 reported to the Command Staff. The six enemies were gathering together to come after Owlam and Hardooth with 1,081 fully armed and battle ready spacecraft. The Mufayton were involved even though they had never been attacked, they were joining in on the attack.

Every member of the Command Staff flopped back in their chairs.

Wymini shook her head. "Oh, *h'oolyach.* We're going to have to prepare for the biggest fight of our lives."